About t

Michael Berns, PhD, FRSB is a distinguished endowed-chair professor at a major California university. He is also founder, chairman and CEO of a non-profit institute dedicated to biomedical research of cancer and nervous system diseases. He has published five hundred articles in leading journals, six technical books, and holds twelve patents. His books and publications have been published in thirteen different languages and he has been featured in *National Geographic* and *Scientific American* magazines five times. He is foreign member of the Royal Norwegian Society of Sciences and Letters, and Fellow of the British Royal Society of Biology and the Royal Society of Medicine. He is well-traveled, having visited and lectured in many European countries, the Middle East, Russia, Japan, and China. He lives a healthy lifestyle particularly with respect to diet and exercise. In addition, he is an accomplished painter and writer of creative non-fiction. Having achieved a pinnacle in his career, he has settled into a more laid-back, take each day at a time, lifestyle, and tries not to take himself too seriously.

THE TINDERBOX PLOT

To: Cynthia Mosser
The best virtual assistant !!
in the world. Thanks so much !!
Michael Berns
10-21-21

MICHAEL BERNS

THE TINDERBOX PLOT

Vanguard Press

VANGUARD PAPERBACK

© Copyright 2021
Michael Berns

A CIP catalogue record for this title is
available from the British Library.

ISBN 978 1 80016 228 0

*Vanguard Press is an imprint of
Pegasus Elliot MacKenzie Publishers Ltd.*
www.pegasuspublishers.com

First Published in 2021

**Vanguard Press
Sheraton House Castle Park
Cambridge England**

Printed & Bound in Great Britain

Dedication

For Robbie

Acknowledgements

I started to write under the tutelage of Laurie Richards whose writing class through California State University San Morcos I took at least six times with a small cohort of dedicated acolytes of this exceptional teacher. Also, I thank Sharyan Lyon for her always insightful comments in the writing groups we belonged to. And the smaller writing group of Ted Fowler and Adriana Briscoe that we formed at the University of California Irvine provided the first sounding board for *The Tinderbox Plot*. Their influence on me was profound, and I thank them graciously. I thank Arthur Fine, my loyal friend for over forty years for being the first beta test reader of *The Tinderbox Plot*. His sharp comments caused me to reorganize and rewrite several key sections. And my two freelance editors, Judy Sternlight and Dana Issacson of New York City taught me how to write fiction. In particular, Judy was crucial in my conversion from a bland science style of writing to one in which the characters were "layered", and hopefully, at times, jump off the page. I also want to thank the editors at Pegasus, particularly Suzanne Mulvey for signing me, my production coordinator, Vicky Gorry, for guiding *The Tinderbox Plot* through the production phase, and in particular my editor/proofreader Joanna Barlow who really put the nuts and bolts of *The Tinderbox Plot* in good order.

Prologue

Eighty miles from Japan's Ryuku island chain, a Delfin IV-class Russian nuclear-powered submarine, the *Moskva II,* hovered at its maximum operational depth of two thousand, six hundred feet while the crew prepared to launch the sub's detachable deep submersible vehicle (DSV).

Upon hearing Captain Kalugin announce over the ship intercom, "Prepare to launch DSV," Andrei Andreievich Grushkov, Director of Russian FSB clandestine operations, and Dr Sergei Alexandrov, a Western-trained Russian cardiac surgeon, followed the DSV pilot through the docking pod into the DSV.

Grushkov strapped himself into a cosmonaut-like harness as the DSV disengaged with a hiss from the mothership. As it slowly descended toward the wreckage far below, Grushkov's heart rate accelerated as he realized this was the beginning of the most important mission in his long career, first in the KGB and now the FSB.

This salvage operation was the centerpiece of the Tinderbox Plot, a plan he and President Nikita Gorky, well-lubricated with iced vodka, developed several years ago over three nights in Grushkov's family dacha. If this part of the mission failed, the Tinderbox Plot was dead, and Grushkov would be forced into early retirement, or worse, considering Gorky's penchant for hastening the disappearance of people who disappointed him.

The DSV was tasked with retrieving the plutonium core of a one-megaton thermonuclear bomb in the wreckage of an American A-4E Skyhawk attack aircraft that rolled off the deck of the *USS Ticonderoga* in 1965. Though Russian nuclear scientists warned that there would be considerable seawater corrosion and a water-pressure-induced implosion resulting in destruction of much of the bomb casing, and virtually all of the electrical wiring, the plutonium pit, surrounded by a thick titanium casing, should still be intact.

Salvaging the pit, however, would require operation at a depth of twenty thousand feet. To achieve this, Gorky instructed Admiral Baranov to assign the *Moskva II* for this purpose. According to US Navy and CIA intelligence reports, the *Moskva's* reinforced hull allowed it to operate at depths greater than two thousand six hundred feet, and with the detachable DSV, the operational depth was extended to twenty-two thousand feet. Little else was known about the *Moskva II* and its DSV, both of which had dropped off the sophisticated American tracking system grid.

As the details of the Tinderbox Plot flowed through Grushkov's head, the DSV pilot announced, "Sonar reading indicates fifty feet above target. I'm turning on the spotlights. There you can see it. It's on its side, broken into three sections. Pressure has shattered the pilot's section, and the tail assembly is several feet from the main fuselage."

"Yes, it's just as shown in our scouting pictures from a year ago," Grushkov said as he flipped through pages of a file labeled *Top Secret*. "We estimated the device was attached to the bottom of the fuselage. At this point," Grushkov said pointing to a marking on a printed picture from last year's survey.

Dr Alexandrov, a Russian surgeon who had performed over one hundred cardiac surgeries using the Mona Lisa robotic surgery system, said, "We will need to position the DSV virtually against the section of the wreckage where we know the device is located. Since its core is a combination of isotopes of plutonium and uranium, we should be able to detect a weak emission signal from the uranium, and pinpoint its exact location."

For the last six months, in between his surgeries at Moscow General Hospital, Alexandrov has been practicing on a mock-up DSV equipped with two external fine claw-like robotic arms that had precision control artificial finger-like projections, much like he used in his robotic heart surgeries. These gave him fine tactile control, as if he were touching the patient. In this case the patient was a partially collapsed thirty-five-year-old nuclear bomb.

Developed specially for this mission by the Kurchatov Institute of Atomic Energy engineering department, was a cold laser knife using a one-hundred-watt picosecond pulsed CO_2 laser. It was mounted on the front end of the DSV and operated on six twelve-volt car batteries. Tests have shown it can etch through solid steel at several millimeters a second. Because the laser's exposure is a series of short picosecond bursts of high energy, the exposed material evaporates in a high velocity steam bubble, so no heat is carried deep into the targeted surface. Heating of the casing would create a hazard because of deteriorated and possibly volatile explosive charges surrounding the bomb core. In addition, the Kurchatov engineers designed a special hollow tube called a hollow wave guide that allows the CO_2 infrared laser beam to bounce down its internal reflective surface and out the end that has to be in direct contact with the target surface, otherwise the infrared beam would simply be absorbed by the surrounding water creating a heat-generated bubble.

After several attempts in shifting deep currents, the DSV was positioned adjacent to the collapsed and jagged bomb casing. "Like a highly calcified heart valve," Alexandrov said. "Need to grasp the jagged edges with the robotic pinchers, cut them with the laser first, and then carefully laser-etch a twenty-inch circular surgical seam in the remaining core casing."

"Be careful as you cut through the casing surrounding the core. You'll need to use the pincer claws to remove the remnants of any remaining explosives that encase the core," Grushkov said.

"Yes, I see some already, and am pulling them out and letting the current carry them away... ah yes, there is the inner bomb casing. I'm positioning the radiometer next to it to confirm radiation emission."

Grushkov read the digital screen out loud in the DSV. "Only five rem per minute, well within the safe range. That's from the decay of the uranium isotope. No alpha particles, detected through the casing from the plutonium isotope."

Dr Alexandrov said, "You can see on the monitor that I have etched the outline of a hole about twenty inches wide on the outer casing. I am now grasping the twenty-inch plate and pulling it off exposing a twenty-inch-wide cavity. I can see the spherical bomb core."

"Be careful," Grushkov said.

"I am now grasping it with the two sets of claws and am slowly extracting it through the opening," Alexandrov said.

"I've got it half out but something is holding it from the other side."

"Possibly wires that have not deteriorated over the years. Can you get behind and snip whatever is holding it?" Grushkov said.

"No, I'm using the two claws to hold it."

The SV pilot said, "I'll try to move the DSV slightly away from the wreckage. Maybe the force of pulling back will cause whatever is holding the bomb to release."

Grushkov weighed the potential outcomes, including the device breaking loose from the claws and plummeting to a final grave. Before he could answer, the DSV swayed as a strong current dragged it a foot from the wreckage. "Whoa, it's broken loose from whatever was holding it," Grushkov gasped.

"I've still got it in my grasp," Alexandrov shouted. "I'm moving it into the lead container fastened to the side of the DSV."

"Now, back to the mothership with our prize," Grushkov exclaimed.

"Then what," Alexandrov asked.

"We go back to the Kurchatov Institute where the plutonium core will become the heart of a new bomb."

"So we're looking at a possible nuclear device that's how much more powerful than what the Americans dropped on Japan?" Alexandrov asked.

Grushkov did some mental calculations. "It depends how much of the plutonium our nuclear scientists use, but it could be ten times more powerful."

"What if it doesn't work?" asked Alexandrov.

"Well, then we will have a dirty bomb explosion in Wichita, Kansas, spewing radioactive plutonium over a wide land area depending on the wind speed and direction. Radioactivity will last for eighty-eight years, the half-life of the plutonium isotope."

Chapter One
Saturday & Sunday

On a humid August Saturday morning, Andrei Andreievich Grushkov, director of foreign clandestine operations of the Russian FSB, the successor organization to the Soviet KGB, arrived at the Mexico City International Airport on a direct flight from Havana, Cuba.

With a rolling carry-on suitcase in tow and a computer case slung over his shoulder, he headed for the Aeroflot Premier Club, where a private conference room had been reserved by the Russian embassy. Grushkov, in his early sixties, ex-KGB, was on a mission so secret it was fully known only to himself and his old friend and boss, Russian President Nikita Gorky.

In a well-appointed windowless room, Grushkov was greeted by a sixty-ish, balding and overweight Viktor Zupin, the senior FSB agent in Mexico City. The two longtime acquaintances embraced in a hearty bear hug.

"My dear Viktor, it's been years since our KGB days. How have you been?"

Zupin backed up and looked Grushkov over. "You've kept yourself fit, Andrei, not like me. It's this Mexican food," he said and belly-laughed.

"The Kremlin and all the embassies and consulates have been modernized with workout facilities. You know, Gorky is an exercise nut."

Zupin laughed again. "Including the famous Lubyanka Moscow headquarters of the KGB… Ahh… I mean the FSB?"

Ignoring Zupin's attempt at humor, Grushkov asked, "How do you like your current post?"

"Kind of crazy. I've become an expert on the war between the Mexican government and the drug cartels, and also the battles *between* cartels. And you, Andrei, what brings you from Cuba?" He gestured for his colleague to sit at the dark wood conference table, on which was a tray with two Perrier bottled waters, glasses, and a dish with assorted nuts.

"This is a safe room," Zupin reassured him. "Our technical team did a thorough bug-sweep."

Grushkov was silent, debating whether he and Viktor should go to the embassy rather than discuss highly classified matters in an unsecure setting. But he also recalled reports that the Mexico City embassy was a leaking sieve. He sat and reached for a Perrier. "I've been going back and forth from Moscow and our Havana station for the past year."

Zupin lifted an eyebrow. "May I assume that your trip here has something to do with the crate we just received from the Kurchatov Atomic Energy Institute in Moscow?"

Grushkov offered a conspiratorial grin. "Viktor, old friend, this will be the capstone of my career." The achievements of his ancestors and memories of many nights as a boy, listening to his grandfather boast of glorious wartime exploits, had long weighed heavily on his shoulders. Grushkov knew this mission was his last chance. If successful, he would return home a *Hero of Mother Russia,* joining his father, grandfather, and great grandfather with that glorious military distinction. After decades of faithful service to his country, this mission would achieve for him the recognition his family heritage demanded. That had been the driving force behind the plan Grushkov presented to Nikita Gorky over two years ago.

"So what's in the crate?" Zupin pushed.

Grushkov shrugged. "Better that you don't know," he said, unwilling to breach his own security measures. However, wanting to satisfy the curiosity of his old comrade, he deflected, and said, "In Havana, I've been training FSB agents to carry out a cyberwarfare campaign in America. They've been embedded for several months now."

"Really? Where?"

"Let's just say that they're wreaking havoc in an already polarized country. Viktor, when the package reaches its final destination, their efforts will be amplified."

Grushkov recalled a meeting early on in the evolution of the Tinderbox Plot, with Gorky and a Russian professor of psychodynamics from the prestigious Lomanosov Moscow State University. The three men had postulated that if the two extreme factions in America were whipped into a frenzy by a well-planned barrage on social media platforms and dark web sites, there would be so much mistrust generated between the conservative right and the liberal left that each would blame the other when confronted with a cataclysmic event. Well executed Russian cyberattacks would bring the two antagonistic American factions past the boiling point when the bomb detonated. And the *coup de grâce,* the crowning touch that had caused Gorky to beam with self-satisfied glee, was that the device's plutonium core had been made at the Los Alamos National Nuclear Laboratory in New Mexico, USA. There would be no Russian fingerprints on the bomb.

For years, Grushkov had tracked the disposition of the American nuclear arsenal, focusing on lost or misplaced missiles. One that had been lost in the Pacific in twenty thousand feet of water had long been written off by the Americans as irretrievable. But not by Andrei Grushkov and his comrades in the Russian Navy.

After the explosion, the Internet and dark web would be flooded with conspiracy theories that what had just occurred was an attack orchestrated from *within* the United States. No doubt this would resonate with extremes on both sides, providing fodder for liberal and conservative trolls whose stock in trade were conspiracy theories and incited violence.

Grushkov pushed aside these thoughts, focusing on the matter at hand. "Where is the package?"

Zupin nodded. "It arrived yesterday on a Russian diplomatic plane. It's in a secure area, protected around the clock by armed guards and two FSB agents."

"Any problems getting it through customs?"

"No. It was labeled as an air conditioning unit. And we made a substantial payment under the table."

"What about its transport to Nogales? It's a long drive."

"The rental truck has a hydraulic loading ramp. The driver, Miguel, is Mexican. He's worked for us for seven years — very trustworthy. He speaks a little Russian and rather good English."

Grushkov stroked his close-cropped salt and pepper beard. "And what leverage do we have over him?"

17

"His wife works in the embassy kitchen. If Miguel does not deliver the package, there will be consequences for her."

"He knows the route?"

"He made a practice run two weeks ago. While there is no GPS access over long stretches, it's well marked on a map."

Grushkov considered all that could go wrong on a long trip, much of it through the Mexican desert. Failure at this point would bring the power of Gorky and the Kremlin down on his shoulders while stranding Grushkov's embedded agents in the US. "Okay. I will accompany him. Miguel and I can share the driving and make it in less than a day."

Zupin's eyebrows shot up. "*You* are going with the package?"

"Absolutely. I'm concerned about the cartel wars you mention. If they know we're sending a valuable package to the border with America, there could be an attempt to hijack it. Miguel will need help, and I will not let this package out of my sight until we reach the safe house in Nogales on the American side of the border." Grushkov leaned across the table and lowered his voice, despite his assurance the room was free of bugs. "We've already paid the Godinez cartel a large sum to dig us a tunnel under the American border wall. I'll need to inspect it before approving transfer of the cartel's next payment." Grushkov paused to gulp the remainder of his Perrier. "With the huge fee we're paying, Godinez and his goons must know we're smuggling something extremely valuable into the US... I don't trust them."

"Which reminds me." Viktor Zupin extracted a compact Glock 23 pistol from his waistband and handed it to Andrei Grushkov, who slipped the pistol into a side pocket of his computer case.

"Let's go to the hangar," Grushkov said. "I want to check the package. How soon will Miguel and the truck get here, so we can be on our way?"

Zupin looked at his watch. "As soon as I call him, he'll be here in twenty minutes. You'll be out of here by three this afternoon, enough time to beat rush hour traffic."

Grushkov pushed back his chair. "Let's get moving."

After being backed into a cargo hangar, using the truck's hydraulic ramp, the square five-foot-by-five-foot wooden crate was loaded on board.

Grushkov instructed Miguel and two muscular FSB agents to be careful. "It weighs over nine hundred pounds. Be sure it's braced with heavy blocks and tightly bound to the truck walls with those straps."

As soon as the package was secured, Grushkov hopped into the passenger seat. Miguel got behind the wheel.

"You know the route?" asked Grushkov. "You have enough fuel for the journey?"

"Of course," said the driver. "Eight gas cans are strapped to the truck's sides, in case we run low."

Grushkov gave a satisfied nod. While unfolding the map that had been sitting on the dashboard, he made sure the Glock now in his waistband was seen by Miguel.

Outside of the city by three thirty, they drove west to Guadalajara on the Gulf of Mexico, then north along the gulf, stopping as needed for water, food and bathroom breaks in isolated towns, lonely oases separated by countless miles of scrub brush and cactus. At Guaymas, they headed north-east into the brutal Sonoran Desert for the last leg to Nogales, Mexico on the border with Nogales, Arizona, USA.

The following day at one p.m., twenty-three hours after leaving Mexico City, Miguel navigated the rental truck through a maze of side streets on the Mexican side of the border.

When they reached a light industrial area with businesses and homes sandwiched together, Grushkov realized they had cell service. He typed in the street address of the Mexican safe house.

"I know where I am going," Miguel insisted.

"One block to two-nine-nine Calle Internacionale," Grushkov said, eying the formidable twenty-foot-high rust-red border fence on his right.

"I hear your people purchased the safe house property," Miguel said.

"Better you don't listen to rumors," Grushkov replied. "And don't start them, either."

At 1.20 p.m., Miguel backed the truck into a large garage stopping near a six-foot square hole in the floor surrounded by chunks of jagged concrete.

Grushkov considered what a lucky find this house was: the perfect location. Alighting from the truck, he was greeted by Alexey Krupov:

fiftyish, muscular, and one of two Russians embedded in the Mexican tunnel construction crew.

"Andrei Grushkov," Krupov extended both hands for a warm handshake. "We are honored by your presence."

Grushkov extracted his hand from Krupov's sweaty grasp. "Thanks, but it's been a long drive, and I want your report before inspecting the tunnel."

"Let's go inside," Krupov said, pointing to a doorway leading from the garage of the partially built residence to the property's main house.

"Miguel, stay in the truck. If anyone comes near the vehicle, warn him away. If he doesn't listen, shoot him with the gun you've hidden under your seat."

From the raised driver's seat, Miguel gave Grushkov a thumbs-up.

In a partially completed kitchen, Krupov placed bottles of orange soda in front of them as the two men sat at a shaky card table. "The tunnel is complete including the railroad track that runs under the border to the safe house on the American side, but we have had a few problems."

Grushkov unscrewed the top and took a sip of the sugary drink, then set it aside. "And what problems are these?" Tugging on his beard, he stared intently at Krupov, awaiting his answer.

"Minor issues stabilizing the tunnel roof. We had to add braces. The electric lights work fine, but we can't get the electric winch to work properly on the Mexican side — the one on the American side works fine."

"So how do you intend to get the package down the forty feet into the tunnel?"

"Not a problem. We'll lower it by hand to the flatbed narrow-gauge railroad cart, like those used in mines to move ore. We have the manpower to push it along the track under the border, all the way to the American side where a hoist will lift it into the safe house. The tunnel's only thirteen hundred feet long."

"Let's walk the tunnel. How many Mexican construction workers are still on the job?"

"Five. There's also a guard with an assault rifle in this house and another on the American side."

Grushkov pushed back from the table. "Let's go."

Climbing forty feet down a wooden ladder, Grushkov noticed chain link cables on either side descending all the way to the bottom. He shouted down to Krupov, a few rungs below. "What are the cables for?"

"They're attached to the electric winch in the garage. We'll use them to manually lower the package even though the winch doesn't work."

At the bottom of the ladder, they had to stoop over to avoid hitting the low tunnel ceiling. A string of lights faded into the distance. The flatbed cart waited on the tunnel track a few feet away.

After checking his surroundings, Grushkov headed through the tunnel toward the American side. He heard the sounds of the workmen finishing the tunnel. After almost a quarter mile of inspecting the narrow-gauge track, Grushkov and Krupov reached their destination.

Grushkov found a wooden ladder and winch-cables, similar to those on the Mexican side. He started up the ladder with Krupov close behind, emerging into a large room, also with chunks of concrete scattered around, and a winch on a tripod stand, its cables dangling into the tunnel. Grushkov surveyed the large room. Several objects were hidden under tarps to protect them from the tunnel's dirt and dust. When he flipped back a couple of the tarps, he discovered statues and antiques. The building had once been an antique mall.

"Where's all the dirt from the tunnel?" Grushkov asked.

"In the backyard," Krupov said. "Yeah, we bought this one-acre property through a Russian shell company. We spread the dirt at night so we wouldn't attract the notice of the American border patrol. They watch the area near the border fence closely. They even installed one of the new American Homeland Security slash camera poles right across the road from this building."

"Back in Havana, I was briefed on that new technology. Apparently, the US Department of Homeland security worked with MIT to develop an infrared digital system to detect people illegally moving across the border. It probably doesn't have the range to reach our location, but better to play it safe and minimize daytime outside activities. What about people who stop by, thinking the antique store is still open?"

Krupov grinned. "One of our guys has a green card and speaks good English. Don't worry, he knows what he's doing."

As if on cue, a dark-complexioned man in jeans and a plaid shirt walked in the front door. With a nod to Krupov, he introduced himself to Grushkov as Xavier.

"I've just been outside inspecting the signs that say the Antique Mall has moved to another location," said Xavier. "I ran into a couple of tourists, and I sent them away."

"Okay," Grushkov said as he did one more visual sweep of the room, turned and descended back down the ladder with Krupov close behind. Two-thirds of the way back they heard a volley of gunshots coming from the direction of the Mexican side. They sprinted the rest of the way, then scrambled up the ladder. Emerging into the garage, the two Russians had their guns drawn, not knowing what to expect.

When he saw Grushkov's head pop up from the tunnel, Miguel yelled, "*Banditos!*" He was on the floor, holding his side. Two bloody bodies lay nearby, and a man with an AK-47 assault rifle was crouched in the house doorway. Before Grushkov could shoot him, Krupov shouted, "He's one of ours."

By now, Grushkov half out of the hole in the floor, another man emerged from behind the rental truck with an assault rifle. But before the bandito could pull the trigger, Grushkov discharged two shots from his Glock, hitting dead center in the man's forehead. He dropped backwards to the floor. Seeing his compatriot gunned down, the remaining bandit dropped his rifle and fled the garage.

Miguel struggled to get up from the ground. "Five guys burst in. I shot one." He pointed at Krupov's man in the doorway with the AK-47. "He was in kitchen and came into garage and shot another." He pointed to another corpse.

"We considered the possibility that a rival cartel might keep a watch on this place, see something going on and want a piece of it," said Grushkov, maintaining a calm demeanor as he placed a hand on his weapon, feeling its hotness before replacing it in his waistband. "Krupov, have one of your men get Miguel to a hospital. And call the construction team. We need them to lower the package and get it moving to the American side. I'll feel better after we winch it up and cover it with the tarps."

Grushkov knelt by Miguel's side and inspected the wound. "This needs to be taken care of. We'll get you back home after you're released from the hospital. You can tell your wife you earned a bonus." He stood up and turned to Krupov. "Once we get the package to the other side, you'll stand guard with Xavier. It may be a week before I get back," he said, thinking of all the details he had to wrap-up, in New York City.

Grushkov took his carry-on suitcase and computer case from the rental truck. From the side of the computer case, he removed four passports. He selected a Canadian one, as well as a Canadian driver's license, then felt around the interior pocket for the five thousand US dollars he kept for contingencies. He slipped Miguel five hundred dollars. "In case you have any problems at the hospital."

Two men from the construction crew arrived and gingerly lifted Miguel into a beat-up Pinto station wagon. Grushkov bent into the vehicle, gently patted Miguel on the shoulder, and said, "You'll be okay."

Hastening towards the tunnel shaft, Grushkov turned to Krupov and said, "Let's get the package over to the American side ASAP."

Minutes later, at the bottom of the ladder, Grushkov shouted instructions up to the five construction workers as they, using the two winch cables and thick ropes, manually lowered the heavy, package down the shaft.

Knowing the explosive power of its contents, Grushkov's heart raced as the wooden crate dangled above. After a few stop-and-goes, and one terrifying bump against the shaft wall, the package reached the bottom. The crew descended from above and securely fastened it to the flatbed railroad cart.

It took them about forty-five minutes to push the loaded-down railroad cart to the American side. Once there, the crate was carefully hoisted up the shaft — a functioning electric winch helping their efforts — and deposited onto the floor of what was once the main gallery of the antique mall. Covered with a large tarp, the package blended in with the other items in the room.

Grushkov turned to Xavier and Krupov, repeating his instructions. "Both of you will live here until I return for the package in a week's time. Guard this package with your lives. Call me on your satellite phone if there's a problem. I contacted Carlos Godinez, whose cartel built this tunnel. I'm asking him for additional men as backup for you. I've never met him, but I think he will want to protect his turf, and his reputation"

"Since you have an American green card and a car," Grushkov said to Xavier, "your job is to buy food and supplies while I am gone." To Krupov, he said, "Your diplomatic credentials will raise embarrassing questions, so don't go outside, and don't answer the door unless Xavier is present. Xavier, I need you to take me to the nearest car rental office, so I can rent a car and then to drive to Tucson."

"Sure," Xavier said. "But why don't I drive you to Tucson? It's only an hour away."

Grushkov was quiet, weighing the risk of leaving a digital footprint when he rented and returned the car, versus leaving the package guarded for two hours by a Russian with diplomatic credentials to be in Mexico, not the US.

"Okay. Xavier, you have a valid American driver's license?"

"Of course, and I live in north Nogales on this side of the border. I make runs to Tucson with cartel product every week. I know the route well."

Grushkov removed the Glock from his waistband and handed it to Krupov, along with a box of cartridges dug from his computer case. "Here's more firepower. I can't take it through American airports on my way to New York City," he said with a smile.

Chapter Two
Monday

At 7.27 a.m., Andrei Grushkov slipped out the service entrance of the Russian consulate in uptown Manhattan. He tilted his head down so only the top of his wide-brimmed hat was visible to any nearby surveillance cameras. He ducked into the back seat of a waiting black Mercedes S-class luxury sedan with diplomatic plates — double-parked on Ninety-Second Street behind the consulate. Once inside, he slid an overnight bag and his computer case across the seat.

"Good morning, Ivan," said Grushkov. "You're taking me to Cold Spring Harbor, Long Island." He peered out the rear window as they sped away from the curb, a black leather briefcase securely between his knees. "I'll give you directions when we get near."

Ivan Krakov, ex-KGB, grinned at Grushkov through the rear-view mirror and barreled east on Ninety-Second Street, heading for the FDR Drive. When he reached the FDR, he headed downtown, weaving dangerously between buses and taxis, laying on the horn in concert with the scrum of other vehicles on this humid August morning. He went through the Queens Midtown Tunnel under the East River to Long Island, where he picked up the Long Island Expressway. In the light traffic on the LIE heading away from Manhattan, Ivan stepped on the gas. Diplomatic plates ensured no stops by the New York police, which enabled them to race with a panache one level below hubris.

"Ivan, what are you hearing about American drones?"

Ivan glanced back at his boss. "We have drone scanners in all of our cars." He pushed a button on the radio consul and a screen lit up. Ivan pointed a black-leather-gloved hand toward the car ceiling. "On the roof is a miniature, three-hundred-and-sixty-degree, seventy-seven-gigahertz micro-radar that detects drone-like objects as small as half a meter for three miles. They trigger a ping and appear as a red circle on the screen.

As you can see, there are none." Ivan reached for the glove compartment, extracted the manual, and handed it over the seat to Andrei in the back.

"Ahhh," Grushkov observed, thumbing through the instruction brochure, after which he handed it back to Krakov. "It is very compact. Our Russian scientists have outdone the Americans on this."

"Andrei Andreievich, Russian scientists cannot take credit for this technology. We pirated the schematics from the Israelis and the operational software from the South Koreans. They both have concerns with drone invasion of their airspace."

"And the Americans, Ivan? They must work closely with Israel on this technology."

"Probably." Ivan frowned. "I understand American radar uses software that can distinguish birds from drones, something we are unable to do yet. The Americans have exceptionally good programmers from MIT and CalTech."

The mention of MIT brought back memories. He was thinking of Lynda Chester, the brilliant MIT-Berkeley postgraduate student Grushkov met thirty years ago when he was posted to the Soviet Consulate in San Francisco. He recalled her blue eyes and full lips. She was just one of several brief flings he'd had over the years, but he recalled Lynda with a particular fondness. He pulled his thoughts away from sentimentality. He was in the US to execute the Tinderbox Plot, and that must be his sole focus. His gut rumbled, nerves, aggravated by an empty stomach, a result of his rush to leave the consulate after having only tea and toast for breakfast.

As they moved through Nassau County, Grushkov was pushed back into the leather seat as the Benz accelerated to eighty on the nearly empty highway. They exited onto a side road and, after a few miles, Grushkov said, "There should be a sign for the Cold Spring Harbor Laboratory on the left, and on the right a fish hatchery. Park in the lot by the hatchery aquarium." Five minutes later, Ivan had followed these instructions and pulled into an empty spot by the hatchery aquarium.

Wearing his wide-brimmed hat again, his black leather briefcase clasped against his chest, and his computer case draped over his shoulder, Grushkov exited the Mercedes, and strolled to one of the hatchery's open-breeding tanks. For several minutes, he gazed at the large tanks like a tourist. Beyond the hatchery was a small lake with a variety of ducks and loons that Grushkov recognized from childhood hikes in the woods and lakes behind the family dacha. The clean air here was invigorating after the polluted air in Manhattan, and Grushkov took a few deep breaths before heading back to the parking lot.

By now, a black Lexus 350C with ordinary New York license plates had backed into the spot adjacent to the consulate car. Grushkov sidled between the two vehicles, grabbed his overnight bag that Ivan had placed on the ground between the two vehicles, and opened the Lexus passenger door.

Grushkov slipped into the empty passenger seat next to an attractive forty-ish woman with blonde hair braided and coiled neatly on top of her head. At the same time, a man about Grushkov's age and build wearing a broad-rimmed grey hat just like his, emerged from the aquarium building and got into Ivan's Mercedes.

Grushkov stifled a smile. It was like looking at himself in a mirror: a man in his early-to-mid-sixties with a greying, neatly trimmed beard, wrinkles around the eyes — even a scar on the left cheek, Grushkov's souvenir of an East Berlin caper gone wrong before the Wall came down.

Once the body double was in the Mercedes, Ivan gunned the engine, exited the hatchery and continued toward Huntington Harbor.

In the Lexus, the driver turned to Grushkov. "Nice to see you again, Andrei Andreievich. What's it been, maybe fifteen years since you taught at the training program for young FSB agents? Do you even remember me?"

"Of course. You're Olga Radinova. You were the best in the class."

She laughed. "And pretty good at extracurricular activities."

He chuckled. "That was a wonderful week in Sochi. The walks in the woods, and swimming naked in the cold stream… I remember it all very well, Olga. We made beautiful music together."

"Who knows what could have happened at a different time? We were at such different points in our careers, Andrei. I was looking to improve my position and, if I remember, you were rising through the ranks of the new FSB."

"I'm not surprised you secured a posting in the US. I had my eye on you for my unit someday," Grushkov said, meeting her gaze in the rear-view mirror. Her eyes were a warm shade of brown, and her mouth turned up ever-so-slightly in a Mona Lisa smile.

"Are you part of the consulate staff in the city?" he asked.

"I'm assigned to the Killenworth Mansion in Glen Cove, about ten minutes from here. I was transferred when the US shut down our other intelligence house. I do mainly computer IT and handle any hacking attacks on the consulate systems in the city. Soon after the Sochi retreat, I was trained at the Russian Cyberwarfare Institute. It was your recommendation letter that got me in."

Andrei smiled inwardly. "I don't know about that, but if it helped, I am glad," he said, as he tried unsuccessfully to smother a belch. "Sorry, Olga, not much to eat this morning."

She leaned over the Lexus front seat to the cramped quarters behind, grabbed a large tote bag from which she extracted a bear claw, an almond croissant, and a bottled water. "These should help. I remember your fondness for pastries."

"*Spasebah*, Olga. You're a dear. What about yourself?"

"I had breakfast," she said. "But I assumed you'd be hungry. According to my GPS, it's thirty minutes to MacArthur Airport in West Islip."

"Good," said Grushkov, starting on the bear claw.

She depressed the ignition button and the Lexus sprang to life. She deftly maneuvered the car onto Northern Boulevard, then through neighborhoods of expensive homes and various Long Island parkways on her way to West Islip.

With the steady hum of the 350C engine in the background and a view of South Bay and the Atlantic Ocean beyond, Grushkov found himself thinking of another day, thirty years ago, near a different body of water: San Francisco Bay. It had been the day Grushkov met Jack Light, his CIA counterpart. It had been a chance meeting, or so Grushkov thought, on a tour boat around San Francisco Bay. He later learned that accidental meetings between CIA and KGB agents simply did not happen. Andrei Grushkov and his wife, Marina, had been taking a rare day off from their responsibilities at the San Francisco Soviet Consulate to take in the sights of the city from the bay. Marina had left Andrei for a restroom visit below deck. He was standing at the railing on the main deck and staring at the grim rock Alcatraz through a low hanging haze when a tall, thin man with sharp, chiseled features appeared next to him.

"They say only three prisoners ever escaped the prison there, but they probably drowned," the stranger said.

Andrei scanned the stranger, taking in his spit-polished black shoes, creased trousers, and beige trench coat. The American wore glasses with thin wire rims that were popular at the time. Andrei knew this was no fellow tourist. But rather than walk away, he played along. He said, "But the bodies were never found, were they?"

The stranger picked up the thread. "No, they never were. But the story has become historic San Francisco lore." He extended a hand. "Jack Light."

Andrei studied the face of this American, searching for a clue to help interpret this unusual encounter. Light could be FBI or CIA. Though the FBI was supposed to focus on domestic security issues and the CIA on foreign, the Russian KGB was well aware that the two American agencies shared information and collaborated on special projects of mutual benefit.

As Marina approached the two men, Jack Light politely smiled, slipped Andrei a business card, and walked away.

Andrei glanced at the simple card that read 'Jack Light' and listed a phone number — nothing else. He said to his wife, "I have just been contacted by either the American FBI or the CIA. I do believe our paths will cross again."

It was a meeting which Grushkov now knew had been staged by the CIA, a means to initiate an acquaintance that would develop into a mutually beneficial friendship over the next several months. When Andrei and Jack reported the contact to their respective superiors, the relationship was encouraged, each side hoping the other would provide valuable information about the operation of their respective organizations, or at the least, provide the opportunity for such in the future.

The opportunity arose a year later, in 1991, after the pair had been engaged in weekly forays to San Francisco wharf bars. Jack Light, apparently in an inebriated state, informed Andrei of secret intel from the CIA Moscow Station. The source, according to Jack, was confident that

Gorbachev was about to lose his grip on the Soviet Union. Revolution, it seemed, was about to befall Grushkov's precious homeland. He suspected the information by a supposedly drunken CIA agent had been carefully vetted with a purpose other than just a Cold War crumb of cooperation between two enemies.

Grushkov had nonetheless felt compelled to personally inform the head of the KGB, Nikita Gorky, whom Andrei had met on several top-brass whitewater rafting excursions on the Akishma River in Siberia. As an expert rafter, Andrei had occasionally been included on these special KGB team-building outings.

On a pretense of returning home to visit his gravely ill mother, Andrei flew back to Moscow where, on a stormy August night in the family dacha, he passed the CIA intel to Gorky. The impending collapse of the Soviet Union was no surprise to Gorky. His own operatives within the Soviet Politburo had kept him apprised of the gathering storm, but the CIA's prediction of the break-up was on a faster timeline than Gorky expected.

Over the next two nights, Grushkov and Gorky had transferred Gorky's secret intelligence files to the Grushkov dacha in the forest on the outskirts of Moscow. On television, they had watched Russian tanks, role into Red Square, and Boris Yeltsin, Chairman of the Supreme Soviet, become the president of a new Russia.

Saving Gorky's secret files, which contained compromising information on just about every powerful Russian politician and oligarch, had been crucial for Gorky's eventual appointment by Yeltsin to head the FSB, the KGB's successor organization. For his loyalty to Gorky, Andrei Grushkov was given the freedom to name his role in the new Russian spy service. He chose to be head of FSB clandestine foreign operations and, over the next twenty years he successfully planned and oversaw numerous operations, including assassinations of Russian defectors and other enemies of the state.

Two years ago, he had presented his rough idea to Gorky, and together they'd developed the Tinderbox Plot into a plan to bring America to its knees including a likely internal civil war. Gorky had promised Grushkov whatever resources he needed. Now, he thinks of his ninety-three-year-old mother in a State-run home for family members of past Russian heroes, picturing the gleam in her eyes when he returned home to receive recognition from Nikita Gorky as *Hero of Mother Russia*.

Grushkov was jolted when the Lexus made a sharp turn. Olga reached out of her open window and inserted an ID card into a slot on a pole-mounted box which resulted in a chain link fence sliding open. She drove straight through the entrance into a brightly lit airplane hangar the size of half an American football field. In the giant building's center, bathed by a bank of bright lights, sat a sleek twin turboprop Cessna Conquest II. To Andrei's horror, his hand-picked Russian engineers, Boris and Sasha, were perched atop the fuselage. They had a large gray power tool grasped between them that they were lowering toward the roof of the airplane.

Grushkov's heartrate tripled and he told Olga to hit the horn. He jumped from the Lexus, shouting, *"Nyet, nyet... nyet!"*

The two men on top of the Cessna looked in his direction and froze.

There was no way Andrei Grushkov was going to allow modification of the airplane commence without a detailed review by the onsite engineers, both of whom had been sent from Moscow to implement the untested changes to the Cessna's fuselage. Grushkov had six days to oversee the plane's modification and flight test it for safety before returning to Arizona for the package.

Chapter Three
Monday

Grushkov unrolled the plans carried by his two Russian engineers and tacked them down to a wooden workbench next to the Cessna. He carefully pointed out different aspects of the modifications of the plane fuselage and floor, necessary to ensure safe transport of the package to Kansas. Satisfied the engineers understood the details of the changes that needed to be made to the airplane, he returned to the Lexus where Olga appeared to be finishing up a cell call. He instructed her to drive to the Clarion Hotel, which they had passed a mile from the airport.

"I need to stay overnight.

"Do you know anything about this hotel?" he asked Olga.

"No. But I have a portable bug-scanner in the trunk. I should do a scan of your room, just in case. Some hotel rooms are routinely wired for video and voice. Kind of like back home. The American intelligence agencies are just as suspicious — or should I say curious? — as we are. Never know what they may pick up, especially in hotels near airports."

In the room, Grushkov sat on the edge of the king-sized bed while Olga scanned the room and bathroom. After ten minutes of sweeping, she said, "It's clean."

"You've learned well, Olga. We can't be too careful."

"Andrei, you're a legend in the Russian intelligence services. I am glad you are pleased with me," she said, standing just a few feet away. "Are you sure you don't need anything more?" she asked, smiling coyly.

He hesitated for a second. "No, I'm fine. See you tomorrow."

As soon as she left, he plugged his laptop into the hotel Internet connection on the small desk in the corner of the room. He opened the browser TOR which gave him anonymous access to the dark web. The program Ghost, downloaded into his computer by the FSB IT team before leaving Havana, allowed him to establish his own Virtual Personal Network (VPN) with fifteen hundred anonymous, untraceable proxy IP addresses to choose from each time he went online. He felt relatively confident that his messages could not be intercepted by the American intelligence agencies, though he also knew they were very sophisticated in their intercept capacities. That's why he used hushmail instead of email, giving him another layer of anonymity. He sent a simple message to Anatoly Chernov, the FSB station deputy in Havana:

On schedule here.

Less than a minute later, he received a single return ring on his throw-away burner phone, signaling everything was okay in Havana. This signal meant that the third Russian team, *Winter falcon*, was ready for insertion into the US. The signal also meant that and there were no outstanding issues with the other two undercover teams; *Snow leopard* had been in Manhattan for almost six months and *Arctic fox* had been inserted in Irvine, California three months earlier.

Assured that his three teams were on schedule and functioning as intended, Grushkov let out a sigh of relief. The plan he and Gorky had massaged into shape as snow had fallen outside Grushkov's dacha two years ago was taking shape. The different strands of the Tinderbox Plot were coming together: recovery of an American nuclear device from the deepest part of the ocean; getting it rebuilt and to its target site in the middle of the United States; and the social media campaigns of *Arctic fox* and *Snow leopard* to foster chaos in an already polarized ready-to-erupt American society. If the Tinderbox Plot succeeded, it would reorder global politics. The stakes could not be higher.

He took a bottle of Stoli from his overnight bag and placed it on the hotel room's small desk. He eyed it but resisted. "Better to wait," he whispered and drifted back to thoughts of his family dacha.

He remembered the summer days in the countryside outside of Moscow listening to his grandfather describe his heroic feats in the First Great War, for which he had been awarded the coveted *Hero of Mother Russia*. Often these stories had referenced his famous Cossack great-grandfather. Since Grushkov's father had been killed early in the Second Great War, the mantle of glory for the family name fell on young Andrei. However, when he reached military age, there was no real war to fight in, but for the Soviet fiasco in Afghanistan. Instead, Grushkov had chosen the clandestine wars waged by the Soviet KGB.

Who would celebrate with him when he managed to cut America down to size? His elderly mother, of course, and his only sibling, Karina. Three years his senior, Karina was a doctor in Vladivostok on the far western coast of Russia where she lived with her husband who served in the Russian Navy. Yes, his mother and sister would be proud of him. But he found himself missing his dead wife, Marina. Oh, how she would have rejoiced with him. He was acutely aware of the void in his life: the absence of a woman's warmth and adoration. His thoughts turned to Olga, the blossoming starry-eyed young KGB trainee he'd spent a week with fifteen years ago. Thinking of her his heart rate elevated.

His resistance to the vodka weakened. He reached for the bottle and poured a double-shot as memories of California in the late 1980's and early '90's surfaced. What was wrong with him? Where was all this emotion and sentimentality coming from?

Despite the numerous briefings prior to his arrival in San Francisco to work at the Soviet Consulate, he'd been unprepared for the city's liberal counterculture. At first, Grushkov had been curious, then intrigued. But ultimately, he'd been repulsed by the lack of political and authoritarian discipline found on the streets of San Francisco and Berkeley. On the latter's university campus, Grushkov had spent innumerable hours trying to recruit smart, disillusioned, young American scientists.

It had been on one of his forays to the Berkeley campus that he had met Lynda Chester, a brilliant post-doctoral student interested in developing computer algorithms to analyze satellite images. Even though Grushkov was ten years her senior, they'd hit it off. Lynda had felt strongly that solving any significant complex problem would require faster and smaller computer chips, as well as the algorithms to control them. She had apparently found in him the maturity lacking in her recently divorced husband whom she'd left behind in Boston. Grushkov was attentive and she was thrilled with his keen interest in her work.

At first, he saw Lynda only as a potential KGB spy destined to make significant contributions to American defense technology which she would then pass onto Grushkov's KGB operation. But over time their relationship became increasingly intense and passionately physical, which likely contributed to the disintegration of Grushkov's marriage.

34

His ailing wife Marina had been allowed to accompany him on his job-posting in the US because of her status as the daughter of a Nobel Prize-winning father. Grushkov poured another shot of Stoli as he remembered Lynda breaking off their relationship so she could take a position with the US government. Then, within a few days of their break-up, Marina died in a San Francisco hospital, following a botched emergency operation for a cancerous blockage in her gut.

Blinking back tears, he was forced to consider that his bitterness towards America may not be anchored in political ideology but in the pain of his wife's tortuous and gruesome death, preceded by Lynda's cold-hearted choice to drop him. He was curious about Lynda's career trajectory. She could play a key role in the American spy apparatus. Her interest and talent analyzing satellite images would certainly serve her well these days in the US defense establishment.

Grushkov was startled by two rings of his throwaway burner phone. Without thinking, he pushed the 'talk' button and heard a hang-up click.

"Shit," he mumbled. "Something's wrong." Two rings followed by a hang-up on his burner phone was a signal from Havana that there was a problem.

Chapter Four
Monday night

Grushkov could not ignore the two-ring hang-up signal from Anatoly in Havana. Whatever the problem was, it had to be dealt with before it metastasized, possibly alerting American intelligence agencies that something was going down on their soil. While these thoughts cascaded through his head, the burner phone again rang: twice.

"*Pizdet*!" He tossed the phone onto the bed and flipped open his laptop, still plugged into the hotel Internet access port. He clicked into Ghost, selected a new proxy IP address, and accessed hushmail through the dark web.

"Father here," Grushkov typed to Anatoly Chernov in Cuba.

In less than a minute, the return message read:

Problem with Arctic fox. Must talk.

Grushkov's breathing rate increased; his temples pulsated. He took out his satellite phone and dialed Anatoly in Cuba. "What's the problem, Anatoly?"

"According to Irene Seminova in California, Larissa Rubin has formed an unsuitable relationship with a Chinese graduate student. Meanwhile, Larissa is concerned that Irene is too friendly with a radical conservative man."

"I'll contact them," Grushkov said, thinking it might have been a mistake pairing these two. Before he hung up, he asked, "How is *Winter falcon*. They should have departed Havana?"

"Left today."

"Good," Andrei said and hung up. He exhaled deeply and forced himself to relax. Anatoly's message indicated that the *Winter falcon* team of Mischa Asimov and Gregory Borisy were on their way to Wichita, Kansas; and Grushkov was relieved that there was no bad news about the *Snow leopard* team of Yuri Khodakov and Peter Petrov, embedded in Greenwich Village in New York City.

But his *Arctic Fox* team of Irene and Larissa was in trouble. He eyed the Stoli, but he needed a clear head, so he carried his laptop to the bed and sat on the edge, pulling his gaze away from the beckoning bottle.

Grushkov considered the situation. *Arctic fox* had been in California almost three months, with only another week before he pulled them out. He recalled his initial concerns when setting up the team of two women from such disparate backgrounds. Irene had been a seasoned veteran, trained to assassinate enemies of the state, while Larissa, a half Russian and half Jewish intellectual with outstanding academic credentials, had been untested in the field.

He remembered his first meeting with Larissa. The beautiful redhead had her hair pulled back, neatly configured into a long braid that extended to the top of her buttocks. She had been leaving the last session of her advanced laser engineering class at Moscow State University when Grushkov took her aside, suggesting they stop at a nearby cafe for a cup of tea.

The twenty-seven-year-old daughter of a Jewish physicist father from Tbilisi, Georgia and a physician mother from Belarus, Larissa's aqua green eyes had boldly locked on his as they sat in a corner of a MSU campus cafe. She had listened intently to his pitch.

Larissa was the middle of three sisters in a close-knit family that — within the confines of their Moscow apartment near the Lebedev Physics Institute where their father worked — acknowledged Judaism as an important part of their heritage. Outside the walls of their home, however, the sisters appeared to be areligious. Still, with the new freedoms that emerged after the collapse of the Soviet Union, their paternal grandmother, who lived with them, openly attended Friday night services at the only remaining Jewish synagogue in Moscow. Larissa was seen attending a few services with her grandma, perhaps out of curiosity rather than belief.

Larissa had an outgoing, gregarious personality and was clearly comfortable with her stunningly good looks. In college she'd had several serious boyfriends, but Grushkov wondered if those relationships had failed when the men realized how much smarter than them, she was. At the time Grushkov had made contact, she was approaching graduation with a PhD in computer engineering after just three years. Her PhD thesis had been on the development algorithms to manipulate social media platforms, an area of great interest to the FSB and other Russian intelligence services.

Grushkov had been observing her progress for months, having access to the records and background profiles of all the MSU engineering graduate students. Larissa stood out as one of the best, and he'd waited until she was ready to graduate with her doctorate before approaching her about joining the FSB.

The conversation at the MSU cafe had been going well until Larissa suddenly expressed concern.

"Andrei Grushkov," she said with intensity, placing her teacup down loudly. "My parents will not approve of my joining a government spy agency."

"Yes, that may be," Andrei replied in a hushed voice. "But your father is a Jew and his job can disappear at the whim of the institute political officer. Your mother's position at the hospital also depends on the government appointed hospital director." He leaned forward and whispered, "I can guarantee they will keep their jobs."

Larissa understood the veiled threat. Grushkov, through his internal spy apparatus, knew that in the privacy of their apartment, her parents frequently discussed their many Jewish friends who'd lost their jobs under the Soviet regime. They constantly reminded their three daughters that old habits do not necessarily change with new politics, especially in Russia.

"And if I accept your offer, I will have access to the newest technology in computer nano-engineering?"

"Of course," he replied. "We want our agents to be as well trained as the Americans."

Grushkov was delighted by her curiosity. Larissa was a natural. Both of them knew that access to cutting edge technology could be a stepping stone for her successful future, whether in the FSB or in the new capitalism taking hold in Russia.

Larissa Rubin signed with the FSB the same day she received her doctorate.

Andrei Grushkov's final briefing of the *Arctic fox* team of Larissa and Irene had occurred three months ago in the humid back room of Havana's Club Muro Blanco, a front for the FSB headquarters in Cuba. It was pitched as a second chance for Irene, who had made a rare and humiliating mistake on her previous assignment. Innocent bystanders in London had been exposed to the polonium she'd used on a pair of Chechen traitors, and this inexcusable error had been documented by a surveillance camera. The camera should have been spotted when she had scouted the area ahead of time; it could have been neutralized, or another site selected for the attack.

After having endured Grushkov's angry rebuke and then his offer of redemption on this new assignment, Irene had vowed, "Andrei Grushkov, I swear to you, there will be no mistakes this time."

Growing up as an only child on the outskirts of Moscow, perfection had been Irene's mantra. Her pharmacist mother would accept nothing less than the best grades in school, and her police-captain father had demanded first-place finishes in the after-school gymnastics program: her ticket to the prestigious Moscow State University. Irene's quest for perfection had continued at the university. After four years of top grades and first-place finishes in the floor exercise on the university gymnastics team, she had been spotted by Russian intelligence officer Grushkov, then tasked with rebuilding the foreign intervention arm of the Russian intelligence agency after the collapse of the Soviet Union a few years earlier.

Having broken up with her third boyfriend in two years and convinced that no male would ever meet her expectations, Irene had jumped at the chance to become part of an organization steeped in mystery and regarded with fear by a Russian populace still grappling with the abrupt disintegration of a government that provided security and an orderly infrastructure for daily life. Grushkov had observed Irene flush with excitement as she thought about being trained as an assassin.

Irene Seminova was smart, agile, and impulsive, so Grushkov had paired her with Larissa Rubin, a more level-headed, socially savvy woman. However, at their first meeting at FSB headquarters in Havana, there had been an instant undercurrent of hostility between them. Upon hearing they'd be a team, Irene had shot covert glances at Larissa, just as she'd done when sizing up competitors, in the many gymnastics competitions from her past.

The timer alarm on Grushkov's computer beeped, jolting him back to the present. On his laptop, he re-established an anonymous IP address and sent a message to Irene and Larissa.

Your behavior reflects poorly on your families. Stop now! Father.

He didn't wait for a response to his veiled threat. Disconnecting from hushmail, he slapped shut the computer. "Old KGB tactics are still useful," he muttered to an empty hotel room.

He would not allow their petty bickering to interfere with their mission. They'd done a good job so far of fanning the flames of the existing polarization in American society, raising tempers to a fever pitch by using social media platforms and infiltrating local fringe groups.

Just another week or two, and he'd pull them out.

Chapter Five
Tuesday

After a hurried seven a.m. breakfast of overcooked eggs and horrible coffee in the Clarion hotel dining room, Grushkov returned to his room, purposefully ignoring his Stoli and instead popping three Tums. Alcohol had long been the bane of citizens under the Soviet system, himself included. Going all the way back to the Stalin era, over many years under the repressive Kremlin, the panacea for prevalent depression in Soviet society was alcohol. A bottle of vodka often replaced the water pitcher on the dining table. Chronic dependency on alcohol was still common. But Grushkov required a clear head on this crucial mission.

He spread the plans for modification of the Cessna on the king-sized bed and reviewed the alterations he and the FSB engineering team in Moscow had designed for the twin engine airplane. Picturing the two Russian engineers on the plane's fuselage, he whispered to himself, "Thank God, I stopped them before they cut into the roof."

Satisfied that the modifications of the Cessna still made sense he called the front office and asked that a taxi be called to take him to MacArthur Airport. The hangar at the airport was rented by a Russian shell company in the Cayman Islands for five thousand dollars a week. It was needed to house the Cessna, also purchased by the Cayman Islands company at a cost of one point five million dollars, four hundred thousand dollars above the going rate for the like-new twin turboprop plane. The owner, a rich businessman from New York, had the plane stored in a private hangar on his nine-hundred-acre winery in upstate New York. According to flight operation logs, the plane had flown less than one thousand miles since rolling off the assembly line twenty years ago. Apparently, the businessman made a killing in trading grain futures and purchased the plane for his son who was subsequently killed in a tragic car accident. The Cessna sat dormant in the hangar until purchase by the Russians. The high price paid ensured there'd be no questions asked, avoiding notification of the American FAA of the sale.

But the airplane and hangar costs were trivial compared with the one hundred- and twenty-five-million-dollar payment to the Godinez Mexican drug cartel to dig the tunnel under the border between the US and Mexico. Gorky was fully invested in this project; its success would solidify his power base among any Russian politicos and oligarchs questioning his leadership. It would demonstrate the weakness and even failure of American democracy, resulting in an increase in Russian credibility and opportunity on the rapidly shifting world stage.

In the hangar, the two Russian engineers who slept on cots in one corner, were milling around the Cessna.

Seeing their disheveled appearance and realizing they probably had not eaten, Grushkov handed them some cash and said, "There's a McDonalds off Schafer Road a block from here. Get some breakfast and be back in forty-five minutes."

After they left, Grushkov circled the aircraft, peering at the underside of the wings, staring up at each of the two engines, not entirely sure what he was looking for. He'd seen pilots routinely do this, and he anticipated the momentary arrival of the pilot, Sergei Popov, from the Russian consulate in Manhattan.

Sergei was a real asset to the team. His reputation as a pilot was solid. Grushkov had been impressed by the tall, soft-spoken pilot when he first met him at the briefing at FSB headquarters in Havana before his being posted to the Manhattan consulate. He reminded Grushkov of himself years ago when he'd debated whether to join the KGB or to apply to flight school in the Soviet Air Force.

Sergei had been posted to the consulate in New York six months earlier, as an assistant political attaché for United Nations activities. In reality, he had been inserted in preparation for this mission. Boris and Sasha, the FSB engineers, were also posted to the consulate three months ago as general engineering support staff, replacing two others who had returned to Russia after a normal two-year rotation.

Grushkov and his FSB superiors in Moscow were careful not to have an inordinate number of personnel changes at the New York consulate. The number and positions of the Russian diplomatic staff was closely monitored by American agencies, including the State Department, CIA, Homeland Security, NSA, and FBI.

Grushkov's attention was drawn to Russian-speaking voices outside the hangar entrance. He quickened his pace and crossed the concrete hangar floor. "Ahhh, Sergei!" He gave the latest arrival a strong bear hug. "You had no difficulty getting rid of American shadows?"

"No problem, Andrei Andreievich," the pilot answered with an impish smile. "I took the subway down to Herald Square, let the early rush-hour crowd pull me into an uptown train to Times Square, where I switched to another uptown train on the west side. At Seventy-Ninth Street, in front of the Museum of Natural History, I flagged a Lyft, which that had just dropped off a family."

Grushkov herded the two engineers and Sergei to a flat workbench near the Cessna. He showed them the tacked-down drawings of the changes needed to be made to the airplane.

They gathered around while Grushkov spoke. "Our task is difficult but absolutely necessary. With perfect precision, we must cut a piece from the fuselage roof that is one point five feet on each side. After, it must fit back into place snugly, so there will be no leaks when the cabin is pressurized. We need to remove the seats, inside paneling, and luggage bins. The package weighs over nine hundred pounds."

"That's near the payload capacity of the Cessna," said Sergei. "Stripped down, we'll be able to carry the pilot and one passenger — maybe."

Sasha, the senior engineer, had a bushy mustache and graying hair. He pointed to the floor area in the diagram. "We can build an aluminum frame to hold the package if you know its exact dimensions. Can you tell me more?" He looked at Grushkov expectantly.

Grushkov drew a sketch in the corner of the plans, adding the package's dimensions for their perusal. "It's a wooden box of one-inch-thick cedar planks. We can fasten it to the aluminum frame, but it must be a tight fit, so it doesn't shift in flight. That could be fatal."

A momentary silence followed that, then Sasha replied, "We'll tap four holes in each side of the aluminum frame so the package's wooden case can be securely fastened." He looked at Grushkov, as if expecting clarification of what was in the box, but no information was offered.

The other engineer, Boris, asked, "What about the floor? Is it strong enough to withstand such a heavy object, especially if you encounter rough weather?"

Grushkov stroked his chin. "That's a good question. I'm not sure, but our Moscow engineers said it should be okay." He and Sergei walked over to the plane, looked under the fuselage, then inside the airplane.

"There's a luggage compartment under the floor," Grushkov said. "I don't know the floor stress tolerance. We can brace it from underneath."

Sergei nodded. "I can keep the plane level in calm weather. But thunderstorms and tornadoes are common this time of the year in Kansas. That could be a problem."

Grushkov instructed Boris to start assembling the frame with the strong aluminum sheets that were stacked in a corner of the hangar. Nodding at the other two men, he said, "Let's get on top of the plane's fuselage and mark the area. We'll cut the roof using a diamond blade saw." He pointed to the saw box next to the aluminum. He had meticulously anticipated all their supply needs, and they had arrived like clockwork. Still, he hesitated to be too proud of himself, knowing he could not foresee every contingency.

As Sasha retrieved the saw, Grushkov continued, "The cabin hull is thin so it will cut easily. Once removed, we'll line it with silicone sealant so it won't blow out under increased cabin pressure."

"We will have to test it in flight," said Sergei, his brows furrowed.

Sasha interjected, "I am an aerospace engineer. I've designed and built many of the shells on our rockets, so trust me when I tell you that we should attach clamps to hold the cut fuselage piece in place."

Sergei frowned. "That could increase the drag as we fly, and it might add instability. I will give further thought to what kind of clamps will not affect the plane aerodynamics."

"I'm surprised the planners in Moscow didn't think of this," said Sasha. He uttered a disdainful *harrumph* and turned away from the plans. "They live at their desks and have little experience in the field."

Grushkov felt a lurch in his gut, realizing *he* should have thought of this. Was there anything else he had overlooked?

Loading the package near the Mexican border in Nogales, Arizona and flying it safely to Wichita was a crucial step, second in importance only to the package contents functioning properly. He wondered if it would be better to rent a U-Haul and drive it from Arizona to Kansas. But that would add another day or two and multiply the chances of detection.

Over a year ago, when he and Gorky had reviewed final plans for the operation, it had seemed perfect on paper. But now, with new engineering eyes on the project, potential flaws were surfacing.

These vulnerabilities triggered further worries for Grushkov, particularly about the *Arctic fox* team of Irene and Larissa. He would hushmail them tonight, asking for an update on their activities. And he planned a personal visit to the *Snow leopard* team, which had been embedded in Greenwich Village months ago. Suddenly, the choice to pay a Mexican drug cartel to build a tunnel and remain silent seemed less of a sure bet.

Now that the Tinderbox Plot was underway, every aspect of it seemed far riskier to Grushkov.

Chapter Six
Tuesday

"Let's take a break," Grushkov announced to the team. "I need to walk. Be back soon."

He set out to walk the perimeter of the airport and gather his thoughts. He feared it was only a matter of time before Irene and Larissa were at each other's throats again; it was his responsibility to insure they work *together* rather than in opposition. The success of their mission depended upon it. They had been tasked with infiltrating social media platforms with online postings, but also to connect with fringe groups through personal contact. Such interactions provided them a better understanding of the conservative movement in America. They'd co-opt elements of that movement for their own objectives.

Though he knew the time for doubts had long passed, Grushkov was nevertheless plagued with them. He had considered the two women's disparate backgrounds a strength, but perhaps he'd been mistaken. Larissa, from a Jewish home of intellectuals, and Irene, raised by a Soviet cop. On top of that, Larissa was gorgeous and Irene, though not unattractive, had a stern demeanor, off-putting to some of those who'd worked with her in the past. Whereas Larissa cycled through boyfriends because she was too smart for them, Irene alienated boyfriends because of her steely, hypercritical personality. Andrei had hoped that Larissa would have a calming effect on Irene, but this clearly had not happened. As he walked, Andrei pondered his options. He was tempted to give them a stern reprimand and let them work things out on their own. He only needed them in California for a few more weeks.

As he rounded the far perimeter of the airport, his thoughts drifted to the *Snow leopard* team. Grushkov had delayed checking on them until he was satisfied with the Cessna modifications; without the successful alteration of the airplane, alternate but riskier alternatives for transporting the package would have to be undertaken.

Grushkov had consulted the FSB Psychology division before making the bold decision to pair Yuri Khodakov and Peter Petrov.

Yuri was a tall, thin sixty-one-year-old ex-Olympian runner with a bushy mustache that had been popular in the Brezhnev years. Considerably older than the rest of the team members, Yuri had been tapped to join the mission because of his vast KGB experience. Further, he and Grushkov had built up a close relationship over the years. Yuri skillfully combined the discipline and patience of the Cold War KGB with the more free-wheeling and tech-savvy sensibilities of the modern FSB.

Yuri joined the KGB a week after the 1980 Summer Olympics at the age of twenty. After failing to earn a gold medal in the long-distance races, he had joined the KGB hoping to further his intellectual development, despite the fact that he had been unable to attend the university. After the KGB had morphed into the FSB, Yuri was selected to attend several FSB workshops on the use of computer technology to wage digital war over the Internet, a key area of importance of the new Russian FSB.

Exhibiting a high level of proficiency for software development and hacking into secure networks, Yuri was subsequently given important assignments capitalizing on his uncanny cyberabilities, which he used to influence the outcomes of the 2016 and 2020 American presidential elections, as well as the British Brexit elections. Yuri had written algorithms to break into secure voting systems in Britain and the US, as well as systems for vote tabulation — important in key American swing states. The consensus within the FSB was that Khodakov had been instrumental in pushing these elections towards outcomes favorable to Russia. His team of expert hackers had been marvelously adept at using both the conventional World Wide Web and the dark web to spread incendiary disinformation and bogus news.

Despite his age, Yuri remained in peak physical condition, running three to five kilometers every day — whether in humid, hundred-degree summers or minus-zero winters. A tall, lanky, rugged-looking athlete, throughout his life Yuri had not exhibited any apparent interest in women. Years ago, when chided by his doting mother, his response had been, "Mother, I train with the other athletes and have no time for girls."

Yuri's commitment to the KGB and the FSB had always been total; he had no goal in life other than to shine for his homeland and defeat its enemies.

Grushkov paired Yuri with Peter, a known homosexual, hoping the two operatives would be able to infiltrate the liberal community of New York City's Greenwich Village. They were ideally placed to hack into the New York University computer systems, with the goal of inflaming America's social media with incendiary fake news.

Being out of contact with the *Snow leopard* team since their insertion, Grushkov had received no updates about their progress. It was time to see them in person, to brief them on the operation's final details. By the time Grushkov had circled the airport perimeter, growing angst over his various teams required that he stop at the main terminal to buy more Tums at the newsstand. After four chalky lozenges, the gnawing sensation abated and, as he finished his circuit of the airport, his thoughts turned to his third team — *Winter falcon* — Gregory Borisy and Mischa Asimov. Their job was the most crucial: unwrap the package and arm its contents.

Grushkov heaved a sigh as the antacid took effect. Borisy was a brilliant applied engineering physics student, one of the most difficult majors at Novosibirsk University. His high level of intellect, plus his facility with complex technological devices, made him ideal for the Tinderbox Plot.

As a scientific attaché, Gregory Borisy had never operated outside the Russian embassy in London. Because it was not typical of a seasoned Russian spy, his boyish appearance — sandy hair loosely hanging from his forehead to shield cobalt-blue eyes — was considered a potential plus by the FSB. From London, Grushkov had dispatched him to a secret military facility for advanced training in nuclear physics, as well as an assessment of his physical stamina. Gregory had passed the rigorous FSB physical challenges and qualified for this assignment.

Gregory had grown up surrounded by technology in the Siberian Soviet scientist-town of Akademgorodok. His father was a professor of computer science at Novosibirsk University, and his mother a biologist at the same university. Gregory had obtained his entire education, including university training in nuclear physics and computer engineering, at NSU. He was a natural, having been mentored by his father even before he could read. When he applied to the FSB after college, his academic parents had been devastated, both wanting him to obtain a doctorate degree and become a professor.

But Gregory sought escape from Siberia. He had been hired by the FSB and posted to the Russian embassy in London as assistant scientific attaché, for the purpose of exposure to Western culture in a large diverse city.

Almost back to the hangar, Grushkov's thoughts shifted to Borisy's partner, Mikhail Asimov — called Mischa by the other team members. Mischa's outstanding feature was his strong-like-a-bull muscular build. His large hands were like the claws of a giant bear.

While this was Mischa's first mission, he had consistently scored at the top of the FSB training class in solving unexpected problems, thanks to training as a fighter and helicopter pilot before joining the FSB spy program. He had served in the military with distinction, having saved an encircled Soviet unit under attack by the Afghan army. While strafing the Afghanis, his helicopter had been damaged by ground fire and he'd crash-landed amid a Soviet unit under attack. Despite sustaining a back injury in the hard landing, he'd discovered an entrance to an abandoned subterranean network used by the Afghani rebels.

Mischa led the unit of twenty Russian soldiers to safety, navigating the complex tunnel system using his compass and pure instinct. While Mischa was the youngest member of the Tinderbox teams, Grushkov was banking on his physical strength and problem-solving skills to steady the team should troubles arise.

Having assessed the strengths and weaknesses of each of his team members, Grushkov turned a critical eye on himself. Was he strong enough to control every detail of this wildly ambitious plan? Ten years ago, he wouldn't have suffered any doubts. But he was not as mentally nimble as he used to be. These days, he checked and rechecked every detail two or three times. He could not afford a single mistake.

Gorky and his close politicos were banking on the mission's success. If it failed, the Russian government would deny any knowledge of its existence. Andrei Andreievich Grushkov and his team would be labeled rogue ex-KGB agents obsessed with regaining power on the world stage after the Soviet Union crumbled twenty-eight years ago. They would be hunted down and turned over to the International Court for War Crimes for prosecution. Russia would make a vain attempt, to gain clemency on the condition the perpetrators of the crimes would be exiled to a Siberian gulag.

Grushkov popped another two Tums as he re-entered the hangar.

Chapter Seven
Tuesday

Pacing the hangar Grushkov reminded himself that it was better to do the job right rather than cut corners and risk failure. With all the parts of the aluminum frame to secure the package now laid out on a tarp-covered floor, it was clear there was no way they could get the wide aluminum frame up the narrow fold-down set of stairs and into the Cessna main cabin.

"We will have to assemble it inside the cabin. Is this something you can handle Sasha?" he said to the senior engineer.

"Yes, Andrei Andreievich," Sasha replied formally. "It will take some time, but we will be ready for the test flight by Friday... or maybe Saturday."

Grushkov turned to the pilot. "Sergei, we must do the test flight Friday. I want us to fly out of here on Saturday."

"It all depends on the test flight," Sergei responded. "If the seal is good, and the plane is stable in flight, it should be okay. I'm planning on flying to Arizona below twelve thousand feet, so we won't need to pressurize. However, I want to do the test flight under pressurization just in case it becomes necessary during the mission to increase our altitude."

"Good thinking," said Grushkov. "I suspect the Americans have realized I'm in the country, especially with all the facial recognition and AI they use. We can't remain in one place too long so let's get cracking."

He popped another Tums.

Grushkov turned to his pilot, Sergei, and said, "I have to head back to the consulate in Manhattan. I'm leaving you in charge."

"Yes boss," Sergei replied, with a military salute.

Grushkov reasoned that while the modifications of the Cessna were underway, this was a good time to check on the *Snow Leopard* team. Also, the Manhattan consulate had a more secure communication system than the Internet and Wi-Fi from a West Islip hotel on Long Island.

He briskly walked the half mile back to the airport terminal and flagged a New York City yellow cab at the taxi stand. He had the driver stop at the Clarion Hotel and he took a shot of Stoli in his room before inserting the half-empty bottle into his overnight bag. He paid cash for the room at the front desk and returned to the waiting cab. "East Ninety-First Street, Manhattan," he instructed the driver.

At five fifteen p.m., Grushkov settled into the Manhattan consulate secure communications room: a basement space fifteen by twenty feet enclosed by a copper mesh grid to diminish any chance of eavesdropping. The room had two workstations connected by insulated cable to a satellite dish on the building's roof. Encrypted communications from here were sent directly to a Russian military telecommunications satellite in a geostationary orbit high above the equator. Because the majority of secure communications between countries and military installations utilized one of the several hundred high speed undersea fiber optic cables, slower communications via satellite were generally reserved for non-classified information. However, undersea cables were routinely tapped, using sophisticated deep-sea electronic technology on US *Halibut Class* submarines. For extra sensitive transmissions, encrypted satellite messaging or even an old-fashioned diplomatic courier were preferred. Using what he thought was a secure satellite link, Grushkov dialed Anatoly's satellite phone in Havana.

After five rings, Anatoly answered, "Dah?"

"It's me, Anatoly," he said in Russian. "What is the status?"

"Boys left last night."

Pleased that the *Winter falcon* team of Mikhail "Mischa" Asimov and Gregory Borisy was on its way to insertion into Wichita, Kansas Grushkov checked his watch and headed to the elevator, ascending to the third-floor guest suite.

The giant flat-screen TV was a luxury. Using the remote, he surfed the major cable news, MSNBC, Fox, and CNN. All three were covering a White House news conference. Grushkov settled on CNN because he liked Wolf Blitzer who he felt was the most objective American news reporter. The American president was being peppered with questions from a gaggle of reporters after a US-owned oil tanker in the Strait of

Hormuz had been attacked and sunk by Iranian gunboats. The Americans appeared to have satellite images of the incident, but Iran was denying the attack claiming it was an Israeli attack designed to blame Iran.

He was about to click over to Fox News for another perspective, but his thumb froze midair as the camera panned the officials flanking the president. Grushkov recognized an old friend: Jack Light. He had less hair, deep lines on his face, and puffiness under his eyes, but it was clearly the CIA operative that Grushkov had befriended over twenty years ago in San Francisco.

They had stayed in contact for a while. Light had been posted to the American Embassy in Moscow several years after their first meeting. And through internal FSB briefings, Grushkov had followed Jack's career with interest after his return to the US following the Moscow assignment. Jack had been steadily moving up through the CIA ranks, but sharing a platform with the American president could only mean he had now reached the agency's highest level.

After a reporter asked the president a complicated question about Middle East intelligence reports, he turned to the distinguished-looking man at his side. "I'd like to introduce Jack Light, Deputy Director at the CIA and I'd also like to take this opportunity to wish Frank Forsythe, our CIA Director a speedy recovery from his surgery. Jack, can you respond to the question?"

"Well, well," Grushkov exclaimed to himself, realizing Jack was in line to be the next head of the CIA.

The sight of Jack rekindled memories of San Francisco and Lynda Chester. She'd be in her fifties now. Andrei could not shake the thought of her: beautiful, witty, fiercely intelligent. In her work, she'd latch onto a problem and not let go until it was completely solved, then incorporate its solution into systems to avoid future snafus. She was precisely the type he had been trying to recruit into the KGB spy network. He wondered where she was now, whether her career had been as successful as Jack Light's. Even after many years, Lynda might be useful to Grushkov.

He left the guest suite and headed to the consulate's second floor, where the FSB intelligence group maintained an office. It was pushing six p.m. and the two occupants of the office appeared to be closing up for the day. They abruptly halted their activity when the legendary Andrei Grushkov entered. He was used to it: often anonymous while out in the world, a revered icon among his own. Some of his notable past exploits had gained him an exulted reputation among the consulate's intelligence officers.

"Andrei Andreievich," said an admiring young case officer, "it's an honor to see you. I'm Nicolai Gameleya. How can I help you?"

Grushkov explained that he'd like to track down an American scientist whom he knew years ago. Nicolai took down Lynda Chester's name, her area of expertise, and other recalled details of Grushkov's. "If she has the same name and is still working for the American government, we'll have her in our database," said Nicolai. "If she has a different surname, it may take a little longer to track her down."

"I will take dinner in the consulate cafeteria and then be in the guest quarters until about nine tomorrow morning," Andrei said.

"Join us for dinner," said Nicolai. "There are so many fantastic restaurants in this part of Manhattan, plus my colleagues in the intelligence office view you as a legend and would love to meet you."

"Sorry," Grushkov answered. "I'm flattered, but I don't want to risk being detected by American surveillance. I came in through the rear service entrance and will leave the same way tomorrow."

"What do you like? Italian, Chinese, Greek? We'll phone it in, and they will deliver to our front door. The food in our cafeteria is just like home: terrible."

"Well, if you insist," Grushkov answered. "Surprise me. I'll be upstairs."

An hour later, there was a knock on the guest suite door. Nicolai stood outside in the corridor; his hands full. "Here is a medium New-York-style pizza, and a special Cantonese-style dish: shrimp in lobster sauce."

Nicolai entered the room and spread out the food on the desktop.

"What a feast!" Grushkov smiled. "Join me, Nicolai," he said, placing the half-full bottle of Stoli next to the food.

"Thanks, but I have colleagues waiting downstairs. Oh, and Lynda Chester is head of a computer imaging unit at the National Security Agency in Fort Meade, Maryland. Pretty important post. She reports directly to the second-in-command at the NSA. Would you like us to dig for more details?"

"Thanks, Nicolai. That's enough for now."

Sitting down to eat, Grushkov recalled her driven nature with admiration. When stationed in San Francisco, he had sought recruits from both Berkeley and Stanford. As a result, he became impressed with the quality of American engineering and science students. After being recalled to Russia following the collapse of the USSR, while working his way up the ladder of the FSB under Gorky's tutelage, for a while Grushkov had followed Lynda's career. But over the last few years, he'd lost track of her.

If she or one of the other bright minds in the American security services had already detected his presence in the US, he was sure they were relentlessly tracking him and trying to figure out what he was up to. His gut told him to move up the launch of the Tinderbox Plot — to keep ahead of detection. Lynda's position at the NSA worried him; his sixth sense, developed over decades as a spy, was warning him.

He downed a double-shot of Stoli and went to bed.

Chapter Eight
Tuesday

Lynda Chester, director of the NSA Wireless Cyber Monitoring Center in Fort Meade, Maryland, sat in her office, surrounded by a bank of computer screens spewing de-encrypted data. It was 6.15 p.m. at the end of a long day mostly preparing for the annual NSA budget review prior to its submission to the OMB. She was looking forward to decompressing in her Jacuzzi tub — recently installed in her condo in the upscale Columbia Heights section of DC. She cleared off her desk and was ready to transfer overnight cybersecurity monitoring to her counterpart at CIA headquarters in Langley when there was a brisk knock on her office door.

Before she could respond, the door swung open and in sauntered Steven Craig, deputy director of the NSA: six-two, Ivy League, wearing his trademark dark suit with an orange and black striped Princeton tie.

"SC." Lynda grinned. "What brings you to the slums?"

"No joke, Lynda. This is a serious visit." He tossed a thumb drive across her desk. "It's from one of the FBI's street-level cameras surveilling the Russian consulate in Manhattan. This was hand-carried to me by one of my contacts in the FBI Image Analysis Center."

Odd that SC would bring sensitive information to her on a thumb drive, in violation of NSA policy, Lynda inserted it into her computer — another NSA violation. Gazing at the image that appeared on her computer screen, her heartrate accelerated. She took a slow yoga inhale and exhale before meeting her supervisor's gaze. "It's Andrei Grushkov, formerly KGB, now head of foreign operations, FSB," she said.

"Bingo," said Steve.

"What's this about? You know I disclosed my relationship with him when I was vetted for this job. That was almost thirty years ago. I was a recently minted PhD from MIT continuing my studies at Berkeley. I was enamored by an older man's charm and attention."

"That's not the issue, Lynda. You can see by the timestamp that this picture was taken yesterday morning. He's leaving the Russian Manhattan consulate through the rear service entrance. He's carrying what looks like a small suitcase, a computer, and a briefcase or pouch."

Lynda nodded. "Looks like he's headed for the double-parked Benz on the street behind the consulate."

"Yeah, it's Ninety-Second Street," said Steve. "We're trying to track his movements by scouring photo recordings from other traffic cams in the city, but it's unlikely we'll get lucky. CIA spotted him in Cuba two weeks ago, then picked him up last week in Mexico City but lost him."

"What about the New York City's tunnels and bridges? The car should be easily tracked by street cameras, especially with that drone-scanner I see on the roof."

"FBI's working on that, but there are three major tunnels and fifteen bridges in the metropolitan New York area."

Lynda more closely studied the image shot from the hidden body-level camera, marveling at how well Andrei had aged. The salt-and-pepper beard was new, but he was still trim and fit.

"What concerns us is that there's no record of Grushkov's entry into the US," said Steve. "He's still got his diplomatic credentials from previous postings, but he should have identified himself upon entering the country. And the embassy is required to notify the State Department and the FBI of all Russian nationals attached to their embassy and consulates."

Lynda felt her cheeks flush, but she was determined to maintain a professional demeanor. "So because he's here under the radar, he must be up to no good?" she asked.

SC responded with a curt nod. "He's a *big fish* Lynda, we want to know what he's up to. You know him, and his habits. He's your baby for now. Don't screw up." SC turned abruptly, leaving her office without bothering to close the door.

She bristled. She'd never messed up a case in over twenty years. SC had gotten the kudos for her work because she was in his division. Now he was number two in the NSA and headed for number one — something Lynda would have a hard time stomaching.

Lynda checked the time — 7.15 p.m. — and muttered, "No Jacuzzi tonight."

Rebooting her main computer, she opened one of her own algorithmic programs. This one she had designed to intercept mobile and satellite phone calls in the western hemisphere. The high gigabit bandwidth detection system had been originally created to intercept cell phone communication on remote battlefields; it not only traced the location of mobile, throw-away burner phones, or satellite phones, it also captured content. This technology interfaced with the Department of Defense global satellite net and was highly classified, accessible by only a handful of intelligence officers, including Lynda.

"Cuba, Mexico, and then over a week goes by before he appears at the Russian consulate in Manhattan," Lynda states aloud to her empty office. It had been a long time since her affair with Andrei, but she remembered how clever he had been, always having backup plans for backup plans, and diversions to throw pursuers off his trail.

Her algorithm would sift through DHS, NSA, and FBI databases, searching for images from airports in the south and western US, matching the recent image of Grushkov in New York. "Watch out, Andrei," she said. "I am good at this too."

Lynda Chester was a 1980 graduate of the Cornell University College of Engineering and Computer Science. For four years, she had been a member of the Cornell ROTC. Her intention had been to join the Navy, following in the footsteps of her father and grandfather who were career Navy. But after taking a course in computer-based pattern recognition and doing research with a truly motivating professor, Dr Sally Spitzer, Lynda had decided to pursue a graduate degree in this cutting-edge field.

Despite striking good looks — long black hair, blue eyes, an almost six-foot-tall athletic body — and warm personality, she'd had no social life. During her last year at Cornell, she spent every free moment in the computer lab, toiling away on her senior thesis project. This was later published in the prestigious journal *Science*, co-authored by Professor Sally Spitzer, a feat establishing Lynda as a significant presence in the rapidly expanding field of computer-based pattern recognition and robotics. After graduation from Cornell, Lynda had earned a PhD in computer engineering at MIT, where she developed an algorithm for extraction of hidden patterns in digital satellite images of planet earth. After her PhD, she obtained a prestigious National Research Council post-doctoral fellowship for studies at UC Berkeley to develop pattern recognition software for artificial intelligence (AI). After two years in California, she had been hired by the NSA to adapt her feature-extraction algorithms for detection of ICBMs hidden under camouflage in remote areas of North Korea. She had risen rapidly through the NSA and was now in charge of the multi-agency Wireless Cyber Monitoring Center.

Lynda puzzled over what Andrei Grushkov might be up to. She was sure that his career and movements have been closely tracked by the CIA for years, especially since Jack Light — likely, the next CIA director — had been a drinking buddy of Grushkov's back in their San Francisco and Moscow days.

While her main computer was searching the airport image databases, Lynda opened a folder on a second desktop computer labeled 'Call Detection Programs'. She clicked on 'Time and Locations'. When the program opened, she typed in the blank entry space: 'All calls, US to/from Cuba, forty-eight hrs."

In fifty-six seconds, the screen displayed: *'1,203 cell, 43 burner, 35 satellite'*.

In the blank instruction space, she entered, 'location & time: burner & satellite'. She reasoned that regular cell calls were probably family or business calls from Florida and elsewhere in the east — areas heavy with Cuban expats. While the facial recognition algorithm was sorting images, Lynda focused her attention on the burner and satellite calls.

In thirty seconds, the computer provided the times and locations of the forty-three received or sent burner cell calls, and thirty-five satellite calls to Cuba. Most of the burner calls were in areas outside the NY metropolitan area, the majority in Miami and South Florida. Ten were in the New York area, six in lower Manhattan. One call was from the Russian consulate on the East side of Manhattan and three others were from West Islip, Long Island.

These three calls caught her attention, none lasting more than a couple of seconds. They had been made from FSB headquarters in the Club El Muro Blanco in Havana. One of the satellite calls, also caught her eye: it was between the Russian consulate in Manhattan and the Club El Muro Blanco. Of the burner calls from across the US, Lynda flagged one from Irvine, California and one from Wichita, Kansas. These calls were suspicious because they also lasted only a few seconds. Further, there was no Russian consulate in either of these locations.

The facial recognition algorithm still crunching, Lynda opened another program that used algorithms to link the NSA-DoD-DARPA satellite network systems. She instructed the program to mine the text of the burner and satellite calls received or sent in the New York area.

The benefit of her innovative phone-intercept software was that each message detected in real-time was digitized, scrambled, and stored in a hack-proof NSA cloud file with unlimited storage capacity. This special cloud environment, known as the Intelligence Community Gov-Cloud, allowed NSA analysts to rapidly connect the dots from multiple data sources.

But these messages had to be retrieved and reconstructed, and that took time. Lynda knew she wouldn't have the results until the morning. And the process wasn't one hundred per cent foolproof. Some calls made at high volume call times might only be partially captured. Still, the confidence level for full retrieval was over ninety per cent.

It was a cat and mouse game. The call to Cuba from the Russian consulate seemed suspicious, especially since Grushkov was recently spotted in both places; and the three calls from the Long Island location were also suspect. Lynda didn't know what to make of the calls from California and Kansas, but they piqued her interest. She pigeonholed them in a mind that rarely forgot anything.

Grushkov had left the Russian consulate on the previous day at 7.27 a.m. On a hunch that he might be involved in the three Long Island burner calls, she sent an encrypted message to her contacts at the FBI, asking for an acceleration of the request to track Grushkov's car at the New York bridges and tunnels. She didn't expect an answer until sometime the next day, and that was assuming all the bridge and tunnel locations had functional cameras surveilling traffic.

She double clicked an icon on another computer she used exclusively for communication with other agencies, sending a summary of her results to senior analysts in the CIA, FBI, and her boss, SC. She turned back to the original bank of computers — still processing facial recognition software and gathering and collating information on every cell phone call made in North America, including calls made but not answered over the past forty-eight hours. Lynda had known for some time now that there was no privacy when it came to cell phones, computer use and normal movements on public streets, airports, and in most buildings with security cameras. Her personal preference for sensitive communication was old fashioned face-to-face meetings outside, preferably in a park.

At nine p.m. she was still at her desk; her computers still churning. They might be at it for several hours longer, and thoughts of her Jacuzzi were gaining traction. It was a thirty-minute drive to her two-bedroom condo in Columbia Heights. It was small, under a thousand square feet and over sixty years old, but it had been renovated and met her needs. Living in DC gave Lynda access to concerts, opera and plays, as well as museums. Her favorites were the Smithsonian's Air and Space Museum and the National Gallery.

But tonight, Lynda was still in her NSA office, thinking of her old flame. She returned to her desk with a full cup of black coffee just in time to see the facial recognition program flashing: '*72% match*'." The details were: '*Hartsfield Airport, Atlanta, camera 116, terminal C, Delta Airlines, gates 20 - 22.*' The time stamp was 11.35 p.m. two days ago.

"Damn," she exclaimed, spilling coffee on her neatly creased pants.

Hunched over her computer, she clicked on zoom image, confirming it really was Andrei Grushkov. She scrolled until she could read the screens behind the two airline check-in counters. For gate twenty, it read *Miami, departure on time, 12.25*, and for gate twenty-two: *Washington-Reagan, departure on time 11.55*. From the image she saw that passengers for the DC flight were boarding. Grushkov was clearly walking away from the gate area.

"Gate twenty-two," she said as she searched for an arrival-departure schedule for Delta.

"Yes!" She did a fist pump. "Arrival from Tucson, Arizona."

Scratching her head, Lynda stared unfocused at the plethora of agency performance awards on the wall opposite her desk. What was in

Tucson? What is near there? Are there connecting flights from elsewhere?

She pulled up a Google map of the south-west US. Tucson was an hour driving distance from the Mexican border.

Her watch said 12.45 a.m. She shook her head to clear the cobwebs. Glancing at the phone-tracing algorithm, she saw it was still mining. Grabbing her purse and heading home, she was determined to indulge in a late-night soak.

Chapter Nine
Wednesday

Lynda had a restless night, waking twice with various scenarios explaining why and how Grushkov illegally entered the US from Mexico. She dragged herself out of bed at five a.m., dressed quickly in dark slacks and a pressed white blouse, and wolfed down an English muffin with strong coffee.

She was on the road by five thirty and sitting at her NSA desk at six. She entered her seven-digit password into her mainframe computer, clicked on the 'phone encryption' folder, typed in a second password, and opened the program that had been running her phone de-encryption algorithm all night.

The results on the three calls to Long Island from Havana were:

First call: one ring, hang-up.

Second call: two rings, hang-up.

Third call: two rings, hang-up.

The call from California was one ring, hang-up; and from Kansas: two rings, hang-up. The GPS identification indicated the Havana calls to Long Island were from Club El Muro Blanco, and the two calls from California and Kansas were also to Club El Muro Blanco, Havana. Lynda opened another file labeled, 'Russian FSB Stations', scrolled to Cuba, clicked, and saw 'Club El Muro Blanco'.

How might these calls be connected? A memory floated to the surface from years ago. When she and Grushkov had their affair, his MO had been to use hang-up calls for signaling. They'd gotten into a spat one night that had started when he'd received a hang-up signal while they were having sex. She'd never forgotten that because it was so bizarre. Now she was onto something — it was palpable.

It was 7.30, late enough for her to call the one person she could always trust: Sally Spitzer. While they hadn't seen each other in several years, they'd spoken by phone two or three times a year just to keep in touch. Sally was the smartest person Lynda knew.

From the NSA parking lot, Lynda pushed Sally's name in her phone directory and after the second ring she answered.

"Lynda Chester!"

"Sally, look. I can't discuss this over my cell, but can we meet today?"

"Sure… Deep State Pub, five."

"See you there." Lynda hung up quickly, knowing cell calls on NSA property were verboten.

The Deep State Pub was two blocks from the White House. Lynda selected a booth at its far end and, exhibiting typical intelligence officer paranoia, she scanned the bar occupants. She hadn't seen her Cornell mentor in several years, not since Sally had given the keynote lecture at Lynda's twenty-fifth class reunion in Ithaca. Way back when, it had been Sally Spitzer who'd persuaded Lynda to pursue a PhD degree at MIT rather than joining the Navy as a commissioned officer after four years of ROTC.

Three years after Lynda graduated from Cornell, Sally had resigned her tenured professorship to become the second-in-command, Deputy Director, of the Defense Advanced Research Programs Agency. DARPA was an independent government organization with close ties to the Department of Defense. Initially stunned that Sally would leave a tenured post at an Ivy League university, Lynda still recalled her mentor's explanation. Sally had been really excited about the challenges provided by DARPA in the development of transformative technologies that would allow the United States to maintain a technological advantage over its enemies. Sally's expertise in artificial intelligence was exactly what DARPA had been looking for. "I was a perfect fit," Sally had said, laughing.

It was Sally's course in advanced image processing and robotics that had motivated Lynda to pursue a graduate PhD, focusing on the complex algorithms necessary for robotic pattern recognition, a key capability in artificial intelligence that allowed computer-controlled devices to discern subtle patterns — like a sophisticated network of satellites under development by China, Russia, Iran, and North Korea.

A fear within US intelligence agencies was that their enemies might link up their multiple satellite systems, resulting in a multiplexed technology array that could overwhelm US capabilities. Sally's job was to support the development of counterintelligence technologies to thwart this effort.

Even though her platinum blonde hair was now white, the six-foot-two-inch Sally was easy to spot as she entered the pub. After big hugs, they sat and for a few minutes caught each other up on the latest.

After a brief pause, Sally said, "Lynda, I'm delighted to see you, but I know this isn't a social visit."

Lynda laughed nervously. "You always get to the point." She bent across the small table so she could keep her voice down. "Sally, my cell phone tracking algorithm has detected something odd in three burner phone calls from Havana, Cuba to West Islip, Long Island. They were no-answer calls. At first it seemed insignificant, but my gut tells me otherwise."

Sally wrinkled her brow. "No-answer calls from a burner phone... Okay, you've got me curious. Is there more?"

"All three calls originated from Club El Muro Blanco, a front for the headquarters of the Russian FSB in Havana. I also tracked two other hang-up calls from the Havana location — one in California and another in Wichita, Kansas. I'm not sure what to make of those."

Sally gazed at a colorful row of bottles above the bar, considering what Lynda just revealed. "A signal was being sent. What else?"

Lynda flushed. She fanned her blouse and explained. This was Sally, after all: a friend to be trusted. "You remember that boyfriend I had, out in California? The one who turned out to be a Russian spy? I know it's ancient history."

"Yeah, Grushkov... years ago."

"I'm always amazed at your memory. Yeah, Andrei Grushkov. He's now head of FSB clandestine operations. Three days ago, he was spotted leaving the Russian consulate in New York... without having registered or crossed through customs at any US entry point. His MO was to use hang-up calls."

Sally met Lynda's worried gaze. "What are you getting at?"

"Two weeks ago, the CIA tracked him to Havana, Cuba."

"Was it to Club…?"

"Don't know. My boss, Steven Craig, just put me on this project, but I sense he's not telling me everything. Maybe because he knows about my affair, which I disclosed when the NSA first vetted me."

"Maybe. But it also could be a turf issue. You know there's a triad of jealousy and competition between the CIA, NSA, and FBI."

Lynda sighed. "Yeah, maybe that's it. We're supposed to work together toward common goals, but the current National Security Advisor encourages competition. I still share openly with the other agencies. Maybe that's why SC holds back information from me."

After a waiter delivered their drinks, Sally waited for him to leave, then sipped her deep red French Malbec. "So Grushkov resurfaced in New York?"

"Yes. But that's not all." Lynda drained her glass. "Using facial recognition, I picked him up two days ago in Atlanta, getting off a Delta flight from Tucson."

"And…" Sally said with raised eyebrows.

Lynda leaned closer. "The border with Mexico is an hour away."

Sally nodded. "Who have you informed?"

"No one yet. I'm still analyzing the phone calls and Grushkov's movements in New York. The FBI is processing images from the cameras outside the Russian consulate, trying to pinpoint the times of his arrival and departure. I'm waiting for those results." Lynda signaled the waiter for refills. She said to Sally, "We still think the Russians are out to get us, despite what some powerful DC people believe. I mean, our beef with the Russians goes back to the Cold War."

Sally chuckled. "Yeah, well, some of us diehards are still stuck in that time warp." The two women paused again while their server set fresh drinks in front of them. Sally took a long sip of wine and cut to the chase. "How I can help?"

Lynda dove in. "Maybe get your satellite folks to do high resolution scans of the Russian activity in Havana? And if your people can spot Grushkov in the US, have them lock onto him with the new multiple satellite technology DARPA has developed. I know you can track individuals in real time."

Sally let out a surprised laugh. "I didn't know anyone outside DARPA knew about RATS."

"RATS?"

That's what we call our new Real-time Algorithm Tracking System. Satellite time, especially if it's a favor, comes with a big 'you owe me' in return, and my favor-card is pretty full."

"Sally, I know it's a fishing expedition, and five hang-up burner phone calls with the Russian FSB headquarters is no proof of a plot. But if we add Grushkov to the equation… well, it's worrisome. That's how we got Bin Laden."

Sally looked hard into Lynda's sparkling blue eyes without replying, and then asked, "Is your past with Grushkov affecting how you are handling this?"

Lynda drained her second glass of Merlot. "Not one iota."

Sally finished her Malbec and placed the empty glass on the table. "Lynda, I respect your intuition, so I'll consult with my super-geeks to see if they come up with anything. Some of the technology we have under development might be useful. Between us, I'm already consulting with the CIA to beta-test our newest satellite communication technology at Langley. If there's another event that involves the Cuban site or you pick up Grushkov's trail in the US, we can be on it. But if nothing else happens, there isn't much I can do."

"Who's your contact at CIA?" asked Lynda.

"Jack Light."

"Jack and I go way back," Lynda said. "Should I approach him directly?"

"No. Let me work this from inside."

"Okay. But my gut says something's going on." She half-smiled. "And I'm embarrassed that it's taken this much time for us to reconnect."

"Me too," Sally winced. "Last time we talked was when your dad died. He was a good man. A fine naval officer."

Lynda thought of her last conversation with her dad before he was wheeled into the OR for heart valve replacement surgery. Groggy from the preop medication, he had squeezed her hand, and with a fading twinkle in his blue eyes, said to his only child, "I'm proud of you, even if you aren't in the Navy."

He never woke up from the surgery.

Thinking of her father's death three years ago, Lynda's eyes teared. "Yes, he forgave me."

Sally reached across the table and squeezed Lynda's hand.

"Sally, my dad was the only man in my life whose love I never questioned. Our bond was rock solid. He was right when he told me it was a mistake getting married to a history grad student right before I finished my doctorate. I thought Dad was jealous, you know that father-daughter thing. But all he wanted was the best for me."

The two women looked into each other's eyes; no need for more words on the subject.

"So you're happy at the NSA?" Sally said, changing the subject.

"I get to write algorithms to solve tricky intelligence problems, but there's also a lot of routine stuff, and of course, the political nonsense."

"Yeah, politics everywhere. Even at DARPA. Our group has a bunch of technical guys and a few women. When I took the job, I thought I'd be in line to head DARPA someday, but when the position opened up a few years back, they brought in an NSF guy to run the show."

"Same at the NSA. I have two male bosses, and no chance of moving up. These guys are old school, the director is stuck in the Cold War and my immediate supervisor is computer illiterate. He keeps a tight rein on me and everyone else under his control."

"Have you considered that you're a smart woman who's viewed as a threat by your male bosses?"

"I've thought about that. But my boss, SC, has got his Princeton education stuck way up his ass. He looks down on my Cornell education as being from a second-rate Ivy League school. He can be quite a snob."

"Sounds like you're ready for a change."

"I've thought about it."

"What about your personal life?"

Lynda said, "What personal life? My first love has always been my work, and there's never been much room left for someone else. I like being independent, coming home when I want, eating when and what I want, going to plays and the symphony. I have a small circle of friends that I do things with. That seems like enough. But there are times I regret not having a family and kids. My parents had a great marriage. Sally, I admire the fact that you're a professional success and also have a great family."

"Jim and I have had some bumps along the way. He gave up a law practice in Ithaca when we moved here. For the first few years he was out of his element, competing with the big law firms. It was stressful for both of us. But when he switched to patent law, he got a good job in the Trade and Patent Office. He's happy now, and our twins are finishing college, so yeah, we're doing well."

They were quiet again for a bit, then Sally said, "You're a genius, Lynda. One of my best students ever. If you want to move to DARPA, just let me know. We are in the R and D side of technology and try to stay two steps ahead of the Russians and Chinese. What we do is pretty exciting."

"Thanks, Sally. Maybe after I solve this Russian puzzle."

They both got up, gathering their purses and jackets. After a farewell hug, they left the Deep State Pub separately, like seasoned spies.

Chapter Ten
Wednesday

When Yuri Khodakov woke up on the couch at five a.m., the Murphy bed was still in the wall. Peter Petrov, the other half of Grushkov's *Snow Leopard* team, had been out all night. This scenario had not been in their original mission prep when they were embedded into Greenwich Village six months earlier. Yuri felt the urge to take out his burner phone and report this situation to Grushkov. Instead, he went for his usual morning run. When he returned at six thirty, there was still no sign of Peter.

At 7.05, Peter returned to their Greenwich Village flat, hair disheveled, pants and shirt wrinkled, uncommon for a guy who was generally meticulous about his appearance.

"Where the hell have you been?" Yuri barked. "I was about to call Grushkov."

"You know where I was," Peter answered. "I spend Tuesday nights with Tom Mahoney. Why do you still get so upset?"

Yuri said. "We are supposed to start our work at seven a.m. Your work ethic is slipping."

"You're jealous of my friendship with Tom," Peter said, and stalked into the bathroom for a shower.

Yuri paced the apartment, thinking about Peter's comment. When Peter returned to the kitchen refreshed and dressed, Yuri said, "Sorry, Peter. I didn't mean to suggest anything personal between us. It's just that Grushkov may have thought of our cover as a gay couple, so we'd fit in the neighborhood better."

"Yes," Peter said. "I think that's why we were paired as a team. And so now you're worried that my dating a different guy does not fit Grushkov's plan?"

"I think that's what bothering me. Now, I realize we could have been a couple, but I rejected that when we first moved in."

Peter blushed.

Yuri ignored it. "I know the NYU professor is an asset; he introduced you around and allowed us to make valuable contacts. I'm okay with you seeing him, and I'm sorry if I overreacted."

"I agree, he's an asset," said Peter. "Thanks to Tom's computer, we were able to hack into the NYU Business School server. So you see? You should be grateful to my sexy American professor." He grinned and opened the refrigerator, pulling out a carton of eggs to make them a hearty Russian ham and cheese omelet breakfast.

Yuri turned on his laptop to scan the morning news. When he spotted a report that a rabbi had been attacked in Rockland County just north of New York City, his breath caught. The rabbi had been stabbed multiple times coming out of his house.

Yuri gasped. "I think our AI-socbots may have mutated, driving violent acts that they were not programmed for. They're no longer *AI*-socbots. Rather, they are mutation-driven socbots… mutbots."

Peter gently folded the omelet on itself at the stove and then peered over Yuri's shoulder to scan the article on his laptop. "It may be a stretch for us to take credit for that attack. Have you checked the American Police Initiative site?"

Yuri clicked into the saved police database site which posted monthly numbers on hate crimes in American cities. Things were definitely heating up across America. And there was little doubt the *Snow leopard* team was partly responsible.

Two weeks after Yuri had launched his AI-socbots, the police database had recorded an uptick in reports of anti-Semitic and anti-gay graffiti scrawled on buildings and walls in large and small towns and cities across America. In the only synagogue in the primarily blue-collar town of Kearney, New Jersey, not far from New York City, windows had been smashed and White Power slogans with swastikas were spray-painted on the sides of the building. Also, an inexplicable rise in lootings had started cropping up; first, in the same neighborhoods as the rise in graffiti and smashed windows, and later in upscale neighborhoods such as Beverly Hills, SoHo in New York, and the Oak Street Gold Coast District in Chicago.

"Sounds like opportunist groups are piggy-backing on our hate campaign," Peter said.

"It's going to increase the impact of what we were sent here to do: divide America further, damage democracy," Yuri said, beaming with pride.

Six months ago, soon after they first arrived at the apartment on Bleeker Street in New York City's Greenwich Village section, Yuri had pushed any romantic feelings about Peter into a deep mental vault. He'd quickly established a routine, running every morning to release his pent-up energy and keep in physical shape. He'd convinced himself that he was concerned with Peter's behavior only because he was afraid Peter might compromise their mission by inadvertently revealing aspects of their backgrounds, particularly growing up in the Soviet Union and studying in Russia after the Soviet break-up.

Several times Yuri had taken out his burner phone to call Grushkov for guidance, but he never hit the call button because he considered that perhaps Peter *was* doing just what Grushkov had wanted. Peter was almost always back by seven a.m. and his blogging and posting on social media had not been affected. In fact, there was an uptick in followers from the NYU community, which Yuri attributed to contacts made through Peter's professor-friend. Yuri had to admit that *Snow leopard* had been far more effective because they interacted with members of the target community, in addition to building remote interactions through social media.

Peter's relationship with Professor Mahoney had paid off a month ago when the professor had indignantly told him that the NYU Business School server had been hacked. A school wide email went out to all NYU faculty, warning that a hacker was using the business school server to send out offensive blog posting and emails, and establishing fake Facebook accounts containing inflammatory, prejudicial messages, several of which had gone viral. According to Professor Mahoney, the NYU police had been notified, and that they were working with other law enforcement groups to track down the hacker.

When informed of this by Mahoney, Peter acted surprised, and when he returned to the Bleeker Street flat early the next morning, he'd excitedly announced in Russian, "Yuri, the NYU police have brought in the FBI."

"We have been too successful," Yuri laughed. He had immediately changed their tactics. Now that the American authorities had been called in, it was time for *Snow leopard* to abandon the NYU server. They'd swiftly moved to the dark web, using the Tor browser and anonymous IP addresses in their next barrage of cyberattacks.

"This is slow and tedious," Peter had complained as they learned the new system. "Do we have to pick a new IP address each time we log on?"

"Not if we use AI-bots," Yuri explained. "They locate anonymous IP addresses through our own VPN. We have untraceable IP addresses, and if we use hushmail with our own VPN , we'll have impenetrable anonymity."

Switching from email to anonymous hushmail through the hacked business school server had kept their identities hidden while their message spread and they gained followers. Now, because of detection by the NYU police, their messaging on the dark web using untraceable IP addresses and VPNs not only kept their anonymity but expanded their reach to far right extremist groups prone to violence. And finally, Yuri's ability to use artificial intelligence bots — developed specifically for the Tinderbox Plot — resulted in a skyrocket increase in acolytes.

Yuri was an expert in social bots, socbots, designed to spread inflammatory messages throughout the Internet and the dark web, the latter being the repository of the most extreme hate. His experience with bots dated back to the 2016 and 2020 American elections. According to FSB cybertrackers, half a million bots were responsible for almost four million fake Tweets in the 2016 American election. It had been even more in 2020, including an additional hijacking of Facebook and Instagram with an overwhelming number of incendiary postings. These platforms were temporarily shut down in early 2021 to allow development and installation of new software to detect and expunge postings and blogs that were aimed at inciting violence and rebellion.

However, *Snow leopard* was using a new type of artificial intelligence software, the AI bot, and now the mut-*bot,* developed by the Russian cybersecurity division of the FSB to counter these changes. These bots were capable of simple machine learning, making decisions on their own. When programmed properly, they functioned independently, and could mutate in response to different virtual environments. They entered a computer, searched its email database, then infected the computers of all the email contacts. Mut-bots were capable of influencing individuals and large groups, causing people to behave according to the bot's programming. They developed and grew their own huge followings. The Russian bot program was flourishing because the American botnet roadmap, which was developed to counter the Russian, Iranian and Chinese efforts, had stalled due to infighting and lack of coordination between the US intelligence stakeholders.

Yuri had spent hours trying to explain these sophisticated concepts to Peter. He'd explained how — just by using conventional social media platforms — botstorms, massive attacks by bots, could self-amplify, carrying fake messages to larger and larger numbers of people.

Over cups of dark, Russian tea, after a typical hearty breakfast prepared by Peter, he asked Yuri whether AI bots could jump like an infectious virus from the social media World Wide Web to the dark web where there was a concentrated reservoir of pent-up anger.

"Dark web is a little more difficult," Yuri had told him. "But the FSB cyberwarfare unit informed me before we left Havana that they've developed an AI-bot that self-selects a new VPN each time it enters the dark web. Can you imagine the potential if we could control botstorms on both the WorldWide and the dark webs? Each bot would be a nano-avatar, amplifying its message through infection, mutation, and self-replication in individual computers. The bots will do the work for us and even continue long after we go home."

Peter's back stiffened at the mention of *home*. "Yuri, I'm not ready to go home. I like it here."

Yuri had given his partner, a cold, appraising stare. "It's not up to me. Grushkov expects you to return home."

Peter forced a smile. "Of course," he said. "And meanwhile, we will continue to stir up trouble."

"True," Yuri returned the smile. "I'm enjoying this work. It's exciting to use the newest tech advancements. The IT group at FSB has developed AI bots that react to the biases of any target group, then push individuals to commit violent acts."

Peter nodded. "Like the violence that happened in Charlottesville, Virginia?"

Yuri set down his tea cup loudly. "Yes, AI mutation bots, the mut-bots, can infect individual computers and cell phones of the white supremacists. They will appear as an email or text from another member of the group, directing the recipient to, for example, throw a Molotov cocktail. Though the AI mut-bots are not programmed for that act, it's the AI machine learning function that detects the level of hate in the recipient by reading emails in their computer; then it formulates an action that the AI mut-bot perceives matches the level of anger."

"We can retire," Peter said, and laughed.

"Indeed," Yuri confirmed. "The fact that the bots are able to use their AI programming to mutate in response to behaviors and facts they detect in targets means that someday we *will* be obsolete."

Peter, with his background in psychology, had created their first social media avatar several months ago. This made-up activist, a consultant in reproductive technology with university degrees, had founded and sold several fake companies that were in the hot area of CRISPR gene editing technology.

With a gleam in his eye, Peter told Yuri, "The hook is the statement: *advocate for gene editing to induce late term abortion.*" He had posted the message on Linked-In, Facebook, Instagram, and Twitter. The post had worked beautifully. Almost immediately, American liberals had responded to Peter's avatar, directing their anger at the fake entrepreneur who they accused of trying to interfere with human embryos' genes.

Peter's stock response to these angry comments was, 'this is a business decision, not a moral one.' This had inflamed the liberal left even more, resulting in comments like: 'All *you* businesspeople think about is making money.'

As Peter had anticipated, his postings resonated with the liberal left. Angry progressives were vehemently opposed to messing with genes, especially in human fetuses. They didn't understand why a liberal democratic businessman would support it. These same postings also stirred up conservatives; the Christian right was against late term abortion. They were opposed to anything that messed with what they viewed as the *natural order*.

As their audience had grown, Peter told Yuri, "It won't take long before the right and left are at each other's throats. We could even post a

YouTube video. We could put you in a white coat with a stethoscope around your neck. It'll go viral. What do you think?"

"Not yet," said Yuri. "I think it will be better initially to use the AI-bots for a simpler message, like 'Too many Jews in powerful positions.' It plays to America's vast reservoir of open and hidden anti-Semitism."

Next, they took on climate change. "It's the perfect issue," Peter announced. "We are speaking of a major divide between the left and the right."

Yuri swiftly designed a blog called *GlobalWarmingFiction* that claimed that energy company scientists had proven global warming to be a hoax.

A week after the anti-science blog hit the blogosphere and went viral, over eighteen thousand responders expressed outrage at the Republican-motivated corporate scientists. And after Peter had sent out a YouTube video on the climate change hoax, *Snow leopard* amassed thirty thousand angry followers on that one issue alone. After they launched their first AI-botstorm, the number of followers had surpassed one hundred thousand, and it continued to grow exponentially.

Given the success of their AI-botstorm in conventional social media platforms, the *Snow leopard* team had turned to the dark web, targeting neo-Nazis and skinheads.

After six months, they had amassed over a million followers and at this point, it was impossible to keep up. They spent their days divided between regular social media platforms like Facebook, Instagram, and Twitter, and the dark web. They alternated between sending out new posts and responding to hate messages generated by their previous posts. They encouraged the senders to bring their friends into the loop. In the evening, they responded to hundreds of disgruntled Americans, many of whom were closet bigots, and were spurred to hit the streets by *Snow leopard*'s messages. They usually broke for a quick dinner prepared by Peter. Occasionally they treated themselves to a meal at a nearby Greenwich Village restaurant, where they always paid with cash from the ten thousand dollars they were given as they left Havana.

On Tuesdays, Peter spent the evening with Professor Tom Mahoney, who had an apartment adjacent to the Sloan Business School. Their

76

relationship blossomed into a full-blown affair soon after their first meeting several months ago at the Think Coffee Cafe.

It had accelerated soon after the day Peter handed Yuri a business card with Professor Mahoney's apartment address. "Why don't you come with me to Tom's? He's having a small party tonight. They'll be other professors from NYU."

Yuri glanced at Peter but did not hold eye contact. "I'll stay here and respond to some of many followers. Contact with the Americans is risky."

"You worry too much," Peter said. "I am careful not to reveal anything about who we really are."

Yuri hesitated. "Peter, are you sure Professor Mahoney does not suspect you are not who you appear to be?"

"I have been incredibly careful. I don't talk about my family or schooling."

"But you share his bed. He must ask personal questions."

Peter was quiet, pondering Yuri's comment. "I remember him asking about my family, whether I have siblings and whether my parents are alive. I avoided answering."

"What was his reaction?"

"I think he respected my privacy. Didn't bring it up again."

"Isn't that peculiar?"

"Well, maybe. But I don't sense any lessening of his interest in me. And he's never brought up that hacking business with the FBI."

"Peter, I must ask how you feel about him. Are you doing this because it is part of our mission or because you are becoming emotionally involved?"

Peter got up from the couch where they were both sitting. He went to the kitchen and took out a chilled bottle of Stoli.

After they had each tossed back two shots, Peter looked directly into Yuri's eyes.

"I love him."

Chapter Eleven
Wednesday

After a restless night in the guest suite of the Manhattan Russian consulate, Grushkov's cell phone alarm woke him at 6.15 a.m. He dressed casually in American-made lightweight jeans and a dark blue Puma polo shirt. After admiring his flat stomach in the bathroom mirror, he headed to the first-floor cafeteria. It wasn't as grim as Nicolai had said. The tea was good, authentically Russian, and the bagels were from a Jewish deli, clearly not made in the consulate kitchen.

He sat in a corner at the opposite end of the cafeteria from a handful of employees, none of whom he recognized. He was thinking of the best way to approach his *Snow leopard* team. Based on FSB reports that closely scrutinized American social media, their activities and those of the troubled *Arctic fox* team in California appeared highly successful, having resulted in a dramatic rise in hate messages.

He mulled the risk of visiting the *Snow leopard* team in person. They didn't know the broader details of the Tinderbox Plot, including the timing of their escape from America. It was too risky for them to have this information while in transit; there was always the possibility they'd be detained and interrogated by US intelligence. Now that the team appeared to be smoothly functioning under the radar from their Greenwich Village site, Grushkov was ready to reveal further details of the plan, as well as providing Yuri and Peter with an exit strategy.

He finished his breakfast, returned to his room for his laptop, and was out the consulate's service entrance by 7.35 a.m. From that back alley, he walked west to Fifth Avenue, hailed a cab going downtown, which dropped him off at Central Park's southern edge. The traffic was heavy, the street jammed with taxis, buses, and commercial trucks, all noisily starting another workday. At Fifty-Ninth Street and Fifth, he descended down a rancid-smelling stairwell to the subway system. Catching an R train to Thirty-Fourth Street, he rode the wave of the morning crush to the F-train platform and into an open subway car after it disgorged a horde of commuters.

He exited the subway at the Washington Square Station. Using Google Maps on his cell, he saw that it was a seven-minute walk to the *Snow leop*ard flat.

At the Bleeker Street address, Grushkov climbed the outside steps and entered the building after a young couple left the front door ajar. Inside, the tiny elevator jerked its way to the eighth floor. , When he pushed the doorbell at apartment eight seventeen there was no response — no noise of movement from inside. After about thirty seconds, he rapped firmly on the reinforced metal door.

After another half-minute, it opened slightly, and Yuri Khodakov's eyes widened. Andrei Grushkov was perhaps the last person he'd expected to see.

"Andrei… Grushkov… ah, ah, it is you," Yuri stammered. "Come in."

Entering the flat, Grushkov scanned the room, and said, "I thought I would deliver your final instructions in person. Where's Peter?"

Yuri's face grimaced. He was quiet wrestling with what to tell his boss.

"What's going on, Yuri?"

"Uhm … Peter has a boyfriend," Yuri said, disapproval apparent in his tone. "A professor at New York University."

Grushkov stared at Yuri for a few seconds, and then asked, "What were your mission instructions?"

"Andrei Andreievich, y-y-you said our objective was to use social media platforms to sow confusion and anger among the liberal left-wing American community."

"Yes, and in addition, infiltrate the local community — something it sounds like Peter has achieved."

Yuri nodded, though his evasive eyes indicated he was not expressing all his thoughts.

"You were chosen for this mission because of your skills at computer hacking and weaponization of the Internet, right?" Grushkov said.

"Yes, Andrei Grushkov," Yuri answered, trailing his boss around the flat.

Grushkov turned and faced him. "And Peter was chosen not only because of his technical skills, but also because he had training in psychology and community relations. And I'm pleased to say your team has been enormously effective." He gave Yuri an affectionate slap on the back. "Mother Russia is proud of you."

Internally Grushkov was not so sure. He had not had direct contact with Gorky since his final audience with the Russian leader a year ago.

"Yes, Andrei Andreievich." Yuri stood up straighter and beamed with pride. "We have over a million followers in both the World Wide Web and the dark web. The numbers are increasing every day because of our use of social bots. I have done a mathematical projection which projects five million followers in another month, and that's a conservative estimate since we don't really know the impact of our AI-botstorms."

The apartment door flew open. Peter was standing in the open door, surprised at the unusual sight of a visitor, and this one in particular.

Grushkov smiled broadly, rushing over and embracing Peter in a bear hug. "Peter, I hear you are meeting with great success. Tell me about your American professor."

Peter stammered, "He... he... teaches neuroeconomics in the NYU business school. He's very kind and generous. I do my job while he sleeps. Early on, I retrieved his IP address, then Yuri and I hacked into the school server, hijacking the network. But other professors eventually got suspicious because of all the hate messages they were receiving, and they notified the police and the FBI, so we switched to the dark web using anonymous IP addresses."

Remembering his first interview with Peter, a muscular fellow with curly dark hair and a broad smile, Grushkov now said, "You have come a long way from the farm in Tajikistan."

"Yes, Andrei. I would still be there if the Soviet Union hadn't fallen apart. My parents were forced to move back to Moscow. I still miss my Tadjik friends."

Grushkov nodded. "Peter, your smile is your secret weapon. Whenever you smile, it's reciprocated, and the door to friendship opens wide. That's why I picked you for this mission."

All three men laughed heartily as the tension in the room evaporated.

Grushkov's stomach rumbled. He looked at his watch. "It's almost lunchtime.

Peter said, "I have pierogi." As he took a package from the freezer he continued. "We found a fairly good Russian restaurant in the East Village. These are frozen but freshly made." He put a pot of water on the stove to boil, adding a sprinkle of salt. "Please Andrei, sit at our small kitchen table and we will have a drink while the pierogi cooks. Tea or vodka?

"Vodka, of course!"

Over the next hour and a half, they consumed a bottle of freezer-chilled Stolichnaya, and between them, two dozen pierogis.

Sated, Grushkov said, "I need a change of clothes, with a hat, and casual shoes."

Yuri rose from the table. "We are about the same size. I have an outfit for you, complete with Adidas sneakers."

"And, please, I will need a razor to remove my beard."

"Happy to accommodate," said Yuri, trailing Grushkov into the bathroom.

As Grushkov shaved his whiskers, Yuri got to what was troubling him. "I think Peter has become too close with his professor."

"Can you be sure you are not jealous?" Grushkov asked as his well-groomed beard fell victim to the razor's edge.

Yuri felt his face get hot, but he ignored Grushkov's question. "Andrei Andreievich, my observations are entirely professional. I believe there is a possibility that Peter will try to stay in America with Professor Mahoney."

Grushkov halted a razor stroke, and focused on Yuri, looking directly at him in the mirror. "You are trained in matters of life and death. You will not leave Peter behind. Do you understand?"

"I do," Yuri said.

At 4.10, Andrei left the flat, walking two blocks to the south-west corner of Washington Square Park. At 4.20, a black Lexus 350C stopped at the curb. Grushkov slipped into the passenger seat and the car re-entered traffic, heading east.

"Nice to see you again, Olga." Stretching to look in the cramped backseat, he said, "I see you got my message and picked up my overnight case from the consulate."

"Of course, Andrei Andreievich. We have good communication between New York and Long Island. Are we headed to the same hotel as before?"

"No, this time to the Hilton Garden Inn, down the road from the Clarion Hotel."

"You didn't like the Clarion?"

"Too risky to stay at the same hotel for more than one night."

A traffic light halted their progress, and Olga turned and gave him a closer look. "You look better without the beard. You shaved off twenty years."

Grushkov smiled, smelling a faint trace of fresh lilacs.

At the hotel, they inspected Grushkov's new room. It had a large king-sized bed and the typical mid-level room amenities.

Grushkov had been so consumed with planning the Tinderbox Plot that he hadn't been with a woman in over a year. Most of his relationships, if you could call them that, had lasted a few weeks, except one with an embassy intelligence officer in London that continued almost six months. Since Marina died, his almost obsessive focus had been to rise through the ranks of the KGB and then the FSB. In addition, four years ago when he'd reached age sixty, he lost interest in women, or so he'd thought.

With Olga, Andrei felt an emotional and physical stirring he hadn't experienced in a long time. He fondly remembered their brief tryst twenty years ago. Following Olga's movements intently as she scanned the room for listening devices and said, "I shouldn't have let you slip away twenty years ago."

She finished the scan, put the device on the dresser, and turned to face Andrei. "So why did you," she said with a wisp of a smile.

He sat on the edge of the bed. "I was busy rebuilding my division for President Gorky."

"So was your interest in me back then merely to satisfy a physical need?"

"Hardly. But at that point in my life, I could not allow myself to become entangled in a relationship. Now I realize that I miss having a real relationship with someone else."

She let out a sarcastic laugh. "Ahhhh, my dear Andrei. You were always driven, married to your job. You grew up in the KGB, with the mantra of 'No personal relationships'."

"This is my last mission," he said. "I want to move out of field operations, and teach, maybe at the university. My goal is to be an *ex*-intelligence officer."

She leaned back against the dresser, gazing intently into his eyes. "Andrei, I was drawn to you back then, and of course I have followed your rise through the intelligence service. That our paths should cross again is mystical. I believe it was meant to happen."

"I am not a strong believer in mysticism. Maybe we are both lonely for a physical connection."

"Just physical?"

"Well, no." he replied. "There has to be an emotional bond too, and a respect for the other person. I haven't thought about this subject in a long time but, Olga, I am drawn to you, and it's not just because you're sexy."

"You think I'm sexy?" She appeared both pleased and bashful, glancing away momentarily.

"I wouldn't say it unless I meant it. But there's always been much more to you than just your *incredible* looks," he teased. "Otherwise, I wouldn't have remembered you so clearly after all these years."

Olga moved from beside the dresser to the center of the room, about six feet from Andrei. Balancing on one and then the other leg, she tossed her shoes across the room.

He rose, walked to her, encircled her body with his arms and gave her a gentle hug. He smelled a sweetness in her hair from her morning bath as he ran his tongue around her right earlobe.

She moaned and ran her hands through his hair, then down his back, lightly squeezing his buttocks.

They separated slightly, looked into each other's eyes, and smiled. No words were spoken as Andrei deftly removed her clothes, conscious of the strong desire and physical presence in his groin. Her breasts were firm and, as he kissed her nipples, they become erect as she moaned again, whispering nonsense in his ear.

They made tender love at first, but as she responded with a warm moistness, he increased the power of his movements until they both, limbs and minds entangled, reached passionate climaxes: she first, and he a few seconds after.

They collapsed on the sheets, falling in and out of sleep. A few hours later, they made love again.

Andrei Grushkov whispered, "It's been a long time."

She whispered back, "For me too."

Chapter Twelve
Thursday-Sunday

It had been three months since the *Arctic fox* team had arrived at their condo in Irvine, California. Since then, Irene Seminova and Larissa Rubin established an online presence with more than seven hundred and fifty thousand followers spread over several activist blogs and radical political sites on both the Internet and the dark web, the latter being Irene's territory.

Despite their success, Grushkov sent the pair an encrypted note of encouragement, but in it he had also pointed out to them that *Snow leopard* was generating significantly higher numbers and instigating more hate crimes and violent acts.

Irene and Larissa were determined not to be outdone. And while it was true, they couldn't stand each other, their common goal led to an uneasy truce.

"Are you sure you don't want to join me on Saturday?" Irene asked. After months of probing the dark web, she had established contact with a number of right-wing fringe groups in Southern California. One of these, a local branch of the National Gun Association, the NGA, was sponsoring an upcoming rally in Hemet, a blue-collar and skin-head community between Orange County and Palm Springs.

"I'm sure," said Larissa. "You have an affinity for gun nuts. I know you'll optimize this opportunity without me tagging along."

Irene studied her glamorous, red-haired compatriot. "And what will you do while I'm making contacts with the NGA?"

"Spending time with Liang." Larissa smiled. "I know you didn't like when I befriended our neighbors but look at how helpful they've been. Thanks to Liang and Zhao, we got access to the University of California's server allowing our entire operation to be set in motion. Besides, Liang will make me a special Chinese meal this weekend."

Irene frowned. "It's true he and Zhao were useful when we needed a way to hack into the university server, but why maintain the relationship? We've gotten all we can get from them and spending more time with them only elevates the risk of exposure. You might do something indiscreet… or say something stupid."

Larissa kept her cool and ran her fingers through her long, auburn hair, well aware that this gesture irritated Irene, who in contrast, took pride in her plain features and lean physique. "You don't think our Chinese neighbors can still be useful?" asked Larissa. "They've been very generous with their time."

"Almost too generous," harped Irene.

When Larissa and Irene had first arrived in California, their two neighbors — graduate engineering students from China — invited Larissa and Irene for dinner, which had subsequently led to an invitation to visit them in the engineering department on campus. Liang spoke English, but Zhao was still learning. So it was Liang who'd given them the tour of the University of California, Irvine campus, including the office he shared with Zhao. He'd also showed them the engineering department's server area, unknowingly giving Irene the passcode when they entered the server room.

Liang specialized in the development of computer chip technology, and he was already collaborating with a private company. Zhao was rotating through the labs of several engineering professors before declaring his thesis topic.

Irene wasn't blind to Larissa's personal interest in Liang in addition to her fawning over his research studies. But she'd held off complaining to Grushkov because Larissa's friendship with Liang had given Irene the information she needed, to slip into the engineering building late at night and emerge with an IP server address. This allowed the two agents to infiltrate professors' email accounts and set up their hate campaign on social media.

"So how will you get to Hemet," Larissa asked with a broad ingenuous smile.

Irene shrugged. "The conference organizers are running a carpool from the Irvine Amtrak station for those of us who don't want to drive to

Riverside County. According to the organizers the remote location is hard to find."

"It would be easier if you rented a car."

Irene scoffed at Larissa's naivety. "That would require using our Canadian licenses and credit cards, unnecessarily creating a digital footprint."

Larissa turned her attention back to her laptop. She was in the middle of adding a new post to *DeportThemNow*, which targeted hate groups against immigrants, ethnic minorities, and Jews. She was blogging and posting under the handle *WhiteForChrist*, a campaign aimed to incite right-wing Christian groups and white supremacists.

"Fine." Irene sighed. "I will pursue this lead on my own." She stood abruptly and headed into the bigger bedroom she'd claimed on their arrival at the condo. The lodgings were clean, spacious, and brightly lit. The Russian FSB was paying for it through a shell company often used for American operations.

Opening her closet, Irene pulled out the military camouflage gear she'd purchased several days ago at a local sporting goods store. Rubbing the stiff fabric, she felt a rumble of satisfaction. She would blend right in.

On Saturday, Irene caught the seven a.m. bus to the Irvine train station and waited with a group of around fifty men and women clustered in front of the station. Two vans arrived with pro-gun stickers plastered on the bumpers and the side windows.

Irene sat quietly during the hour and a half ride to Hemet, listening to discussions about perceived threats to the Second Amendment, and different strategies to throttle the criticism by the liberal 'lame-stream' media. These included firebombings, physical threats, and attacks at rallies.

Thoughts of violence got Irene's heart pumping; it was what she'd been trained for, but she hadn't had a chance to use deadly force on this mission. She thought about throttling Larissa. Irene suspected the stuck-up redhead was having an affair with Liang. She had to figure out how to use it to her advantage when she returned from the NGA meet-up.

The bus arrived at a large brown field, that looked like it had once been a cattle grazing area. Exiting the vehicle in front of several tents and booths, they noted the carnival-like atmosphere among the gathered crowd. One large white tent had a sign announcing: 'The Neo-Nationalist Nation, NNN'. Just a few feet from Irene, a boy, maybe twelve years old, was wearing a swastika armband and handing out flyers advocating violence against Jews as the 'final solution'.

At another tent, she encountered a scruffy, grey bearded man in dirty jeans talking with a lean, smartly dressed, fortyish guy about six feet tall. He wore light brown chino pants and an open Izod knit shirt. They introduced themselves as members of a new organization, Concerned Citizens for Nationals News, the CCNN.

Irene smirked and looked at the pair. "That's kind of close to CNN.'

"That's the point," said the well-dressed man, introducing himself as Vance. "It's a parody. We plan to saturate social media with a true American nationalistic message."

"Love it or leave it," Irene said, recalling her Havana briefings and the many rehearsal lessons on proper without-an-accent California diction.

"And expel those damn foreigners," added the scruffy guy.

Irene's pulse quickened. She felt sweat meander down her back in the ninety-degree heat of Riverside County. "I'd like to be part of this effort," she said to Vance. It was an ideal connection for the mission she had undertaken.

Vance linked an arm under hers and guided her toward a wooden bench under a massive California oak with trunk girth at least six feet wide. At his initial touch she had stiffened, but as they sat together under the oak's massive branches, she relaxed. She felt oddly comfortable with Vance. She couldn't remember the last time she'd been with an attractive man she was not competing with in some way. Or stalking to kill.

Vance leaned in close. "So you want to be part of our effort? Do you believe in the values of our Founding Fathers?"

"Of course," Irene said, extracting her arm from his. "Tell me more about CCNN."

"It's simple, Irene. We want to encourage the emergence of true American nationalism. But we need a vehicle."

Irene blinked, confused. "You need a car?"

Vance gave a deep belly laugh. "That's a good one, Irene. I'm talking about a platform. A way to distribute our articles and push our conservative values."

"What about Fox News, or conservative outlets like Breitbart, the Daily Caller and Infowars?"

He raised his eyebrows. "You've done your homework. But those are all run by fat cats with mixed agendas. Our approach is direct: make America white again."

Irene couldn't ignore the illogic. "But is that even possible?"

"Let me finish," he said, moving closer on the bench until their thighs gently touched. "We need to organize rallies, protests, and get our message into the lame-stream media through these efforts. We're planning on starting CCNN once we figure out how to circumvent restrictions on new broadcast licenses. But we can hit social media right away, and hard."

"A television network costs serious money," Irene said.

"We have wealthy backers. But we need a core staff to implement this effort and run the operation."

Irene's pulse quickened. "I might be able to help. I work in communications."

Vance's face lit up. "Wow. A true patriot! So you're still interested?"

"I might be." She felt his body heat, even though the temperature was over ninety degrees. Not wanting to appear too eager, she looked at her watch. "Do you know when the return van leaves?"

Pointing to the picnic tables atop a nearby hill, Vance said, "There's a barbecued ribs lunch in the picnic area. I expect the vans will leave sometime after lunch, but I'd like to drive you back. I'm from Corona del Mar, between Laguna Beach and Newport Beach. Do you know the area?"

Irene was silent a few seconds. Offering him a tentative smile, she said, "That would be nice."

Vance stood and offered Irene his hand. They walked arm-in-arm toward the wisp of barbecue smoke.

89

Meanwhile, Larissa was pursuing Liang.

At four in the afternoon, she knocked on Liang's condo door.

It opened instantly, and he invited her in, greeting her with a rapturous smile. Instinctively, she hugged him, much as she did whenever her extended Jewish family visited in Moscow. But her hug with Liang lasted a bit longer, and she purposefully allowed her breasts to linger against his chest.

He didn't resist. In fact, he tightened his embrace ever so slightly.

After the hug, he stepped back and said, "You are very ravishing Larissa. I like your dress. The yellow flowers remind me of a field of summer flowers in the countryside outside Beijing."

She didn't bother resisting his charms, smiling and blushing. "It's my favorite dress. I save it for special occasions." She looked over Liang's shoulder for Zhao.

He realized what she was looking for. "Oh, Zhao is in the lab, running experiments. I encouraged him to go in on a Saturday, saying he won't be bothered in the lab by all the undergraduate research students crowding the labs during the week. I don't expect him back until after midnight."

"What, do the other students go off and surf at the California beaches on weekends?"

Liang belly-laughed and said, "Not the Chinese students, but maybe the other undergrads do. They are cooked golden brown by Monday morning, and then during the week, they practice on their skateboards, traveling between buildings for their classes."

"Yes, I've almost been hit several times."

Liang suggested they go to the back patio and sit. Along the way, he stopped in the kitchen and retrieved two glasses of white wine. They sat on a well-used outdoor two-seater couch with a view of sprawling distant hills.

"This couch was left by the previous renters," he said as he fiddled with his cell phone until music came from a wireless speaker just inside the open patio door. They were sitting close. Larissa consciously brushed against his right hand. He reacted by encircling her hand, gently squeezing, and not letting go right away.

Liang sipped his wine and said, "I'd like to know more about you. Where are you from?"

Using the cover story that had been drilled into her by Grushkov, Larissa said, "I grew up on Long Island in New York. My father owned a restaurant in New York City, and my mother was a doctor."

The conversation between them lasted about an hour: Liang wanted to know as much about Larissa as possible, and Larissa, careful not to slip up, as Irene had warned, kept turning the conversation back to what it was like for Liang in China, and what his plans were after graduate school at UC Irvine.

After another fifteen minutes Liang said, "I think it is almost time for dinner. Will you please excuse me while I work in the kitchen?"

"Oh, let me help. I spent a lot of time in the kitchen with my grandmother growing up. She lived with us and was from the old country."

"The old country?' Liang asked, with raised brows.

Realizing she had made a mistake that Irene would jump on her for — if she were present — she said, "Oh, my grandmother came from Europe when she was little. We call it the 'old country'."

"I understand. Many Americans have roots in other countries. Have you cooked much Chinese food?"

"No. We eat rice occasionally, but my experience with Chinese food is mostly at restaurants."

"Okay, so you are in charge of the rice." Liang handed Larissa a plastic bag half full of white rice. "There is the pot," he said, pointing toward the stove and water. "Add a little salt, but not too much."

"Yes, I know what to do," she said and gently tapped his shoulder, keeping the physical connection alive.

While Larissa focused on the rice, she was aware of the clatter of dishes and pots as Liang worked on the rest of the dinner. After twenty minutes, multiple unfamiliar but enticing aromas filled the kitchen.

"You sit at the table in the dining room. I will bring the food in soon." He handed Larissa the steaming bowl of white rice she had just prepared.

The dining room table was a rickety card table with a white tablecloth. It had been pre-set with chopsticks at each place setting, plus plastic utensils.

From the kitchen, Liang shouted, "I don't know if you have used chopsticks so there are forks for you. Sorry they are only plastic."

Liang emerged, deftly balancing three dishes between two hands and his arm. As he placed them on the table, he said, "The first dish is eggplant with onions and pork. It is not spicy. The second is shrimp with a red spice sauce. I am sorry that the shrimp were frozen and not fresh. The third dish is steamed vegetable, chestnuts, snow peas, and broccoli. California has exceptionally good fresh vegetables. As you Americans say, dig in."

"This is very kind of you." Larissa reached over and gently squeezed Liang's hand. He reciprocated the squeeze.

After most of the food was eaten and the bottle of white wine consumed, Liang returned to asking Larissa about herself and family.

"Your mother was a doctor?"

"She did general family practice and saw her patients in an office in our home."

"So, she was home a lot with you. Do you have sisters or brothers?"

"No, I am an only child." Larissa again tried to focus the conversation back on him. "And do you miss your parents, being here in America?"

After dinner they again sat on the patio, the sun now setting over the horizon. She snuggled close to him and, before they both are aware of what was happening, they were kissing.

"What time did you say Zhao is due back?" she asked.

"Midnight," he said, taking Larissa's hand.

The next day, though the air between them was heavy with mistrust and suspicion, both women sat at their desks and worked at their laptops, studying the analytics of their efforts while stoking the flames with more incendiary posts. Since they first arrived three months ago, Irene behaved as if the dark web was her exclusive domain, relegating Larissa to using hushmail on the World Wide Web.

Even now, well into the mission, Larissa's comment, "We're vulnerable using hushmail on the open social media platforms," only strengthened Irene's resolve to keep Larissa under her thumb.

Irene, whose mood seemed to fluctuate between a slow simmer and an overflowing boil, paused her typing but did not look up. "You need to do as I say. The purpose of hushmail is so the recipient of the post won't know its source."

"Understood," said Larissa. She resumed typing for a few seconds. Irene smiled; she could tell she had gotten under her partner's skin.

Irene's past successes in the spy business had been linked to her ability to think outside the box, perhaps not always following prescribed procedures to a T. Though this attitude had gotten her in trouble — the polonium incident in London a few years back — her goals were invariably achieved, and she received praise from within the Russian intelligence apparatus. "I don't think Grushkov will argue with the million followers projected by the end of the month."

One of her early dark web blog posts titled *Take Back America*, had really taken off. It had quoted fake government statistics purporting that Jews controlled more that ninety per cent of the money in America through their ownership of financial institutions, high tech companies, and entertainment businesses. Also, she had claimed that Jews and other minorities held most of the power in government: the Federal Reserve, the Supreme Court, and chairmanships of key congressional committees. Her post had ended with the phrase 'Take Back America'.

The response was quick. There was a flurry of comments: *Right on, kill the Jews; Write laws that allow only white Christians to hold high positions in industry and government; Purge the Jews from the Supreme Court*. One message in opposition to the blog said, *You bigot bastard; crawl back into your hole.*

Irene said, "We're creating an army of hate."

Larissa's post *DeportThemNow* had received equally venomous comments: *America for whites; Time for a new holocaust; Send the spics back to Puerto Rico.*

Even now, the results were surprising. "I did not think there was so much pent-up anger in America," Larissa said. "The people we've met have been so nice."

Irene rolled her eyes at Larissa's naivety. "When a democracy like America is under stress, subliminal hatred will bubble to the surface and be directed at minorities and Jews. The increase in racist and anti-Semitic acts was proof of this."

Irene's comment about minorities resonated with Larissa. Her paternal grandparents had been orthodox Jews from Odessa. She remembered as a little girl her grandmother in tears recounting the 1905 Odessa pogrom that had resulted in her parents being shot in the town square while she'd watched. Larissa was vaguely aware of a stirring deep inside. It was not a good feeling.

One of Larissa's blogs with the banal title *LiberalsSuck*, blamed the liberal left for global warming and denounced their desires to make America a socialist state. Respondents to this post threatened violence against liberal voices in Congress and in certain media outlets such as CNN, the *New York Times*, and the *Washington Post*.

As a follow-up to these comments, Irene penned a blogpost: *When Violence Is Necessary*. She described a scenario in which the Democrats achieved control of the Senate and the House of Representatives, with enough votes to override any veto. The post suggested that the first legislation to pass both houses would be the total ban of all long rifles and automatic weapons. She claimed the Democrats would institute strict controls on handguns, including revocation of all open and concealed-carry laws. Without openly calling for violence, the post clearly implied that the Second Amendment of the American Constitution was in jeopardy, and drastic measures had to be taken to protect it in the name of the Founding Fathers. Though this post went out on both the World Wide and dark webs, the responses had been most vehement from followers of the dark web.

Within fourteen hours, there were ten thousand followers. By the end of the first week, over one hundred thousand people had viewed the post, resulting in more than three thousand comments supporting violence as the only effective solution. To amplify the situation, someone read aloud the post on YouTube as a manifesto. That also went viral on Facebook, WhatsApp, and Twitter: all platforms run by Facebook.

And again, the dark web responses were even more overtly violent.

Chapter Thirteen
Thursday & Friday

SC walked into Lynda Chester's NSA office, closed the door, and dragged a straight-back chair to the front of her desk, taking a seat.

Lynda turned from her computer screen to face her boss' cold stare. "This must be serious, SC."

He tossed another thumb drive across her desk.

She stared at it for a few seconds, stifling feelings about SC's arrogance and rudeness. She knew, and he knew, that she was a lot smarter than him. It was probably why he perceived her as a threat to his aspirations to be the next NSA director, so she smiled and inserted the thumb drive into her computer.

She recognized Grushkov's image immediately.

"Timestamp is 7.35 Wednesday, yesterday," said SC. "He left the Russian consulate's back door to Ninety-Second Street. FBI had it covered with a snoop-camera in the alley."

Lynda's brain tumbled the facts like the numbered balls in a bingo cage, trying to make sense of why Grushkov was moving around Manhattan incognito. She had not informed SC that she had already backtracked Grushkov to Tucson, and possibly Mexico. She needed to dig further into that, but she could also use some help.

She laser focused on SC, debating how much to reveal to a man she felt was driven by his own political agenda. "We should bring the FBI into the loop," she said. "Their job is boots-on-the-ground surveillance, not ours. They have secret ghost units trained exclusively for shadowing suspects."

SC stared back but said nothing.

She continued. "Our mandate is communication gathering and interpretation. We should also alert the CIA. Grushkov is a foreign agent on our soil."

SC pushed back from the chair and paced in front of Lynda's desk. After half a minute, he stopped, placed both hands on Lynda's desk and arched forward until his orange and black Princeton tie was an inch from her nose. "This is our baby, and you're in charge. I won't have another agency taking credit for our discovery. Don't fuck it up, Lynda."

She instinctively pulled back from his saliva spritz.

She glared directly at him. "So what do you want me to do SC? Something is going down, and we don't have a clue as to what and when."

He bantered back. "You've got all that fancy software we've been supporting for years. Figure it out. You have direct access to the DOD satellite network. If you need to, hack the FBI imaging center. I'm disconnecting with my FBI contact. The more images of Grushkov I ask for, the greater the likelihood they'll swoop in and grab credit."

Lynda wasn't about to reveal that she'd already connected with the DOD and DARPA satellite net. "Let me understand. You're telling me to hack the FBI?"

Rather than answer, he turned and abruptly left her office.

"What an ass," she whispered to an empty room. She was leery. SC had done this before, telling her she was in charge, then later on, when it suited his political agenda, pulling the rug out from under her and taking credit for himself. She'd thought about sending her résumé to her contacts at the FBI and the CIA. But at the CIA she'd be under Jack Light, who she trusted even less that SC. The head of the FBI, Celia Starks, was an unknown, but word on the street was that she was a hands-on director, liked by staff and field agents.

Lynda looked at the most recent image of Grushkov on her monitor. He was in stylish casual clothes, as if he was out for a stroll. Again, he had left through the consulate back door, so obviously he didn't want to be tracked. She took her mouse, clicked on the NYPD website, then on NYPD Mobility Platform, followed by Technology. She typed LCNSA and her access code zero-zero-zero-one-seven. In a few seconds, she had access to all three thousand five hundred traffic cams that were used by both the NYPD Traffic Division, and various crime divisions, including the special terrorism prevention unit. She clicked on the NYPD Domain Aware System (DAS) which pooled livestreams of data from multiple sources, including all three thousand five hundred traffic cams.

She downloaded the Grushkov image into the NYPD DAS facial recognition program, used its software and her mouse to outline Grushkov's head and body, then selected 'Upper West and East Side' and imputed yesterday's date, from 7.20 to 7.30 a.m.

One of the most powerful facial and body-type match programs she had helped develop as a consultant to the National Geospatial-Intelligence Agency was activated. This had been the software used to locate Bin Laden, and it was now utilized by all major US metropolitan police departments, as well as the FBI and DOD.

In seven minutes, she was looking at Grushkov entering a cab at Ninety-Second and Fifth Avenue. "Damn," she blurted. Lynda could not make out the cab license or the cab ID number. Just that it was headed south on Fifth. On a hunch, she pulled up the search menu and clicked 'lower Manhattan' and entered 'eight a.m. to five p.m.' She debated her next move while waiting for the DAS pattern recognition program to scan images from roughly one thousand street and building CAMs.

Given the number of images that needed to be scanned, Lynda knew it was a long shot to locate Grushkov, but it was still worth a try. Considering SC's turf war paranoia, she figured it was not a good idea to alert her usual FBI contacts, even as she felt it would make good sense to put a tail on Grushkov the next time he surfaced. Though her initial instinct had been that SC was jesting about an FBI hack, his abrupt departure when she'd pressed him on it suggested he was serious but didn't want his fingerprints on it.

By the time she finished this thought, a message popped up on her computer screen: twelve terabytes: ninety-two minutes'.

"Shit," she mumbled, seeing that it was already 5.10 p.m. Finding Grushkov was going to be difficult, so while the NYPD program was scanning thousands of images, she decided to dig further into the only other lead she had: the five, hang-up burner-cell calls.

Based on the GPS site identification, she used Google Maps to study the Long Island location of the calls. The only significant feature nearby was MacArthur Airport, a general aviation airport with heavy usage for private charters, airlines supporting the overflow for the major metropolitan airports serving New York City, and private light aircraft. The Wichita, Kansas call appeared to be from a mixed residential and commercial area with several small private airstrips., and the California call was from Irvine, near a university and John Wayne Airport. All near airports, she noted.

Normal protocol would require that Lynda request the FBI to initiate onsite investigations. However, based on SC's instructions, a request to the FBI would be viewed as tantamount to cavorting with the enemy. For Lynda to check out the closest location, she would have to fly to Long Island, rent a car, and sleuth on her own — an activity not in her job description — but thinking and acting 'outside the box' had served her well over the years.

Using the internal secure communication system, she messaged SC:
Would like to travel to New York to check out site of Havana calls.
An immediate response:
No. Stay put.
She felt a migraine coming on, something that happened rarely — only when she let herself get overstressed.

Her computer screen flashed: 'Search complete: zero matches'.

Reverberating in her head: "This is your baby. Don't fuck it up."

The nascent migraine morphed into a full-blown shitstorm.

Despite SC's warning and her lack of trust in Jack Light at the CIA, she wrote Light an encrypted email:
Detected Russian agent undercover, NYC.
After sending the message, she muttered, "Fuck you, SC, I'm covering my ass."

She transferred overnight monitoring of her phone tracking program to Langley, logged out of her computer, and headed home to her Jacuzzi.

On Friday at eight thirty., after another restless night, but minus the migraine thanks to an hour-long soak, Lynda saw the late Thursday notification from the NYPD DAS system: 'One sixty-one per cent match, SW corner Washington Square'.

She downloaded the clip from the Washington Square traffic cam. She understood why the match was only sixty-one per cent. Traffic cams did not have pixel resolution needed for facial recognition programs. Lynda scrutinized a fuzzy image of a beardless man stepping into a dark vehicle. The shoes and clothing were different from the image taken earlier in the day, but the body type, size, and facial bone structures matched. Based on her personal familiarity with Grushkov, Lynda was reasonably certain it was him.

She focused on the car: a black Lexus coupe with an odd bump on its roof. She vaguely recalled an interagency email about miniature radar detectors for drone detection.

A keyword search surfaced the email which illustrated several models, one of which clearly matched the Lexus roof protrusion. She scrolled through sequential images of Grushkov entering the car, freezing on one. Zooming closer she had the license plate number!

Using the network of state and federal agencies accessible to the NSA, she entered the license plate number into the New York DMV data base. In fifteen seconds, the result: 'Russian Federation, Glen Cove, Long Island, non-diplomatic'.

"I'm fucking onto something," she said, then got up and closed her office door. Back at her desk, she used the NYPD DAS system to try and track the black Lexus. The problem was that the car had left Greenwich Village thirteen hours ago. By now, the Lexus might be out of Manhattan and back at its home in Glen Cove. However, this was another trail leading to Long Island.

She could follow her earlier hunch and try to secure SC's approval to task one of the NSA-DOD satellites to image the Clarion Hotel: the GPS location of the hang-up calls from Havana.

Three burner calls to the same location from Havana, and a satellite call from the Russian consulate in Manhattan to the Clarion Hotel a day apart was not coincidental, especially when paired with Grushkov's presence in the New York area in the same time frame.

Despite his limitations, it was time to educate her boss.

She rode the elevator to the top floor of NSA headquarters, where SC and the director had their highly staffed suite of offices. She gestured to SC's executive assistant, Gretchen. "Is he in?"

Just then, SC's office door flew open and the director of the NSA, Jim Hall, emerged, with SC close behind. Upon seeing Lynda, Director Hall said, "Lynda, SC just briefed me on the Russian situation. Good job. Any new developments?"

She glanced at SC behind Hall who gave her an affirmative nod, which she interpreted to mean it was okay to respond. "As a matter of fact, yes."

The director's face brightened. "My office." He pointed down the corridor to his corner suite. "C'mon, SC, let's get the latest."

Inside Director Hall's expansive suite, the two men sat in posh leather chairs. Lynda perched on the edge of the leather couch. The room was well appointed with flowers in vases and pictures of Hall with various dignitaries.

Both men look at her expectantly.

"I've detected a pattern of burner cell calls between the Cuban headquarters of the FSB and various points in the US. Some correlate with known locations of Andrei Grushkov who is presently in the US without the required notification of the State Department, or any other agency." She didn't mention the calls from California and Kansas, wanting more time to investigate them.

"What's your next step?" asked Hall.

"It appears that Grushkov left Greenwich Village last night in a black Lexus registered to the Russian consulate in Manhattan, but without diplomatic plates. I'd like a satellite scan of the Clarion Hotel near MacArthur Airport, on the chance he's still there."

The director turned to SC. "This is yours. What do you want to do?"

Up until now, SC had been quiet, but now he was on the spot. Lynda knew he was in a pickle.

"We could notify the FBI field office on Long Island," SC said.

"Yes, that would make sense," said the director. "But then they'll want to know why, and you know what we were just discussing. We're coming up on our OMB budget cycle and could use a *hit* on something big."

Lynda saw her opportunity. "We could task one of our joint NSA-DOD satellites to scan the area of the Clarion Hotel, as well as others in the area."

Both men were silent for a few seconds, laser focused on Lynda, who stared right back. SC had his hands in his lap, and Lynda saw his thumbs rubbing against each other — a tell of his she'd noticed in the past, when he was stressed or in a jam.

"Let's do it," said Hall. "I'll make a few calls but repositioning one of the DOD satellites will have to be run up through the Defense Department chain of command. I'll call the deputy assistant director of Defense and give him a heads-up."

"What about one of the CIA spy satellites?" asked SC.

"I'll call Jack Light at Langley, but their satellites are shared with DOD, and right now they're in orbits to spy on everywhere *but* the US. Plus, I'd have to brief him on what we're on to."

Lynda had another idea. "We might try the NOA weather satellites."

"Not the kind of resolution we need. Mostly wide-angle images of large areas," answered the director.

There was another silence as the three of them mulled over the options. Each decision would have a ripple effect. Sharing knowledge had serious consequences.

Lynda cleared her throat. "How about the National Geospatial-Intelligence Agency? They're best known for satellite-generated maps, but they also have the capability to employ real-time, three-dimensional images throughout the spectrum, including infrared."

The director's eyes widened. "Damn, Lynda, you're right. The NGA provided the imagery that was key to getting Bin Laden."

"Using my algorithms," Lynda added.

"The NGA is part of the Department of Defense and run by a rear admiral. My wife and I have had the pleasure of entertaining the admiral at our home," Hall said.

"Their analysts are able to determine at a long distance what an object or a building is made of," said Lynda, keeping mum about the fact that she'd already been using the NGA pattern recognition software through the NYPD. She expected both her superiors at NSA to take credit for any successes on this project, leaving her out in the cold. Keeping the details of her methodology close to her chest gave her control while simultaneously protecting her from her bosses' intention to usurp the kudos if the NSA efforts bore fruit.

The director half-smiled at Lynda. "I'll speak with the assistant secretary of defense and see what kind of read I get. If I run into obstacles, I can also bring in the national security advisor and the director of National Intelligence. But that might bring it to the president's attention." He sniffed. "I'm not sure we want that, at least not yet."

The director stood, an indication the meeting was over.

"Lynda," he said, "thanks for your hard work and insightful input. As usual, you're doing a great job. SC and I will come to a decision on this and get back with you ASAP."

Lynda figured it will be at least two or three days before any satellite could be repositioned to image the hotels in the MacArthur Airport area. By that time, it would be too late to thwart whatever nefarious plan spymaster Grushkov was up to.

Lynda left her boss' office, then stuck her head into the large NSA image analysis and programming facility that she oversaw. To the twenty programmers and computer geeks working there, she shouted, "I'm going out for a run."

She needed to clear her head while avoiding another migraine.

Chapter Fourteen
Thursday & Friday

Olga stepped from the hotel's shower in the small bathroom and squeezed around Grushkov who was shaving at the sink. Her wet naked body caused a cascade of neural and hormonal impulses in him. He focused harder on moving the razor across his face without cutting himself. He could feel the passion in his briefs; he concentrated on not turning to face her. Last night was wonderful, feelings and emotions he had buried for years had erupted. But today was business; he had to keep the Tinderbox Plot on course — a lot of work to do — emotions must be put aside.

She wrapped herself in a large bathroom towel and started to blow-dry her hair with the hotel's drier in front of the large mirror in the bedroom. When done she twirled and clipped the blonde hair to the top of her head. "It's my professional look," she quipped and smiled at him seductively while slipping on her bra and panties, and the same cream-colored blouse and black slacks she'd worn yesterday.

"I prefer it down, but that's our secret," he said.

Grushkov packed his overnight case while Olga dropped the room key at the Hilton's front desk. He preferred not to be seen by the desk clerk.

On the drive to the hangar, she asked, "Will you be back in the city soon?"

He gave the question some thought before answering. "A lot to do today. How about Moscow in the spring? I'd like to show you my country dacha. Been in my family for generations. It's an incredibly special place."

"I'm here for another year — unless I get expelled for spying." She laughed.

"Do you want to be recalled sooner?"

"No. I want a full posting to the US on my record. It'll be valuable for my assignment to other foreign consulates. Plus, I have this wonderful car at my disposal and my own flat in Glen Cove." Olga drove the Lexus into the hangar where the Cessna sat, its twin engines loudly humming.

Upon seeing the plane, Grushkov stiffened in his seat. "They were supposed to wait for me."

Olga put her hand over his.

From the open plane door, Sergei beckoned for Grushkov to come on board. He shouted to be heard above the sound of the engines. "Just waiting for you before we test fly."

Before Grushkov got out of the Lexus, not wanting to be seen by his team, he bent toward Olga and kissed her gently. "Don't leave. We should be back soon."

In a few minutes he was in the co-pilot's seat. Sasha and Boris were also onboard, gripping straps fastened to the inside of the stripped-down fuselage. They taxied out of the hangar to the main runway. Sergei identified the plane to the tower as a Cessna Conquest II-light. Receiving take-off clearance, he accelerated down the runway. When airborne, he made a wide turn to the right, climbing to four thousand feet, and gradually to ten thousand feet.

Boris released his straps and inspected the seal on the cabin roof. "No leaks."

"Okay," Sergei said. "I'm pressurizing the cabin and climbing to fifteen thousand feet."

When the Cessna reached fourteen thousand, Boris exclaimed, "Geez, we've got a leak in the corner on the right side of the cabin roof."

"The internal pressure is pushing out on the epoxy seal," Sasha said, after inspecting it.

"Let's head back before it gets worse," Grushkov shouted above the noise of the engines.

Then the seal separated completely. The cabin air rushed out through an opening that was now six inches long.

"We've lost cabin pressure," Sergei yelled. "Grab onto the straps and hold on!"

But Grushkov did the opposite. He unhooked his co-pilot harness and stepped into the cabin as Sergei put the plane into a steep dive. Trying to keep his balance and tumbling backward as the plane lost altitude, Grushkov managed to grab a free strap attached to the cabin wall. He pulled himself up toward the widening rent in the ceiling. With his free hand, he grabbed the piece of the cabin roof that was lifting off and pulled it back toward where it had split off.

He shouted to Boris and Sasha, who were still clasping their straps, "Help me. We can't lose the ceiling. My hand is fucking freezing!"

By the time Sasha and Boris relinquished their grasp on the straps, Sergei had the plane leveled off at one thousand feet and was circling back to the airport. Together, Grushkov and Boris maintained a grip on the ceiling piece. It was now separated from the cabin roof by about a foot, though fortunately it was still attached to the rest of the fuselage by the epoxy seam.

Back in the hangar, they deplaned and gathered round the workbench. Olga was in the Lexus, talking on her phone. She looked up and caught Grushkov's eye, offering the hint of a smile.

He tried smiling back but couldn't quite manage it. He had problems to solve.

Grushkov turned to his two engineers. "What do you think?"

"We can bend the ceiling back and reseal with new epoxy. Maybe use more and let it cure longer," Sasha said.

Sasha added, "As I suggested earlier, we can attach small latches along the cut seam that will hold the ceiling piece tightly to the fuselage."

"We can fly under ten thousand feet, unpressurized," Sergei announced. "That is the safest considering what just happened."

"Okay," Grushkov said. "But when we load the package into the plane, first we will remove the ceiling piece, next we will lower the package in, and then we replace the cut roof. I need to be sure it can be resealed without leaks when we fly to our destination."

"No problem, Andrei Andreievich," Sasha said. "We have good solvent you can take with you to your destination. It will dissolve the sealant. We have attached a small handle you can pull on, to remove a section of fuselage once the sealant is dissolved."

Sergei interjected, "As I said, I think it safe if we fly below ten thousand feet. Then we don't need to pressurize the cabin. But I will test again with pressurization, just in case we have to climb over a storm."

Sasha said, "Okay, we can fix and test again later today."

"No," said Grushkov. "I want you to remove the ceiling section, clean all the edges completely, and refasten it with fresh epoxy sealant, like we will do when we load the package. Let it set and harden overnight. We'll do another test flight tomorrow, and if it holds, we'll be out of here by Saturday.

While Grushkov observed, Sasha and Boris removed the ceiling piece. From their box of sundry bolts, screws, and latches they selected six latches that they attached to the cut roof segment and the fuselage, that should hold it tightly in place.

Grushkov looked at his watch and turned to his men. "It's almost lunchtime. You go to McDonald's for lunch. I'll stay here."

After they left, Grushkov went to the Lexus, where Olga was flipping through a magazine. He slipped into the passenger seat. "They need to redo the plane modifications and test again tomorrow."

"Andrei, you are needed here?" she asked smiling wistfully.

"You have something in mind?"

"I have a friend with a beach house on Fire Island, about an hour away. She uses it rarely. We can have it for as long as we want," she said with a sparkle in her eyes.

Back from lunch, Boris and Sasha cleaned the edges of the removed cabin ceiling as well as the internal edges of the cut fuselage in the plane. They let the surfaces dry completely, and then applied fresh epoxy sealant on the inside and outside surfaces while Sergei watched closely. They reinserted the cut segment into the fuselage opening and then closed the clamps that held the cut piece even tighter to the fuselage. Grushkov watched too but was distracted by thoughts of Olga's supple skin and her lilac scent. He decided to take her up on her offer.

At three o'clock, Grushkov said to the engineers and Sergei, "I'm going back to the consulate in Manhattan. I'll be back tomorrow afternoon and we can do another test flight."

On the ferry to Fire Island, Grushkov gazed at the water, inhaled the salty air deeply, and exhaled slowly. His body relaxed as he closed his eyes and pushed thoughts of the Tinderbox Plot to a far corner of his brain. The rest of the day and the evening would be his and Olga's. He felt a calm he could not remember experiencing in many years.

Olga's idea to go to Fire Island was a good sign she felt the same as he. While these thoughts percolated, she moved closer to him as they both leaned against the ferry railing and gazed at the sea. Her hand encircled his.

The beach house on Ocean Way opened directly to the Atlantic Ocean, which crashed dramatically onto pristine white sand. It was a stone and wood-frame cottage with two bedrooms and a loft. The large central room had a high ceiling, with a stone fireplace in its center. The master bedroom had a king-sized bed and cedar-framed sliding glass doors that opened onto a patio… and then the ocean.

Olga disappeared into the walk-in closet. Ten minutes later, she emerged, blonde hair cascading about her shoulders. She wore a yellow sheer bathrobe that was loosely tied with a white sash.

Without a bra, her breasts swayed gently as she glided toward the bed, where Grushkov was sitting and gazing out the doors at the ocean. He stood and turned to face her. Looking into her azure blue eyes he undid the sash: she gently removed his clothing. He moved both hands gently up each side of her naked body, over her buttocks, back, and to her shoulders. He lifted the gown until it fell to the floor next to the bed. Her arms encircled his shoulders, and she pulled him to her. They tumbled backwards onto the bed and soft down pillows. He felt an incredible peacefulness as he inhaled her sweetness. They kissed each other all over, with tenderness and abandon, ultimately moving in synchrony toward mutual satisfaction.

As they cuddled, limbs still entwined, Grushkov whispered, "I imagine us in a dacha deep in a forest in Russia, the only sounds, wind and rain through the trees."

"Ahhh, but we are here, dear Andrei, on a beach — alone, away from everything."

"Yes, Olga, this is our time." He untangled from her warmth, stood next to the bed. "Let's go for a swim. There must be bathing suits somewhere."

Olga rose, their naked bodies entwined as they kissed deeply.

"No need for bathing suits. This is Fire Island, a very permissive community," said Olga. She took Grushkov's hand and led him through the doors and onto the sand.

Without a stitch of clothing, she let go of his hand and skipped toward the glistening Atlantic. Grushkov pursued her, and they splashed into the water together. They turned toward each other, water covering two-thirds of their bodies, kissing for a long moment before parting. Both plunged headfirst into the surf.

After the swim and a shower together, they lay languidly on the bed in each other's arms.

Olga glanced at the clock next to the bed. "It's seven. We should think of a meal. There is wine in the kitchen and fat steaks I took of the freezer when we arrived."

She went to the closet and returned with two terrycloth robes.

"I'll open the wine," Grushkov said.

Over dinner on the patio, as they watched the waves break against the sand, they didn't say much, just enjoyed the sound of the waves as the August daylight slowly extinguished.

Inside, after they finished eating, Grushkov lit a flame under logs in the fireplace. In the dark with only light from the fire, they sat on the floor, close enough to feel the warmth of the flames. They lay back on the plush carpet and turned to face each other.

Andrei took Olga's hand in his. "What would you do if you were free to do whatever you wanted?"

She squeezed his hand. "Do you mean now or the future?"

"The future, Olga. Now is as perfect as it can be."

She was quiet for a moment, then she leaned forward and kissed him lightly on his lips. "I think I'd like to have moments like this last forever."

"The memory of today will be with me forever. But, really, what would you like in your future if you had your choice?" he asked.

The fire crackled in the background. Ghosts danced across the ceiling as the flames in the stone fireplace twisted upward.

A tear crept down Olga's cheek. "My mother is gone, and I have just a sister who is in St Petersburg. I wish she was with me here in the US."

"You will see her again when your posting is over in a year, or even earlier if you would like."

"Andrei Andreievich, I am torn. I have made many friends outside the Russian diplomatic core. Since I have my own flat, I have the opportunity to live similarly to many Americans. My friend owns this beach house and has many parties here with all sorts of open minded and free-spirited people."

"I understand, Olga, but deep inside you, like me, are generations of Russian descendants."

"Oh, Andrei." Another tear streaked her cheek. "I love Mother Russia. I won't abandon loyalty to my ancestors. But that doesn't change that I have many dear friends in America. I wish we belonged to one world, with no separations by borders… or ideologies."

Grushkov pulled Olga closer and kissed the tear still on her cheek. He said, "You wish for a utopian world. It will not be." As soon as he said this, he felt a knife slice through his inner fiber. He saw the bomb in its cradle.

Olga seemed to sense a change in mood as he pulled away. She moved closer and embraced him. Her robe opened so her breasts were taut against his chest.

Grushkov's breathing quickened. His loins awoke, and his hands caressed her buttocks and pulled them toward him. Andrei pushed the bad thoughts from his mind as he and Olga writhed in unfettered passion. The fire snapped and crackled to their rhythm.

They woke up on Friday morning as the sun peeked above the horizon. The fire behind them was out. They looked deeply into each other's eyes, embraced, and kissed deeply again, words unnecessary to convey their bond.

After a light breakfast with the sun moving higher above the horizon, they again dashed naked toward the warm Atlantic for a brief swim, then back to the house.

On the drive back to the airport, they spoke little. Grushkov leaned across the front seat and kissed Olga's cheek, again with tears.

"Why the tears?" he asked.

"My tears are for us, Andrei. I am afraid I will not see you again."

"Olga, my dear, I will not lose you again," he said, not really knowing how this could be.

Olga stopped at the airport gate rather than drive into the hangar. Andrei exited the passenger side and went to the driver window. Olga extended her head partly out the window and they kissed for a long time before she drove away.

He walked the hundred yards to the hangar. On one hand, Grushkov felt alive like he hadn't felt in years, and on the other hand, he had a momentous mission to carry out.

Sasha and Boris were once again atop of the plane, now smoothing over the epoxied juncture between the inserted cut ceiling segment and the surrounding fuselage. Sergei was inside the cabin, smoothing out the seams from the other side.

Grushkov called out, "How soon before we can do the test flight?"

"Anytime," Sergei said. "But it is lunchtime, and we should eat."

"Okay," Grushkov said. "The three of you go to McDonald's and bring me an egg muffin-something."

"Egg McMuffin," Sergei said, sticking his head out the cabin door.

After lunch, all four men piled into the Cessna for another test run. Since the cabin has been stripped of seats, they brought along the two blow-up mattresses they'd been sleeping on, putting them on the cabin floor. Boris and Sasha used the seatbelts that had been looped around the posts of the aluminum frame to hold the package. Grushkov sat in the co-pilot seat.

At ten thousand feet Sergei said, "I'm pressurizing the cabin now. We'll climb slowly to twelve thousand feet, then fifteen thousand."

Grushkov's heartrate accelerated as he considered the riskier backup plan: trucking the package from Arizona to Kansas. Meanwhile, the two engineers unclicked their seatbelts and, with thin tissue paper in their hands, they slowly moved the tissues along the seam between the cut ceiling segment and the rest of the fuselage. After moving the tissue along the entire seam, they saw no suction pulling the tissue.

Boris yelled above the sound of the props, "No leaks."

"Great," shouted Sergei. "Let's head back."

Using the headphones and microphone connected between the pilot and co-pilot, Grushkov asked Sergei, "Can you fuel up so we can leave first thing tomorrow?"

"Yes, of course. But I need to know our final destination so I can check weather and file a flight plan."

"We won't file a flight plan," said Grushkov. "We will fly Visual Flight Rules."

"Okay," Sergei said. "VFR. We will not file an official flight plan, and we will not be tracked by traffic controllers, but I still need to know our destination. Weather during this time of year can generate thunderstorms too high to climb over. I'll have to fly around, which uses more fuel. I need to know possible airfields in which to land."

"We're going to Nogales, Arizona — two thousand one hundred miles from here — where we'll pick up a valuable package and fly it to Wichita, Kansas."

"Okay," Sergei said, making mental calculations. "Range of aircraft is two thousand five hundred miles, but we have added wing fuel pontoons, so we should make it easily without stopping. We cruise at two hundred and fifty miles per hour, so it will take about nine hours, depending on wind and weather. I'll check for airfields along the way if we need to refuel."

"There must be fields without control towers," said Grushkov. "We do not want to be identified."

"I don't think that should be a problem. There are many Level Three general aviation fields in Texas, without control towers."

Chapter Fifteen
Saturday

After a sleepless Friday night on the blow-up mattress inside the hangar, Grushkov used a small bathroom in one corner of the hangar to brush his teeth and massage his face with a towel soaked in hot water. In the mirror, he saw red-rimmed eyes and stubble sprouting for a new beard. His time with Olga — plus, last night on the rubber mattress — reminded him that he was no longer thirty years old. But the thought of her and what may be possible in the future energized him, nonetheless.

Grushkov's thoughts shifted to the Tinderbox Plot. Media reports of an increase in violent acts against liberal groups and their businesses and similar acts by liberals against conservatives indicated that his operatives had been highly successful in fanning the flames of violence. After the bomb goes off in Wichita, America will spin off its axis. He didn't doubt that the American intelligence agencies now suspected something was up but, based on his early experience in America and his tracking the myriad of US spy organizations over the years, he was banking on internal turf wars and multiple bureaucracies hindering any one agency putting the pieces together before it was too late.

Boris and Sasha returned at eight a.m. with two fresh breakfasts, this time from Starbucks. "Andrei Andreievich, we will send you off with a breakfast other than the egg mac." They spread out the food on the worktable, now cleared of the construction blueprints.

Grushkov and Sergei looked at the food, puzzled.

"They are sausage, egg and cheese on fresh biscuits," said Boris.

Sasha added, "Just like your babushka made when you were little, dah? We brought enough for eight hungry Russians."

After a satisfying meal, they cleaned the hangar to erase any evidence of their presence. They made several trips to large metal garbage bins behind the neighboring hangar, about fifty yards away, removing all traces of the aluminum they'd used to make the frame to hold the package in place. The workbench was cleaned and moved to a corner of the hangar and the floor was swept to remove any aluminum fragments.

They threw the remains of their breakfast into the bin behind their hangar just to show any potential snoopers that nothing out of the norm had occurred in the hangar.

Grushkov and Sergei took off from MacArthur Airport at 10.33 a.m. on Saturday. The Cessna Conquest gradually climbed to ten thousand feet. Sergei programed the onboard navigation system for a direct route to Nogales, Arizona that would take them over St Louis. On an early morning visit to the New York Jet weather office for private pilots at MacArthur Airport, he had reviewed projections for thunderstorms over the south-west corner of West Virginia and Northern Kentucky.

Sergei said, "Our onboard Doppler radar will show any storms, so we can fly over them if they are not too high, or fly around them, if necessary. I've placed the plane on autopilot, which will follow the direct route to Nogales, but since we are flying VFR, we need to keep an eye out for other aircraft."

"I see we have blankets if we get cold," said Grushkov.

"They're just in case the heating system fails. After all, this plane isn't new."

Three hours into the flight, Grushkov unbuckled his harness and used tissue paper to check the ceiling for leaks. He didn't find any. "And now, I will take a leak myself," he announced to Sergei. "Sixty years old, you know," he laughed.

He returned to the cockpit slightly out of breath. "Yes, activity at ten thousand feet is tiring. I need to get in better shape." He carried a Starbucks bag and removed two chicken sandwiches. "Sasha handed me lunch before we left."

Halfway through the meal, there were a series of beeps from the weather radar. "Pretty big storm about twelve miles ahead," said Sergei. "Top of thunderheads are over thirty thousand feet. I'll plot a course around it. Buckle in tight."

"What does it look like?" Grushkov asked in a higher-than-normal voice.

"I can detour about fifty miles off course, but we'll probably get hit by wind gusts at the storm's edge."

"This should be a good test of the roof," Grushkov said.

"Yeah, good thing we don't have the package onboard," said Sergei, just as the Cessna was lifted and pushed sidewise by a wind gust. "Hang on, Andrei. It'll be this way until we get around the storm. I'm going up to twelve thousand feet. The closer to the ground we are, the more severe the winds."

Grushkov didn't understand the meteorology, but he trusted his pilot. He was less confident in his engineers and the ceiling holding up under pressure. But it was better to test it now, as opposed to when they were carrying the package to its final destination.

For the next half hour, they were buffeted left to right, up and down. Grushkov deposited his partially digested lunch back into the Starbucks' bag and gripped both sides of his seat as tightly as he could.

When they emerged into clear sky and returned to their normal course, Sergei declared, "Four hours to Nogales. That was a good test of our structural integrity. However, if we'd had the package and it snapped loose in the cabin, that would have been disastrous."

Grushkov remembered that the area around Wichita was prone to tornadoes this time of year. "What if we encounter a tornado?" he asked.

Sergei's response was simple. "Then we're screwed."

Chapter Sixteen
Saturday

Lynda reasoned that government bureaucracy and ego-driven turf wars would delay if not kill approval to redirect any satellite to image the MacArthur Airport site. At six thirty on Saturday morning, after another restless night, Lynda considered what her NSA bosses would say to cover their asses: "We saw no clear threat to national security."

She took a quick morning shower and dressed in neatly-pressed slacks and a light blue blouse. After a breakfast of a toasted English muffin generously garnished with raspberry jam direct from her aunt's farm in Rochester, Vermont, and strong caffeinated coffee, she clicked the Uber app on her cell.

"Reagan Airport," she confirmed with the Uber driver as she climbed in the small car's backseat. She was entirely aware that what she was doing was risky. SC would flip out if he knew about her plan. If this spiraled into a full-blown terrorist crisis, which she felt was a distinct possibility, SC's boss would need to show he had not been sitting on his butt. The more Lynda ran through the details of what she'd already uncovered, the more excited she got; it was like the rush before a college judo match. Her heart was racing as the Uber sped toward the airport.

In forty-five minutes, Lynda was boarding a United Airlines shuttle to New York's La Guardia Airport.

By ten fifteen, she was renting an Alamo economy sedan car. Using the car's GPS, fifty-two minutes later, she arrived in the parking lot of the Clarion Hotel in West Islip, Long Island, the site of one of the burner cell hang-up calls to Havana's FSB headquarters. MacArthur Airport was nearby, and she wondered if that was significant.

After a careful inspection of the lot around the hotel with no detection of a black Lexus coupe, she went to the reception counter, flashing her NSA ID. After explaining what the NSA was and that she was there on official business, the receptionist summoned the office manager.

"No," said the manager. "I don't remember a black Lexus or anyone matching that physical description."

Rather than trying to interview the entire hotel office staff, Lynda's training as a detail-oriented scientist-investigator kicked in. She scanned the surrounding area and spotted the Hilton Garden Inn a few blocks away.

She motored over to the Hilton, scanned the parking lots for a black Lexus, then asked the hotel desk clerk about a black Lexus and described Andrei Grushkov.

"No, I haven't seen that man. But there was a black Lexus sports coupe here a few days ago, I think maybe Wednesday or Thursday. It belonged to a blonde woman who spoke with an accent."

"Is there a registration card?"

The desk clerk rummaged through paperwork and showed Lynda a card signed by Francine Drake. She had checked in at 7.05 p.m. Wednesday evening.

"Any record of check-out time?"

"No. Customers just turn in the keys and leave."

"Do you have security cameras covering the parking lot and entrance?" Lynda asked, scanning the lobby walls, looking for a camera.

"Yes, the entrance and parking lot are covered."

Lynda checked her watch, debating if she should head over to the airport or spend an hour looking at the hotel tapes. Time was critical when pursuing a suspect, but in this case, it wasn't even clear why Grushkov had arrived in the country under the radar. Unless he committed a crime, there wasn't much that could be done, other than ordering him out of the country.

"Okay, I'd like to review the tapes from Wednesday seven p.m. until Thursday ten a.m."

At 9.02 p.m., Wednesday, a black Lexus 350c pulled into the temporary parking area in front of the hotel. A woman with blonde hair emerged from the driver's side, entered the lobby, and left at nine fifteen. She drove to the side of the hotel where there was no camera coverage. At eight fifteen on Thursday morning, she walked into the lobby and dropped something — a room key — at the front desk. She emerged from the building and walked around it, disappearing from the range of the camera.

Lynda played the arrival scenario again. She saw a shadow of someone in the passenger side of the Lexus, but the resolution of the old analog surveillance camera was not good enough for any identification, even using the most sophisticated NSA pattern recognition programs at her disposal. Still, the Lexus matched the previous images that Lynda had, of a car with the drone detector on the roof.

She figured there was a good possibility they had headed to MacArthur Airport. On her own, without any backup or additional support, she decided to follow her gut instinct and head for the airport.

At 12.05 p.m., she parked her rental car in a no-parking zone next to the airport entrance. Noticing a full array of surveillance cameras, she felt optimistic about spotting the Lexus if it had come here.

Inside the terminal, she located the TSA office and introduced herself to the on-duty TSA supervisor, providing just enough sketchy details to convey the importance of her request.

"We have security cameras covering all the public spaces," said Glenda, the TSA officer. "And others on the entrance and exits to the tarmac. I'll assign Shareena from my staff to help review the tapes, but there are over twenty cameras."

"Hmm. Okay, let me start with yesterday, Thursday from 8.20 to ten a.m." Lynda reasoned they may have stopped for breakfast on the way from the hotel to the airport.

In a cramped office with a dozen monitors projecting images from different cameras, Lynda and Shareena squeezed into a small desk space and started reviewing past surveillance tapes. They spent forty-five minutes scanning digital camera images projected on two desktop computers. "Darn, no black Lexus," Lynda exclaimed. "How about the entry roads to the airport?" she asked Shareena.

"We have them on the main road starting at Veteran's Highway."

After another twenty minutes looking at every car entering the airport area off Veteran's Highway between 8.20 and ten, Lynda exclaimed, "There it is!" But the Lexus continued toward the main terminal and turned left onto another road before reaching the main terminal. "What's that road?" asked Lynda.

"Schaffer Road. Goes to charter and private aircraft hangars."

"Any security cameras?"

"Of course. At every entrance to the airfield."

"How many entrances?"

"Don't know. Maybe four or five."

Lynda's stomach growled. Her watch said 1.28 p.m. She stretched at the computer desk and turned to Shareena. "Are you up for a lunch break?"

"Yeah. There's a McDonald's or Starbucks just down Veteran's Highway."

Lynda drove Shareena to McDonald's. After a twenty-minute lunchbreak, they were back in the preview room, reviewing images from cameras monitoring several side roads and entrance gates to the private portion of the airport. At the 8.27 Thursday timestamp, a black Lexus coupe passed through a security gate on the side of a large blue hangar. "What's that street and building?" Lynda asked.

"Hering Drive, and New York Jet charter terminal."

Viewing the tape further, the two women observed the Lexus travel about a hundred feet, make a sharp left turn, and head for the private plane hangars. The car circled around one of the hangars and disappeared. "Must've pulled around to the front," said Lynda.

"Yeah, the plane entrances are on the other side."

"I'd like to see that side. Any cameras we can look at?"

"Nope," answered Shareena. "We're a general aviation airport with a lot of private charter flights and limited domestic commercial flights. Not enough to warrant more surveillance."

Lynda scrolled forward. Skimming through several hours of video, she saw several small aircraft, taxi to the row of hangars, but the images were not good enough to make out the tail numbers. She'd ask for a copy of the images just in case she could bring out enough detail to identify the planes by registration numbers, but it was a laborious longshot.

As she scrolled forward, three men walked around the hangar, out the gate, and turned right on Hering Drive.

"Where are they headed?" Lynda mumbled.

"Probably to one the restaurants off Veteran's Highway, about half a mile," Shareena said.

They returned after thirty minutes, carrying a paper bag. The time stamp was 12.35 p.m. Thursday. Lynda continued to fast forward the surveillance tape and, at three fifteen on Thursday, the black Lexus left the hangar and the airport. Three men exited the hangar on foot at six fifteen, leaving the airport and heading in the same direction as in the morning. They returned an hour later, passing through the security gate, and disappearing into the hangar.

Shareena said, "Must've been for dinner."

"Okay, let's see what happens the next morning," Lynda said.

Friday, at 7.35 a.m., three men left the hangar, passed through the gate, and in forty minutes they returned, one of them carrying what looked like a McDonald's bag.

Lynda excitedly said, "These guys pass right under the surveillance camera. I can see some of their facial details. I'll need a copy of these images."

"You'll have to ask Glenda, but I don't think there will be a problem."

As the tapes continued forward, at one thirty p.m. on Friday, the black Lexus stopped at the tarmac gate but did not go through. The camera angle was not good, but it appeared there was movement inside the car. Then the passenger door opened and a man emerged. He went over to the driver's side and a blonde woman extended her head slightly out the window.

Lynda's heart jumped into her mouth. "It's him!" she exclaimed.

Lynda watched Grushkov kiss the blonde driver for over twenty seconds, according to the time stamp. Next, he walked to the tarmac gate, appeared to insert an entry card, and walked through, in the direction of the hangar.

As the Lexus backed up and did a U-turn, the surveillance camera recorded the license plate. "Bingo!"

Lynda was on a roll. She continued to view the tape and, at the 1.40 p.m. mark, she spotted movement: a twin engine airplane exited the hangar area and headed for one of the main runways and disappeared. At

2.20 p.m., the plane returned and went out of sight in front of the hangar. Friday evening, the same three men made a dinner run.

Lynda fast-forwarded to Saturday, the present day. At seven a.m. this morning, the three men made a breakfast run and returned at 7.55, this time carrying two large bags. It struck Lynda that this food run was different.

At the timestamp 9.32 a.m., Lynda exclaimed, "Looks like they're carrying stuff from their hangar to the next hangar. Can we zoom at all?" She couldn't find a zoom control. "Crap, no. I'll need to requisition these video records," she said impatiently.

On the tape, the same twin-engine plane left the hangar area at timestamp 10.28 a.m. and taxied towards the main runway. Lynda fast-forwarded the surveillance tape to thirty minutes ago. There was no evidence of activity from the hangar, and the plane did not return.

She scrolled back to 11.11 a.m. Two men walked from the hangar through the gate, toward the main airport terminal and down Schaffer Road. "Can we pick them up on other cameras?"

"Yes, I'll search for you," Shareena answered.

"Thanks. I need to know how they left the area. It'll help us to track them down."

"This is cool stuff, Lynda. I think I'm in the wrong end of security."

"No, what you're doing is really important, Shareena. We rely on every bit of information to keep this country safe. You've been incredibly helpful. I want to see if there are records on which planes departed between nine and ten thirty this morning."

As Lynda walked from the preview room back to the TSA office to request copies from Glenda of the surveillance images, she debated how best to inform SC and the NSA director. They didn't even know she had traveled here on her own, but their approval would be needed for a search warrant to enter the hangar. This would involve bringing the FBI, Homeland Security, and the Department of Justice into the loop, something she was well aware her superiors were reluctant to do. At least that had been their position yesterday.

Figuring out who had access to the hangar would involve searches of the legal records on the hangar ownership, lease agreements, and determining if there were facial recognition matches of the men captured on the airport surveillance cameras. That was a lot of work and it included a lot of ifs, but there was nothing to stop Lynda from inspecting the outside of the hangar and the contents of any garbage dumpsters in the area.

Once onsite, Lynda pulled on a pair of disposable gloves she'd bummed from Glenda. She had no intention of contaminating the aluminum fragments she extracted from the outside garbage bins with her own fingerprints. DNA and fingerprints would be valuable in prosecuting and/or expelling from the country individuals involved in this scheme — whatever it was. She stacked scraps of aluminum from the dumpsters into a neat pile. With the discarded food garbage from the suspect hangar, she knew there was a strong likelihood of extracting DNA evidence from the plastic food utensils.

She jotted Saturday, 3.32 p.m. in her notepad, then dialed SC's secure private number on her cell. Her heart raced and she felt a clammy sweat on her back through her clothing as she waited for her boss to answer.

Chapter Seventeen
Saturday

"We'll be passing St. Louis on the right in a few minutes," Sergei said, banking the Cessna gently to the left to get back on course. "We should have clear skies the rest of the way. We'll arrive in Nogales in approximately four hours, six thirty Arizona time."

"And our fuel supply is fine?" Grushkov said.

"Yeah, we'll make up the lost time pretty easily. Also, with the extra fuel pontoons, we've got a good reserve."

"Good." Grushkov nodded. "The package is in a safe house in Arizona. Not hearing anything from my men there is good news." Still, the sooner he got the package in the Cessna and on the way to Kansas, the better.

Grushkov thought about the complexity of pulling this operation off. The package's travel from Moscow to its final destination had been kept from everyone but a few, and even the select group of engineers and physicists from the Kurchatov Institute who'd fabricated the device around the salvaged plutonium core had no knowledge of how and where it would be used. All they knew was that it had to be an exact duplicate of an American bomb. The plutonium core, the pit, salvaged from an American nuclear bomb lost at sea during the Cold War, was crucial to building the device. Later, after the dust settled, the bomb would be identified as American.

The specific design details had been secured through bribes and strategically placed spies in the US Los Alamos and Livermore National Labs, along with publicly available information from the UN's International Atomic Energy Agency.

The bolts, rivets, and screws had been surreptitiously purchased at the American PX in Wiesbaden, Germany. Because of the extreme level of secrecy surrounding the Tinderbox Plot, after completion of the device four months ago, all members of the design and construction team had been threatened with dire consequences to their families if they breathed a word to anyone about the project.

Grushkov's satellite phone rang, jolting him back to the present. It was his team in Arizona, guarding the crated bomb.

"Dah," he uttered.

"Another attack," said Alexey Krupov. "Package safe. Xavier dead." The call ended abruptly.

Grushkov phoned back, but there was no answer. He felt a tightening in his chest; he took a few deep breaths to relax and considered his options.

The first thought that came to mind was to withhold the second twenty-five-million-dollar payment to the Godinez drug cartel — due when the package was safely on board the Cessna and on its way to Kansas. The cartel had agreed to provide protection up to that point.

After mulling over the situation, Grushkov used his sat phone to call Havana. "Anatoly, problem in Mexico. Do you know what's going on?"

"No, Andrei. Haven't heard from Krupov."

"Don't make the second payment yet," said Grushkov. "Wait until you hear from me after we land."

"Andrei, these shady characters think nothing of killing if they can make a better deal elsewhere."

"I am aware, Anatoly, but we made the first payment on schedule when the package reached the Mexican safe house. So they know we're honoring our end."

Grushkov ended the call, sighed, and said to Sergei, "There is a problem between competing Mexican gangs. The situation on the ground is unstable. We will need to proceed cautiously when we land. Do you have any weapons?"

"Yes. In my travel case in the back. Got two NYPD Glock 17s on the black market while I was in New York."

"Good. We may need them."

Grushkov considered the one hundred and twenty-five million dollar deal, he'd made with Carlos Godinez, head of the Godinez drug cartel. The first twenty-five million dollars had been transferred to a numbered account in the Cayman Islands when the package arrived at the safe house on the Mexican side of the border. The second twenty-five million dollars was to be transferred into a numbered Swiss account after the package transited the tunnel to the safe house in Arizona and then was safely loaded onto the Cessna. The final seventy-five million dollars, held in an overseas escrow account by Deutsche Bank in Berlin, would be paid after Grushkov and his team escaped to Mexico through the tunnel, following the successful execution of the Tinderbox Plot in Wichita.

If Grushkov did not emerge from the tunnel on the Mexican side of the border within seven days of the package being moved to the American safe house, the final seventy-five million dollars would not be transferred to the Godinez cartel account.

Grushkov feared that Carlos Godinez might sell them out to the Americans for even more money. He remembered discussing this possibility at the final planning meeting with Gorky in his ornate Kremlin office two years ago.

As they drank tea from an antique samovar, Gorky said, "Make sure Godinez knows that if he betrays us, every member of his immediate and extended family will be eliminated — no matter how long it takes. And we'll start with his youngest son, a member of the Mexican embassy staff in Moscow."

Grushkov had admired the ruthless gleam in Gorky's eyes when making this threat. It reminded him of their younger days in the KGB.

The money was not an issue with Gorky. It was trivial compared to the vast resources at his disposal.

Also, Grushkov knew that this particular Mexican drug lord was in dire need of a cash infusion because of escalating pressure from the US enforcement agencies. In addition to one of his sons essentially being held hostage in Moscow, an additional motivation for Godinez to cooperate with the Russians was that — once this operation was over — the tunnel would become his, for use in ongoing illegal smuggling activities.

Grushkov remembered Gorky's eyes lighting up when reviewing the plan. His boss could not pass up any opportunity to further destabilize an already-degenerating American social and political system. If all went according to plan, Russia could step up and fill the resulting international power vacuum, restoring the power and prestige they had enjoyed prior to the breakup of the Soviet Union.

Gorky's response to his proposal had been powerful. The Russian president rose from his ornate chair towering his six-foot six-inch frame over the seated Grushkov. "Andrei Andreievich, we have the opportunity to ignite race wars in America, like already exist in their prisons, except now it will be in the streets. There's a core of white Americans terrified of the brown and yellow races becoming the majority. We shall exploit that fear."

Grushkov couldn't help adding, "Already we see the open hostility towards the Jews, a group with more power than their meager numbers deserve. We can manipulate the latent antisemitism in America through social media as well."

Gorky had smiled. "The American states will peel off, just as our republics did, and there will no longer be a 'united states' of America."

At this point, the Russian leader removed a bottle of rare, aged Jack Daniel's Gold 17 whiskey from a cabinet, pouring two double shots into fine crystal snifters. Raising a toast to the Tinderbox Plot, he said, "The Americans still make the best sour mash whiskey." He had peered at Grushkov over his glass and said, "Of course if you fail, I will disavow any knowledge, and label it as a misguided plot by a bunch of crazy ex-KGB agents."

This proclamation by the president of Russia still weighed heavy on Grushkov.

He was determined to succeed, despite the operation's reliance on a shady criminal like Carlos Godinez. The Mexican drug lord had assured Grushkov that many of the engineers and workmen who'd constructed the famous sixty-foot-deep El Chapo tunnel under the US-Mexico border in Douglas, Arizona had also been secured for this job.

"What about the Americans?" Sergei shouted over the din of the plane. "Are they on to us?"

Grushkov stared out the window at cloud clusters. "They are smart and have vast resources. I expect they are picking something up from phone or Internet chatter. I just don't know how close they are."

He was silent, then suddenly had a new idea. He took his satellite phone from his case and dialed the secure FSB number at the Manhattan consulate.

"Nicolai, it's Andrei Grushkov. I need a favor."

"Anything, Andrei. Just name it."

"I need you to send an FSB team to the Hilton Garden hotel near MacArthur Airport on Long Island. Have them inquire discreetly whether anyone has been there in the last couple of days, asking questions about someone that resembles me or Olga Radinova."

"No problem Andrei. I will go myself with my best man."

"Good. Call me back as soon as you have anything."

Three hours later, as they approached the single runway airfield in Nogales, Arizona, Sergei called out, "No tower at this airfield, so we have no requirement to identify our aircraft or our destination."

"That's why I chose it," replied Grushkov. "We've rented that large, white hangar past the terminal building. It's been used for years to store an old DC3."

"Yes, I see it."

"We've got it for a week, along with six of Godinez's men. There's a rented winch to lift the package into the plane. I'm figuring we'll need a day to get the package moved from the safe house to the hangar in a rented U-Haul. Another day to remove the aircraft cabin roof, lower the package into the frame, and securely fasten it. We'll let the epoxy set overnight and leave the next morning. Can we manage that?"

"Of course, Andrei. But I am worried about the Mexicans. Can we trust Godinez's men to keep their mouths shut about our operation? There's already been one breach of security."

"Godinez shows no mercy to those who betray him," said Grushkov. "That's why I picked him for this project. That said, I'll be relieved to get in the air with the package."

The Cessna touched down smoothly on the airport's single runway. While taxiing toward the open hangar, Grushkov's satellite phone rang.

"Dah. Nicolai?"

"This morning around ten thirty, a tall fiftyish woman in pants and a blue blouse asked the manager of the hotel about a black Lexus. She identified herself as NSA. She then left for the airport."

"Is that it?"

Nicolai hesitated for a few seconds. "She left a business card. Her name is Lynda Chester."

"Shit," Andrei said, raising his voice above the prop noise. "Sergei, we're only a half day ahead of the Americans. Repaint our tail ID numbers as soon as we're in the hangar. This woman who is pursuing us is relentless."

Chapter Eighteen
Saturday

At 3.35 p.m., Lynda phoned SC. "I'm at MacArthur Airport on Long Island. I'm here on my own time. I think you'll want to hear me out, but this is not a secure phone."

She endured the predictable rant by SC about her operating outside of protocol as a rogue agent, but at the end of the vitriol, he relented. "Okay, I'm listening."

"I've tracked the person of interest to a hangar at this location. Have not entered the hangar as per protocol but have found items of interest in garbage bins in plain sight."

"So what are you asking?" SC said.

"I need a search warrant, facial recognition analysis of suspects caught on airport security cams, and high priority for DNA and fingerprint analysis."

There was a twenty second pause. "That's a shitload to ask for. Give me details."

"On an unsecure line? *Your* protocol, remember?" *Bonehead*, she was thinking. She took a deep breath before continuing as vaguely as possible. She wondered if he would be discounting her initiative and instincts if she were male. "I've uncovered illegal activity by a foreign agent who's operating undercover. We've identified a car and the female driver associated with the agent's consulate. And I suspect an aircraft with ill intentions is at this moment headed somewhere in the US. SC, we can't let this get too far ahead of us." She let her words sink in, then added, "This is on your watch."

"Okay, I'll run it by the director."

"It's imperative that the FBI enter the hangar and process the scene asap."

"Just sit tight until you hear from me, Lynda. It's late Saturday, and our boss will have to contact Director Starks at the FBI. That makes it a national security matter. You better be right." He hung up.

While waiting for an answer that might not come the same day or even the next, she headed back to the TSA office, where the same supervisor was on duty. "Glenda, can you get me into the control tower? I'd like to find out what private aircraft took off around ten this morning."

"You'll need to talk with the tower supervisor. His office is on the ground floor of the tower. C'mon, I have a golf cart. It's about a half a mile from here."

After introducing Lynda to Jack Becker, the air traffic control day supervisor, Glenda headed back to her own office.

Lynda showed her credentials to Becker and established how important it was to find out where this plane was headed. Jack logged into his computer. "We have all the conversations with every aircraft stored, encrypted, and backed up. From what you say about the hangar location, we can eliminate all commercial and private jet traffic." He typed in instructions and in a few seconds, a list of aircraft and transcripts of voice communications appeared on his monitor.

"Pilots identify their aircraft by registration number and in some cases by type of aircraft and destination."

"Jack, look, one plane on your list departed at 10.33 a.m."

"Yeah, I see. It's a Cessna Conquest II-light, tail number N217X. He asked for clearance to ten thousand feet. That's an even number altitude, so he was likely headed west. He didn't file a flight plan; he was flying VFR. No way to tell where he was going."

"Can't radar track him?"

"Ms Chester, there are thousands of flights every day from three major airports and several small ones in the New York City area, and hundreds heading west at any moment. Unless he was in voice contact with Air Traffic Control along his route, there's no way to know which one of the hundreds of blips at ten thousand feet is your aircraft."

"Do you know the maximum range of that Cessna?"

Becker typed into his computer and located the operational specs on the Cessna Conquest II. "Fully fueled, twenty-two to twenty-five hundred nautical miles, depending on weather and air speed. But if he

129

refueled or the aircraft had wing pontoon tanks, he could go anywhere in the US."

"If he lands to refuel, he has to identify his plane by tail number, right?" Lynda asked.

"Only if he lands at an airstrip with a control tower. Otherwise, there's no requirement for ID. And there are plenty of small fields without control towers that have aviation fuel."

"If I want to send out a national alert for a Cessna with this tail number, how would I do that?"

"You'd have to contact Homeland Security, or maybe the FBI and the FAA."

"Okay, thanks," she said, and turned to leave the control room. Suddenly she stopped, turning back to Becker. She was remembering the image of Grushkov in the Atlanta airport. "Can you bring up a map of Tucson on your screen?"

"Sure." He opened Google Maps and clicked on Tucson.

"What airports are between Tucson and the Mexican border?"

"Only Nogales, Arizona."

"Shit," she muttered under her breadth.

Becker looked at her with raised eyebrows.

"Sorry." Lynda hustled out of the control room.

Walking back toward the hangar, Lynda wondered what it might be like to confront her old flame. Grushkov was likely armed. Her own Beretta was in the nightstand next to her bed. She made a mental note to transfer it to her purse when she got home. But it had been years since she'd gone through the field training program required of all NSA agents regardless of whether they were going to be manning a desk or in the field. Lynda was not even sure she could fire it at another human being, unless maybe he fired at her first.

She was not surprised at SC's reluctance to ask other agencies for help. He was so focused on the need for NSA successes to aid his climb to the top of the agency that he'd lost sight of the need for collaboration with the other agencies. She could follow up her initial contact with the FBI on this, but going behind SC's back would surely come back to bite her. She would just have to wait and hope NSA's decision will be to bring in the FBI or some other agency.

Meanwhile, there was nothing stopping her from contacting the FAA and seeing if she could persuade the agency that there was a national security matter that needed the Cessna registration number sent as an alert to every air traffic control center in the US.

Back at the suspicious hangar, she walked to the adjacent hangar and knocked on the side door. She waited half a minute with no response. Then she heard someone inside, so she pounded on the door until it opened.

She was staring at a man in coveralls with grease on his hands. He looked blankly at her as she identified herself.

"What's NSA?"

"We're like police but... uhm... we track down spies."

His face came alive.

She asked about the recent occupants of the hangar next door. "Yeah, I seen 'em. Odd group. They lived there and spoke to each other in a foreign language."

Lynda opened her phone to the Internet, searched around, then played some Russian dialogue.

"Yeah, yeah. That sounds like it, but I don't know what else I can tell you. They kept to themselves, and I got no idea what they were saying."

"Could you describe what they looked like?"

"Not really. I was pretty far away and didn't pay them much mind."

"Here's my card. Please call if you remember anything else. It's important."

Walking back to the suspects' hangar she rummaged through her shoulder bag for her lock-pick tools. There had to be more evidence inside. But before that thought translated into action, her phone rang.

"Lynda, SC. Director wants you back in DC asap. He'll talk with the FBI on Monday."

"But—"

"No buts, Lynda. He's pissed you went out on your own on this, especially after we told you we'd handle it. Now get your ass back here and stay put until Monday." Before she could respond, he hung up.

"Fucking chauvinistic bonehead," she mumbled.

Chapter Nineteen
Saturday & Sunday

Grushkov was met in the Nogales airport hangar by a Mexican who identified himself as MJ, a member of the Godinez network. Jerking his head nervously from side to side, in heavily accented English, he said, "I have Xavier's car. We must leave quickly."

Sergei located cans of black and white paint in the corner of the hangar to change the tail number, but Grushkov said, "Do it tomorrow. I need you by my side at the safe house with the Glocks."

Alexey Krupov, disheveled and with a few facial bruises, greeted them at the antique store safe house, an AK-47 slung over his shoulder. "We had another attack by the Ayala cartel. This is their territory. Carlos finally worked out a deal with them, but only after they killed Xavier."

Two other Mexicans with AK-47s were slouched against a wall. "They're Godinez men, just in case," Alexey said. "They have a pickup truck so we can load the package and take it to the hangar."

"It's over nine hundred pounds. We must be very gentle with it," Grushkov said.

Alexey nodded in agreement. "We have mattresses for the back of the truck. But it's too heavy for the four of us to lift." He waved to the Mexicans, speaking to them in Spanish. One of them used his cell phone.

Forty-five minutes later, four men emerged from the tunnel.

Together, the four lifted and positioned the package in the middle of one mattress on the truck bed. But before they had time to wrap the second mattress around the package, there was a loud bang as one of the tires blew out.

After rapid fire Spanish chatter between MJ and two of the Mexicans, Alexey turned to Grushkov. "No spare tire and no jack to lift the truck."

"Damn." He's thinking, his well-thought-out hi-tech project, has turned into an amateurish comedy of errors.

Grushkov shot an accusatory glare at Alexey, who said, "We still have Xavier's car."

"Won't work. It's too heavy. We need a truck."

He considered the group around him. There were eight undocumented Mexicans and three Russians, two of whom were undocumented. And Sergei had a diplomatic visa that required he remain in New York. "Unload the package and get it back in the safe house," he snapped. "Can't have it sitting in the street on a truck with a flat."

Grushkov took a moment to consider the options. He glared at the slash camera pole by the border fence across the road. Then he dialed Carlos Godinez's satellite number. "Carlos, we have a problem. Need an enclosed truck or van to move package to airport."

"Andrei Grushkov, I can help but it will take time for me to get one of my men with green card and American driver's license through border checkpoint and then to a truck rental company."

"Don't you have proper vehicles in your operation in Mexico?"

"Yes, but it will take a day to get it here and through American customs."

"Let's do that. I would rather wait for your truck as opposed to renting on this side."

"Okay Andrei. I'll call you when I have an ETA on the vehicle, but don't expect it until tomorrow afternoon. And this will cost extra."

"I'll notify our Mexico City embassy to transfer half the second payment with an extra half a mil when the truck arrives, and the remainder when the package is on the airplane."

"Okay. Be in touch," Carlos said.

"Not so fast, Carlos. What about the Ayala gang? Are you sure they are going to stay away? They already shot up one of my men and killed Xavier."

"I've taken care of it. But be prepared, just in case." Carlos hung up.

Grushkov took Sergei and Alexey aside. "I don't trust these guys. We will share guard duty through the night. We'll need two of their assault AKs and here are my two Glocks. Sergei you and I will take the first eight hours. Alexey, you and MJ will take the second."

"We should eat," Sergei said.

After removing two hundred dollars from the side pocket of his computer case, Grushkov said to MJ, "You and Alexey go to MacDonald's for food. Find out what your guys want. I'll have a cheeseburger."

At four a.m., during Alexey and MJ's guard period, there was a scuffling sound at the bottom of tunnel shaft. Alexey yelled in Spanish for anyone down there to identify themselves, but there was no response.

Grushkov awoke instantly from a fitful sleep. Grabbing his Glock, he joined Alexey and MJ at the opening to the tunnel shaft.

"Could be big rats," Alexey said.

Grushkov's KGB training kicked in. "I'm going down there. Give me one of the AKs and keep an eye on the sleeping Mexicans."

Slowly descending the wooden ladder with an assault rifle slung over his shoulder and a Glock in his waistband, Grushkov paused every few rungs and listened for any movement below. At the bottom, he used his cell mag light to illuminate the tunnel. There were two partially smoked cigarette butts, one of which was still warm. He shone the light as far as it would illuminate down the tunnel, about twenty yards, and saw nothing. He scrambled back up the ladder to where Alexey, MJ and two of the other Mexicans were standing.

As soon as Grushkov reported the hot butt, MJ whipped out his cell and dialed. He spoke excitedly in Spanish and hung up. "I alerted our guys in the other side. They were asleep but will check the tunnel from their end."

In less than five minutes, they heard a prolonged volley of gunfire followed by shorter bursts from the Mexican end of the tunnel.

"Automatic rifle and handgun," Grushkov yelled. "Encircle the tunnel shaft. They may be coming back our way."

Ten minutes later, there were sounds on the shaft ladder. Grushkov and his men raised their weapons, poised to let loose a barrage of gunfire.

A head emerged from the tunnel shaft.

MJ yelled, "He's one of ours."

Fingers eased off the triggers as the lone Mexican climbed out of the shaft and reported that they killed two Ayala gang members at their end.

"So much for Carlos' guarantee," Grushkov said to Alexey and Sergei.

Turning to the rest of the group around the shaft opening, he said, "We need to be extra alert until the truck gets here." Grushkov checked his watch. "We've got a long day ahead of us. Sergei and MJ, make a breakfast run at six. Those MacDonald's egg muffins are surprisingly good. Get two for everyone, and a lot of coffee." Grushkov pictured the Stoli in his carry-on case, but resisted, knowing he could not afford a slip-up at this critical moment.

At three p.m. a moving van with a rear hydraulic lift backed against the entrance of the safe house on the American side of the border. The driver was a Mexican man in jeans and a cowboy hat. A trim, neatly dressed man in chinos and a white polo knit shirt got out from the passenger side. He had slicked-back dark hair, was wearing aviator sunglasses, and had a red scar that extended from the corner of his mouth to his right cheek.

MJ jumped forward. "Andrei Grushkov, this is Carlos Godinez."

The two men eyed each other before Godinez extended his hand. "I'll accompany you to airport."

Grushkov offered a weary smile. Clearly, Godinez wanted to make sure that his client would authorize the second payment, along with the extra half mil.

"Great, Carlos. It's nice to finally meet you. You speak really good English."

"I went to Occidental College near Pasadena for three years but never finished because of a family business matters," he said, removing his sunglasses and fixing his dark eyes on Grushkov.

In an hour, the package was loaded in the truck on a bed of two mattresses and securely fastened with straps. Six of Godinez's men rode in the back of the truck for the forty-five-minute drive to Nogales airport. Godinez and his driver, along with Grushkov, were in the truck cab while MJ followed behind, driving Xavier's car with Alexey, Sergei, and two more of Godinez's men.

The truck backed into the hangar, six feet from the Cessna, right next to the rented tripod winch.

After the package was lifted out of the truck and gently set on the hangar floor, Sergei got on top of the airplane and, using the epoxy solvent, dissolved the seam that had been fastening the cut segment to the fuselage. He uncoupled the clips and grasped the handle on the cut piece. Lifting it off the fuselage, he passed it to Grushkov and Alexey, who stood below the Cessna, arms raised.

It took another thirty minutes to attach the package to the heavy iron hook on the winch hoist cable and slowly lift it, until it was positioned directly over the opening in the roof of the Cessna. Sergei guided the package as it was lowered. Grushkov got inside the plane to guide the package into the aluminum frame, already bolted to the floor and cabin walls.

"It's a tight fit," Grushkov said.

"It should be stable, as long as we don't hit any rough weather," said Sergei.

Carlos Godinez was standing at the bottom of the steps, a pistol jutting from his pants belt. He watched Grushkov's team lower the package into the plane.

Using his satellite phone, Grushkov dialed Anatoly in Havana. "Andrei here. Transfer second payment. Need another half million. Trouble at this end." He hung up.

"We will wait until I have confirmation from the bank," Carlos said.

Grushkov frowned. "It could be few hours. The money is being moved into your Swiss account from a Bulgarian bank."

"It's five o'clock. I will send MJ for some good Mexican food. This MacDonald's shit is for you gringos," Carlos grinned broadly. "I trust you Andrei — just want to share a meal with my Russian friends."

After a feast of enchiladas, quesadillas, mole chicken on rice, and carnitas spread out on two, fold-down tables in the corner of the hangar, Carlos said, "We have our favorite restaurant on this side of border. They do almost as good job as the ones in Mexico. What do you think, Andrei Grushkov?"

"Definitely better than Big Macs."

Carlos felt a vibration in his trousers and extracted his cell phone. "Si, Bueno." He nodded to Grushkov. "Money transferred. We leave now, my good friend. I await your return and the final payment." He slapped Grushkov on the back.

Grushkov winced. "One minute, Carlos. Leave the car, the mattresses, and two AK-47s."

"Sure, no problem, Andrei, but it will cost," Carlos said, his hand moving to the gun in his waistband.

Grushkov said nothing but hard stared at Carlos.

Carlos waited a few seconds, then laughed uproariously. "Just kidding, Andrei."

He turned to MJ. "Give Andrei the keys to the car and two AK-47s."

After the Godinez gang departed, Grushkov said to Sergei, "Let's get the roof epoxied back in place, and change the tail number." Turning to Alexey, he said, "You share guard duty with Sergei and me tonight. Take the car back to the safe house tomorrow and then get back on the Mexican side of the border and wait for our return in a few days. But I need you tonight. I don't trust these cartel guys."

Chapter Twenty
Sunday

At seven a.m., Lynda stepped out of her DC condo for an early morning jog and virtually bumped into a buff-solid guy in a dark suit.

Before he could say anything, she said, "FBI or CIA?"

"You're Lynda Chester?"

"Who wants to know? Let me see your ID."

He extracted his flat ID, flipped it open, and she saw Conrad Wilson, Central Intelligence Agency.

"Let me see your driver's license," she said.

He scowled and produced his license, which matched the name and photo on his CIA ID.

"Can't be too careful," she quipped, as she showed Wilson her NSA ID badge, the only identification she carried when she did her morning run.

Wilson gestured her toward the front seat of a black SUV double-parked in front of her condo, hemming in her own parked car. She got in and he started up the engine and drove away.

"You know it's Sunday?" she said.

"We work twenty-four seven. You'll be met at the memorial wall," he said, barreling down empty streets onto the Beltway, and then to CIA headquarters in Langley, Virginia.

"It's about the burner cell calls alert I sent over," she said, being careful not to ask directly. This was her project, and she didn't want to seem tentative or weak.

"I'm just the errand boy today. At the wrong place at the wrong time when they sent down orders for a driver. All this is above my pay grade." He shrugged. "I don't have a clue why you're being summoned."

Once in the main building at Langley, seeing the stars on the memorial wall caused a lump to form in Lynda's throat. If she'd taken her commission in the Navy, maybe she would have had more opportunities to face danger. This was only the third time in more than twenty years that she'd been able to get into the field, and she reveled in the adrenalin rush, reminiscent of her judo days at Cornell.

There was a light touch on her shoulder, and a voice said, "It does get to you, doesn't it?"

Lynda turned and gazed into Sally Spitzer's gray eyes.

"We've got something interesting," Sally said. "Meeting's upstairs. Follow me. Here's a day badge that will get you through security checkpoints."

They walked down a corridor with rows of rooms, each with a combination key padlock, reaching an elevator that required each occupant to insert a security card.

Alone with Sally in the elevator, Lynda whispered, "You're DARPA, not CIA. Why are you here?"

"You know those algorithms you wrote for intercepting sat phone calls? Well, the CIA's been using them to track bad guys on the terrorist watch list. DARPA's been subcontracted to develop satellite phones that can't be traced. CIA figures it's just a matter of time until the international bad guys are capable of developing software like yours — if they haven't already."

"So it's a game, keeping one step ahead of the opposition?"

"Yeah, a never-ending game of hopscotch, and you're one of our stars. Your message about the mystery undercover high-level Russian has piqued considerable interest over here. This is an agency that's paranoid about coincidences not being coincidences."

Seeing Lynda's questioning expression, Sally continued. "You'll see what I mean in a few minutes."

They exited the elevator on the third floor and walked down a long, sterile corridor before reaching a conference room with an open door. The room was stuffy and dark, except for a PowerPoint projection already on the screen. Three men were seated at an oval conference table, speaking in muffled tones. They stopped speaking when Lynda and Sally entered.

Lynda recognized the oldest of the three as William Boyd, Assistant Deputy Director, the number three guy after Associate Director Jack Light. She went directly to him, extended her hand, and said, "Lynda

139

Chester, Director, NSA Imaging Center. Give my regards to Jack. He used several of my algorithms to track Bin Laden back in 2011."

The other two men looked like they were in their early thirties. They introduced themselves only as Tom and Frank. After the two women sat across from them, Boyd took a seat opposite the screen, which displayed a map of the United States with dots scattered across the continent.

Frank pointed at the screen with a red laser pointer. "Each dot represents a hate message sent through the Internet during a random one-hour period over five days in one week."

"It's over a thousand points," Lynda observed.

"One thousand one hundred and ninety-two," Tom said. "Our numbers geeks say we're probably looking at hundreds of thousands, since these are taken from just five random hours in a single week."

"That's why you're here, Dr Chester," Boyd said. "Since you developed the applicable algorithms, we'd like you to try to find a pattern."

"Have you considered a bot attack? At the rate the messages are spreading, it could be a classic bot-storm. NSA's detected rudimentary artificial intelligence bot attacks from North Korea and in Europe, likely from Russia," Lynda said.

"We're considering that," Boyd responded.

"Bill," Lynda said, slipping to a more casual tone, "I'm sure you know that the president tasked the creation of an interagency Roadmap Against Botnets in 2018. A 2020 update report made it clear that our different agencies were having difficulty in developing a coherent plan."

Raising his tone an octave, Boyd replied, "Dr Chester, I am familiar with those reports and am well aware that they warned of 'bad guys with evil intents' using AI-bots against us."

At this point, Lynda realized that she had not been summoned to the CIA because of Grushkov's sighting — at least they were not saying so right now. She was one of those intel skeptics who did not believe in coincidences.

Putting aside that thought, she refocused. "Can you project the patterns from each successive day, starting with day one?"

Boyd, who was controlling the PowerPoint projection from his laptop hit the advance arrow. As they were projected in successive order,

Lynda's photographic mind processed the images. After several minutes of examining the patterns of hundreds of dots on the US map, Lynda said, "I'll need the raw data so I can run it through my pattern extraction programs to confirm."

"What do you *think* you see, Dr Chester?" Boyd said, his tone gruff.

She took the red laser pointer from Frank. "There appears to be clusters of messages from Southern California and New York City. Starting on the second day, you can see dots springing up randomly across the US, in rural and city areas. What's different between California and New York is that the New York area has a high density without the gradual build-up we see in California. Do you have New York data going back for a few weeks or even months?"

Before any of the CIA men could answer, Sally said, "Maybe the New York area started before California, so the curve looks different?"

Lynda smiled. "I guess that's why you were my best professor. Yes, that's what I'm thinking; I'd like to see if we can detect a build-up in New York from earlier data." She looked to Frank.

"What do you think this means?" Boyd interjected.

"Give me the raw data, and I'll see what I can come up with."

"We'll load what we've got on a high-capacity thumb drive." He nodded at Tom, who left the room.

Sally asked, "Have you traced the messages to the source-computers in California and New York by the IP addresses?"

"We're working on it. We have strong indications about which messages are from the source computers, but when you have so many data points from one area, it's hard to look at them all." Boyd continued. "The ones we're focusing on are using hushmail and untraceable proxy IPs that are changed each time they connect through a VPN."

Surprised, Lynda asked, "Don't you have software to penetrate the hushmail system?"

"We're not there yet. There's also a legal question about violating freedom of speech. There's already a class action lawsuit against the government by hushmail users."

Lynda frowned. "But if it's a question of national security, the legal question should be moot, right?"

"Yes," Boyd replied. "But we haven't proven that yet."

141

Lynda was thinking *bonehead* — just like SC at the NSA. She cleared her throat. "Bill, I'm interested in your New York site. I've tracked an FSB Russian to New York and intercepted SAT phone calls from the Russian consulate in Manhattan to FSB headquarters in Havana. But my Russian has gone dark, and I don't know where he is. My gut's telling me there may be a connection between your hate messages and my Russian."

"Yeah, I remember your message last week about the intercepted burner calls. We're also thinking there may be a connection with the rise in hate messaging and your mysterious Russian."

Lynda strongly suspected that Boyd was holding back more than he was revealing. She shot Sally a side glance, who returned a subtle smile.

"Not sure we can help any further, Lynda," Boyd said. "We're already giving you the raw data."

Not satisfied with his answer, she persisted. "Bill, how come this is a CIA project and not FBI? CIA's mandate is overseas intelligence and spying, not domestic intelligence. Anyway, CIA, NSA, and FBI are supposed to share information, especially as it relates to national security."

Lynda knew she had hit a nerve when Boyd stiffened.

"We extracted this information from a foreign asset. That's all I can reveal."

Before Lynda could pursue this further, Tom returned and handed her a thumb drive. He said, "This drive contains the raw data on almost two thousand hate messages. You can break-out the data by day and time."

Boyd jumped in with a command. "Get back to me as soon as you have something." He snapped his laptop shut, got up, and leaned across the table to Lynda, handing her a business card. "My private cell is on the back. A car will be out front to take you back."

"What do you think?" Lynda asked Sally as soon as they were outside in front of Langley.

"He sure was evasive when you asked why CIA and not FBI is on this."

"Yeah, I don't like being stonewalled, but I'm already in hot water with my boss and don't want to alienate the guys over here, too. And I

142

wonder about his *asset*. Could be a mole on the other side, or someone they water boarded to get the information. They still do that, you know."

Sally laughed. "You came down hard on Boyd. As far as CIA having a mole on the other side, that doesn't surprise me — as well as water boarding."

"As long as it's not on American soil," Lynda said.

Outside, a black SUV pulled up, but with a different driver.

Lynda gave her mentor a hug. "When you get a chance," she said, "I'd like to learn about that new anti-snoop phone technology you're working on. It could help us at NSA."

"How about Saturday morning, once a month?" Sally answered.

"Deal. Let's check calendars."

Chapter Twenty-one
Monday & Tuesday

At 7.05 a.m. on Monday Grushkov held his breath as concrete rushed toward them, disappearing at an alarming rate. With a few yards to spare, the Cessna was airborne.

Sergei said, "The weather report in the Wichita area is scattered clouds with fifty per cent chance of thunderstorms. "It's three and a half hours of flying time. I'll stay under ten thousand feet. I don't trust the cabin roof under pressurization."

"How's the plane handling?" Grushkov asked.

"Heavy on take-off and sluggish on turns. It's not designed to have so much weight concentrated in one position."

There was a tightening in Andrei's gut, but he pushed it away.

Two hours into the flight, Sergei observed, "Two thunderheads about twenty miles ahead. Radar shows enough space between them to pass through. It looks good, but there may be some jostling."

"Package can't take much," Grushkov said. "Can we fly over?"

"Are you willing to risk the ceiling blowing out?"

"No. Fly between."

A blast of turbulence threw the Cessna into a steep climb, followed by a vacuum effect and the plane plummeted downward. The unusual weight distribution of the heavy package made it difficult for Sergei to keep the plane level while being buffeted by gusts coming from different directions.

Grushkov twisted in his seat to look at the package. "One of the bolts has been pulled up. If we hit another rough spot, the entire aluminum frame could pull out of the floor." He pictured the bomb exploding, turning him and Sergei and the plane into pulverized powder. For a moment, he wondered if the Tinderbox Plot was worth dying for.

"Check the map to see what airfields may be nearby," Sergei yelled while trying to keep control of the tossing plane. "We should land, wait out the storms, and repair the cage as much as possible."

"The delay could be too much," Grushkov answered, knowing that Lynda Chester had picked up his trail, and was only a half-day behind.

"It's not safe to continue," Sergei shouted above the prop noise. "We should be near Amarillo, Texas."

"I see a small airport called Tradewind near Amarillo, on the map," Grushkov said.

"Probably has no control tower. We can't fly VFR in this storm. I will contact the Amarillo control tower, see if they can find us on radar and vector us in."

"Cessna N297X light calling Amarillo, out. Cessna N297X light calling Amarillo, out."

"Cessna N297X, this is Amarillo."

"Amarillo, we are experiencing heavy turbulence and need vector guidance to land VFR. N297X out."

"Roger, Cessna N297X light, we have you on radar fifteen miles south-east. We'll vector you in."

"Roger, Amarillo. We have your beacon acquired. What is your visibility and wind? Cessna N297X out."

"Cessna N297X, visibility one mile and closing, wind gusting ten to twenty miles per hour north-north-west. You are cleared to land on runway alpha-one, south south-west."

"Cessna N297X, roger Amarillo. See runway lights. Proceeding VFR. Thanks Amarillo, out."

Buckled in tight, Grushkov stared intently at the package in its aluminum frame that looked ready to pop; he was willing it to stay in place.

"It's a long runway," Sergei shouted. "We'll be okay if I can set it down evenly on both wheels."

Suddenly the Cessna jolted to the left, and to Grushkov's horror, he saw the second of four bolts holding the cage to the floor shear off, causing the cage to slide toward the fuselage wall. He opened his harness and stumbled back into the cabin. Grabbing one of the small mattresses left over from the recent test flight, he shouted, "Keep us steady, Sergei.

145

I need to wedge this mattress between the cage and the cabin wall before it smashes through."

But the Cessna tilted to the right as another gust hit, causing the cage to move in the opposite direction, away from the cabin wall. Grushkov lunged and shoved the mattress into the larger space created when the cage moved away from the wall. When the Cessna tilted back to the left, the cage compressed the mattress against the bulkhead and did not move.

Sergei put the plane down with a thud in the center of the runway; they decelerated and began their taxi towards the terminal area.

"We need to find someone who can fasten the aluminum frame securely back to the floor and add more braces," Grushkov said. "Someone who won't ask too many questions."

Sergei wiped a trail of sweat from his face. "As soon as I am cleared to taxi off the runway, we can head for those hangars. There's usually a few maintenance crews looking for some extra work, especially in bad weather when so many flights are redirected."

The Cessna taxied into a large maintenance hangar where Sergei persuaded two men engaged in a card game with a half dozen other men, to repair the inside frame of the Cessna.

Since Grushkov and Sergei would spend the night on the mattresses in the Cessna, Grushkov walked to the main terminal for a bite to eat and to bring something back for Sergei. While eating at a table in McDonald's, he watched the TV mounted on the wall. A newscaster was describing an unexplained increase in violence, especially against African Americans in Houston as well as firebombing of an NGA office in Dallas. Knowing this was likely the result of his embedded teams' efforts, Grushkov smiled.

At 6.10 on Tuesday morning, Cessna N297X taxied to Amarillo airport runway alpha-one to start the last leg to Wichita, Kansas.

"Cessna N297X light, you are cleared for take-off. Do you want ATC tracking? Amarillo, out."

"Cessna N297X light, Amarillo we are good for VFR, out," Sergei said into his microphone.

Grushkov took out his satellite phone and dialed Anatoly in Havana. "ETA Kansas eight fifteen a.m."

146

After the Cessna departed Amarillo, one of the air traffic controllers beckoned her supervisor. "That Cessna that just left could be the plane we received an alert on. It came through on Sunday from some federal agency. I think a printout was posted," she said, walking over to the alert board.

She and her supervisor reviewed the alert from the FAA. On it was a phone number and email address at the National Security Agency in Fort Meade, Virginia. "Did you get the tail number on it?" asked the supervisor.

"Yeah, it's off by one number. But I got a squirrelly feeling about it. The pilot was flying VFR in marginal weather. And he left real early this morning VFR, with no mention of destination."

"Doesn't hurt to notify the feds. Who's the contact person?"

"Says Dr Lynda Chester."

Chapter Twenty-two
Monday, one week earlier & Tuesday a week later

Tired and irritable, Gregory Borisy and Mihail 'Mischa' Asimov — Grushkov's third team — exited the Wichita Amtrak train station. Gregory said, "My uncle's pigs wouldn't eat that train food."

Mischa answered, "I'm sure your uncle's pigs wouldn't eat any American food."

They both chuckled and decided to take a taxi from the station to the address provided by Grushkov. The taxi wound through downtown Wichita, an upscale neighborhood of old multistoried homes with well-kept lawns, and finally to an industrial neighborhood with many large hangar-like buildings situated next to an aircraft runway. Gregory recalled Grushkov's background information on Wichita and surmised that these large buildings were connected to the aircraft industry that had once flourished.

They were dropped off at a large concrete building without windows that looked to be a block long and three stories high. Mischa said, "This is the address, but it sure isn't a flat, and we don't have a key."

"Not a problem," Gregory said. He walked toward what appeared to be the entrance to the building. Instead of a door with a conventional doorknob or handle with a lock, there was a heavy iron door with a keypad. With a satisfied smile, Gregory typed in a series of numbers that Grushkov had instructed the *Winter falcon* team leader to commit to memory.

He remembered his mentor saying: "You'll know when to use them."

Inside the building, Mischa's eyebrows lifted. "Pretty big space."

Gregory said, "Before we explore, we should signal that we have safely arrived." He took out his burner cell, and dialed Anatoly's number in Havana.

When he heard, "Dah," he hung up.

Gregory turned to Mischa. "Message will be relayed to Grushkov. And now, our job is to sit tight."

"For how long?" Mischa asked.

"As long as necessary. We're just one part of a larger operation. Andrei needs to prepare the plane and get it here with its payload. That's all I know. Now let's examine our new home."

They started to walk the length of the building, with numerous aircraft tire marks on the concrete floor. Gregory looked up at a ceiling at least twenty feet high; he saw metal tracks running the length and width of the building. There were two electric winches with thick chains for lifting heavy items, such as aircraft engines. Gregory grabbed one of the hanging control boxes and inspected the toggle switches and colored buttons. He pushed a green button, and a heavy chain started to lower from one of the winches. When he pushed the red button, it stopped.

Gregory, with Mischa close behind, walked to the other end of the building, where he found two heavy floor-to-ceiling sliding doors controlled by a series of buttons on the adjacent wall. He pushed the green button.

With a rumble, the doors slowly slid open.

There were other buildings across the airstrip with similar taxiways. Several of the hangars were open, revealing single-engine, and in one case a twin-prop, planes. The adjacent building had a large banner that said, 'For rent', and the two buildings further down had similar rental signs. Grushkov had mentioned that Wichita had a depressed aircraft industry. Many empty buildings on small airfields were used mainly on weekends by private pilot enthusiasts.

In one corner of the hangar was a door to a room with a large glass window looking out at the hangar floor. Inside, the room was spacious, about twenty-by-twenty feet. It had two single beds against one wall, and against the other wall, a kitchen sink, a microwave, an electric convection range, cupboards with dishes, and a kitchen table with four chairs. There was a shiny refrigerator-freezer fully stocked with fresh vegetables, eggs, milk, a twelve-pack of bottled water, and an unopened bottle of Stolichnaya. The freezer was stocked with steaks, chicken, burgers, and frozen vegetables — enough to last two weeks. A bathroom with a sink and shower was behind a door at another corner of the room. There was also a desk with a computer modem, its five lit green lights indicating active Internet access.

"Ahhh," Gregory sighed. "We have a lot of food and Internet access." He removed his laptop from its carry-on case and plugged into the USB port. Following protocol learned in Havana, he opened his dark web Tor browser and clicked on Ghost. This took him into the web using an anonymous IP address. He checked his hushmail account and saw no messages. "We will check each day at seven a.m., noon, and nine p.m. for the package ETA signal."

"Wow, look at this," Mischa exclaimed as he scrolled the MSNBC news website. "Their reporting a surge in negative, even violent, postings on many social media sites. There's been an increase in threats against the liberal newspapers like the *New York Times*. They're even quoting FBI sources that there appears to be a concerted effort by foreign entities to infiltrate social media platforms like Facebook and Instagram." He pulled up another news site where a pundit warned that the country seemed to be escalating toward widespread violence. A confederation of extremist groups was threatening civil war.

"Doesn't surprise me, Mischa. Remember the goals of *Winter falcon* and *Snow leopard* was to achieve exactly that — capitalize on the existing American polarization, build upon it and raise the level of American angst to a fever pitch — drive the extremist groups on both sides to violence."

"I get the big picture," said Mischa. "When our bomb detonates, America will descend into a chaos — the two extreme sides blaming the other."

"Yes, the different *united states* will peel off just like the Soviet Republics did thirty years ago," said Gregory.

While Mischa continued to surf the Internet, looking for more reports, Gregory removed an envelope taped to the desk. Inside was a note dated the previous week, which he read aloud:

Fresh food will be left at the front door every Tuesday morning at six a.m. Take it in by six thirty a.m. Also, leave your garbage in a large plastic bag by the front door by six a.m. Tuesday. If you have special needs for food or other items, leave a note in this envelope and place inside the bag on top of the garbage.

"Strange," Mischa said. "Someone knew we were coming but wasn't sure what day we'd arrive."

"A sleeper," Gregory replied, taking the note from Mischa. "Someone under deep cover that has a respectable life with family and job. We may never meet him."

Seeing that Mischa's curiosity was piqued, Gregory elaborated. "According to Andrei Grushkov, when the Soviet Union broke apart in '91, the Americans saw it as an opportunity to attract some of our scientists. The travel restrictions in the Soviet era were strict, especially for Jews, many of whom were the brightest scientists we had. Given the chance during the break-up, when control of emigration was lax, many fled to the US and Israel."

"But what about the sleepers?" Mischa asked.

"Well, according to Grushkov, he and Gorky devised a plan, to let some Soviet scientists defect to America as refugees. Russia labeled them 'traitors of Mother Russia'." Gregory walked toward the kitchen table, gesturing for Mischa to sit while he retrieved from the fridge two glasses and the bottle of Stoli.

Sitting across from Mischa, Gregory poured three inches of cold Stoli into the glasses and slid one across to Mischa. "America was willing to accept them because their immigration rules on political refugees were very lax. So they accepted Russian scientists as refugees, not knowing they were actually KGB-trained spies."

Gregory tossed back his drink. "But now tell me about yourself, Mischa. How do you come to be here?"

"I spent six years in the military as a helicopter pilot and then a fighter jet pilot at the airbases in Tajikistan and Uzbekistan."

Gregory refilled his glass and added a fresh inch to Mischa's. "So how did Grushkov find you?"

"One day he came to our air base outside Moscow and asked if anyone was interested in a dangerous job as a spy. I was bored, fighting a losing war, so I volunteered, and here I am." Mischa took a gulp of Stoli. "These are pretty good accommodations compared to places where I was stationed during the Afghan War. Too bad we are confined to quarters. Maybe at night we can walk the runway. I doubt any of the local private pilots fly at night."

Gregory leaned across the table, so he was a few inches from Mischa who leaned forward also. He said just above a whisper, "You know what we are asked to do on this mission?"

"Yes. I know what you are getting at. I am a soldier. I've killed many enemies."

"And innocent people too?"

Mischa drained his glass. "Of course. It's unavoidable."

"How… how many?" Gregory stammered, the vodka now in full effect.

"I don't think about it," Mischa replied.

Gregory pushed his empty glass to the side of the table, signaling he'd had enough. "I am worried we may start a nuclear war. I question whether we will be recognized as heroes of Mother Russia. How do you feel?"

"I am trained not to question orders," Mischa replied.

"Yes, I think that is why Andrei Grushkov paired us." He allowed the words to sink in.

"I've trained for missions like this. When the Cold War ended, I thought my life was over. As the Soviet Union, we were on top of the world. We flew the Americans to the space station because their space program was a mess after the Challenger exploded."

"Golden days." Mischa nodded.

"We even had agents in key positions in NASA, and in the facilities that manufactured and assembled the American space shuttles."

"How do you know?"

"My father was KGB in the 1980s. He went through a training program for an undercover assignment in America. However, at the final physical exam, they found a heart murmur. But he trained with several KGB guys who were smuggled into America by mercenary Mexican drug dealers."

Mischa laughed loudly. "So we have a history of working with the Mexican drug lords that give America such trouble these days, and who are key to the success of our current mission."

"It's ironic," Gregory said. "Gorky was making a name for himself in the KGB when we were the Soviet Union and forging relationships with the drug cartels that these days drive the American president crazy."

"Yeah, who would have predicted that five years after the Challenger blew up, our glorious empire would be dismembered, republic by republic?" Mischa said.

"But we're back," Gregory responded. "Especially if we are successful on this mission. We must celebrate tonight before tomorrow. Let's cook nice big steaks, finish the bottle of Stoli, and if we need more there's the bottle in your suitcase."

"How did you know I had the vodka, Gregory?"

Now it was Gregory Borisy's chance to laugh loudly. "We are KGB! I've got a bottle too."

"Yes, let's celebrate. We will change history."

"Perhaps even more than you think," said Gregory. "Because the bomb will be identified as one of America's own. And with the efforts of *Snow leopard* and *Arctic fox*, America will explode in a civil war. The right-wing extremists will blame the left liberals and vice versa; and the anarchist groups will take advantage of the mass confusion"

Mischa Asimov looked at Gregory with eyebrows raised and a wrinkled brow. "How do you know all this? I know nothing of the other teams and even less about the package that will arrive."

Whether it had been the vodka or the fact the Gregory felt paternal toward Mischa, he now realized he may have revealed too much.

Mischa scratched his head and gazed at Gregory. "I don't see how each side will blame the other. Neither have control of America's nuclear weapons."

"I don't think it will matter," Gregory said, and continued. "Once the bomb is identified as American-made, both sides will blame the other. Accusations will fly, violence will erupt, and chaos will occur."

"Wait—you mean it's an American device?"

"Yes." Too much Stoli speaking. "I thought you knew. Let's eat a good meal and finish that Stoli," Gregory said.

Tuesday, six thirty a.m. after one week in Wichita, *Winter falcon* received a hushmail from Anatoly Zupin in Havana:

Baby born at 8.15 a.m.

Gregory looked at his watch and said to Mischa, "Package arrives in an hour."

At eight a.m., Mischa pushed the green button on the wall and the hangar doors slid open. He and Gregory peered outside into a light rain on a cloud-shrouded gray day, not ideal flying weather. At 8.15, there was no sign of the airplane.

Mischa said, "Must be the weather." He reached for the button to shut the doors but stopped when he heard the faint drone of a plane gradually increasing until the running lights were visible in the distance. A sleek twin turboprop with extra fuel pontoons at the tips of each wing touched down on the runway landing stripes, decelerating until it was two-thirds of the way down the runway. The Cessna turned and taxied toward the hangar where the *Winter falcon* team was waiting.

The pilot feathered the engine closest to the two-man greeting party and taxied through the open doors that slid shut behind.

Touchdown to hangar door closure took less than three minutes.

Two men were visible in the cockpit. The pilot, a tall, slim man in his forties exited first. Gregory and Mischa's jaws drop as Andrei Grushkov stepped down the folding stairs. The legendary spymaster rushed over and bear-hugged his two agents.

Gregory exclaimed, "Andrei Andreievich Grushkov, we did not expect you here."

"You didn't think I would miss the final phase of an operation that has taken three years to plan? Anyway, with so much complicated logistics, it was imperative I accompany the package. We had fun and games with some Mexican bandits and a little trouble with the weather, but we are here — package safely delivered." Grushkov introduced Sergei Popov, the pilot, then walked away, strolling the hangar's periphery to familiarize himself with its layout.

After greeting the two agents, Sergei circled the plane, checking the undercarriage and the tires which were slightly compressed from the heavy load still onboard. He said, "We really should start to unload. It will be tricky."

Gregory eyed Sergei suspiciously. Even though he came with the boss, he was an outsider. "So you are from New York?"

Sergei said, "I'm part of the New York consulate staff, cultural attaché, and I come from Murmansk. I will go home with you once we are done here."

Gregory frowned. "What was the problem with Mexican bandits?"

Grushkov interrupted Gregory's interrogation. "We must get the package from the plane. We have a lot to do."

The three of them walked over to the plane and watched Sergei climb onto the wing, then lift himself onto the top of the main fuselage. On hands and knees, he inched down the fuselage toward the tail of the plane. He removed a wrench from his back pocket and proceeded to unfasten bolts sunken into the skin of the aircraft. After fifteen minutes, he tossed eight bolts onto the hangar floor, flipped several latches that held the cut segment in place and, with both hands, tugged on a handle recessed in the top of the fuselage.

Grushkov yelled, "Apply the solvent Sergei."

After application of the epoxy solvent and several more attempts, the curved section of the fuselage top came free, exposing the airplane cabin.

Andrei Grushkov said, "We went to great effort to select the right plane so we could remove a section of the fuselage cover and replace it without difficulty."

Mischa Asimov laughed. "Yes, like a T-Bird convertible."

Sergei balanced by straddling the fuselage and slowly bent to a squat. With both hands, he lowered the fuselage section to Mischa and Gregory below, who rested it on the hangar floor.

"Now we remove the package," Grushkov said, glancing up at the ceiling winches.

Mischa maneuvered one of the winches so its hanging cable, with a curved iron hook, was directly over the opening in the roof of the plane. He lowered the cable to the crate and slightly adjusted it. Sergei had dropped into the fuselage with a wrench, and he unbolted the package from its frame; he then slipped the winch cable hook through the ring on top of the crate. Mischa controlled the winch so it slowly lifted the crate through the opening in the fuselage with about an inch to spare on either side. The crate was hoisted out, moved a few feet beyond the aircraft, and then slowly lowered to the hangar floor.

Mischa and Gregory lifted the removed aircraft roof back to Sergei, still on top of the plane. He cleaned the edges, reapplied fresh epoxy, and fastened it back into the fuselage.

Using a crowbar and hammers with nail-removal prongs at one end, Grushkov and his two agents carefully pried off the sides of the wooden crate, revealing a rectangular metal container resting in a nest of splintered wood. The only markings on the metal box were a serial number and the small yellow and black decal displaying the international symbol for radiation.

The four Russians stared at the deadly symbol. No one spoke or moved.

Finally, Grushkov said, "Time for more vodka."

Chapter Twenty-three
Monday & Tuesday

Lynda was back at her NSA computer, trying to extract patterns from the hate messages provided by the CIA. As she'd observed at Langley, there had been a gradual increase in hate messages from a California site that after a week was obscured by a larger number of similarly volatile messages spread across the US. Her GPS tracker pinpointed the California site as a residence near Irvine University, with a secondary site actually on the university campus. There was also a heavy concentration in the New York City area that Lynda reasoned could be due to the area's dense population. In order to see if there was a pattern in the New York data that matched the California pattern, she dug into the raw data provided by the CIA. She tasked one of her algorithms to track New York hate messages for several months prior to the spike in the California data.

As her computer crunched, she reflected on SC's scathing rebuke on Saturday morning while she was at MacArthur Airport. The interagency competition and politics she had encountered — from SC and the NSA director — was downright alarming. She had no doubt there was a developing threat in America. Her job as an intelligence officer was to do everything possible to expose and thwart the perpetrators, not bend to politics and jealousies.

Before her computer spat out results, her cell rang.

"Lynda," Sally said. "CIA wants to see both of us in an hour. I'll pick you up at your office in twenty. We can talk on the way."

She turned back to her computer just as it completed its data mining. She did a quick scan of the results and saw that, when analyzed as far back as five months, the New York data on hate messaging on social media had a similar pattern to the California data: a progressive increase in hate messages originating from a GPS site in Greenwich Village, which, in four weeks, had spread across the East Coast, eventually leading to a heightened level of vitriol across the US, apparently merging with the results from California.

"Damn!" She popped a high-capacity thumb drive into her computer and, in violation of another NSA policy, copied data from her NSA computer to a thumb drive that would leave with her. "Fuck SC," she muttered under her breadth.

Lynda hopped into Sally's Beemer. "What, no private agency car?"

"It's my DARPA cab," Sally jested, jerking her head so her snow-white hair tumbled to the opposite side of her head.

Being alone gave them the opportunity to catch up on developments over the last week. Sally seemed initially reluctant to provide details, but when Lynda pressed her she said, "Using image analysis software that's based on your algorithms, we found something interesting. I can't say more until we're in a secure room."

"I can see why they want *you* involved," said Lynda. "You're assigned to the CIA to help install and run DARPA's new technology, to troubleshoot when needed, but why me? Is it because the CIA image analysis programs are based on my algorithms?"

"I think that's part of it. But Jack Light is jockeying to be the next CIA director. The position is going to open soon. He remembers you from your stint in California and has followed your rise through the NSA. He's short of talent in the software development area, which is NSA's strong suit. You're being female, I'm sorry to say, will also look good."

"Shit, its plain old boy sexism in reverse. I wouldn't work for that prick, period."

Sally laughed. "Play along, especially if you really are convinced there is a serious Russian plot afoot."

In the same conference room as before, with the same three men, Lynda and Sally took seats at the table across from Tom and Frank.

Boyd started the briefing. "Dr Chester, the FSB Havana calls you brought to our attention provided support information from our counterintelligence asset that suggests an evolving terrorist plot against America."

No shit, Lynda was thinking. At least someone was taking her seriously.

Boyd continued. "Thanks to Dr Spitzer's geek-team image analysis software and Dr Chester's detection of a Kansas call to FSB spy headquarters in Havana, we've detected an unusual activity pattern in Wichita."

Sally interrupted, "Software based on Dr Chester's algorithms."

Boyd coughed and said, "Right. Tom, run the digital movie."

Tom narrated while pointing his red laser beam at the screen. "This is a composite time-lapse sequence of digital images taken from a low orbit geostationary surveillance satellite equipped with a ten gigabit Peltier-cooled high-resolution camera. It can grab, process, and transmit an image every second, but if pushed, as many as two hundred frames a second."

Sally interrupted again. "The camera is the newest technology developed by DARPA in conjunction with JPL in Pasadena. It's still in beta testing, and highly classified, but I pushed to have it authorized for this situation, to take a crack at the Wichita problem. Combined with Lynda's software, it worked!"

Lynda asked, "What's the spatial resolution?"

"One centimeter." Sally grinned.

"That's amazing," Lynda whispered to Sally.

"That's what DARPA's all about," she answered.

"Wait a minute," said Lynda. "You said images from a low orbit geostationary satellite? That's physically impossible. Geostationary orbits need to be thousands of miles up. At that distance, it's impossible to get decent images of anything except maybe regions of continents."

Silence.

Boyd finally spoke. "This is too classified to discuss. But we have been able to put low orbit geostationary satellites, LOGS, in space. We're also transitioning to a military version of Starlink. Several thousands of small satellites are in orbit simultaneously, so that any object or person can be tracked continually over time. As one satellite disappears over the horizon, another in the network takes over, and so on. This system should be operational in a manner of months, and it could replace or complement the LOGS system "

Tom picked up the ball. "We scanned Wichita continually over successive forty-eight-hour periods since your visit last week. The digital images were downloaded to our servers here, then analyzed with your software, seeking any pattern of vehicles or pedestrians that were suspicious.

"Why Wichita?" Lynda interrupted.

Boyd said, "We used the GPS location of the burner cell call you detected between Havana and Wichita, and information from our asset. The two matched."

The time-lapse movie continued to its end, covering a forty-eight-hour period in four and a half minutes. He said, "Now I'll play it again, but with image magnification on one building in an industrial area of old airplane hangars and rarely-used airstrips."

As the movie played in magnification mode, Lynda stifled a gasp. "My gosh, according to the timestamp, there's a guy delivering a package to the hangar at six a.m."

Sally added, "A suspicious occurrence picked up by the software. And it looks like he's also collecting a bag that's left at the front of the building."

"Right," Tom said. "It's almost one week since this movie was made. If someone is living in that hangar, we're guessing there could be another weekly delivery and pickup tomorrow at six a.m. Kansas time."

Lynda was skeptical. "You're telling me that based on my detection of a burner call from Wichita to Havana, you started round-the-clock satellite surveillance on the Kansas hangar?"

Boyd cleared his throat. "Dr Chester, your detection of that call corroborated information we'd already received from our informant. So, yes, we've been keeping an eye on the Wichita site since getting your alert last week."

"Now what?" Sally asked.

Boyd said, "We can notify the FBI field office in Kansas City, and send Wichita law enforcement to check it out. We can't do an intervention yet, because we don't have probable cause. Living in a hangar isn't illegal."

Lynda's jaw muscles tightened. With a raised voice, she said, "What are you, a lawyer?"

"Yes," he answered.

"So we wait?" Sally asked.

Agent Tom said, "As I said, it's ten a.m. here and, if it's a weekly pattern, we should see repeat activity around seven a.m. our time tomorrow. We'll want to process the new image data before we meet, say, at eleven tomorrow morning?"

"The evidence of a weekly pattern is pretty thin," Lynda tersely quipped.

"Successful intelligence gathering often hinges on seemingly insignificant observations," Boyd retorted, and to twist the knife a bit, he added. "It's your software, Dr Chester. That's why you're here. Associate Director Light thought you might spot things we may miss. We'll see you tomorrow at eleven," he repeated, then stood, indicating the meeting was over.

In the car on the way back to NSA headquarters, Lynda said to Sally, "*Process the data* means look for anything they don't want us to see. And what about their mysterious *informant*? They know a lot more than what they're revealing.*"

Sally laughed. "CIA spooks. Every day is Halloween to them. You know how careful they are to protect their sources."

"And dropping Light's name. It's kind of deprecating to suggest I am here because of their boss rather than based on my own accomplishments."

Sally laughed again. "Need a thick skin working with these guys. Believe me."

On Tuesday at seven thirty a.m., Lynda was at her NSA computer, answering communications from several agents she'd tasked with tracing Grushkov since leaving MacArthur Airport three days earlier. At 7.35 her cell rang. She saw it was from Amarillo, Texas.

"I'm Nicole Yokomori, air traffic controller from Amarillo international. Saw your alert on a twin turbo Cessna Conquest. We had one leave here about half an hour ago, flying VFR north-east. Tail numbers were not an exact match for your alert, but they were close enough. He flew in yesterday VFR in heavy weather, which was unusual, and he bugged out of here first light."

Lynda's heart ticked-up listening to Nicole. "Did anyone see the pilot or any passengers?"

"Don't know, ma'am. But I think he headed to one of our maintenance hangars for repairs. I have a break in half an hour. I can walk over there and make inquiries."

"Nicole, this is really important. I'll text you a photo of a person of interest. Can you see if anyone at that hangar recognizes him?"

Lynda retrieved the digital image of Grushkov that SC had shown her last week, copied it into a file and sent it to Nicole. Her pulse was racing. She checked her watch, knowing she needed to leave for Langley in an hour.

Her cell rang at 8.22.

"Dr Chester, I talked with the maintenance crew that worked on the Cessna and they said there was a man accompanying the pilot, but he kept in the shadows so they couldn't get a good look at him.

"Did the workmen hear anything about the aircraft's destination?"

"I didn't ask."

"What about the repairs? Any details?" Lynda was already wondering who she might send to Amarillo to interview the engineers and collect evidence.

"They said they were paid cash to reinforce an aluminum frame in the main cabin that had broken loose in the turbulence. That's all I know."

"Thanks Nicole. You've been a big help. Can you text me the names of the maintenance men and their contact information?"

"Of course, but we're shorthanded here so it may take me a little while."

Lynda hurried out of her office and took the elevator to the top floor. She had to persuade one of her superiors to bring the FBI into the loop. They likely had a field office in Amarillo and could interview the maintenance crew that had worked on the Cessna. She would love to break protocol and head to Texas right now, but she had that meeting at the CIA in less than an hour.

"Need to see either of them," she said to Gretchen.

"They're both out, should be back later this afternoon."

"It's really important, Gretchen."

"I'll tell them you were here."

Lynda stalked away and took the elevator down to the garage. Before she got in her car to head over to Langley, she texted SC:

Have lead on POI.

Eleven a.m. on Tuesday morning: same room, same seats, same five people watching a digital movie taken earlier that morning, a week after the previous recording. The men in the room obviously had already watched it because when the man appeared with the bag at six a.m. Kansas time, only Sally shouted, "Yes!"

The movie continued and sure enough, after the man deposited a bag at the door of the hangar, he collected a bag put out by the hangar occupants and hurried with it to his car. The images continued to stream until noon Wichita time.

Lynda called out, "Wait! Replay from eight a.m. Wichita time at a slower image rate."

At the slower rate, about five hours after the grocery delivery, there was a blur of motion on the airfield runway. Lynda's ability to zero in on details that no one else could see caused her to yell. "Play it frame-by-frame from the point of that blur."

When this short clip from 8.18 a.m. Kansas time was repeated frame-by-frame, a twin-engine plane was seen landing on the runway; it taxied into the open hangar at the rear of the same building where the packages had been delivered and picked up earlier in the morning.

"That's less than two hours ago, our time," Lynda practically shrieked.

Tom said, "You're one step ahead of us, Dr Chester. We're still analyzing the movie."

Lynda gasped. "Still analyzing? A goddamned plane just landed and went into that hangar. It's time to interdict." Her heart sank. She realized these were not the right guys to inform about the call from Amarillo.

Boyd, who had been quiet until now, said, "Wait a minute. What do we have? A plane lands in broad daylight at an operational civilian airfield and goes into a hangar that may be its normal home. We have someone living in a hangar. Maybe they've rented it, or they own it. They could be handicapped, which might explain the grocery deliveries and

163

the garbage pickup at a convenient hour. Bottom line, we don't have probable cause."

Sally said, "Can't we put the Kansas City FBI field office and Wichita law enforcement agencies on alert and ask them to check out the hangar?"

Boyd closed his eyes. "That's fine. But all they can do is knock on the door. They don't have cause to enter the premises without the occupant's permission. I'll contact the FBI and see what I can stir up."

"FBI got my alerts a week ago on the Havana calls, so they're already partly in the loop," Lynda said. "Can you gather satellite IR thermal images of the inside of the hangar?"

"We have the capability," said Boyd. "But I'm not sure I can persuade my superiors to move on it."

"We need infrared satellite imaging," Lynda said, knowing full well from Sally that the technology had been deployed.

Boyd glared at Lynda, "We called in a lot of favors just to get continual twenty-four-hour LOG satellite surveillance. I'd have to take this to the director of National Intelligence and the DNI may feel he needs to inform the national security advisor who might inform the president, and no one wants POTUS involved until we know what we are dealing with."

"Does the request really have to go that high?" Sally asked.

Lynda shot Sally a look, and she rolled her eyes in response, confirming in Lynda's mind that turf battles among Cabinet members could stall progress.

Boyd had witnessed the subtle exchange between the two women. He said, "I think, in this case, I can get my boss, Jack Light, to deal with the Secretary of Defense. They're golf buddies."

"How soon will you know?" Lynda asked.

"Depends on which satellite is available and if it has to be repositioned," Boyd said. "Most of our intelligence gathering satellites look at other parts of the globe, not the US. Let's wrap up this meeting so I can consult with the folks upstairs. Why don't you ladies take a break in our cafeteria, and we'll meet back here in an hour?"

In the hall, Lynda pulled Sally aside. "The LOGS must have the thermal cameras. Why is Boyd talking about 'positioning other SATS'?"

Sally answered, "He's stonewalling."

Lynda frowned, replaying this morning's events in her head. "Sally, I didn't want to say anything without running it first by SC at NSA, but I got confirmation this morning that a twin-engine Cessna left Amarillo, Texas, heading north a little after six our time this morning. Wichita is about two hours north of Amarillo."

Sally nodded. "That matches the arrival time of the plane that entered the hangar at 8.18 Kansas time. Was Grushkov identified?"

"Not specifically. But the maintenance crew that worked on the Cessna in Amarillo said there was a passenger on the plane. Sally, it had to be him."

Lynda was silent for a few seconds. "All the evidence points to Grushkov."

Lynda grabbed Sally's arm and turned towards the elevators. "Let's talk to Jack Light. He can get the FBI to send someone to Amarillo to interview the maintenance crew that worked on the Cessna."

When they exited the elevator on the top floor where the top brass of the CIA had their offices, they learned from a stone-faced executive assistant that Light was out of the building and would not return until later in the afternoon. They left their names but didn't expect to hear back soon. In the hall, waiting for the elevator and violating a CIA rule, Lynda texted SC but really didn't expect to hear from him either.

In the elevator, Lynda said, "Once we get out of this meeting, I'm going to ask my contact at the FBI to send an agent to Amarillo to interview the airport maintenance crew."

"Without SC's approval?" Sally asked.

"I'm on record trying to contact him," she said and shrugged.

"So you really think Grushkov was on the Cessna that flew into Wichita this morning?" Sally asked, as they headed toward the conference room and the meeting with Boyd.

"Goddamn right."

Chapter Twenty-four
Tuesday

At ten a.m., Grushkov, with Mischa's help, lifted the top from the outer metal box, revealing dense padding. Grushkov snapped open a razor-sharp knife and carefully sliced the padding, revealing a metal case that was three feet wide by four feet high. Its top was secured by six flat-head Phillips screws.

Gregory hustled to a corner of the hangar and returned with a large Phillips screwdriver.

"Dah, *spasebah*," Grushkov said. Meeting Gregory's gaze, he added, "This is a crucial step. If you believe in a god, say a prayer."

Using the screwdriver, he removed the screws, then said to his muscleman Mischa, "Help me lift the top, be careful we don't jolt anything.

As they lifted the metal top, they felt a rush of warm air. In the center of the box, a frame held a black spherical object the size of a basketball.

Grushkov whispered, "In the center is a plutonium core surrounded by carefully positioned explosives."

Attached to the inside wall of the case, about six inches from the top edge, was a small, rectangular control box. A digital counter on its front had six buttons labeled one to six. From the bottom of the control box, a spaghetti-like cable of wires extended to components further down. Three color-cladded wires hung unattached and had phone-jack-like plastic connectors at their free ends.

Being careful not to touch the ball containing the plutonium pit, Grushkov gingerly picked up one of the free wires and snapped it into a connector deeper in the box. The digital counter lit up: zeros in all six channels. "Battery-powered," Grushkov said softly as he stepped back from the weapon, beads of sweat on his forehead and the tip of his nose.

Grushkov wiped the sweat from his face and said, "Time for a break. Gregory, you have Stoli and food?"

"Of course, Andrei, our kitchen is fully stocked with food and vodka from a mystery person," he said, trying to inject levity into a tense situation, but no one laughed.

Turning to Mischa, Grushkov said, "It's not safe to be exposed to the bomb for more than twenty minutes at a time. Help me lower the metal plate very gently over the open box."

The four Russians adjourned to the kitchen-bedroom observation room. Gregory retrieved two bottles of Stoli from the refrigerator and set them in the center of the table next to slices of thick brown bread and deli-sliced roast beef.

After the first bottle was emptied, Gregory Borisy said to his chief, "Andrei, the mission ops did not specify if the device is a plutonium or uranium bomb."

Grushkov answered with a slight slur. "Mischa, you're the physicist. Tell us about the bomb."

Mischa replied, "It's an implosion plutonium bomb, miniaturized to fit into a ballistic or tactical missile." He glanced at Grushkov and said, "But I don't want to bore you with the details of how to build an A-bomb."

Gregory said, "I didn't know they could be so small."

"That's how I can tell it's plutonium-based," said Mischa. "Uranium bombs are long and narrow. Plutonium bombs are spheres and can be small, like this one."

"So why is it like a basketball?" Sergei asked.

Mischa looked at Grushkov expectantly, who nodded for him to continue.

"It's a sphere because in order to initiate fission in the plutonium core it must be surrounded by carefully positioned explosives. When the explosives detonate simultaneously, the force of the explosion compresses the core so much that fission is initiated in the plutonium: the bomb explodes with tremendous force."

Sergei asked, "I still don't understand why it has to be a sphere."

"It's geometry," said Mischa. "The explosives are positioned with extreme precision in three dimensions around the plutonium core. The only workable shape is a sphere. The explosive energy is focused into the plutonium core from all sides, causing equal compression of the core to the critical point where nuclear fission occurs. That's why it's called an implosion instead of an explosion A-bomb. A lot less force than a fusion bomb which operates on a different principle and is a hundred times more powerful."

"But still more powerful than either of the bombs America dropped on Japan."

"Go on," said Gregory, as he opened the second bottle of vodka and filled everyone's glasses.

Mischa complied. "If the explosives surrounding the plutonium core are not precisely aligned when the bomb is built, or if they get misaligned later on, the explosion is asymmetrical. As a result, there's no nuclear fission of the core. Instead, there's just a big explosion. The radioactive core material is dispersed in a large plume, essentially it's a dirty bomb."

Andrei Grushkov added, "This basketball-size atomic bomb will release three times the amount of energy than the one that destroyed much of Nagasaki in 1945."

Everyone was silent.

"But we've been exposed to the bomb's radioactivity just working on it outside its two metal cases?" Gregory asked.

"Don't worry," said Grushkov. "The plutonium core emits alpha particles, which are pretty harmless unless ingested into the body. They're absorbed by clothes and just about any other material. But skin is susceptible, so better to limit exposure."

Before he could elaborate further, his satellite phone rang. He saw it was from Nicolai Zhukov at the New York consulate. Grushkov walked to one corner of the hangar, out of earshot from the rest of his team.

"Andrei," Zhukov said excitedly, "we intercepted a cell phone call from Amarillo, Texas airport to Lynda Chester's unsecure personal cell phone."

"Dah, dah, Nicolai?"

"In response to an FAA alert, Amarillo reported a suspicious Cessna leaving the airport this morning heading north-east. It stopped for repairs of an unusual looking structure inside a stripped-down cabin."

"Was there any mention of me?"

"No. But Chester asked about a passenger and sent a picture for identification."

"Thanks, Nicolai, good work. Sometimes we get lucky monitoring cell calls—especially unsecure ones from intelligence officers."

"Andrei Andreievich, when you expressed interest in Dr Chester and we detected her near the Long Island airport, I increased surveillance on all cell calls to the NSA, especially hers. Most are scrambled, but yes, we got lucky on this one because it came from an unsecure airport in the middle of Texas."

"Nicolai, you will get a commendation for this. It's this kind of initiative that leads to successes."

Grushkov hurried back to his team while processing the information he had just received. "We need to move quickly," he said. "The Americans are close."

"How do we get out of here before the bomb goes off?" Gregory asked.

Grushkov's eyes lit up. "The same way we got the bomb here. We fly to Arizona and escape through the tunnel under the border."

Gregory said, "I remember the news reports about a tunnel with a railroad track and an electric cart that the drug lord El Chapo used to escape from the United States."

Sergei laughed. "Our tunnel is forty feet deep and goes right under the Americans' wall."

"Now let's get finished before the Americans, barge in on us," Grushkov said to his team before downing another shot of vodka.

Grushkov noticed Mischa looking at him askance.

Gregory patted Misha on his back. "Don't worry," he said, smiling at Grushkov. "A joke on one of our previous missions was that 'Andrei Andreievich has vodka in his veins instead of blood'. He knows our lives are in his hands. He does not make mistakes."

Chapter Twenty-five
Tuesday

In their cramped Bleeker Street kitchen, over an herbal tea and latte they'd picked up on their morning walk, Peter and Yuri blogged and posted on the dark web via their own autonomous VPNs. Their combined use of AI bots and mut-bots to infect the computers of liberals and conservatives had exponentially grown the number of followers in their orbit.

"Look at this comment," Yuri said. "It's in response to my last blog post, *America is a Melting Pot*, where I say, 'People of color will be the majority before your children are grown'. This response came within twenty seconds: 'Charlottesville was piece of cake compared to what's next'."

"And look at this one," Yuri crowed ten minutes later. "Here's a response to the same post that was carried by one of our AI-bots from the computer of one right-winger to a computer of another."

"It's funny," said Peter. "We're helping *Arctic fox* stir up the conservatives even though that wasn't our mission."

Peter took a break from his morning posts and he streamed CNN. Wolf Blitzer was breaking a story about a firebombing at the *Washington Post* offices in DC.

"We need to think about how we're going to get out of the country," Yuri said after draining his cup of herbal tea. He set the cup down loudly on the tabletop.

Peter looked away from Yuri, clearly upset at the thought of leaving Tom Mahoney.

Yuri noticed Peter's reaction. He also recognized that Peter's connection with Professor Mahoney had given their team valuable insight on the best buttons to push within the liberal left. Being accepted into that establishment had given the *Snow leopard* team unique insights into the thinking that drove the liberal movement and, thus, ways to stir them up more effectively.

However, Yuri still had concerns about Peter's relationship with Tom Mahoney. Since Peter's proclamation of love for Tom, he had been spending even more time at Tom's. Yuri had thought the opposite would occur after NYU brought in the police and FBI to investigate the hack of their servers. As a result, *Snow leopard* switched to posting on the dark web. Instead, the relationship between Peter and Tom seemed to have intensified. Yuri vividly remembered Grushkov's comment that Peter could not stay in America, and it was Yuri's responsibly to see that that did not happen. The implication of Grushkov's comment was that Yuri would be justified in using deadly force. Yuri didn't know if he could bring himself to kill Peter. But if Peter defected, the impact on the mission and on the Russian intelligence service would be disastrous.

Through her connection with Vance from the NGA event in Hemet, Irene had established herself as a key member of his CCNN white supremacist group. In the three weeks since attending the Hemet meeting, she had established a routine. Three days a week, she went to the new headquarters of the CCNN in nearby Santa Ana, about a fifteen-minute bus ride from the Irvine condo. There, working with Vance and three young social media whizzes, they blitzed the World Wide and dark webs with CCNN messages, glorifying a love for America while denigrating immigrants, minorities, and any other liberal group that did not espouse the white supremacist CCNN philosophy.

As her credibility increased within the CCNN, Irene gradually injected a Kremlin-based conspiracy theory into the organization's messages to its followers. She knew it would galvanize right-wing organizations and fringers, that already embraced conspiracy theories involving a deep state. The right-wing conspiracy believers were easily persuaded that the liberals were planning an event that would plunge America into further chaos. This fear could be used to drive the right-wing and extreme fringe groups to violent insurrection.

"I've got a team of white nationalists doing our work for us," Irene said to Larissa, an uncharacteristic smile on her face. She was heading out the door to meet Vance. "It's just what Andrei wanted. Infiltrate the groups we are targeting. Get them to work for us."

Meanwhile, *Arctic fox's* success using the IP address of the UCI engineering school's server had allowed the Russian team to hack the email accounts of faculty members, staff, and graduate students. Only when the professors started to get nasty messages from people responding to the incendiary blogposts did the school IT department realize their system had been hacked forcing *Arctic fox* to switch to the dark web, similar to *Snow leopard* in New York.

Returning from a day at CCNN, Irene gloated. "Andrei will be delighted. I've got my own American team working for Russia, and they don't even know it."

"And you have Vance as well," Larissa quipped.

"No. Not the way you think," she said, feeling her face flush. "It's all business with me. My purpose is to carry out the mission, not get distracted like you."

Larissa forced a thin smile. "C'mon, from what you have told me, he's interested in you as well as your computer skills."

"I rely upon other skills to achieve my goals. I don't flutter my eyes to get what I want."

Larissa glared.

After almost three months, *Arctic fox's* efforts on the World Wide Web and the dark web had resulted in over two and a half million followers. Some bloggers were conservative zealots urging violence and others, though fewer, were extreme liberals also advocating violent solutions to their issues. Since the bloggers were engaged in their own back-and-forth escalation of hate, the campaign took on a life of its own.

Irene's attendance at the NGA event in Hemet had gotten her access to another neo-Nazi nationalist group, the NNN, which focused on threatening all ethnic minorities. The NNN encouraged armed white supremacists to storm the capitals of Michigan and Ohio, deep red states because of Democratic policies of the two governors, actions that fit well within *Arctic fox's* Kremlin-driven objectives to foment chaos. While previously submerged in dark web postings and secret meetings, these feelings erupted in plain sight first in Charlottesville and now across middle America and even in rural pockets of the most liberal of states.

After attending three NNN monthly meetings in Hemet, Irene had helped to form several splinter NNN groups that had since taken hold in rural Orange, Riverside, and north San Diego California counties. As the level of computer savvy in these largely blue-collar groups was not very high, Irene's expertise with computers solidified her position in the NNN, though her main focus remained with the CCNN. Her demonstrated organizational and operational abilities complemented Vance's financial and fundraising skills.

Arctic fox was now spewing hate not only through its own blogs and posts from the Irvine condo, but also from NNN splinter groups and the CCNN.

Alone in the condo, Larissa considered how Irene was so comfortable among the hate groups. So comfortable, Larissa thought, that she may want to stay in the US. Larissa thought it would probably be wise to inform Grushkov of her suspicions.

She opened her laptop and sent a message to Havana.

At the same time Larissa was reporting on Irene, Irene was thinking, *Larissa is a liability to my efforts. It's time I informed Havana about her and Liang.* Later that evening, alone in her bedroom, she sent a hushmail message to Anatoly in Havana.

She knew it would be communicated to Grushkov, wherever he was.

The next morning both Irene and Larissa received email warnings from Grushkov. It was clear they needed to bury their differences and work together as a team, or dire repercussions would occur upon their return to Russia.

Chapter Twenty-six
Tuesday

Lynda and Sally were back in the Langley conference room by twelve fifteen, any appetite for lunch suppressed by the importance of the situation.

At precisely twelve thirty, Boyd, Tom and Frank arrived. Lynda focused her gaze on Boyd, but he avoided eye contact.

He cleared his throat and then looked directly at Lynda. "I've discussed the situation with my superiors, and they concur that your expertise can be helpful, especially since it's your image analysis software we're using to analyze Dr Spitzer's DARPA images."

Boyd removed two red badges from his jacket breast pocket and tossed them across the table to Lynda and Sally. "Please put these on before accompanying us to the CIA Satellite Image Retrieval System. You'll need to display these badges at all times while in the SIRS facility."

As they followed the men down a long corridor toward two elevators at the end, Sally whispered to Lynda, "I get the sense this dude really doesn't want us here."

"Yeah. I think someone overrode him on this. It's that spook thing again, paranoid about sharing with outsiders — and naming their facility 'SIRS' — c'mon, give me a break," Lynda said, and rolled her eyes."

Lynda, whose mind was spinning like a top on afterburners needed to bounce her ideas off her mentor before they entered the SIRS. Turning to Boyd, she said, "Need to make a pit stop."

He pointed to a restroom, and Lynda nodded for Sally to follow her.

As they stood in front of the sink, Lynda said, "I'm seeing things these boneheads are missing."

Sally turned on a couple of taps and let the water run. If anyone tried to eavesdrop it wouldn't be easy over the running water. "Yeah, well, that doesn't surprise me. You were always able to see the big picture before anyone else. So what aren't these guys seeing?"

"The burner cell calls that my algorithms tracked to the Russian FSB center in Havana and Grushkov's undercover presence in the US are connected. I sent CIA my intel on this. Also, something was done to a twin-engine Cessna in a MacArthur airport hangar on Long Island, and now a similar plane secretly lands in a deserted Wichita airfield. It all adds up, Sally."

"Adds up to what? But you're absolutely right: the plane suggests a well-financed operation." Sally pulled out her lipstick and casually applied it.

Lynda met her eyes in the mirror. "And then there's the wild card: the CIA's *mystery* informant."

"Sounds like you don't believe there really is an informant."

"No, I think they have one, but I don't get why they are not sharing with the NSA or the FBI."

"The NSA and FBI have a lot of resources to complement the CIA's," Sally added.

"Do you think it's nothing more than a turf issue?" asked Lynda.

"Maybe. Certainly, Jack's got his eye on the directorship of the CIA. He's second in command, and his boss is undergoing cancer treatment. Let's see how the afternoon goes."

Lynda turned the water off and they exited the bathroom.

As they got on the elevator, Boyd said to Lynda, "Are you with us, Dr Chester, or is your mind engaged elsewhere?"

"Both, sir," she replied, forcing a smile.

Before he could respond, the elevator door opened, and they headed down a dimly lit hall leading into the SIRS facility. At its end was a steel door with a keypad lock, guarded by a Marine MP with a sidearm. Boyd typed in a series of numbers, and the door clicked open. After stopping Lynda briefly to read the date stamped on her red badge, the MP scanned her from head to toe.

The room was about a thousand square feet with a bank of large flat screens mounted on three of the four walls. They were surrounded by live streaming satellite images of various corners of the earth. In addition, about a dozen computers were being worked, some by uniformed personnel, others by civilians.

A uniformed colonel with ribbons on his chest cleared his throat and pointed to the screen directly in front of them. Instead of introducing himself, he plunged right in. "You are looking at relatively real-time images of your Wichita target building from one of our high-resolution Sat-2s. They generate... "

Ignoring protocol, Lynda interrupted, "What do you mean *relatively* real time?"

Unfazed by the interruption, he launched into a condescending explanation. "Each satellite image is a distribution of pixels of different intensities. The brighter areas in the images have more bright pixels than the darker areas. It takes two to three seconds to process each terabit image, so what you are seeing is *almost real time*. Is that clear, ma'am?"

Oblivious to the others in the room, Lynda said, "Colonel, I'm not sure you're aware that you are using my algorithms. I know how pixels create an image. What I want to know is this: what's going on in the Kansas hangar?"

Sally added, "Thermal images would be helpful. Aren't the SATs equipped with this imaging capability? It's technology DARPA provided under an interagency cooperative agreement."

Unflustered by Lynda's rebuke and Sally's query, the colonel pointed to the screen. He said, "These are... err... *almost* real-time IR thermal images from our advanced LOGS-3 satellite of the target building. You can see four thermal signatures of human bodies." He turned and pointed to another screen to the left of the center screen. "Ma'am, these are stored streaming IR-thermal images of your target since we were tasked with this project over an hour ago. We are well aware of your desire for thermal imaging," he added.

Lynda said, "Colonel, it's our need, not our desire. Now, can you drop out the human thermal signatures?"

The colonel responded with, "Ahhhh," and was interrupted by a young female civilian manning one of the desktop computers.

"Sir, that's a sub-loop of the algorithm that I can control from my computer."

Lynda bypassed the colonel and asked the civilian operator her name, which was Sophie.

"Sophie," Lynda said politely, "can you stream on the left screen the thermal images you have from when they first started a little over an hour ago, until just before the *almost* live-streaming images on the right screen? Then remove the thermal signatures of what looks like four persons."

Sophie looked to the colonel whose face had reddened, but he nodded okay. "Yes, ma'am," Sophie replied before rapidly typing on her keyboard.

In about thirty seconds, the thermal images of the four individuals disappeared. Lynda scrutinized the relatively dark streaming images recorded over the past hour while she also processed the live images projected on the right screen. She used her innate ability to process multiple images simultaneously. After a minute or so she shouted, "Wait! Did you all see that?"

When there was no response, Lynda glanced at the clock on the wall: 12.50. "Sophie, go back to Kansas time stamp 10.40 on the left screen, and play it forward at a much slower rate, say one-tenth the streaming rate... ah, yes there — freeze that image at 10.51."

Sophie followed the instructions.

"Now capture one of the *almost* live current images; just grab any image frame that's streaming live and project it somewhere else. Can you split-screen and project both images, the current Kansas 11.52 time and the earlier Kansas 10.51 image on the right-hand screen?"

Sophie did not respond, just worked her keyboard. In twenty seconds, the older image and the new *almost* live image were side-by-side, both minus the four human bodies.

Lynda turned to face the three CIA men, Sally, and a room of about fifteen computer operators. Her back was to the colonel. "Now can you see it?" she almost yelled in exasperation.

Sophie was the first to say it. "There's a thermal hot spot in the older image that's not in the recent image."

"Right," Lynda said, trying not to yell. "I don't know the resolution on the satellite thermal camera, but I suspect that hot spot is twelve to eighteen inches wide, about the size of a basketball."

The special IR camera had been developed under Sally's DARPA program, so she chimed in. "Yes, that camera has a resolution of four inches, so that hot spot looks to be in that size range."

CIA agent Frank said, "About the size of a missile nuke—"

"Let's not jump to any conclusions," Boyd interrupted.

Sally asked, "Lynda, why do you think it's in the early image, then gone in the later image?"

"Maybe a shielded container with 'hot' material was briefly opened, then closed."

CIA agent Frank said, "Possibly to arm the device."

"Okay, this meeting is over," Boyd barked at 1.07 p.m.

As Lynda and Sally prepared to leave the room, Boyd added, "I don't need to remind everyone that this is highly classified sensitive information. No one is permitted to discuss any aspect of this with anyone unless expressly approved by either me or Associate Director Light."

Out in the hall, Lynda said to Sally, "This might be out of our hands."

"Possibly." Sally shuddered. "I hope they don't do anything stupid."

"Like what?"

"Like get so bogged down in a turf war that they can't take decisive action when it's called for."

Having been part of the NSA since leaving her post-doctoral position at Berkeley thirty years ago, Lynda was more than familiar with the complexities of having seven different government entities tasked with intelligence gathering on foreign intervention. Under different political administrations, she'd witnessed the boundaries between agencies shift as well as the level of cooperation. She was bothered that the CIA was not sharing the information about their Russian informant, especially if that person could shed light on Grushkov's intentions. Lynda knew that Jack Light and Andrei Grushkov had once had a close working relationship from opposite sides of the Iron Curtain. If Sally was right, that Jack was interested in luring Lynda away from the NSA, he must know about her early affair with Grushkov. Maybe that was why he was holding back. She decided to confront Jack directly. If he really wanted to recruit her, holding back important information to her current

178

efforts was not the way to do it. But she also knew, based on years of experience intelligence gathering, that the identity of an informant was always closely guarded, even from other agencies. However, holding back information that could help another agency, was another story.

Lynda nervously looked around the empty hall. "We don't have time for a tug of war between agencies. Someone's got to get a look at the Wichita hangar. That plane can go just about anywhere in the US."

"Since I'm on a contract with CIA, I'll see what I can do to get this moving on a fast track," Sally said.

"I'll do the same at NSA," Lynda added.

Before they left the building, they again stopped before the wall with the stars of fallen CIA agents.

"It's a shame they can't be recognized openly for their heroism," Lynda remarked. "All their families know is that their loved ones died in service to their country — no details, not even a name."

"I agree," Sally said softly. "They could wait, say, ten or even twenty years, and then at least post a name. That would give the families closure, and the chance of exposing any sensitive information would be minimal. All the contacts of that person would likely be gone by then."

At the curb outside the building, Lynda stopped and turned to Sally. "My ultimate boss at the NSA has a direct line to the president's national security advisor."

"Are you sure you want to short circuit the normal process and go that route?"

"If there's a nuke in the hangar, you bet! But it will be my boss' call, not mine."

Sally quickly looked over her shoulder at people exiting the building. "Let's head to my car." When they were out of earshot of anyone, she said, "If it gets to the president, what will he do?"

"Impossible to say," said Lynda. "Everything is circumstantial right now. Until we have hard evidence, I doubt NSA will go forward. It's really up to the FBI, Homeland Security and CIA to gather the hard evidence."

When they reached Sally's car, Lynda said, "It sure would be helpful to have more specific information about the CIA's *informant*. There could be strong corroborating evidence from that source."

Sally laughed. "You know that's unlikely. You should focus your efforts on getting approval to enter the Kansas hangar."

"Yeah, I know you're right. But it bugs me anyway."

"You've done everything you can up to this point. If you push your boss and I use my influence within the CIA, maybe we can speed up a raid on the Wichita hangar."

"It's my bosses at NSA that worry me. Each time I give them what feels like solid evidence, they pull me back. Like at the airport on Long Island."

Sally unlocked the car, and both women settled into their seats. "Is it your gender?"

"That's part of it. These intel guys belong to the Old Boys Club. Even if they recognize that I'm pretty darn smart, they still want to take the credit."

"What about your contacts at the FBI?"

"SC pulled me back, but I sent information over there anyway. I don't think they'll bury it, but they just don't know what they're doing. They don't have the full picture. What we need is a strategy to pull the different agencies together, so they all see the same data, and realize the urgency of the matter."

Sally's eyes lit up. "What do you have in mind?"

"DARPA's mandate is technology development, not intelligence gathering, so maybe they'll listen to you since you don't have an agenda," Lynda said. "I'm prepared to break protocol again and book myself on the next flight to Wichita. I've got the credentials to bluff my way into that hangar. It's worth another slap on the wrist if it turns out I'm wrong."

"But if you're wrong, it could be your job," Sally said, meeting the gaze of her prize student. There was a brisk rap on the passenger window.

"Are you Dr Lynda Chester?" asked a dark-suited guy with brown hair parted in the middle. He stood outside the car, along with a blonde guy in a grey suit and tie.

"Who wants to know? Show me some identification."

They held up two open flat wallets with FBI in large letters clearly visible. "We're here on a matter of national security. The director would like to see you. Right now, please."

Lynda said, "This is Dr Spitzer, Associate Director at DARPA. She will accompany me to the FBI."

The two agents nodded okay.

"We have a vehicle," one said, pointing to a black government SUV at the curb, its motor running.

Chapter Twenty-seven
Tuesday

With lights and sirens blaring, they arrived at the J. Edgar Hoover Building at 1.35 p.m. The FBI agents whisked Lynda and Sally into an elevator and up to a boardroom adjoining the director's office. They were directed to seats halfway down a long table of expensive dark-grained wood, not a scratch on its shiny surface. The two agents that had brought them sat against the wall, under a picture of the smiling president.

Five minutes later, the director of the FBI entered the conference room from her office. Washington DC had been astonished when the president — not known for his deference to women or minorities — had appointed Celia Starks, a fifty-one-year-old African American woman, as the first female to head the FBI. Her credentials were impeccable: Yale undergrad, Harvard Law, and she had worked her way up to Associate Director of the Justice Department. Despite her compact, muscular five-foot-seven-inch frame, Celia was unusually soft spoken while still savvy enough to work a room like a polished politician. She'd been in the job for almost two years and had received generally good reviews from both Democrats and Republicans, a rare accomplishment in the nation's polarized capital.

Unlike other agency heads, Starks was known as a hands-on boss who rubbed shoulders with rank-and-file field agents. Though her approach had ruffled a few feathers, the vast majority of agents appreciated their director's desire to run the FBI from the ground-up rather than top-down.

Lynda and Sally stood when the director entered. She shook their hands, greeting them by name before introducing her senior agent, Stan Nelson, who followed a few feet behind.

The director took a seat across the table from Lynda and Sally.

Director Starks turned to Lynda. "Thank you for the alerts on the Russian phone calls and identification of Mr Grushkov. I've been in contact with your supervisors at NSA and with Jack Light at Langley. Your efforts played a crucial role in exposing this threat, so I want your assessment… Give it to me unfiltered."

It took about ten minutes of back and forth, but Director Starks was quick to grasp the situation, while Agent Nelson took notes on his laptop. She asked Lynda, "What's your level of confidence that there's a nuclear device in the Wichita hangar?"

"My gut says it's there."

"Gut feelings don't get convictions. Any direct evidence? Intercepted calls where a bomb is mentioned, radiation detection… anything I can take to the Attorney General and the DNI?"

"The infrared imaging, the communication with the Russian FSB headquarters in Cuba, the airplane in the Wichita hangar, and the appearance of a top FSB operative in the US, who, I'm confident is in that Cessna," said Lynda.

The director gave a decisive nod. "The FBI is now the lead organization on this. I've cleared it with the DNI, CIA, Homeland Security, Defense, and NSA. Our job is to work as a team with input from each agency. I've also spoken with your superiors, and you are now both on loan to the FBI. Any questions?"

"No ma'am," they replied in unison.

"Good. I'll be setting up a joint meeting asap with the directors of the CIA, NSA, DHS, and Sec-Defense. Just so we're clear, I'm urging the DNI and the National Security Adviser not to brief the president until we have definitive proof there's a nuclear bomb in Kansas."

Lynda blurted , "There's something else."

"Okay, let's have it," Starks said.

Lynda described the unprecedented onslaught of hate speech on social media, and her belief that there was a connection between that and the calls between Havana and sites in the US.

Celia Starks said, "The FBI has full authority to pursue individuals involved in the incitement of riots, sedition, or plotting a conspiracy against the US government. I'll put my best IT people at your disposal. You can work right here in our Image Acquisition Facility. Our IAF has direct feeds from the same satellites as CIA and NSA. But I need you to monitor that hangar. Contact me if anything changes."

"Director Starks, I'm not sure you need my help," said Sally. "Lynda is the one to work with. My job at DARPA is R and D."

The director smiled warmly at Sally. "I want you to stay onboard in case we run up against a tech issue that may benefit from something DARPA has in the pipeline. Plus, you understand the operational specs on the visible and IR satellite cameras. Lynda is the software developer. Bottom line? You're a team I don't want to split up at this time. My folks are good at using new technology, but they don't have your level of expertise."

"Of course, Director Starks. With your approval, I'd like to brief some of my department heads at DARPA. They're bright people, and something they're working on might help, either on the Wichita problem or the social media hate blitz."

"Okay but be discreet. This absolutely cannot leak out or we'll have panic in Kansas and a media frenzy." The director turned to Lynda. "We're dealing with a potential national disaster. I need you to work with my team and push forward, regardless of what you hear about agency turf wars. We need to brush politics aside and act decisively, or we'll be too late."

Lynda realized that she was clenching her jaw. Forcing herself to relax, keeping her voice calm, she said, "I think there's a high probability that there's a thermal-emitting device about the size of a nuke that would be sufficient to wipe out much of Wichita. And if the device is armed and loaded onto an airplane, they can fly it just about anywhere in the US."

Director Starks frowned. "What concerns me — besides having a possible nuclear bomb in one of our cities — is how they got it there. It's possible they smuggled it through one of our borders."

"Or brought it in, component by component, through different portals, then assembled it here," Lynda said.

"Maybe it was stolen from one of our nuclear stockpiles," Sally added.

"We keep good watch on our nukes. If one goes missing, we — Homeland Security and half a dozen other agencies and departments — would be notified immediately. And why Wichita, and why the airplane?" Starks probed. "It doesn't add up."

Lynda said, "Whatever the motivation and the methods, it doesn't change the fact that the Russians appear to be plotting something in Kansas. But as pointed out to Sally and me at Langley, the evidence is still circumstantial. We have no proof there's a bomb."

"Many criminals are convicted on circumstantial evidence," Director Starks said. "It's a probability game. Can we take a chance that it is a nuke, and do nothing? That lowers the bar. I'm thinking we need to act, based on what evidence we have, and take our lumps if we're wrong."

Director Starks said to agent Nelson. "Take Drs Chester and Spitzer downstairs to the IAF. I'll call the IAF director and inform her that she is to put her top people on this and spare no resources. We need to know more about what's going on in that Wichita hangar." Before departing, she said to Lynda and Sally, "Keep in touch with me by cell. Agent Nelson has my contact numbers; both our phones are secure."

On the way down to the FBI IAF, Lynda, and Sally had another impromptu meeting in the restroom. Washing her hands in the sink, Lynda said, "I'm giving this another day, and if nothing breaks, I'm heading to Wichita. Inaction is capitulation."

Sally offered a rueful smile. "So if you're wrong, you'll get rebuffed by another agency head?"

"The FBI director can't fire me; I'm only on loan. And I can't just sit around while our enemies are plotting on our soil. Let's check the imaging, see what our quarries are up to, then plot our next step."

Chapter Twenty-eight
Tuesday

Andrei Andreievich Grushkov glanced at Mischa and Gregory; based on their body language and facial expressions he sensed doubt. He did not want to openly confront them, as he also had qualms about the level of carnage that would result when the bomb detonated. But as their leader and the originator of the Tinderbox Plot, it was important to him that they function as a team and feel that what they did was for Mother Russia.

He addressed his two agents. "You were chosen for this mission among many candidates who applied to be part of my team. I have confidence we will be successful and bring glory to our new Russia."

Mischa answered first. "Andrei Andreievich, I have killed many people in the Afghan War. Some were innocent non-combatants. Of course, I wonder about the need to kill so many with such a deadly weapon. But I am a loyal soldier and am proud to follow your lead."

"I am trained to get information by any means possible," said Gregory. "I do not question our mission, Andrei Andreievich."

Grushkov was reassured. "The spy business has challenging moments, but we must not lose sight of our purpose to serve Mother Russia." It sounded hollow as he said it, but he let the words stand.

He recalled conversations at the family dacha when he was a child, about his duty to carry forward the family tradition of heroic military service when he was a grown man. But now he worried his actions could be condemned as cowardice rather than heroic; his name might one day reside in the dung heap of historical villains. He pictured his mother's gentle smile and wondered what she would think when she heard of his exploits. He imagined the sweet lilac smell of Olga and pondered how she would feel about him after the destruction of Wichita.

When did he become so sentimental? This would not do, at all. He said to his team, "We are soldiers, dedicated to our country in times of peace and war. America blames Russia for aggressive intentions around the world, when all we want is to reunify the republics that rightfully belong under the Russian flag." Grushkov recalled a similar speech Gorky had given him when he expressed concerns after the details of the Tinderbox Plot were finalized.

That encounter had been in an ornate gilded room in the Kremlin. Gorky had been in a high-backed ornately upholstered chair. On his right — in smaller chairs — were the heads of the Russian Nuclear Energy Agency, Russian military forces, and the FSB.

"Andrei Grushkov," Gorky said, in a smooth and earnest tone, "you have misgivings about the plan?"

In the silence that followed, all eyes shifted to Grushkov.

Gorky rose from his gilded chair, like a czar from two centuries ago. He paced a few steps, then turned to face Grushkov, who had stood to meet his boss whose six foot plus frame towered above him

"I remember the stories of your grandfather's triumph in the first Great War against the German invasion of Russia. Many innocent lives were lost, but that is the cost of war, Andrei."

"I understand," Grushkov said, and Gorky continued.

"We are engaged in a new kind of war, one fought from computer terminals and satellites and other devices we control remotely. But your victory will involve Russian secret soldiers on the ground, amongst our enemy. What an honor we're offering you. Your challenge is great, Andrei, but the result will lift our country to a higher level of dominance in a complex world. You will be a *Hero of Mother Russia*, like your grandfather."

Back in the Wichita hangar, Grushkov went to the kitchen table and emptied what was left of the Stolichnaya into four glasses.

The glasses clinked and were drained. In unison, they shouted "*Na Zdorovie*," and, following Grushkov's lead, smashed the glasses against the blank wall.

Gregory and Mischa eyed each other with a hint of skepticism while Sergei stared blankly at the wall as the glasses fragmented.

"Now to piss, and then I arm the bomb," said Grushkov.

Bladder emptied, Grushkov gestured to Gregory and Mischa to lift the metal plate from the black box. "Gently," he said, glancing at his watch. The time was 1.50 p.m.

When the plate was removed, he leaned over the open nuclear cradle and, being careful not to brush against the sphere containing the plutonium core, he inserted the two remaining cladded wires into color-coded wire receptacles on the bomb's underside.

The weapon was armed. Grushkov held his breath for fear that even a puff of errant exhale might set it off, even though this was impossible.

"Two more steps," he said. "Set the six-digit activation code, and then the detonation timer." Blotting his brow with his shirt sleeve, Grushkov backed away from the bomb, turning to Sergei and asked, "You have our flight plan back to Arizona?"

"We'll fly VFR at ten thousand feet, below commercial traffic. Distance is eight hundred eighty miles. Should take about three to four hours at two hundred and forty-five miles per hour. Piece of cake, as Americans say."

Grushkov was not so sure. He knew how close Lynda was getting, and he would not underestimate her determination, or that of her cohorts in the different American intelligence agencies. Working with Jack Light over the years, he understood the American apparatchik better than any other Russian agent. He suspected by now, that the CIA, FBI, and NSA had parlayed their resources and were closing in.

Grushkov knew *Snow leopard* and *Arctic fox* had succeeded in bringing social media to a frenzy. He'd seen reports of physical attacks on the offices of liberal news media outlets, followed by another report of a Molotov cocktail tossed through a window of Fox News. He saw these as direct results of the social media blitzes of his two embedded teams and hoped they had caused the American security agencies to divert some resources to that threat, as opposed to the Kansas plot.

"What about fuel?" Mischa asked.

"We have plenty," replied Sergei. "With those fuel pontoons, I could fly to California."

Grushkov checked his wristwatch again. "It's almost two o'clock. Now that the bomb is armed, I will set the detonation time for seven p.m. today, plenty of time to reach Arizona and get out of America through our tunnel. Mischa, once it's set, I'll need your muscles to gently lift the metal plate and lower it onto the black box, so the screw-holes are exactly aligned."

"Why set the timer with such a long delay?" Gregory asked.

Grushkov straightened up and glared at his disciple. "The sleeper who has been delivering your food and collecting your garbage is taking his family on a road-trip to the Grand Canyon Park. I want to be sure he has enough time to leave Wichita, considering he has three teenage daughters who would rather stay home and be with friends than do a road trip to a national park."

Andrei bent over the box and once again, slowly reached for the flashing control panel, careful not to brush against anything, especially the cradle holding the dark sphere.

He took a deep breath, and slowly exhaled to steady his hand. Then he depressed each of the six buttons on the detonation clock, setting it for nineteen hundred hours. He slowly straightened up and backed away, nodding at Mischa to replace the metal plate over the open bomb-box. He gestured to Gregory, and said, "Here's the six screws and screwdriver. Make sure the plate is fastened firmly but not too tight."

The bomb case was closed at 2.25 p.m. Kansas time.

Grushkov observed intently as Mischa and Gregory replaced the top on a device that would disrupt forever the early evening hour of thousands of innocent Americans. He mumbled to himself, "The poor little children."

Chapter Twenty-nine
Tuesday

In the sub-basement of the Hoover Building, Lynda and Sally huddled with two MIT-trained computer engineers in the FBI's IAF. The room had several rows of computers and three large screens in the front. Two IT guys proudly explained that this was where the FBI had sorted through all the footage from the Boston Marathon bombing to track and identify the Tsarnaev brothers.

A livestream of the Wichita hangar was projecting on the center screen when Lynda and Sally had arrived. However, the images were not thermal, but rather black and white, high resolution images of the outside of the building. Lynda knew the CIA was streaming IR thermal images at Langley, so she approached Agent Nelson to get those to stream into the FBI center. He placed a call to Director Starks.

It took fifteen minutes, but at 2.25 DC time, the FBI was streaming IR and visible images of the Wichita hangar.

"Look at that," Lynda exclaimed. "The small hot spot is back." She turned to the IT engineers. "I need to know when it reappeared."

Jim, the older of the two engineers still in his mid-twenties, started typing while the other one explained, "We get the same satellite feeds as the CIA, DHS, and several Defense Department facilities."

Jim asked, "How far back on the thermal imaging stream do you want me to go?"

"Until the hot spot appears for the second time."

Lynda watched over his shoulder as the images streamed on his desktop computer CRT. "There," Lynda said. "What's the time stamp?"

"Right there in the top right corner," Jim called out. "It appeared at 1.50 Kansas time. That's 2.50 our time."

Lynda looked at the clock on the wall, which read three fifteen. She turned to Sally. "Based on the live IR images on the big screen, assuming the hot spot means the bomb is exposed, it means the casing is still open."

"Langley is seeing the same. They must be going bonkers trying to figure it out. *Whoa*! It just disappeared, 3.25 our time. So, the heat signal lasted thirty-five minutes. About the same time as before."

"Agent Nelson," Lynda said, "we should inform the director."

"I'm on it." He pulled out his cell.

Lynda turned to Sally. "Does DARPA have anything that can detect remotely alpha particles through what is probably one to two-inch steel?"

Before Sally could respond, Celia Starks strode into the IAF and gestured to the team huddled around the computer to join her in a small conference room where the occupants could see the giant screens while they conferred.

"Can you follow the movements of the four bodies in the hangar?" Starks asked.

Sally said, "Director Starks, that's the advantage of the DARPA satellite imaging. We don't have to rely on ground-based detection systems, which have limited scope."

Jim answered the director's question about tracking the IR images. "Sure, I can kick in a program that will outline each of the bodies and generate a line-track that shows the movements of each one for as long as you like. It's a program I wrote when I was pre-med." He left the room and came back with his personal laptop. "It's in here somewhere," he mumbled, typing furiously.

Director Starks warned the two IT engineers that what they were about to hear was top secret. "Keep your mouths shut."

"Yes, ma'am," they both said.

Starks said, "What the CIA lawyer told you is true. We need probable cause to interdict the hangar. We need something more. The Wichita police have driven by the hangar several times and established surveillance from an adjacent building. But so far, nothing incriminating."

"What about the license plate on the garbage man's car?" Lynda asked.

"That's a dead end. Satellite imaging can't read the plate. Bad angle."

"What else can be done?" Sally asked Starks.

"DNI is trying to get a meeting with the relevant parties. Just don't know how long it will take to get us all in one room or zoom-conferenced-in. All we can do now is closely monitor the thermal signatures in the hangar and wait for a report from our field agents who will approach the hangar." She abruptly stood. "I've cleared my calendar and will be in my office. Lynda, please come with me." She departed the conference room, Lynda, close behind.

As they walked briskly, Starks said, "I'm concerned about the social media frenzy you mentioned. Langley has shared their data, and your analysis on the enormous increase in hate messages. We've detected criminal activity against media platforms of both the right and left, and an increase in attacks on synagogues and firebombing of the homes of some of the liberal members of Congress. It looks like we may have underestimated the amount of repressed anger in the country."

"It's such a dramatic escalation," Lynda said. "I'm not surprised that the anger is spilling into the streets. It seems organized though; radicalized groups seem to be working together for the first time."

"It's more than just spilling into the streets, Lynda. The media is pointing at the politicians for lack of action over the past year. And polarized factions in Congress are blaming each other for what's happening." Director Starks lowered her voice. "The president is fit to be tied, frustrated with everyone and haranguing against the media for distorting the events."

They reached the FBI director's office. Lynda took a seat across from Starks who was at her desk.

"I'm afraid to think what will happen if a bomb goes off in the middle of America," Lynda added.

"You think the bomb plot and the social media attacks are connected?" asked Starks.

"Yes, it's weaponization of the Internet, including the dark web. Think about the impact of both together. We're sitting on a virtual tinderbox. One spark sets it off."

"Who do you think is behind this?" asked Starks.

"The Russians. It's too sophisticated an attack. They're using software that only the Chinese and maybe the Iranians have the capability to develop. At the NSA, we detected intricate bot technology under development in Russia about a year ago. The dark web botstorm attacks we're seeing look very Russian."

Starks said, "I'm not up to speed on bots, but have heard them alluded to by our tech guys. What else leads you to believe this is a Russian plot?"

"The detection of Andrei Grushkov in this country under the radar coordinates with these attacks. Phone calls from the Havana FSB station to the Russian Consulate in New York as well as to California, New York, and Wichita, Kansas all are part of a carefully planned plot."

"That's going to be a hard sell without concrete evidence." But before Starks could go further with this thought, she received a message on her cell.

Meeting with the agency heads and the DNI in forty-five minutes.

She grabbed a laptop-sized shoulder bag, headed for the door, and said, "Get back downstairs and keep me informed."

When Lynda returned to the IAF, she found Agent Nelson on the phone with Wichita. He looked at Lynda and Sally, shook his head and mouthed, "Nothing new."

Lynda looked at the wall clock: four thirty.

Chapter Thirty
Tuesday

On Tuesday at 2.25 p.m. local time in Kansas, Grushkov walked to the desk in the hangar with his laptop. When plugged in and connected, he used the TOR browser to send hushmail messages to *Arctic fox* in California and *Snow leopard* in New York:

Holiday over. Come home immediately.

He wanted them out of the country when the bomb detonated. They could continue their social media cyberwar from the FSB headquarters in Havana, if that was even necessary. At this point, both teams' social media campaigns were self-sustaining. In addition to the AI-bots which operated independent of human control, there were now several millions of followers, many of whom were recruiting new disciples every day.

With the messages sent, he returned to the main hangar area where Mischa and Gregory were finishing their work. "Make sure the top is tightly fastened, but don't jar the box even the tiniest amount. The bomb is armed and ready to explode." He raised his voice. "Be careful attaching the outer plate."

Gregory, who knew Grushkov from previous operations, sensed his boss was on edge. He left Mischa to finish the tightening and went to his mentor's side. "Andrei Andreievich," Gregory said, using a familial address usually reserved for family and close friends, "What bothers you?"

Grushkov looked into Gregory's deep blue eyes, and softly said, "We will kill many innocent children."

"What are you saying, Andrei? This is the plan developed by you and President Gorky, isn't it?"

Gregory's question hit a nerve. He remembered his meeting with Gorky. It was soon after Russia's invasion of Crimea. Gorky had been under a lot of criticism from the world, especially through the UN. This criticism had been spearheaded by the United States. It was then that the two had devised the Tinderbox Plot, designed to devastate America. Imperative to the success of the plot was an indelible trust between the two men, a trust that had been established in 1991 when Grushkov helped Gorky secure his secret files as the Soviet Union crumbled.

Gregory responded angrily. "I didn't know you were a fan of America, a country where the rich run a society that makes them richer; a country that bullies the world with its vast armies. Are you getting soft, Andrei Andreievich?"

"You misunderstand, dear Gregory. I am not sure we will be 'Heroes of Mother Russia'. Rather, I fear, we will be labeled war criminals, hunted down, tried, and executed. Our family names will be disgraced. You and Mischa are my team, my pupils, my children, so I am concerned about your fate. That is what troubles me."

Grushkov turned from Gregory, surveyed the hangar, and said, "We must lift the bomb almost to the ceiling. That is the instruction from the scientists who claim it is the best configuration to maximize the explosion, but I think it is mainly to keep it out of the hands of the Americans if they arrive before it explodes."

"You think the Americans know what we are doing?" asked Mischa.

"Don't underestimate them. They have intelligence capabilities and agents who are very good," he said, knowing Lynda had tracked him to the Long Island airport, then picked up his trail in Amarillo heading toward Wichita. They are not far behind."

Mischa took the controls for the ceiling winch and maneuvered the machinery over the bomb case. He lowered the chain-link cable and moved the winch to the left, then right, on its track until the cable was directly over the metal ring on the bomb case.

"Gently," murmured Grushkov. But his compatriots did not need this caution. They were fully aware of the danger.

Gregory slipped the cable hook into the ring.

Grushkov said, "That looks good, Mischa. Now slowly lift it to the ceiling."

They all watched as the black box was hoisted toward the ceiling. At twenty feet up, there was a *crunch* and the cable stopped moving. The bomb stopped with a lurch and swung from side to side. The four Russians gasped and held their breaths until it stopped swinging.

Sergei walked over. "Could be a fuse, or something jamming the cable as it winds into the winch housing."

An attempt to fix the problem could easily cause the box to jerk and swing until the cable broke. Grushkov said, "Leave it. Raising it was a stupid idea anyway. When the bomb goes off, the effect will be the same whether it is twenty feet up or on the floor… just leave it. It's time we left. Take your laptops. Everything else will be vaporized."

Gregory said, "What if the bomb does not detonate?"

Then many lives are saved, Grushkov thought to himself. But he said, "Good point, Gregory. We must go through the hangar and bedroom and remove anything that may identify us as Russians. Any notes, newspaper articles, books you may have brought. Put everything in the plane. And we will need the pillows and cushions from the bedroom for the plane ride."

It took forty-five minutes to scour the hangar for anything that might potentially identify its occupants. Grushkov checked his watch: almost four. He looked at Sergei. "Are you ready?"

"Yes. If we leave now, we'll be in Nogales in three hours, if the weather holds. There should still be plenty of daylight. We will arrive about the time the bomb detonates."

"I'd like us to be out of the US when that happens," said Grushkov. "Can you push the plane to fly faster?"

"I can try. Maybe shave off fifteen minutes."

Meanwhile, Gregory and Mischa were finishing the tidying up. "What about fingerprints and DNA?" Gregory asked.

Grushkov considered the question. Doing a thorough cleaning would take at least another two hours, and they could not spare the time. DNA was difficult to remove. One cell or a single hair could yield a DNA fingerprint. Neither Gregory nor Mischa were in the American databases, but because of his previous assignment in San Francisco, he was.

"No, we don't need to clean any more. We leave now." He programmed the hangar door timer to close in five minutes. "Let's go."

Grushkov was the last to enter the airplane. Before he ducked into the cabin, he glanced at the black box, hanging precariously from the hangar ceiling. His watch said 4.03.

196

Chapter Thirty-one
Tuesday

At the FBI Image Analysis Facility, Lynda's team was analyzing the movements of the hangar occupants. In Wichita, FBI surveillance teams were stationed across and down the street in a vacant building. They were recording real-time images of the building and remotely monitoring for evidence of radioactivity. Another FBI team was recording real-time images of the other side of the hangar. The FBI surveillance teams were in constant contact with the FBI IAF facility in DC.

In the IAF, Lynda, Sally, and the IT team watched the four IR body images as they seemed to move randomly about. Then two of the figures appeared to hover at the spot where they saw the suspected bomb heat signature.

Jim, the senior IT engineer said, "Okay, now they've moved away from that location. You can see the individual tracks by following the dotted line. My program's cool, isn't it?"

"It would be cooler if it could tell us what they're doing," Sally said.

After twenty minutes, they observed a congregation of all four heat signatures at the suspected bomb location, where they remained for another ten minutes. Then the four thermal images separated and darted around the entire hangar complex for another thirty minutes.

Closely following the behavior of the thermal images, Lynda tried to picture what was actually going on in the hangar.

At five p.m. DC time, all four moving heat signatures merged into one and appeared to move toward the hangar door. About thirty seconds later, there was a gasp from the FBI personnel who were watching the large screen non-thermal images of the outside of the hangar.

Lynda looked up and saw a twin-engine plane exiting the hangar. It taxied toward the runway and accelerated out of sight. "Shit!" she exclaimed.

Agent Nelson was already on his cell. The wall clock said 5.03.

In less than thirty seconds, Nelson handed his cell to Lynda. "It's the director."

"Director Starks, the plane just took off from the hangar," Lynda said.

Starks answered, "I'm in a meeting with the DNI, agency heads and some of the president's Cabinet. We just got the same message from Langley. I'm putting you on speaker, so you are now part of this meeting. I've briefed everyone on your role in uncovering this plot."

"This is Joe Green, Homeland Security. What makes you so sure we are dealing with a nuclear device?"

Lynda responded, "I am not sure, but the heat signature we obtained is the size of a plutonium isotope core, called a pit. I'd have to ask the nuclear physics folks what the thermal geometry looks like for that kind of core , but I don't know what else it could be. I don't think we should gamble that it *isn't* a nuclear bomb. It could be on the plane that just took off. It can fly anywhere with those extra fuel tanks."

"This is Ben Cousins, Defense. We're tracking the plane with ground radar and over-the-horizon radar. Right now, it's heading south-west at two hundred forty-five miles per hour at ten thousand feet. No major cities in its path until Amarillo, Texas if it keeps on its current course, but that could change any moment."

"NASA Headquarters and several military bases are in Houston," said DHS secretary Joe Green.

FBI Director Starks wasn't sure about his inference. "Ben, the plane can turn at any time and reach the East Coast, including DC."

"What are you suggesting, Celia," he asked. "Shoot it down?"

Starks said, "We could interdict with military aircraft and try to force it to land. And if that doesn't work, yes, I would shoot it down."

There was silence in the room for about fifteen seconds, then Lynda heard muffled conversation in the background. She imagined what it was like in the room with so many powerful people. As long as she had been left alone to develop new algorithms that impact national security, she'd been happy. At least that was what she had thought until now. But the rush of actually tracking an adversary down was thrilling, like her days of college combat on the judo mat. She stored away that thought for later.

Secretary Defense Cousins said, "Celia, shooting down a civilian aircraft is stuff of movies. I'm not even sure we can do it without the president's approval, especially if we think there's a nuke on board. But I agree, we should put aircraft in the air and try to communicate with the pilot and convince him to land at the closest airfield, preferably military."

Chairman of the Joint Chiefs, Admiral "Wolfie" Wolfseifer who was attending the meeting on a secure zoom line said, "I'll check which military assets are available. It's time to brief the secretary of the Air Force and others that need to know."

Lynda asked, "What about the president?"

Secretary Cousins answered quickly, "POTUS is at a state dinner for the French president. He's been briefed by his chief of staff."

"What about the Wichita hangar?" Lynda asked.

"FBI is coordinating the efforts," he replied.

Celia Starks chimed in, "We have reconnaissance teams in place and an FBI SWAT team coming from Kansas City. We've activated a rapid deployment HAZMAT unit that's equipped to handle chemical and radioactive material. The nearest HAZMAT is in Detroit. They'll fly into McNally Air Base just outside of Wichita. ETA is four hours."

"Why so long?" Cousins asked.

Celia responded, "The FBI and DHS have teams strategically placed around the country, but it takes time to move all the protective and detection equipment to locations as remote as Wichita. We've also alerted the FEMA special response team that was established as part of President Bush's Homeland Security Presidential Directive Nineteen after nine eleven."

Lynda tried to suppress her angst but found herself shouting, "The airplane took off and it could have the bomb onboard: a flying nuclear weapon. Or it's possible a bomb is armed and ticking in the hangar. Waiting half a day could be too late for the half million residents of Wichita."

CIA Associate Director Light who'd been quiet during the meeting said, "Lynda, we don't know there's a bomb either in the air or on the ground. A prudent course is to follow established protocols. Proceed cautiously until verification."

Lynda's heart pounded against her chest. She started to speak into the cell, "But—"

Celia Starks cut her off. "We'll try to coax the pilot to land the plane and follow procedure in executing a search of the Wichita hangar. I don't want CNN or Fox accusing us of not following established procedures."

The secretary of defense, the senior Cabinet member present, agreed. "That's how we will proceed."

The phone connection cut off. Lynda handed the cell back to Agent Nelson and said, "I hope that plane doesn't have the bomb on board. If it's in Wichita, at least we know where it is. It's going to take several hours to get a HAZMAT team there from Detroit. I'm beginning to think that's why they picked that place. It's the middle of nowhere. I've got to get to Wichita: now!"

Chapter Thirty-two
Tuesday

Two Navy F16Cs scrambled out of the Fort Worth Naval Air Station approached the twin-turbo-prop Cessna over Amarillo, Texas. The difference in airspeeds made it impossible for the Navy jets to pull alongside the slower flying aircraft and signal the pilot to land, so the Navy pilots put in a call for a slower aircraft. Rather than return to their base, they purposefully crossed directly in front of the Cessna, so their engine exhaust wash violently rocked the Cessna.

"Geez, what the hell was that?" Gregory yelled from the back of the Cessna as he was flung up toward the ceiling, then violently slammed down and to the side.

Sergei exclaimed, "Severe turbulence. Use belts attached to cabin wall. Are you all okay?"

There were groans from Grushkov and Gregory in the back, but the cushions that they'd thrown into the cabin appeared to have helped. There were bruises but no broken bones or head injuries. Papers and garbage from the hangar were strewn about the cabin.

Mischa, who was sitting in the co-pilot seat with his seat harness secure, said, "That was not natural turbulence. It was too quick and much too violent." He scanned the horizon. "It was high-performance jet turbulence. There's two of them circling around for another pass. Everybody, brace yourselves! Get into those safety belts and hold on."

A few second later, the two F16s passed the Cessna on either side but did not cross in front. The message had been delivered.

Mischa said to Sergei, "Give me the controls. I'm taking us down."

Sergei stuttered, "You... you... "

"I'm a trained fighter pilot. I know what I'm doing. Give me control."

"Do it, Sergei," Grushkov yelled from the back.

Once at the controls, Mischa said, "Hold on."

He put the Cessna into a steep dive. All the loose material in the cabin flew to the tail end. The two passengers clung to the straps attached to the sides of the cabin. At one thousand feet on the altimeter, Mischa started to level off. By the time the Cessna was at four hundred feet, it was flying level.

Mischa told Sergei, "We need to watch the terrain for anything that's taller than three hundred feet. This part of west Texas is pretty flat, but there may be hills that are more than three hundred feet. I'm dropping our speed to one hundred forty miles per hour, just short of stall speed to ensure those military jets can't harass us."

Grushkov, who had recovered from being flung about, said, "We've been discovered. I'm afraid we need to scrap Nogales. They'll arrest us as soon as we land. I may be able to claim diplomatic immunity, but the three of you are spies who blew up an American city. Where are we Sergei?"

"Just south of Amarillo, Texas. At this speed, we're about an hour from El Paso and an hour and a half from Nogales."

"Sergei, do we have enough fuel to make it to Mexico?"

"Yes, of course. We can fly deep into Mexico before we run out, but the Mexican Air Force will be alerted by the Americans, and who knows if they will be quick to shoot us out of the sky?"

Mischa said, "I doubt the Americans will let us enter Mexican airspace."

Grushkov's watch said 5.32, still at Kansas time. "If we are in American airspace when the bomb goes off, the Americans will shoot us down rather than let us escape. The bomb is set to detonate at seven Kansas time, so that should give us enough time to get over the border."

"I'll calculate," Sergei said. "At our normal speed of two hundred forty miles per hour, we would arrive at the Mexican border near El Paso, Texas in about an hour and a quarter, which would make it around six forty-five Kansas time. So, yeah, we should be okay, but it will be close"

"Shit," Gregory exclaimed from the back of the Cessna. "If we are delayed any longer, we could still be in American airspace when the bomb goes off."

"Calm down Gregory. We have no choice," Grushkov said. "We can't go to Nogales, so we'll try for Mexico near El Paso, Texas, if the

Americans leave us alone." He rummaged through his small carry-bag and pulled out his satellite phone. He punched a number into the satellite phone but got no answer. He tried a second number.

"Ahh, Carlos," he said. "It's me, Grushkov. Change of plans. We can't land in Nogales and use the tunnel. It looks like we have to fly across the border at El Paso. It's closer. We need a place to land."

"That's a major change, Andrei. I will have to make new arrangements for you. It will cost another... "

"I will talk with my superiors when we land."

"I need confirmation."

"Carlos, I'm in a small plane being pursued by the Americans. I can't authorize an additional payment until we land."

"Call your bosses in Moscow."

"Doubt I can get through to Moscow at this time of day. We may never make it to Mexico if the Americans shoot us down. You'll have to trust me on this. You already have fifty million plus the additional one million for the truck in Nogales. That's a lot of dineros. We need to figure this out if you want the final payment of seventy-five million plus the additional million I agreed to, for the truck in Nogales. I'll call you back if I get through to Moscow. Goodbye, Carlos."

"That doesn't sound encouraging," Mischa said.

"Just playing his game. Everything is a negotiation. There's no way I can reach anyone in Moscow who will authorize more money."

Grushkov waited fifteen minutes and dialed Carlos' number. "Okay, as I thought Carlos, no one is there to authorize more money. I will talk to the Russian ambassador in Mexico City, but it is too late today to get anyone. I can persuade him to arrange for the final seventy-five mil to be moved to your account once we are safely on the ground in Mexico. But for any more, I will need to speak with Moscow." He paused. "Have to go. We have two jet fighters on our tail. Here's my pilot. Give him the map coordinates in Mexico and details on where he can land this plane."

Sergei opened an aerial flight map of the south-west US, including northern Mexico. He matched coordinates provided by Godinez with those on the map, and said, "An hour south-west of El Paso, it's just desert. He said it's a staging area for his operations. There's a flat dirt road we can land on. He'll line up vehicles to guide us. It should still be light out when we arrive."

Mischa was visibly excited and seemed to be relishing an operation that reminded him of his days in Afghanistan. "Not to worry. If it's night, I can land, using the car lights to guide me."

Before anyone could respond to Mischa, there was a loud varoom, and one of the F16s flew past at about six hundred feet. It turned to the right, followed by another F16, which turned to the left.

Mischa said, "They just want us to know they're still on us. If they wanted to knock us out of the sky, they would have already done it."

Grushkov was thinking about his other two teams, hoping they'd made it out safely. He suspected that by now, American intelligence had likely figured out that the social media hate campaigns and the bomb plot were part of the same Russian operation. But *Snow leopard* and *Arctic Fox* were well-trained and were familiar with their escape routes. Now that he'd signaled them, they should be on their way.

Chapter Thirty-three
Tuesday

Lynda hit redial on Nelson's cell. "Director Starks, this is Lynda. I need to go to Wichita right away, but there are no direct flights."

"Lynda, we're establishing an interagency team as we speak."

"Sally and I are confident that the social media attacks are coordinated with the bomb threat. We can examine the hangar with the background of the entire plot; we may find clues that are missed by teams that do not have a full perspective on this operation, and we're ready to go right now."

After a pause, Director Starks said, "Okay, you've convinced me, but I'm going with you. Be there in thirty minutes. We'll have an FBI Gulfstream ready at Reagan."

"Yes, that would be great. Bye."

She turned to Sally. Her pulse was racing and she was feeling that old judo competition rush. "We're heading to Reagan International where an FBI plane is fueled and ready to fly to Wichita."

"Great. Being on loan to the FBI means no approvals from our supervisors are needed," Sally said. "Not what I signed up for when I left Cornell for the DARPA job, but this is sure more exciting than sitting behind a desk — or puttering around in a lab."

Her heart pounding, Lynda wondered what her parents would think if they knew where she was. Her mom would be terrified, even though, as a Navy wife, she'd had to wait out tense situations when Lynda's dad was in action. Her father would be proud, excited, and concerned for her safety. Growing up as an only child, she had been his tomboy. This would be a vindication; it could justify her decision to pursue science rather than a military career. All of this swirled through her mind before she focused on getting to the hangar — proving to all the doubters that she was right after all.

Agent Nelson, who has been listening to the exchange, added, "I'm pretty sure the director will have called ahead for a helicopter. She doesn't like ground traffic. The FBI jet is a Gulfstream 700, very fast, capable of going eight hundred miles per hour. We should be on the ground in Wichita by six forty-five and at the hangar by seven."

At five fifteen, Agent Nelson's cell rang. "Right, we'll be there in five." He turned to Lynda and Sally. "She's landing on the roof. Follow me."

Up on the roof, holding their hair from flying around in the rotor wash, Lynda and Sally climbed through the open door of the FBI Sikorsky S760D executive helicopter. Nelson jumped in behind them.

They were airborne ten seconds after the door slid shut, banking right toward Reagan International as they passed the Capitol Building and Washington Monument. The noise was too loud to allow for conversation, but Director Starks handed them headphones with built-in microphones.

As soon as all three had them on, she said, "The secretary of defense and the chairman of the Joint Chiefs are seeking approval to shoot down the plane before it enters Mexican airspace. Mexico has voiced concern that some of the ordnance could strike Mexican territory, or worse, people in Mexico could be injured. They want a guarantee that the United States takes responsibility if the plane crashes in Mexico, especially if there's a nuclear device onboard. In other words, the situation is fluid. I hate to lose these guys in Mexico, but we need to concentrate on our immediate goal: get to that hangar and see what's there."

At five p.m. Kansas time, the FBI Gulfstream was an hour and fifteen minutes into the flight.

Lynda turned to Starks and Nelson, who were seated across from her. "Can we land at the suspect airfield?"

Nelson shook his head. "The runway is too short for this plane, but we're making good time. We'll touch down in Wichita in fifty-two minutes."

When they landed, a sheriff's helicopter was on the tarmac, with rotors spinning. Starks, Lynda, Sally, and Nelson bounded down the Gulfstream fold-out stairs, loped the fifty yards to the waiting chopper, and were helped aboard by a crew member. Airborne by 6.54 Central Daylight Time, they banked to the east and gained altitude to a thousand feet.

Starks shouted above the rotor noise, "How long to the hangar?"

"Eight minutes," answered the co-pilot. "The interdiction team is gathered on the runway and in front of the building. They want to blow the front doors and send in a robot. HAZMATs been mobilized, with an ETA in about an hour. They're waiting for your instructions whether to go in or wait until HAZMAT arrives."

"Who are you talking to?"

"Supervising Agent MacDougal, Kansas City field office."

"Give me the mic," said Starks. "Mac, it's Celia Starks... Yes, no HAZMAT yet... Still on the way from Detroit... I know the risk, but we can't wait any longer. Go! I'll be there in five."

Chapter Thirty-four
Tuesday

"Where are we, Sergei?" asked Grushkov. "It's 6.38 in Wichita. The bomb detonates in twenty-two minutes."

Sergei answered, "I'm not sure where we are exactly. Judging by the homes and buildings, I'd say we're above south Texas. Wait, I see something ahead."

Mischa had been keeping the plane at one hundred and fifty miles per hour at one thousand feet, barely above the few hills and treetops in this barren part of Texas. "There are three choppers coming right at us! They're military, look like Blackhawks."

"Are they armed?" Gregory asked.

"Yes, of course," Mischa replied. "They have high caliber ordnance. They could cripple us and force a landing or send heat-seeking missiles to blow us out of the sky."

Grushkov said, "Likely they will try to force us to land, and if we don't, then they will shoot us down."

Mischa pulled the altitude flap controls back to a steep climb position, throttled the Cessna to full power, and headed right at the lead helicopter. Caught by surprise when the Cessna accelerated from one hundred and fifty to two hundred and seventy-five miles per hour, two choppers dove to the right and the center copter dropped below the Cessna.

"They'll circle back on us, but their top speed is only one hundred and eighty miles per hour , if I remember correctly from my military war games," Mischa chuckled. "They could be faster now. No sign of the F16s."

He increased both engines above their rated maximum RPM, hoping to pick up a few more miles per hour of speed. But after several minutes of pushing the plane beyond its rated specifications, a 'low oil' indicator light flashed for the right engine. A few seconds later, the temperature light alarmed, indicating it was overheating. "Someone, look at the right engine and tell me if you see an oil leak. I'm throttling back."

"Yes," Gregory said. "There's a thin stream of fluid coming down and off the wing."

Mischa looked at the temperature gauge. It was still flashing, and the needle was in the red. "Sergei, keep your eye on the temperature and the oil pressure on the right engine. Gregory, keep watch out the windows for any sign of the Blackhawks. I can still outrun them if I stay above two hundred miles per hour. Have to cool down the right engine, though."

Mischa scanned the airspace and horizon on either side of the plane and said to Sergei, "I'm going to decrease the power of the right engine to about half and keep the left one at full power so we'll have to correct for the right yaw, using the horizontal stabilizer. Can you handle that?"

"Dah, Dah," Sergei replied excitedly.

Mischa pulled the left throttle back to its halfway point, keeping an eye on the right engine RPM gauge. The Cessna drifted to the right and started a slow roll, with the left wing starting to rise. "Sergei, correct with the stabilizer," Mischa said loudly, as he throttled back a bit more on the right engine.

The Cessna flew for about ten minutes with only a small decrease in the engine temperature. The airspeed had dropped to under two hundred miles per hour, closer to the Blackhawks' speed.

Mischa said, "I may have to feather the right engine to get the temperature down or take the plane up to twenty thousand feet, where the outside temperature is a lot colder." He scanned the horizon and saw a large cloudbank about two miles to the left. "What do you think, Sergei? Can we reach that cloudbank before they catch us?"

"Worth a try."

"Okay, here we go." He throttled both engines to full power, banked to the left and did a steady climb toward the cloudbank. Air speed increased to two hundred and fifty-five miles per hour and in eight minutes they entered the cloudbank at fifteen thousand feet. There was no sign of the pursuing Blackhawks. He throttled back to two hundred miles per hour. "The engine temperature is starting to drop. Sergei, give me a corrected heading to El Paso."

Grushkov's watch, still on Kansas time, said 6.58 p.m. He closed his eyes for a second and took a few deep breaths. His heart was pounding, not because of his current predicament, but because of what was about to happen in Wichita. He wondered if he would be remembered as a Hero of Mother Russia or a villain of the twenty-first century. He recalled his shaking hand as he had connected the final wires in the bomb casing.

He tried to remember the prayer his grandmother — a devout believer in the Russian Orthodox religion — would recite over his bed at night, but he could not. He had a vivid picture of his mother reading him stories of the glorious days of the czars and the Cossacks when he was a child, and now he pictured her today, ninety-four years old, in a state retirement facility, gazing at a gold-framed picture of him, but in his mind Grushkov could not tell if she was smiling or crying.

"It's about twenty to thirty minutes to El Paso," Sergei said. "I think the Blackhawks will learn our direction from their military controllers."

Chapter Thirty-five
Tuesday

The shock wave from the blast lifted the Wichita sheriff's helicopter almost a thousand feet, its nose pointing straight up before it stalled and free fell. Lynda's seatbelt kept her from hitting the ceiling. On the ground, the roof of the hangar blew out. The heavy double doors also blew out, mowing down the staging unit like pins being hit with a bowling ball.

The helicopter pilot, an ex-Marine, regained some control of the stalled chopper and auto-rotated to a grassy patch halfway down the runway from the hangar that now had a large, dark gray smoke plume extending several thousand feet up and still expanding.

As soon as they touched ground, FBI Director Starks jumped from the chopper and started running toward the catastrophic scene, but Lynda leapt out of the helicopter just after her. One corner of Lynda's brain assessed the scattered debris and twisted bodies while another corner of her mind registered the debris cloud and the damage to the hangar. There was no bright flash or devastating shock wave. Lynda grabbed Stark's arm and shouted, "It's not a nuclear explosion, but likely has radiation. We've got to get out of here… pilot says he can get the chopper back in the air."

The strong, athletic FBI director dragged Lynda a few yards toward the demolished hangar before stopping. "We need to help the injured and secure the area. Where the fuck is that HAZMAT unit?"

Nelson and Sally, who stumbled from the chopper, were gazing at what was left of the hangar a thousand yards away. Mangled bodies were near the hangar area. A dozen people were wandering around aimlessly amongst the debris field, many with tattered fragments of clothes hanging from their bodies. Flames had engulfed most of the blown-out building.

Sally's DARPA physics training caused her to shout, "The debris cloud needs to be tracked by meteorologists. It's loaded with radioactive material. We've got to head back up!"

FBI Director Starks shrugged off Lynda's grasp and sprinted back to the helicopter. Once onboard, she grabbed her satellite phone from her shoulder bag on the floor.

The pilot shouted to the others, "Get in! We're leaving now. The debris is moving away from us, but we can't take any chances."

They climbed back into the helicopter and, before they were seated, the rotors were moving and the chopper was airborne and banking away from the remnants of the hangar.

Starks was pushing her SAT phone buttons to inform the other agency heads, plus the director of National Intelligence. No doubt they had been monitoring the operation and were well aware of the situation, but it was imperative they were informed that it had likely been a radioactive dirty bomb as opposed to an atomic bomb explosion.

Nelson was jabbering into his satellite phone. He turned to Starks and said, "I've notified our liaison at the White House." He handed her the phone. "You'll be connected to the president. Hold on."

"Shit, Nelson," she exclaimed above the rotor noise. "See if you can get a casualty report. Contact the Kansas City field office. They'll know who was dispatched to Wichita."

She heard the president's voice on the sat phone. "Yes, Mr President. We believe a radioactive bomb has been detonated in Wichita... No, sir, it was not a nuclear explosion. Wichita is still fine, but we think there's substantial radioactive debris, plus a radioactive cloud that could impact a substantial number of people in the area. And if the wind shifts it could impact Wichita directly. I suggest that the FEMA response team be activated under Homeland Security Presidential Directive Nineteen. We don't know how extensive, but we lost a good part of our FBI interdiction team based in Kansas, City. Yes, sir, I can be at the White House in three hours."

Starks shouted above the copter noise to Lynda, who was sitting behind her. "The president is calling a ten thirty emergency meeting this evening of his national security team plus related Cabinet and agency heads. It'll take a few hours to get everyone into the White House Situation Room or connected by secure zoom."

The chopper turned sharply away from the damaged hangar and an increasing plume of dark black smoke. The co-pilot said, "Wind direction is away from downtown Wichita for now.

The FBI Gulfstream was waiting on the runway, engines running. Starks, Lynda, Nelson, and Sally ran from the chopper to the Gulfstream boarding stairs. Before they could even belt in, the jet was barreling down the runway.

Once airborne, the steward offered all manner of drinks and asked if there was a preference for a cold or hot dinner. They all refused food and alcohol. Lynda asked for water. Initially, the conversations were minimal, each introspectively dealing with their close brush with death. But after the immediacy of the event sunk in, the conversations turned practical.

Starks said to Nelson, "I'll connect with Jack Light at CIA and see if he has anything new from his informant." Glancing over at Lynda and Sally she added, "The FBI should have a lead role, since we've been heading the investigation. But there will likely be fingers pointed at us for not preventing the explosion. As members of the NSA and DARPA on loan to the FBI, and being most familiar with this plot, I want both of you to have key roles in sorting this out."

Lynda said, "Sounds like a good plan if the other agency heads agree."

"Let's hope they do the right thing," Starks said grimly. "It's up to the DNI and the president."

Lynda said to Director Starks, "Sally has the technical expertise to be more useful than me. I'd be glad to help in any way you decide, but I'd like to pursue the source of those hate messages that ignited social media to a point where the anger is now in the streets. I think the Wichita event will generate even more ferocious responses."

"You're right," Starks responded. "We need to look at the big picture, especially if you can show a connection between the social media cyberwarfare campaign and the Wichita event. We're freewheeling in the shadow of a harrowing event. You have my approval to delve into the weaponization of social media as it relates to this bombing."

An hour into the flight, the pilot walked the cabin, asking how everyone was. He informed them that the plane would land at Reagan International in forty-five minutes. "We'll be going through a special portable HAZMAT unit that's been set up in one of the government hangars. We need a decontamination assessment in case we've been exposed to radioactive material."

Since the initial discussion, Director Starks had been on her satellite phone, discussing the situation with her associate directors and department heads. They, in turn, were sending out encrypted messages to the FBI field offices, placing them on high alert for any activities out of the ordinary. She'd also contacted Jack Light to ask if his informant had been able to provide anything helpful. His answer had been a terse, "No."

Her call to Joe Green, Secretary of Homeland Security, was less polite. "Geez, Joe, you need to secure the borders with Mexico and Canada. We have at least four suspects who may be fleeing the country if they haven't already. There are others who have been fomenting hysteria on the web, and they may be *getting out of Dodge* too. We need to review video footage of people departing over the past twenty-four hours. My team will spearhead this activity, as we did in the Boston Marathon bombing case." Starks listened to him rant for about fifteen seconds. "Joe, take it up with anyone you want, but I'm taking charge of the video analysis until I'm told otherwise. We developed these facial recognition programs. If you have a problem, bring it up when the president asks how the hell these bad elements got into the country in the first place."

After hanging up, Starks turned back to Lynda and Sally. "I'm sure I'll have similar conversations with other agency heads. In a way, everyone has a legitimate argument that a piece of this falls under their jurisdiction, but if we all work together, we'll solve it a lot sooner than if we waste time trying to undercut each other."

The captain announced they were landing in Reagan International in ten minutes. Celia Starks looked at her watch: nine fifteen. Allocating another thirty minutes for the HAZMAT scan, she figured she had time for a quick trip to her townhouse a few blocks from the White House. Even with a hastily called meeting, she needed to look clean and sharp.

Lynda's hair was a mess and her blouse was missing a button, which must have been pulled lose when she'd tried to restrain Starks. The FBI director said, "Lynda, come home with me. You can borrow a fresh blouse, wash, and work on your hair a bit. You're coming with me to the White House meeting."

"Yes, ma'am," Lynda responded in a shaky voice. "This is way above my pay grade," she stammered.

"You'll do fine. I need you there in case we get technical questions I can't answer. I'm not sure what they know about your Grushkov and his involvement, but it may come up, and if it does, I may turn to you. You can bet the other attendees will have their own experts sitting behind them."

"What about the CIA's secret informant?" Sally shouted above the jet noise.

"That's up to Jack Light to divulge. It's kind of a wild card. But every agency is fiercely protective of their sources."

Lynda stayed silent but was thinking the CIA informant could be a key piece of the puzzle… if there really was an informant. Knowing that the friendship between Grushkov and Light went back many years, Lynda had suspicions that there may not even be an informant, but that Light had invented the informant to detract from his compromising relationship with Grushkov. But she was not prepared to make such an accusation without concrete proof. That could end her career.

Chapter Thirty-six
Tuesday

"That's El Paso to the right and Ciudad Juarez, Mexico on the other side of the Rio Grande," Sergei called out as the Cessna exited the clouds into a clear, early evening sky.

"How far?" Grushkov asked.

Sergei replied, "About five miles."

"Everyone, watch for Blackhawks or any other aircraft that may have been scrambled to look for us." No sooner had Mischa uttered the warning when a stream of tracer bullets from below the Cessna shot across their path.

"If we run for it, those Blackhawks will likely take a real shot," Mischa said. "They have heat-seeking missiles, so we will be nailed."

Everyone in the Cessna knew the Wichita bomb should have detonated by now. They couldn't know whether word had reached the Blackhawks, but if it had, they were in immediate peril, especially if the American choppers were not able to force the Cessna to land on the US side of the border.

"I have a plan," Mischa said. "I'm going down full throttle to about four hundred feet and fly right toward downtown El Paso." Just then another stream of tracer bullets crossed just in front of the Cessna. "That's a second warning across our bow. The next will be real."

Mischa pointed the Cessna toward the center of downtown El Paso, plunged the plane into a dive at max speed. The ground and buildings rushed toward them and, with difficulty, he managed to pull the plane out of the dive at three hundred feet. Mischa continued to head the aircraft toward the center of town at two hundred and forty miles per hour.

He laughed. "The Blackhawk top speed still is one hundred and eighty miles per hour. We can outrun them, but not their missiles. So we'll stay over the populated city until the right moment."

Grushkov said, "Mischa, I knew you were an ace pilot. Let's hope our luck holds."

Mischa's eyes glinted. His pulse was in overdrive. He had the confidence he'd had when he flew in combat. He was gambling that the Americans had strict rules about firing their weapons over populated areas, especially highly dense ones like El Paso. He checked the gauges and saw the right engine temperature was climbing into the red zone, but he couldn't worry about that now.

He kept the plane flying parallel to the Rio Grande, past the bridge connecting El Paso with its sister city, Juarez, and then he made his move. He banked the Cessna sharply to the left, which raised their altitude somewhat, but he kept the aircraft in a bank until he saw the Rio Grande at a right angle to the plane. He leveled off and shot across the border into Mexican airspace. The three Blackhawks did not follow and did not fire.

There were no Mexican aircraft waiting for them.

Sergei loaded the coordinates provided by the Mexican drug lord into the plane's navigation computer, and said, "It's a two-hundred-twenty-mile straight shot south-west over desert. I'll need to cut the speed to around two hundred miles per hour, so we should be there in a little over hour."

"If our engines hold out," added Mischa. He wrinkled his brow as he again checked the gauges. The oil pressure was low, but not falling any more. He checked the right wing and saw a trickle of oil dripping off the flap. "I'm going to cut back on our speed and climb to twenty thousand feet to cool down the struggling engine. We don't want to ditch. It's desert as far as I can see. I'm pressurizing the cabin."

After fifteen minutes at the higher altitude, there was a hissing sound from the main cabin. Grushkov looked up at the ceiling and shouted, "There's daylight along one edge of the seam."

"Damn," Sergei yelled. "The seal is coming undone. The engineers told me not to go above fifteen thousand feet because the pressure differential may be too great for it to hold."

Mischa initiated a gradual decline down to five thousand feet, willing the cabin ceiling to stay in place. "I'm turning off the pressurization system now so there's less stress on the ceiling," he said.

"And I'm dropping the oxygen masks in case anyone feels faint, but at this altitude you should be fine."

At the lower altitude over a searing August desert, the air temperature outside was ninety-two degrees Fahrenheit. The right engine temperature responded by climbing to the top of the red danger zone. After ten minutes, the red engine light flashed and an alternating low-to-high claxon blared through the cabin. There was a fire in the engine.

Sergei pressed a switch that activated fire extinguishing foam built into the engine housing while Mischa feathered the engine, and said, "Okay, everything under control."

Gregory and Grushkov clutched the dangling straps in the stripped-down cabin. Gregory's hands turned white from his grasp of the hanging straps, and his face was ashen. Grushkov was unfazed, having been in worse situations.

Mischa shouted, "I can fly this plane on one engine. It's designed to do that. We just go slower and do not arrive at destination on time." He looked at his watch. "Maybe another hour."

Gregory mumbled, "If nothing else happens."

But the hour was uneventful. As they approached Carlos' designated landing spot, what appeared as barren scrub desert now had brush and large cacti. In the distance, they saw several one-story barn-like buildings with expansive reflective tin roofs. Numerous parked vehicles, mostly pickup trucks, were parked near the buildings. There was a group of about half a dozen people standing around in front of the largest building. Mischa brought the aircraft down to eight hundred feet and flew directly over the buildings, looking for a flat area to land.

Sergei said, "They're waving at us to fly around again. They're running to the trucks."

Mischa flew a wide circle and lined up with the largest building again, except this time he saw a row of four trucks on each side of an area empty of all plants and large rocks. He extended the wing flaps to forty degrees to lower the stall speed. He instructed Sergei to lower the landing gear. His airspeed was now a hundred miles per hour and dropping fast as they approached the ground. He throttled back the left engine to an airspeed of ninety miles per hour. He shouted, "Prepare for a hard landing!"

The Cessna cleared the largest building by about twenty feet. Its wheels touched the ground by the first two trucks, but the plane bounced up and glided another twenty yards before touching down again with a thud.

Mischa cut the engine, and the plane traveled at a ground speed of about sixty miles per hour down the dirt path, bouncing on small rocks along the way. By the time it reached the fourth and last pair of trucks, its ground speed was down to thirty miles per hour, and the brakes were straining to slow it down before the Cessna hit a large cactus about fifteen feet high. Mischa applied the left brake, and the plane did a slow cartwheel to the left, its right wingtip slicing off the top of the cactus.

He turned to the two passengers, smiled, proud of his skill at landing safely. "I am trained well."

The four Russians exited the plane into searing heat. A pickup truck barreled towards them, stopping ten feet away in a boil of sand and dust. A deeply weather-tanned man in a battered American cowboy hat jumped out of the passenger side and pointed an AK-47 at them. Grushkov yelled, "Where's Carlos Godinez?"

Chapter Thirty-seven
Tuesday Evening

Lynda took a seat directly behind Celia Starks who sat at the long rectangular conference table in the White House Situation Room. She was flanked on one side by Stark's assistant, Stan Nelson, and the other side by a military man seated directly behind a heavily decorated admiral whom Lynda recognized as Wolfie Wolfseifer, Chairman of the Joint Chiefs.

With her heart pounding, Lynda was trying hard not to stare directly at any of the powerful people in the room, most of whom she'd seen regularly on CNN and Fox News. Her NSA boss, SC, was at the table and she imagined his stare drilling through her as she assumed he felt she had no business being there without his expressed permission. And at the other end of the table was Jack Light, whom she feared may publicly reveal her past relationship with Grushkov, just to knock her down a peg in front of the president and those in the room. Lynda took a deep breath and calmed herself by picturing her father.

Everyone rose, as the president entered the room dressed in a dark suit, white shirt, and striped blue and red tie. He motioned everyone to sit. He plopped into his seat, folded his arms tightly across his wide chest, and with a defiant set jaw said, "Who the hell set off an atomic bomb in the middle of America?"

Secretary of Defense Ben Cousins said, "We're trying to assess and contain the radioactivity before entering what's left of the building. And, Mr President, it wasn't an atomic bomb, it was a dirty bomb. There's a big difference."

"I know the difference, Ben," said the president, glaring at Cousins.

Tim Holt, the national security advisor who was attending by zoom, jumped in before the president launched into a rant. "As soon as the building is safe to enter, teams from Los Alamos and Livermore National Labs will collect bomb residue so they can fingerprint the radioactive material. But they have to be assembled and flown in from California. A HAZMAT team is on the scene and assessing the radioactive debris and fallout, but I think it's imperative you activate Presidential Directive Nineteen, so FEMA and DHS can implement their extensive detection and mitigation plans. We need to know exactly what the material is and then how to contain its spread."

The president said, "Yes, yes." He turned to the secretary of DHS and said, "Get it done,"

The president asked, "So what do you mean 'fingerprint' the bomb?"

Celia Starks seized the opportunity. "Mr President, scientists at Los Alamos have developed a sensor that analyses the radioactive isotopes and other elements of the bomb core. The proportions of these elements can be used to 'fingerprint' the material, in other words, identify its source, sometimes down to the mine where the radioactive isotopes were extracted, or the facility where they were enriched."

"You mean identify the country that made the bomb," the president said.

"Yes, Mr President," Starks replied. "The US and the International Monitoring System have established a 'fingerprint' database of the ratios of these elements, so we can pinpoint the country that's the source of the radioactive material. But that might not tell us which country actually delivered the bomb."

The president ignored the second part of Starks' statement, asking, "How long before we have results? Once we know where it came from, we'll need to develop an appropriate response."

Associate Director Light — still sitting in for the CIA director who was recovering from cancer surgery — said, "The National Labs were under the Department of Energy until it was disbanded last year. Now the labs operate independently with spotty coordination with the different intelligence agencies."

The president laser-stared at Light, turned to Starks and said, "Get in touch with whoever the hell is in charge out there in California and tell them to get their asses in gear. How long will this finger-printing take?"

Everyone was silent. "This is our first bomb assessment under real — not simulated — test conditions," Starks finally answered.

The president turned to the vice president, who had just arrived at the meeting due to flight issues. "Jimmy, find whoever was the last secretary of the Department of Energy, and get him here. I need a scientist I can trust." He turned again to his FBI director. "What makes you think this was intended to be a nuke as opposed to a shit-load of radioactive waste bundled with high explosives?"

Since this event happened on her watch, Starks knew she was on thin ice, so she figured it was best to be transparent. "Mr President, we've had our eye on the Wichita hangar for a couple of days. We detected an unusual pattern of cell phone activity that led us to surveil the hangar by satellite." She hesitated. "We've been working with CIA and NSA to assess the phone activity and any potential threat associated with it." She looked at Jack Light and SC, both of whom gazed back at her coolly.

Lynda took all of this in; she recognized that Celia Starks was laying the groundwork for shared responsibility. It was a dangerous tack, but it seemed to Lynda that Starks did not want to be left holding the bag, especially since she believed the CIA had information they were not sharing.

"So you were onto this for a few days, and we did nothing to stop it?" the president said in an accusatory tone.

Before Starks could respond, Jack Light said, "Mr President, I think we need to focus on what's happening in Kansas right now."

SC added, "And how we want to handle the media."

The president turned to the vice president. "Get the press secretary in here."

The chairman of the Joint Chiefs, Wolfie Wolfseifer, interjected, "We've been attacked, Mr. President. We need to increase our military readiness level until we know whether this is an isolated incident or the first in a chain of attacks."

Everyone in the room was thinking *nine-eleven*.

The president asked, "Does anyone disagree with increasing our military readiness by one step?"

Hearing no objection, the president nodded at Admiral Wolfseifer, who whispered to his aide, who then left the room.

Celia Starks said, "We should have information from the HAZMAT team shortly. Preliminarily, I've been told that the radioactive cloud is moving over west Kansas and dissipating over Missouri farmland. Until we know the exact composition of the debris cloud, we can't make an accurate assessment of the hazards."

"How long will this take?" the president asked.

The secretary of HHS said, "The meteorologists can come up with pretty good dissipation models, but until we know how much and what kind of radioactivity was released, it's going to be hard to assess the health risk."

Starks said, "I suggest we activate the Nine Eleven Protocol. That gets our top experts in key areas together to analyze the data as it comes in, so we can inform the public in a coherent way and take appropriate mitigation actions."

The director of National Intelligence, Frank Frankel, who had been quiet up to this point, said, "Mr President, according to the protocol adopted after the nine eleven attacks, we have a precise set of steps to follow in assessing an attack of this nature. It is my job to call the group together, which includes several people in this room, representatives of our fourteen intelligence agencies, plus key scientists and technical experts."

"Then get started. I'd like briefings twice a day," the president said. "Is there anything else?"

The press secretary and chief of staff had arrived. The president turned to them. "Draft a brief statement for me to address the nation. I want to calm everyone down." He looked at his chief of staff. "Can you get it set up in an hour?"

"Yes, Mr President. We'll do it from the Oval Office. It's wired for short-notice addresses."

"Good. I'll have the First Lady at my side. It will be more calming with her there."

He turned to FBI Director Starks. "Find out from your team in Kansas what the immediate loss of life was. And how do you know it was a nuke and not just a mass of explosives? I'm still confused about whether this was a *dirty* bomb or an atomic bomb."

"Mr President," Celia Starks cut in, "I called it a 'dirty bomb' because the explosion injected radioactive material from its core into the atmosphere. That has to be of concern."

223

Starks continued. "Mr President, a scientist on loan to the FBI from the NSA was the first to suggest this might be a nuclear device. I'll let her answer your question. Dr Chester," FBI Director Starks turned to face Lynda.

Lynda was on a stage grander than she'd ever imagined; she was about to brief the president of the United States and half of the Cabinet, plus other power brokers of this administration. She found herself recalling her PhD oral exam when she'd suddenly faced a challenging question from an obstreperous old professor who was best known for pinching female students' butts. Today he'd be impeached from his tenured professor job, but not back then. She had known, back then, that if she couldn't answer his question, she'd fail the exam, which is how she felt now.

Drawing on an inner reserve of calmness, Lynda rose to her feet and said, "Sir, I mean, Mr President, first the heat signature was definitely similar to a plutonium bomb core signature; second, the damage to the building and the force of the blow-out of the heavy doors suggests enough explosives to induce fission in the core, and thus a nuclear explosion that would have wiped out much of Wichita. I was there with Director Starks when the bomb detonated, and it definitely wasn't a nuclear explosion. There was no high-altitude mushroom cloud." She hesitated and added, "If it were a nuke, we wouldn't be here."

There were snickers and a few chuckles. Celia Stark frowned at Lynda as she shook her head ever so slightly.

The secretary of Defense said, "Mr President, we've been tracking a twin-engine plane that left the Wichita hangar a few hours before the explosion."

The president stared blankly at the ceiling, arms across his chest tightening even more. Finally, he blurted out, "A god damned plane, and no one told me!" He switched his gaze first to the secretary of Defense, then to DHS, and finally to Admiral Wolfseifer. "Wolfie, where the hell is this plane? I want those pricks, preferably alive."

Before the chairman of the Joint Chiefs could respond that this was the first he'd heard about a plane, his Air Force colonel aide, who had just returned to the room, whispered in his ear for about twenty seconds.

"Wolfie, let's have it," the president nearly shouted.

"Mr President, we had tactical ordinance in pursuit of the Cessna, but they escaped into Mexican airspace."

"Jesus." He looked at the undersecretary of State, then to the veep. "Jimmy, get me the president of Mexico on the phone, and you, Madam Undersecretary, get me the Mexican ambassador… now! Both of you out of here! I want to nail those bastards and find out where they're from. We've got our own bucket of nukes, and they won't fizzle."

A shiver went through everyone in the room. Lynda sat down, glad she was out of the spotlight. She felt her heart ready to jump from her mouth.

Turning back to Starks, the president said, "You said you were tracking phone calls."

The FBI director explained that they had tracked calls from the Russian FSB center in Cuba to several sites in the US that have been flooding social media with vitriol to raise the angst of the American people. One of these sites in Wichita, Starks explained, had been a mystery until the bomb exploded. "We believe they are all connected," she said.

Lynda held her breath while the FBI director's words sank in.

"So you think this is a coordinated attack on America?" the president asked.

Jack Light answered before anyone else had a chance. "Mr President, it's likely that this is a foreign plot. The calls from Cuba and the escape to Mexico point to foreign intervention."

FBI Director Celia Starks refrained from upstaging the CIA associate director, who had lofty aspirations. She knew this president was unpredictable, so she was content with letting Jack Light stick his neck out.

"If it's foreign, why didn't your agency have a clue, from all the spying you do, and all those confidential informants you use at my expense?" the president demanded, engaging the associate CIA director in a stare down.

Light responded, "We're working on it, Mr President. We believe this is a highly organized and well-funded terrorist group. We have an informant who we're milking for details."

"Then it can't be the Cubans. They're always on the brink of bankruptcy," said the president.

"No, Mr President, but it could be any number of suspect countries that have a presence in Cuba."

Celia Starks maintained a poker face, stifling the smile she'd save for later. It was clear no one was quite ready to accuse the Russians, knowing they would simply deny it. Waiting for the fingerprinting of the bomb debris made the most sense before pointing fingers.

The vice president and the undersecretary of state returned to the meeting. "Mr President," the veep said, "we're trying to locate the Mexican president, and the Mexican ambassador is somewhere in California. He'll be back in DC tomorrow."

The president's face turned crimson. "I want results, not excuses!" he shouted. "That goes for everyone at this table." Glaring at each person, in turn, he added, "What about the media? How are we going to contain this? They're everywhere, like rats on a hunk of cheese."

The vice president said, "Mr President, the chief of staff and communications director are working on the statement you'll be delivering in about forty-five minutes. We have the First Lady prepped as well. She'll look great at your side as you read the statement."

FBI Director Starks said, "Mr President, it's already all over the news and social media that there was an explosion in Wichita. People in Wichita and the nation would appreciate some words from you. We don't yet know how many were exposed to radioactive material, other than those in the immediate vicinity of the hangar."

"You were there when it went off?"

"Yes, Mr President. My team and the pilots have been checked for radioactivity, and I'm pleased to say, we weren't exposed."

Joe Green, Homeland Security Secretary, piped up, "Mr President, why don't you authorize the US Geological and Meteorological agency to broadcast hourly updates on the TV weather channel and on Internet platforms, similar to the updates given for major hurricanes?"

"Will that satisfy you, Madame FBI Director?" the president asked mockingly.

"Yes, Mr President," Celia said emphatically.

The president looked at the vice president and said, "Put that in my remarks to the nation."

Lynda had been carefully observing the body language and demeanor of the president and Celia Starks. She wondered how much longer Starks would have her job.

The president got to his feet, signaling the meeting was over. As he left the room, he said, "We'll meet again in two days… or sooner if I think it's warranted. Wolfie, come with me. I want to talk about my nukes."

Upon hearing the president's comment, everyone in the room froze in place for a second.

Chapter Thirty-eight
Tuesday

As the meeting broke up and participants milled around outside the Situation Room waiting for the president's national address, FBI Director Starks pigeonholed Jack Light. She said, "The explosion was over three hours ago. We need to contain the media hysteria. What are you hearing from ground zero?"

Light furrowed his brow. "I know as much as you. As of now, it's all public information. Within ten minutes of the explosion, social media was exploding with YouTube clips from local residents. At twenty-five minutes, the local broadcast media TV trucks were on site."

"What about radiation?"

"Your FBI teams were there. What are you getting at?"

"The two FBI reconnaissance teams and the SWAT team that were directly affected by the explosion were in a general state of shock and confusion at the hangar site. First responders arrived, but they were held back until radiation protection suits arrived and were distributed."

Director Starks stared at Jack Light, wondering about the informant he'd just revealed to the president.

"So your informant said this was a well-financed operation. What else did he say?"

Jack took Celia Starks arm and guided her away from the other meeting attendees. "I can't reveal the identity of our informant. I can only tell you that he is peripherally involved with this plot, but not an active participant."

"We're supposed to be cooperating, Jack," Starks said, and she felt her face flush as her blood pressure rose. She fought the temptation to call him out in front of other committee members, but that would be embarrassing and counterproductive. It would further alienate Light. She needed to know what he knew without pushing for the identity of the informant. If Grushkov's role was confirmed by Jack's informant, it would be further confirmation from another source of Lynda's conclusion: that this was a Russian operation.

Starks said to Light, "The lack of concrete information about the perpetrators of this attack will spawn wild stories blaming everyone, including a government sanctioned Deep State or radicalized domestic terrorists. A whole host of crazy theories will surface. Before we have facts confirmed, any number of countries at odds with America could be blamed. I'm skeptical that a message from the president will calm the public."

"I'm hopeful he will," Jack said and abruptly turned away from Starks, heading back to the Situation Room where everyone was gathering to listen to the president's address.

Lynda, who'd been hanging out in the hallway with agent Nelson and aides to the other committee members, hurried to Stark's side as they returned to the Situation Room.

"Director Starks, Nelson is picking up Internet chatter on his cell suggesting that the bomb was American-made. He says other staffers are getting the same information."

Starks abruptly stopped walking and looked at Lynda. "Just what I've been afraid of: wild conspiracy theories. The social media angst is so high, it wouldn't surprise me if the right blames the left, and vice versa. I want you both to get on this asap. We'll connect after the president's address."

In the Situation Room, all eyes were on the monitors around the room. Celia Starks was processing the information she just had gotten from Lynda. If the bomb was foreign made, identifying the source through fingerprinting the core would channel American anger at the culprit nation; the crazy theory that it was an American bomb would be debunked. But if the bomb was American, that changed the dynamic. It could galvanize those millions of hate-motivated followers of the New York and California bloggers. Liberals would retaliate and attack conservative businesses, the homes of Christian Right congressmen and congresswomen, and the offices of the NGA. Since the bomb debris hadn't been analyzed yet, Starks knew there was no reliable scientific evidence on its source, unless someone else had known it was an American bomb and had released that information ahead of time.

Extremist trolls from both sides could milk the scenario. Then the Russians would have achieved their goal of creating widespread havoc without actually nuking an American city. Jack Light's informant seemed even more important now. He could point a definitive finger at Russia as the bomb culprit. She turned her attention to the TV monitors as the president began speaking to the country from his teak desk in the Oval Office.

Following the president's brief address to the nation in which he implicated *foreign entities* as the perpetrators of the Wichita bomb explosion, FBI Director Starks managed to get a few minutes alone with the president in the Oval Office.

"Mr President, the current casualties in Wichita are six FBI and four local SWAT team members who lost their lives. Another twelve responders have been injured. Two are in critical condition. Others on the scene have broken bones and bruises, but they're also likely to have been exposed to substantial radiation, as they were in close proximity to the explosion."

He responded dismissively. "I know about the casualties."

Before she had a chance to ask where the president got his information, he was whisked away by his chief of staff.

Celia left the Oval Office, retrieved Lynda from the frenzied White House Situation Room, and headed for the portico, where government vehicles were lined up.

Once in the FBI SUV, Director Starks turned to Lynda. "I think Jack Light is feeding POTUS information before we have it. At first, I thought the CIA had a network of sources inside the country, but now I'm thinking he has a mole inside the perpetrators' operation, what he calls his informant."

Lynda cleared her throat and hesitantly said, "Have you considered that Jack might be the informant and working for the other side? He has a long history with Grushkov."

Starks faced Lynda and said, "No, Jack is a loyal patriot. If he was working with Grushkov, I'm sure he'd be using the relationship to gain an advantage for our side. What have you and Nelson found out about the conspiracy bomb rumor?"

Riding in the front, agent Nelson swiveled in his seat and said, "Nothing yet. I've got queries out to our wide network of contacts in social media and the other agencies."

"In the past we've run up against platforms like Twitter, Telegram, and Facebook hiding behind First Amendment freedom of speech, and refusing to reveal sources," Starks said.

Lynda said, "I've contacted my geek squad at NSA. They're experts at sleuthing social media and tracing posts back to the source computer IP addresses. The NSA supercomputer, Vesuvius, can penetrate just about any privacy shield. That sounds simpler than openly challenging the First Amendment."

Chapter Thirty-nine
Tuesday

"I know it's late, and it's been a crazy day, but I'd like to brainstorm a few ideas with you," Starks said to Lynda as the FBI SUV inched forward in the White House driveway.

Lynda was surprised by the FBI director's desire to confide in her since there were many senior FBI staff who she must bounce ideas off of on a regular basis. Or it could be that since they both were almost killed earlier in the day, they shared a special bond.

"Okay, I'm a night owl anyway," Lynda said, somewhat stretching the truth.

"We're just a few blocks from my condo," Starks said. "Let's go there. I'll have my driver drop you off at home after we've had a chance to chat. C'mon, we'll walk. The night air will refresh us after all that posturing."

Starks opened the SUV door and she and Lynda stepped out between a row of black government cars. Nelson jumped out of the front seat to trail them just out of earshot.

There was a light DC drizzle in the humid August night, but they were undeterred on the short walk. Starks got right to it. "How long before you can get answers using the NSA supercomputer?"

"Maybe a day, if I can get access right away," Lynda said. "Vesuvius is incredibly fast, making over a billion calculations per second. It can read a million emails and texts in one second. It can pick up a cybertrail from just a few key words."

"Unless we get on top of this conspiracy theory soon, I'm afraid it will fan the flames of public discontent even more," said Starks.

"My NSA team developed all the cryptanalysis algorithms for Vesuvius," said Lynda. "It's the biggest and fastest we have."

"Just what we need," Starks responded. "We have to tamp down this American-made bomb rumor before it undermines our efforts to control what happened. It's got to be a conspiracy theory coming from a fringe element, and I worry it won't take much for it to go viral and gather traction amongst the rebellious and the on-the-fence populace."

Lynda said, "It could have been released by the perpetrators themselves as part of their plot to create even more confusion after the bomb detonated. I'd like to get to Light's informant, if he really has one."

Starks pondered Lynda's remarks for a few seconds, then said, "That might provide additional clarity on who's behind this."

"Yeah, separate confirmation that Grushkov was really behind this attack," Lynda chimed in.

As they turned the corner toward the block where Starks lived, Lynda changed the subject. The more she got to know Celia Starks, the more she considered how it would be working permanently under her at the FBI. She'd get out from under her two male NSA bosses. "Not like the days of J. Edgar Hoover, is it?" Lynda asked.

The director chuckled. "Yeah, he thought he was more powerful than the president... and he was. But yes, it's vastly different now. Better, mostly, but there are also multiple layers of bureaucracy, which makes it more difficult to get things done, especially in a crisis. It's taken me two years to figure it out." She paused, then asked, "How did you feel about the meeting with the president?"

"I'm still processing. Certainly, there's a lot of concern about the attack, but also a lot of posturing."

"Yes, crisis brings people together against a common enemy, but there were a lot of agendas in the room."

They'd arrived at Starks' moderate condo; two bedroom, nicely appointed furniture, but also displaying an efficiency of space resembling a Zen Buddhist abode. As Starks and Lynda made their way up the front walk, agent Nelson got back into the FBI SUV that had been following closely behind.

Inside, Celia offered, "Coffee, tea, or wine?"

"Tea's fine."

A few minutes later, sitting at the kitchen table with their ginger teas, Celia Starks said, "I'm with you on the CIA informant. I'm concerned at Jack Light's reluctance to provide any details about him to the FBI or NSA, two agencies most concerned with domestic terrorism."

"Also, Homeland Security," Lynda added.

"Well, Joe Green can't keep his mouth shut. He's hoping for a higher Cabinet position or maybe even a political run. I don't trust him."

Lynda was thinking, *turf battles*, but pushed aside the thought and said, "Why won't Light share the informant's identity with us? Protecting his source?"

Starks said, "That's what I initially thought when I first heard about it from you and Sally. But we meet regularly with the Langley folks in small meetings, as well as in a monthly meeting run by the DNI. The informant was never mentioned, and you only found out about it because one of the lower-level CIA agents let it slip."

Celia sipped her tea. "I was surprised with Light's emphatic accusation at the president's emergency meeting that we had been attacked by a foreign power."

"You mean, like he knew something no one else knew?"

"He chose his words carefully, saying it could have been any number of countries, when he had the same information we had, that the calls were from the Russian FSB site in Cuba, and he knew we were tracking a Russian agent in this country," Starks said.

Lynda understood the point. Jack Light could have implicated the Russians, but he didn't.

Celia filled their empty cups with fresh tea and brought out a tin of macadamia nut cookies. "Analysis of the bomb debris isn't complete. Either someone knows the bomb was American-made and has leaked the information, or a false story was fabricated and disseminated."

"You think this could have come from the CIA informant… and then was leaked by the CIA?" asked Lynda.

"Anything's possible in the spy business, but I'm not going to stick my neck out and start accusing the CIA. That's a battle I can't win. Light is in line to be the next CIA director and he will report directly to the president. I'm not going to burn that bridge," she said and smiled ruefully. "I report through the attorney general to the DOJ, several steps below the head of the CIA."

"I can understand why you don't want to discuss it within the FBI, but why are you telling me?" Lynda asked.

"Innocent ears maybe." Starks laughed. "We need a conspiracy theory of our own to combat the American-made-bomb one."

Now Lynda laughed. "Not in my job description."

"But it *is* one of the functions of the National Counterterrorism Institute," said Starks.

"I know. The NCI was set up after nine eleven by *W* and is comprised of top antiterrorism experts, plucked from different agencies. They report directly to the DNI and president," said Lynda.

"They're into dark ops that even the FBI won't touch. I'm going to give you the name of a contact at the NCI, but the FBI footprint can't be on this."

"I'm beginning to understand," Lynda said. "You want me to work with the NCI to develop a counter theory to the American-made bomb one, and flood the Internet with that?"

"That's about right," said Starks. "But rather than a counter theory, I want you to uncover the truth. And perhaps we need to cool our heels on accusations against the CIA. Jack will bring us into the loop when he's ready."

Despite it being almost two a.m. Lynda's analytical brain was churning a mile a minute. The informant issue was a challenge that must be approached carefully, lots of eggshells along the way. She could task her supercomputer algorithms to search all intercepted phone calls as well as much of the texts of the thousands of hate messages for keywords such as 'informant', 'mole' and 'snitch'. It would provide her the opportunity to add short-cut loops to her algorithms. These were ideas she had been incubating for some time but had yet to implement.

And in the deep recess of her mind, two seemingly unconnected facts wobbled toward each other: thirty years ago, Andrei Grushkov and Jack Light had been drinking buddies while both were stationed in San Francisco, the same time Lynda had been having her affair with Grushkov. Subsequently, both men were stationed in Moscow, on opposite sides of the Cold War. Lynda wasn't sure whether or not these dots connected, or if she should share this with Director Starks.

She yawned.

"Time for my driver and Nelson to take you home," Starks got up from the kitchen and went over to Lynda, giving her a friendly hug.

"Let's continue the discussion tomorrow, first thing. Is seven too early? I have a busy day."

Lynda, who was not a huggy person, was surprised at the embrace, but accepted it as a friendly gesture. They had both shared a near death experience, and this brought them closer than what would be acceptable in the FBI pecking order.

"Seven's fine," she said.

Chapter Forty
Tuesday

Enduring a bumpy, half-mile ride in the back of the pickup truck from the Cessna to the largest of the squat buildings in one-hundred-degree heat was not what Grushkov had expected after paying the Mexican drug cartel seventy-five million dollars, and an additional fifty-five million about to be delivered. The pickup ground to a halt in front of the large main building, showering those in the back of the truck with dust and sand.

A door to the building swung open and two scruffy, bearded men with AK-47s emerged, ambling over while the driver unlatched the back tailgate.

The first gun-toting Mexican waved the AK-47 at the Russians clinging to the sides of truck and yelled, "*Vamos, vamos,*" as he swung the gun muzzle back and forth. Meanwhile, six more men came out of the building, gathering around the truck as Grushkov and his team jumped from the back, brushing off the dust and dirt.

Grushkov surveyed the group of armed men and demanded, "Take me to Carlos Godinez."

The thuggish man who had waved them out of the truck now pointed his gun at Grushkov and jerked it toward the building. "Go, go, go."

Andrei Grushkov, with his limited knowledge of Spanish asked again, addressing the man swinging the gun, "*Senor, estás tu* Carlos Godinez?"

The Mexican was quiet for a second, then he smiled, showing a few brown teeth with empty spaces between. "Godinez... no," and he laughed. Others in the crowd also started laughing.

Grushkov turned to his team and said, "I guess Toothless here is saying Godinez is not on the premises."

They were herded into the building. Its interior was even hotter than outside. It was a large warehouse the size of an American football field with many bales of hay stacked from floor to ceiling. Near its entrance was a dilapidated wooden desk, along with a half dozen chairs and several mattresses on the floor. Several large fans blew hot air around the warehouse, doing little good. The muzzle of an AK-47 waved them towards the chairs.

Mischa whispered, "There's probably a dozen bricks of coke in each of those bales. That's how it was transported in Afghanistan."

One of the Mexicans went over to a refrigerator that looked like it was from last century and took out four bottled waters, giving one to each Russian.

"Looks like they have electricity out here in the middle of nowhere," Gregory said.

"Generator," said Sergei. "I saw cables coming from that small building next door."

The toothless Mexican opened a battered wooden cabinet that had a microwave on top and removed a satellite phone. He went out the door, dialed, and started speaking in fast, indecipherable Spanish. After about a minute, he returned and handed the phone to Grushkov. "Senor Godinez."

"What's going on, Carlos? We're being held like prisoners."

"Andrei, I did not tell them you are friendly. They don't know about the Nogales operation."

"Okay, so they don't know anything, but they do not have to treat us this way."

"They have not assaulted you, have they? And they gave you water, yes?"

"Yes, they gave us water, but the conditions are unacceptable."

"Andrei, we built your tunnel and helped get your package into the US, but we knew nothing about your real intentions. I'm still not sure exactly what you did, but America is very upset, and your government has contacted the Mexican government to help catch you. So you are a *hot* commodity."

"Carlos, I didn't know the media would pick it up so soon. So now you know."

Grushkov looked at his watch. It was almost nine in Wichita, over two hours since the bomb was set to explode. He asked the drug lord, "What's the media saying, Carlos?"

"They said, someone tried to blow up Wichita, Kansas. Apparently, it was not an atomic bomb, but the explosion released radioactivity and killed many Americans."

On hearing the news about the bomb, Grushkov exhaled deeply and felt a wave of relief. "That's sad, but we were just doing our job. How are you going to get us to Mexico City?"

"It's a little complicated, Andrei. There is a lot of pressure to turn you over to the Americans."

"Carlos, you're dealing with the Russian government. You made an agreement with President Gorky. It's not an agreement you can break, especially since you've already received a lot of money from us and will receive more when we are safe in the Russian embassy in Mexico City. When are you coming for us, Carlos?"

"One of my product drivers will pick you up and bring you to Mexico City. He's already on his way to your location. I'll call him. Bye."

After handing the phone back to Carlos' thug, Grushkov looked at his team, all of whom had paid close attention to the conversation.

"We're about five hours from Mexico City by car. Carlos is phoning the driver of a cartel truck that's already on its way here. Anyway, that's who will take us to Mexico City."

"Was he was trying to back out of the agreement?" Sergei wanted to know.

"The agreement was that once we exited the tunnel in Nogales, Mexico, he would deliver us safely to the airport on their side of the border where we'd catch a commercial flight to Mexico City. He knows we were pursued by the American military, and he heard that a bomb exploded in Kansas. It's all over the news. I think he's toying with the idea that the Americans might pay a big ransom for us."

"In other words," said Mischa, "we don't know what he will do."

The cell phone on the desk rang. The toothless hombre picked it up, listened, and handed it to Grushkov.

""Carlos here. The driver will soon arrive at your location. As instructed, he will take you to the Russian embassy in Mexico City."

"Si, Carlos, the Russian embassy, gracias... Bye." After setting down the phone, he looked up at his countrymen. "We'll be delivered to the Russian embassy in Mexico City. At least that's what he said."

Grushkov rubbed his chin and considered their situation. With the Mexicans it was all about the money. "Let's assume they put us on the truck. We could overpower the driver. But they may have several others accompany us, especially if they plan on delivering us to the Americans."

"I counted eight of them here," Mischa said. "But I see only three AK-47s. And there's four of us. That's decent odds, especially if we surprise them. We're all trained in combat, except maybe Sergei." Drawing on his Afghan experience, Mischa offered a suggestion. "It would be better to overpower them here and take their weapons. When the truck arrives, we tell the driver to take us to Mexico City or we will kill him."

Sergei nodded. "You see how the Mexicans have rested their AK-47s against the wall by the refrigerator? Only Toothless keeps his, probably in case we try anything."

Grushkov said, "We must do this soon, before the truck arrives."

"Okay," Mischa said, speaking in a low voice, though none of the Mexicans appear to understand Russian. "I will finish my water and go to the refrigerator for another bottle. When I am there, the three of you start arguing and make a commotion. I will grab one of the two AKs and take down Toothless with the gun at the door. The rest is easy."

"Okay, let's do it," Grushkov said.

Mischa drank the remaining water in his bottle, got up from the chair, waving his empty bottle for the Mexicans to see.

Four Mexicans were in the warehouse, making space for an incoming shipment. Three were in the area with the Russians. Toothless was leaning against the wall next to the door with an AK-47, and the other two were lying on the mattresses, resting. One was out front of the building, smoking pot, judging by the smell seeping under the door.

Toothless did not move to stop Mischa from crossing the room. When he opened the refrigerator to get a fresh bottle, Gregory started shouting at Sergei, who lunged and started a physical fight with his compatriot. Grushkov rushed to separate them.

When Toothless saw the Russians fighting, he started towards them.

Mischa sprinted to the wall, grabbed one of the AK-47s, flipped off the safety, and fired a short burst at Toothless.

Mischa's aim was true. There was a splatter of blood and bone against the wall. Toothless flopped to the floor, mortally wounded.

Gregory sprinted to the fallen man and secured his gun. Mischa grabbed the third AK-47 and tossed it to Sergei.

As soon as they heard the gunshots, the four men in the back of the warehouse ran toward the front, but they stopped halfway, throwing their hands over their heads when they saw that the Russians were now armed.

The Mexican who was smoking in front of the building came through the door and stumbled over a dead comrade, who had fallen across the door jamb. Gregory stuck the barrel of the AK-47 in his face. The two Mexicans who were dozing on the mattress stared down the barrel of Sergei's AK-47. Like their comrades, they threw their hands in the air.

Grushkov shouted instructions to his team. "Move them to the back of the warehouse behind those bales and tie them up with the baling string. Sergei, you guard them. Keep them together behind the bales. Mischa and Gregory, we will wait for the truck. Hopefully, it will be just the driver, but we must be prepared if he is not alone."

Mischa shouted to Gregory, "We must capture the driver alive. He knows the route to Mexico City."

After twenty minutes, they heard the sound of a truck approaching.

Grushkov peeked out the warehouse window and saw its faint headlines. "Let's wait in the building until the truck stops, and we see how many they are."

Five minutes passed and the sound of the truck engine was deafening in the quiet desert night. There was a grinding noise as the brakes were set.

Through the window, Grushkov saw one man exit a modern cab of an eighteen-wheeler. "At least with all their drug money they have a modern truck to haul their product," Grushkov said.

The driver opened the door to the warehouse and was greeted by two AK-47s; one pointed at his belly, and the other, his head.

"What the fuck?" he said with a strong Texas twang. He was clean-shaven, wearing cowboy boots and a fancy shirt.

"You're American," Grushkov said.

"You're goddam right. True, red, white and blue Texan. Tommy Mack's my handle. What's going on here?"

"Not your concern. Can you unhook the rig from the cab?"

"Sure, that baby can hit a hundred miles per hour without the rig. It's a beaut. Now point that goddamn muzzle somewhere else. I'm paid to drive, not to get shot."

Grushkov swung the AK-47 around and pointed it at the dead Mexican. "Okay, here's the plan, and if you don't like it, we'll shoot you just like that one there on the ground."

"Hey, just tell me where you want to go."

"Where were you told to take us?"

He looked around nervously. "Well, Mr. Godinez said I should call on his sat phone when I got here, and he'd tell me where to deliver you."

"Did he use that word: deliver?" Grushkov asked.

"Yes, sir."

"Time to leave," Grushkov shouted. "Mischa, grab the sat phone, and do a quick sweep to make sure there are no more phones. We need all the keys from the trucks. Gregory, grab a half dozen waters, and anything in the fridge that looks reasonable to eat while we are on the road. C'mon, Texas, let's go outside, and unhook the rig from cab."

"What about our prisoners?" Gregory asked.

"We leave them. Not much they can do without phones and vehicles."

"I make sure," Mischa said. He went out the door and soon there were series of bursts from the AK-47.

Texas' tanned face blanched.

Mischa came back and said, "Can't go far without tires."

Grushkov and Mischa squeezed in the front seat with Texas, the name they decided for the driver since 'Tommy' didn't seem to suit the tall

Texan. Sergei and Gregory were slouched in two bunks in the back of the cab, with three AK-47s for company.

"So you're a drug runner?" Grushkov asked Texas.

"Never thought of it that way, but I guess so. After three years of drought in west Texas and a herd of four hundred Herefords to feed, plus a mortgage on this eighteen-wheeler, I came south to find good hay, which I found, but there were strings attached."

"You mean the drugs?"

"Yes, and my life. These cartels have a long reach into the US Godinez paid off the money I owed on this rig in return for me taking his product to key cities on my route home. It's worked out well for both of us."

Mischa said, "So the tunnels under the American wall aren't used any more?"

"Some are. I deliver product to several tunnels. The border and its wall are a joke, like a sieve. There are plenty of tunnels the American DEA haven't found. When they destroy one, these guys build two more. My delivery is an insurance policy that product gets through, even if the tunnels are found. Keeps the cash flowing."

After ninety minutes, about halfway to Mexico City, the satellite phone in Grushkov's backpack rang.

"Yes, Carlos, it's Andrei."

"You shot up my men."

Grushkov's thinking "Shit, we must have missed a cell phone."

"Had no choice. We were treated as prisoners, not as paying customers, so we took possession of the warehouse. I am sorry some of your men were killed, but we had no choice."

"Okay, Andrei. You will be delivered to the embassy, but first you must have the final payment transferred," Carlos said.

"No, Carlos. If you want the final payment plus the added million, we must arrive at the Russian embassy unharmed," Andrei said, and hung up.

"That didn't sound good," Mischa said.

Grushkov turned to the driver. "Texas, are you familiar with the route to Mexico City?"

"In my sleep. This is my seventh run. What's going on?"

"Carlos is pissed. Is there a place along this route where he might ambush us?" Grushkov asked.

"Hmmm, only one place I can think of. When we exit the desert, about fifty miles from the outskirts of Mexico City. It's a blind curve with rock formations on each side. But Carlos has a helicopter."

"Yeah, that's bad. Gregory and Sergei, make sure those AK-47s are loaded and ready to fire."

"Mr Andrei," Texas said, "we're comin' up on the blind curve."

"Okay. Take it as fast as is safe, and then maximum speed after."

They accelerated through the curve at fifty miles per hour. Texas put the pedal to the floor and the cab flew down the straight paved road at ninety-eight miles per hour.

"There's someone behind us," Texas said. "Looks like one of their rundown pickups. They'll never catch us."

"Yeah, they probably cobbled together enough spare tires from all the shot-up trucks." Mischa said. "But look what's ahead," He shouted.

"A chopper!" Texas yelled above the roar of his rig. "What do we do?"

"Pull over in front of that group of palm trees," said Mischa. "We're no match for them in a moving vehicle. Have a better chance to neutralize the chopper from cover. But we need to get that pickup truck first."

Texas positioned the rig in front of the stand of palm trees blocking them from view from the road. The pickup that had been in pursuit slid to a stop on the pavement about twenty yards down the road. Three armed men jumped out.

They were immediately mowed down by Mischa and Gregory, firing AK-47s.

The helicopter did a low pass over the scene and banked to the right as it gained altitude.

Mischa shouted, "They're assessing our position and strength. They don't know we have a third weapon. Sergei, take your AK and run to the pickup truck. They won't expect fire from that direction. When they hover and start shooting at us, aim for where the rotors attach to the top of the copter, or at the pilot if you get a side shot. Texas, Andrei, get under the rig and stay there. Gregory, come with me." Mischa ran to the stand of palm trees.

The helicopter hovered about thirty feet above the rig. Men with automatic rifles were perched at the open doors on each side, looking at the abandoned rig cab when Mischa and Gregory opened fire. The chopper turned broadside so one of the armed men onboard could start spraying the trees with automatic fire.

Sergei took aim at the pilot and opened fire. The glass canopy shattered, but the man at one of the open doors facing the rig had enough time to spray the palm trees where Mischa and Gregory were pumping bullets in the direction of the helicopter.

Without a glass canopy, the helicopter could not fly so the pilot settled the chopper onto the pavement.

Gregory rushed from behind the trees, spraying the helicopter before the occupants could get out and return fire. One of the gunmen got hit in the face, brain tissue and bone splattering the inside of the chopper. As he jumped out of the chopper, a second gunman took several rounds in the torso, and the pilot slumped forward, shot through the neck.

Gregory looked around but could not find Mischa. He yelled to Grushkov and Texas to get out from under the truck and look for Mischa.

Gregory ran back to the palm trees where they had been firing at the helicopter and found Mischa slumped against one of the trees, three bullet holes in his torso. Gregory knelt next to him and saw he was still breathing. He yelled for Grushkov to bring the first aid kit from the rig.

He held Mischa closely as he would a brother.

Just as Grushkov got there with the first aid kit, Mischa looked into Gregory's eyes and said, "I die for Mother Russia. Please tell my mother."

Grushkov blotted his eyes with his shirt sleeve. "We will take Mischa to the embassy in Mexico City," he said. "We'll send him home where he will receive a hero's burial. Now we must get to the embassy before Carlos sends more men."

"It's only about forty-five minutes," Texas said. "But I'll be hunted by Carlos for helping you… I'm dead."

"Yes, that's a problem," Gregory said. "But I have idea." He lifted the AK and fired a round that grazed Texas' head.

Texas grabbed his head which was bleeding profusely and, startled, looked at Gregory in disbelief.

"Are you crazy, Gregory?" Grushkov bellowed.

"Andrei, it's what Mischa would have done. We leave Texas here with the Mexican's satellite phone. He can push redial and connect with Carlos. When Carlos' men get here, they will see that Texas was not assisting us. We forced him to drive. Texas' rig is easy for me to drive. I'll get us to the embassy."

Grushkov tossed a rolled bandage to Texas and said, "I'll leave the first aid kit with you. Gregory is a good shot. It's only a slight flesh wound. Good luck, Texas."

Chapter Forty-one
Tuesday

Irene and Larissa were finishing a light lunch in their condo when both their laptops chimed, indicating an incoming message.

Larissa reached her computer first. "It's Grushkov!" she said and turned her computer so Irene could also see the screen.

'Holiday over, return home immediately. Father.'

Irene opened her laptop. The message was the same.

Larissa said, "This is sudden. I wonder what happened."

Irene, her brain churning, stared blankly at Larissa.

Larissa turned away, not wanting to engage Irene's stare, for fear of revealing her secret message to Anatoly about Irene's relationship with Vance. She had to be cool and not give Irene, a trained assassin, any reason to be suspicious . "We should clean the condo, and then I will say goodbye to Liang."

Irene weighed her options. She interpreted Grushkov's instructions not to kill Larissa, unless Irene was positive she was going to defect. Irene was suspicious, but not sure.

They quickly cleaned the condo, making sure there was nothing left behind that would identify them or their mission. Their last Internet session revealed almost two million blog, Facebook, Instagram, and Twitter followers, far more than they could keep up with. Some of the most vehement dark web white supremacist groups had spilled into the mainstream World Wide Web, using their anonymous IP addresses, and thus, were difficult to trace. Hate speech was everywhere online and violence was erupting in many cities across America.

"We've fulfilled our mission. We must leave now before we are discovered," Irene said standing in her bedroom door, suitcase packed, staring at Larissa with suspicion.

Larissa glanced around the place that had been her home in America. She gathered her computer shoulder bag and large purse, and said, "I'm going to say goodbye to Liang. I'll be back in a few minutes." She set her overnight bag at the front door with a loud clunk specifically to assure Irene that she would be right back.

After forty-five minutes, Irene's gut told her something was wrong. She eyed Larissa's suitcase for a couple of seconds, and then hurried over, flipped it on its side and opened it. Larissa's clothes were neatly folded. Irene ran her hand through the layers of clothes and the side pockets, searching for a clue about Larissa's intentions. On the bottom of the suitcase, under all the clothes, was the flap with straps that would normally be used on top of the contents to hold them in place during travel. Underneath the flap was a plain brown envelope. Inside were two airline tickets from San Diego Airport to Reagan Airport in Washington.

"Shit," Irene exclaimed. "They're going to defect."

Since the *Arctic fox* exit plan was to take Amtrak to San Diego and then exit the US at the San Ysidro border checkpoint, Irene figured Larissa planned to slip away and meet Liang after they arrived in San Diego.

Irene stuffed the envelope back under the flap and slammed the suitcase shut. The pieces fitted: Larissa had been spending a lot of time with Liang, and twice during the last week she had spent the night in his condo. When queried by Irene, she simply said, "It's my personal business. It doesn't affect the job I do."

It was one thirty. Larissa had been gone almost an hour. Irene stalked to the Liang's condo and knocked loudly at the door. Finally, Zhao opened the door a crack.

"Is Larissa here?" Irene demanded.

"At Starbucks. Back soon."

"Send her home when she returns," she told Zhao, who nodded okay and closed the door.

Back at the condo, Irene recalled Grushkov's instructions about removing Larissa if she jeopardized the mission. Larissa knew too much to be left behind, even if it was only to be with Liang. It would be treason if she revealed information about the mission and how the FSB operated.

Irene's assessment of Larissa was that she was not loyal to Russia. Irene was confident that she had the authority in this situation to act.

She was an expert killer with a variety of methods at her disposal. The challenge, in this case, was to avoid the appearance of murder. Larissa's death must look like an accident.

In missions in which when she had carried out assassinations, the steps had been well planned out ahead of time. This situation was different. She would have to do it quickly so she could get out of the US, per Grushkov's instructions.

When Larissa returned to the condo, Irene would suggest they toast the success of their mission with cold vodka from the freezer, the classic Russian way to drink vodka. She would spike Larissa's drink with a few drops of the date rape drug, Rohypnol. That would knock her out, after which Irene would inject her with a ten-cc solution of potassium chloride. Autopsy would show an unexpected heart attack: no evidence of foul play.

In preparation, Irene placed a bottle of vodka in the freezer. She retrieved a ten-cc syringe and twenty-gauge needle from her night case, loaded the syringe with the potassium chloride that she had been keeping handy, just in case.

A thrill coursed through her body. Assassinations gave her a power rush; a giddiness she had not felt since the polonium operation in London. Taking a life, especially of a Jew who had been a thorn in her side, caused an extreme level of anticipation and gratification she could only compare to a massive orgasm.

Irene was at a peak mental state, ready to carry out the final phase of the mission. It was imperative that she get Larissa back into the condo and under her control. It had been over an hour since Larissa had left to say goodbye to Liang.

At two p.m., Irene stalked back to Liang's condo and knocked vigorously on the door. There was no answer. She picked the lock, went into the condo, and found it empty.

Back in her condo, Irene realized Larissa was gone and the situation was now out of control. She had been outsmarted. The airline tickets had been a ruse to throw her off. It had worked. Irene did not know what to do. Grushkov's message to *Arctic fox* was to leave asap.

She took out her burner phone and dialed FSB headquarters in Cuba.

Anatoly answered after three rings. His response to Irene's situation was, "Find her, and do what you are trained to do."

Larissa and Liang had planned for this situation, including the purchase of two airline tickets to trick Irene about their plans.

As soon as Larissa had gone to Liang's condo, he had emailed his friend, Tim Whatley, who picked them up within fifteen minutes. They drove to a Laguna Beach hotel they had previously scouted.

Larissa and Liang were in each other's arms in a corner room at the top of the Surf and Sand Hotel in Laguna Beach, about twenty minutes from Irvine. They sat on their private patio with an expansive view of the Pacific Ocean, and the island of Catalina twenty-six miles away.

"You will be in big trouble with your government," Larissa mused.

Liang answered. "Yes, China will put pressure on the university to send me back, and they will threaten my parents. What about you?"

Larissa was quiet, thinking Russia would send someone to kill her if Irene failed. She was glad she'd revealed to Liang her Russian identity soon after they'd first started their relationship. But she was afraid to reveal that she was a spy because he may balk at defecting. She knew she would need to confess once in the hands of the American authorities. Meanwhile, it was time to relax and enjoy the sun and beautiful setting in Laguna Beach.

"They will not be happy that I have encouraged you to defect," she said.

"At least you're not a Russian spy," Liang said with a laugh.

She shuddered at his comment but maintained her composure. "It's complicated, Liang. It's better we don't discuss it now. What will we do next?"

Liang said, "Tim says he can get us an appointment with the American Immigration department. But first he wants us to meet with the elected government official that represents this area of California. He thinks she will support our request for political asylum."

Larissa took his hand and led him back into the bedroom. "Let's enjoy our time together for a couple of days," she said. "And not think about our complicated situation."

At two o'clock, Irene realized that unless she found Larissa quickly, she would have failed in another mission. She vividly recalled the rumbling threat in Grushkov's voice when he told her that this was an opportunity to redeem herself for the London polonium mishap. He had specifically said, "Keep an eye on Larissa."

Irene was a perfectionist and letting Larissa slip away was out of the question. She could not imagine returning to Russia having failed again. Taking out her laptop, she hacked into the university engineering server, just as she and Larissa had done several weeks earlier. Once in, she located Liang's email account and started scanning his emails, focusing around the time Larissa went to his condo.

"Aha," she exclaimed. Five minutes after Larissa had left the condo to say goodbye to Liang, he had sent an email to Tim Whatley.

Irene found Whatley's email account and saw that, three minutes after receiving Liang's email, Whatley used his Mozilla browser to open the website for the Surf and Sand Hotel in Laguna Beach.

Irene checked her watch: two thirty p.m. She figured she could take an uber to Laguna Beach and arrive by three, find Larissa, and do what had to be done. But Liang would be there, too, and it would get messy.

She carefully filled the syringe with enough potassium chloride to kill two large persons. She placed it in a plastic bag, along with a small bottle of Rohypnol knock-out drops. She put the bag into a side pocket of her laptop shoulder bag, next to what was left of her stash of money. She looked around the condo out of habit, then headed for the front door, phone in hand to call uber.

As soon as Irene stepped out the front door, she almost crashed into a man and woman dressed in business suits. They were stern, unsmiling, perfectly groomed.

The woman spoke first. "Are you the resident of this condo?"

Irene's training kicked in. "Who wants to know?"

They identified themselves as government agents and showed flat wallets with shiny gold badges on the surface.

Irene's heart pounded her chest, and a chill knifed through her body. "Yes, I live here," she said coolly.

"Can we see some identification please?"

"Why don't we go inside?" Irene smiled stiffly while her brain was churning possible options. She turned to enter before the agents could respond to her question. Back inside the condo, she offered them seats in the living room, and said, "Would you like some water?"

"No thanks, we're fine," said the male agent. "We would like to see some identification please. A driver's license or passport?"

"Here's my passport." She slipped her hand into the side pouch of her computer bag, the pouch with the plastic bag with the syringe. She groped around, pulled out the Canadian passport and handed it to them. "What is this about?"

But the agents ignored her question.

While they both examined the passport, Irene nonchalantly moved her hand into the computer pouch, grasped the plastic bag with the syringe, and deftly tucked it into the waistband of her slacks under her loose-fitting blouse.

The woman said, "You are Canadian."

"Yes. I live in Vancouver."

"May I photograph your passport?"

Not knowing her rights, Irene figured it was best to agree. "Why not?"

The man said, "I see you have a computer in that case you are carrying. May I see it?"

Irene's computer had all the records of her emails and the special hacking software provided by the FSB IT people in Havana. But it also had special facial recognition features; it would not turn on without scanning and confirming that access was allowed.

She handed the computer to the male agent and watched him open the top of the computer and push the on button. The computer camera scanned his face and activated a program that destroyed the software, programs, files, and records of all Internet and communication activity.

While the feds were focused on the computer, Irene said, "Will you excuse me for a moment? I need to use the bathroom." Rather than ask their permission, she walked into the guest bathroom just off the entryway.

The two agents exchanged glances. Since they had not arrested Irene, or read her any rights, they had no reason to prevent her from using the bathroom. All they knew was that they had received a message from CIA headquarters in Langley to determine the identity of the occupants of the Irvine condo, and confiscate any computers. For detention or arrest, they would have to call in the FBI or local law enforcement. But that did not prevent them from speculation.

The female agent, Nancy Jensen, said, "I think this investigation is related to the massive uptick in social media violence."

"Yeah, internal chatter points to foreign involvement, possibly Russian," the male agent said.

The thin bathroom door allowed Irene to pick up bits and pieces of the conversation. She heard 'social media', and 'Russian', and assumed she would be arrested and interrogated as soon as she was done in the bathroom. It was possible that Larissa had already made a deal with the Americans and informed on her, in which case her fate may be worse than just interrogation. She was a spy, in the US illegally, and she might just disappear at the hands of the Americans. She had been warned by Grushkov that if caught, the Moscow government would denounce her activities as that of a disgruntled ex-KGB operative.

In the bathroom, Irene activated a scenario she had rehearsed many times on previous missions; a rote process drilled into the conscience of the highest-level Russian agents when they are certain to be caught. She took the syringe from the plastic bag and inserted the needle in a vein in her left arm and injected the lethal dose of potassium chloride.

As her heart accelerated into extreme tachycardia, she pictured her parents' smiling faces. Within a few seconds, Irene Seminova dropped into an irreversible coma. Her last thought was that she was sacrificing herself for Mother Russia.

Upon finding Irene's body sprawled on the bathroom floor, CIA agent Nancy Jensen checked for a pulse. "Damn it! She's killed herself."

"Take her computer, and let's get the hell out of here," said the male agent, Bob Wright.

"Not until we search the place. Might be something else here," Jensen said as she headed to check the bedrooms. After a few minutes she said, "Damn, there's two of them. Bob, look for another computer."

After a ten-minute search, all they had were some women's clothes, one burner phone, and a compromised laptop computer.

"Maybe our IT folks can extract something from the computer," said Bob. "Let's get the hell out of here."

On the east coast, Yuri sat in the window seat of the train from Penn Station to Montreal, watching the fading daylight reflect off the summer green forests of upstate New York. Under different circumstances it would have been a calming view but given what had happened that morning Yuri was barely aware of his surroundings. He was on autopilot.

A mere twelve hours ago, Peter had returned from a night at Professor Mahoney's. His face had been bright and happy when he announced to Yuri that, despite Grushkov's previous day's message to immediately leave America, he had decided to stay in the US to be with Mahoney.

"You have family in Russia that you will never see again. Think of the embarrassment your parents will feel," Yuri said, trying to calmly apprise Peter of the consequences to his family back home.

Tears welled in Peter's eyes. He turned away and said, "I'm taking a bath," and he headed toward the bathroom.

Yuri, seeing he'd hit a nerve, hurled another comment at Peter before he disappeared. "Your parents are in their eighties and enjoying the luxury of a top retirement home paid for by the FSB. They'll be tossed out if their son is disgraced."

Peter whirled around, choking back tears. "You know I can never be an open gay man in Russia. You have been in the closet for most of your life."

Though the comment stung, Yuri knew it was true.

When Peter emerged from the bathroom, his eyes were red. Pulling on a clean pair of khakis and collared knit shirt, he announced, "I've thought about what you said. You are right. I am Russian. My parents are Russian, and they will be retaliated against. I'm going to meet Tom and explain why I must leave him."

By noon, there was no sign of Peter's return. Yuri paced back and forth in the flat, considering what do to. He had Mahoney's home address and knew the location of his office at NYU. He could go there or wait for another hour. He could phone Anatoly in Havana and ask for advice. As he thought more about it, he decided to walk by Mahoney's apartment, not sure if he would knock on the door.

As Yuri approached Mahoney's flat, the street was blocked by three New York police cars. There was a gaggle of people at a yellow taped-off area. Yuri asked a college student what had happened.

"Not sure. I think someone fell from the building."

A man with a scraggly beard and a grocery cart filled with clothes and discarded items, pointed up and said, "Guy was killed. Fell fifteen floors from the balcony."

The rest of the day was a blur as again and again, Yuri recalled the events that soon followed.

A policeman came out with Tom Mahoney in handcuffs. His eyes were red — like he'd been crying. As soon as he saw Yuri, he pulled free of the cop and ran towards him. Before the cops got hold of him again, he said to Yuri, "It was an accident, he told me he was leaving. We quarreled and he lost his balance and fell."

Later that day Yuri had left the flat with nothing but his and Peter's laptop computers sandwiched into one case.

As the train wound its way along the Hudson River and then through the farmland of upstate New York, Yuri tried to deal with conflicting emotions. Over the time they lived in New York a strong bond had formed between them. Yuri, the oldest of Grushkov's team members, felt like a big brother to the younger Peter. He knew Grushkov had selected him because the inexperienced Peter needed a guiding hand — someone to keep him out of trouble. A mixture of sadness at his loss plus a feeling of guilt because he was the one who pushed Peter to break off the relationship with Tom, consumed Yuri as the train headed north. A tear trickled down his cheek.

When the Adirondack pulled into Montreal station ten minutes late, Yuri pointed to the commotion outside the train window and said to the conductor, "What's going on?"

"Looks like a checkpoint," replied the conductor.

Yuri felt his breathing accelerate. He tried to slow it down while he joined the other passengers in line.

A female officer at the impromptu checkpoint asked for his travel documents. She looked at his fake FSB US passport, checked that the photo matched the face and asked for another ID. He showed her his bogus New York driver's license, which she checked against the passport photo. "What is your purpose in Canada?" she asked.

"Sightseeing."

She peered behind him. "No luggage?"

"Just staying with friends and returning tomorrow. I travel light."

The line behind had grown considerably, and a man yelled that he had to catch a connecting train to Toronto. With no specific orders other than to look for suspicious characters, she ignored her instinct and waved Yuri through.

"What happened?" Yuri asked. "Why the checkpoint?"

"Terrorist attack. All I know."

Chapter Forty-two
Wednesday

After a restless night, Lynda woke up a few minutes before her alarm went off at five thirty. Lying in bed, she replayed the late-night discussion with FBI director, Celia Starks. She forced herself to look at all the pieces of the giant jigsaw puzzle.

The idea of a CIA informant nagged at her. She understood Stark's explanation that informants are often held in close confidence by whatever agency had them. It was for both the informant's safety and the need to keep the information stream flowing. But in this case, Jack had been unwilling to provide any information about the contribution his informant was making to solving this case. His informant had not identified any of the Russian terrorists, and in fact had not even implicated Russia in the plot. And then there was the American-made-bomb conspiracy theory that Lynda had been tasked with neutralizing.

After twenty minutes of mulling it all over, she got up, did her bathroom chores, and headed to the kitchen. She wolfed down her typical toasted English muffin with her grandma's jam in between sips of steaming black coffee, then left for the FBI Hoover building at six thirty, with plenty of time to spare for her seven a.m. meeting with Director Starks.

Director Starks gestured for Lynda to sit in one of the well-upholstered leather chairs in her office while she took a seat on the adjacent couch. There were two water-filled glasses on the coffee table between.

Starks began. "We've got a complicated situation, and the president is understandably impatient for answers. We don't know where the radiation cloud is going, or even how much radiation is being spread over Kansas and Missouri, though our meteorological experts have said it's dissipating — mainly over farmland."

"Who's in charge of the investigation?" Lynda asked.

"The DNI is coordinating the overall effort. We'll have the first meeting of the National Intelligence Committee, the NIC, this morning."

"Will all the key people be there? Has FEMA been brought in to coordinate the identification and mitigation measures?" Lynda asked.

"No. It will take several days to get everyone together and up to speed. Information will be coming in from the field and will need to be assessed and assembled into a cohesive picture. I assume that FEMA's rapid response team will be brought in to help with assessment and mitigation members. That takes time too, which is something we just don't have a lot of."

Lynda took a drink, waited a few seconds and asked, "I thought the FBI was in charge?"

Starks thought for a few seconds before answering. "We have key responsibility for coordination of much of the on-the-ground responses and in the collation of the various pieces of intelligence from the other agencies. But the overall big picture coordination falls under the DNI. He will be the one to brief the president, but he will not have the responsibility of the nuts-and-bolts execution of our responses. That's our job, working with the other agencies."

Lynda absorbed this explanation, but still wasn't sure she understood the complex bureaucratic operation of the multiagency intelligence network. There had to be some central coordination of the efforts or else something major could slip through the cracks, or worse yet, decisive action could be hampered by the government morass. After many years in the military she remembered a quote from her dad: *The bureaucratic mentality is the only constant in the universe.*

Before she could express her fears, Starks asked, "Who do you think is behind this, Lynda? You've been involved with this since the beginning."

"It has to be the Russians," Lynda said. "A Cessna similar to Grushkov's departed from Amarillo, Texas, heading north toward Wichita on the day the bomb exploded. All the calls to and from the Russian spy agency in Cuba and the different sites in the US foreshadowed the Wichita explosion. This information needs to get to the DNI's committee and to the public. If the finger can be pointed at an outside enemy, America will re-focus on that threat, where it should be, and put a lid on the mushrooming conspiracy theories."

"I agree, Lynda. But the government committee will operate deliberately and slowly. I'd like you to move on your own, and use the NSA supercomputer to track down the source of the fake it-was-an-American-bomb theory."

"And put out our own theory?" asked Lynda

Starks took a drink of water while her comment to Lynda sunk in, and then continued. "We want the truth, not fake conspiracy theories of our own. And keep Sally involved. She has the imaging expertise which complements your cyber wizardry, plus, she's consulting for the CIA, so she has a direct line to Jack Light. She knows all their technical people. Maybe the two of you can get a line on the CIA's informant. I think you may be right: the informant may be a link to the Russians."

"Proof that this was a Russian plot will defuse rumors that it was an American-made bomb, and a plan of internal insurrectionists to drive the country into civil war," said Lynda.

"Yes," Starks said. "But we need to go on the offensive on social media, spin our own idea that it's the Russians, whether or not we get conclusive proof from Jack's informant. Here's the name of my confidential contact at the National Counterterrorism Institute." She handed Lynda a slip of paper. "Just remember, no FBI fingerprints on this," she added.

If something went awry, Lynda considered her own vulnerability with her bosses at NSA, especially since she's been using the NSA supercomputer.

"Can you contact SC at NSA, and solidify that I'm still on loan to the FBI and reporting directly to you?"

"Of course. Will that be a problem?"

"Not for me." Lynda laughed. "Personally, I'm loving this assignment and working under you. But SC and NSA director Hall are intent on *not* being left out in the cold on this. They'll want credit — that is if it all works out well."

"Got it, not a problem. Hall is on the NIC with me. I'll take care of it during our meeting later today."

"There's a few other things, Director Starks."

"Let's have it."

"Jack Light and Andrei Grushkov were drinking buddies when they were both posted to the San Francisco Bay area in the '80s. Even though they were on opposite sides of the Cold War, they were very tight."

"Are you sure?"

"Absolutely. At the time, I was having an affair with Grushkov."

"Damn, Lynda."

"I disclosed my relationship with Grushkov to the NSA as part of my vetting process, and now I'm disclosing it to you. But that doesn't alter my concern about the Light-Grushkov connection."

"I'll follow up. It's pretty dicey, but the FBI's good at this," Starks said.

"If there really is an informant passing information to the CIA, it should be shared with us," Lynda said.

"I don't see any advantage of Jack inventing the fact that there's an informant. Eventually the truth will come out. I bet it's an issue of protecting his source."

After Lynda left Stark's office, the director of the FBI considered that Lynda's disclosure about her affair with Grushkov should disqualify her from further involvement on this case. FBI policies on conflict of interest were pretty clear—but Lynda was too crucial to this effort. Starks pigeonholed Lynda's disclosure hoping it wouldn't come back and bite her.

Starks spotted her opportunity to question Jack Light before the first meeting of the National Intelligence Committee. They were both in the hallway while final materials were being laid down at each seat for the committee members. Other members of the NIC were in a cluster at one end of the hall, so Starks deftly inserted her arm under Jack's and said, "Can we chat?" as she guided him further from the group.

Before she could pose the question, he said, "Yes, we have an informant."

Celia Starks, who was usually not caught off guard, raised her eyebrows.

"It took a lot of spade work to get our informant to turn. He's well placed but has only peripheral knowledge of the Russian plot."

"Jack, if this informant was aware of a plot against America on US soil, you should have notified me." Starks' felt her face getting hot.

"I need to protect the informant's identity. I have no doubt he will be in danger the more people who know about him."

"So you're going to stonewall me on this?"

"Look," Jack said, glancing at the other members of the committee starting to enter the conference room, "We don't have much time, but I will share with you that those hate messages that your gal Lynda analyzed for us, well, they came from a location in Irvine, California. I sent agents out there, and one of the perps triggered a self-destruct on her computer, then killed herself before she could be interrogated. We found high quality bogus US and Canadian passports. The quality was so good that it feels like Russian FSB, but we're not sure."

"Where's the computer now? We have the resources to reverse engineer it, and extract information."

Light held Starks' gaze. "We have the same capabilities you have, but as a gesture of cooperation I'll see that you get it, and also the burner phone we recovered."

Celia Starks wondered what he wasn't telling her. Offering up the dead perp's computer was an uncharacteristically generous gesture.

"I can see that you're skeptical." Jack Light gave her a pained smile. "There's another perp. We found clothes indicating two persons had been living at the Irvine condo. And we're trying to locate the landlord so we can track the source of the rental money. Maybe the FBI wants to put the condo under surveillance?"

"Of course, we do," she snapped. "I want a forensic team to go over the place. We do this for a living, Jack. We may recover DNA and fingerprints that will help identify the perps."

They slipped into the meeting as the door closed.

Returning to FBI headquarters after the DNI's committee meeting, Director Starks called a meeting in her office of her own team, including Lynda, Sally, and the heads of FBI forensics and IT divisions.

To the head of IT, she said, "We'll be getting a computer from the CIA that has activated self-destruct software. We're interested in seeing what you can salvage. Also, a burner cell that we need to deconstruct."

She turned to the head of forensics. "We have a site under surveillance in California where there was an apparent suicide of a key perp. We know there was another person living there. I need you to get a forensic team out there and go through that condo with a fine-tooth comb. CIA has had a team there, so I don't know what they may have contaminated. I want our team to examine the body. I'll call the LA coroner and arrange it."

To Lynda, she said, "As we've discussed, I'd like you to lead the effort with our IT team and put a damper on the social media cyberattacks."

"Of course," Lynda said. "But I'm perplexed about how and why CIA got to the California site without coordinating with the FBI."

"I confronted Light when he informed me of this. It's like he wants us to bail him out for their screw-up in California."

There was a brief silence in the room before Lynda asked, "What happened at the meeting with the DNI?"

"We should have a read on the origin of the bomb material by tomorrow. The fingerprinting process is being done on fragments recovered from the hangar, as well as samples from the atmosphere."

Lynda was looking at an urgent message on her cell from one of her NSA staff, and she made an announcement to the team in the room. "CNN is claiming the bomb was made in the USA. They're quoting a reliable source."

Starks turned on a small flat screen in the corner of her office. Wolf Blitzer was summarizing the current crisis. He concluded with the comment: "CNN has learned from a credible source that the chemical analysis of the bomb debris indicates the plutonium core material was made in the USA."

"Jesus Christ," Celia exclaimed. "The president announced on national TV that the bomb was from a foreign country." She walked to the screen and back. "Maybe the president can address the nation again and calm things down. We've got to get control of social media and the press on this."

Lynda asked, "When is the next briefing with the president?"

"Tomorrow morning. I suspect with the media frenzy spinning this bogus American-bomb scenario, it'll be a top item on tomorrow's agenda." She looked at Lynda with raised expectant eyebrows.

On TV, Wolf Blitzer cut to a live press conference with the speaker of the Congressional House and the president of the Senate. Both were demanding full disclosure from the president and other members of the Cabinet with respect to what they knew about the source of the bomb. Both indicated that key committees of the Senate and the House would implement full investigations of the event, as well as the effectiveness of the US intelligence agencies in detecting and acting on information relative to attacks on America.

Lynda observed Starks' posture stiffen as she listened to the politicians announcing their investigations.

Chapter Forty-three
Wednesday

The president strode into the joint meeting of his Cabinet and DNI's Intelligence Council in the White House Situation Room. He waved for everyone to sit and started without any greeting. "Media's out of control, saying the bomb was American-made."

The DNI, whose intelligence council had been collecting and collating all the information on the bombing, said, "The final fingerprinting has determined the bomb looks like an American bomb. But there's disagreement among the scientists about the bomb core, what they call the pit. Some say it's American, others say not."

Jack Light cleared his throat loudly, waited a few seconds, and said, "Mr President, a CIA informant is implicating Russia in the bomb plot."

FBI Director Celia Starks, who had been sitting directly across from the president, stared at Jack Light, waiting for him to reveal what she knew was coming — consistent with his propensity to grandstand.

Jack continued, dropping the additional shoe before anyone else had a chance to speak. "Mr President, our informant is a woman, not a man, and as we have indicated previously, we have kept her identity secret as a way of protecting her . She has directly implicated Russia in the social media cyberwar campaign."

Celia Starks could not let the second-in-command of the CIA have the final word on this. She looked at the president and said, "Mr President, we need to get what we know about the bombing out to the public . It will defuse a lot of the angst about an internal plot."

"Yes, Celia, I am well aware of the need to inform the public." He looked at the people in the room for a few seconds, allowing his comment to sink in, and continued, "I plan to address the nation later today. I'm waiting for the latest information from meteorology and the scientists about the radiation risk to the public. So far, they're telling me that because of storms in Kansas and Missouri, most of the radiation is landing on farmland."

He turned to Jack Light. "Before I make any public accusations, I want to know how credible your informant is."

"Mr President, our informant is part of the Russian delegation at the New York City consulate. Revealing her identity publicly will put her life in danger."

Celia Starks now realized that Jack's secretive behavior with respect to the CIA informant made perfect sense: protecting his informant's identity, then using her to advance his own goal to be the next CIA director.

The DNI said, "We are working on a guarantee of political asylum and enrollment in the witness protection program for the informant."

Jack Light added, "I will personally convey our offer of asylum."

"Okay. Get that done asap."

The president turned to Celia Starks. "So where are you with all this crazy activity on the Internet? It's mushroomed into a full-blown pain in the ass, a crisis in its own right."

"Mr President," Celia said, "We believe these attacks were coordinated with the bomb attack in Kansas. One suspect in California committed suicide before she could be interrogated, but we are executing a complete forensic autopsy to see if her country of origin can be ascertained. We're closing in on the second suspect and hope to make an arrest soon."

"That's good, Celia. And get those smart cybergeeks of yours to flood social media with messages that blunt the fake hysteria generated by our enemies. And Jack, I want daily reports from you on progress with the informant."

To DNI Frankel, the president said, "I'm going on national TV this afternoon to announce that the bomb was foreign made to look like an American bomb. But I am not prepared to publicly accuse the Russians. Any problems with that?"

"No, Mr President," said the DNI.

"Good. You all heard the congressional leaders on the tube. They're starting their own investigations. I want to be in control of this, not other politicians. Many members of Congress are more interested in their own re-election than the good of the country."

"Mr President," Celia Starks piped up, "I'm concerned that our scientists are not in agreement on their analysis of the bomb core. If this leaks out, things could spin out of control."

Glaring at DNI Frankel, the president said, "Make those Los Alamos scientists button their lips, and that goes for everyone in this room."

Jack Light said, "Mr President, our public position on this can be that this was a well-financed group of terrorists, from one of several countries who are our enemies."

"You mean China, North Korea, Russia, or Iran," the president said.

"Yes, Mr President, the *usual suspects*."

The president continued. "Okay, I'll reassure the public that there is no significant danger of radiation exposure, and that we're making progress on identifying the foreign perpetrators of this attack." The president looked around the room. "Now, who can tell me what's going on in Mexico? When I talked with the Mexican president, he promised to track down the terrorists who escaped in the plane."

Jack Light jumped in. "Mr President, it looks like the plane crashed in the Sonoran Desert, south of El Paso, Texas. The terrorists are in the hands of a Mexican drug cartel."

"Do we know their country of origin?" the president asked, jaw set, arms tightly crossing his chest.

"Mr President, as I mentioned previously, according to our informant, they're Russian," said Jack. "But we need to have them in our hands to confirm."

FBI Director Celia Starks bit her lip. Jack knew it was Grushkov and his people, but she kept silent. She and Jack Light had made the case for the Russians, and that was clear to everyone in the room. But the president appeared to have his own agenda.

Jack Light responded. "Mr President. I have a team on their way to Mexico City. We've made a deal with the Godinez drug cartel to hand over the terrorists before they reach the Russian embassy there."

"That's great Jack, but I won't publicly blame the Russians. It will put Gorky in a difficult position, just when I'm negotiating with him over a joint space program, and another oil pipeline through the middle of Europe."

FBI Director Starks, thoroughly annoyed with Light's hijacking the meeting, asked, "Who are we going to blame, Mr President?"

The president glared at Starks, clearly annoyed at being put on the spot. After a few seconds to think before answering he said, "Maybe Iran. They're the major destabilizing influence in the Middle East, with the ability to cause wild fluctuations in world oil supplies simply by blocking the Strait of Hormuz or blowing up Saudi refineries with cruise missiles. Or North Korea. They're always a good punching bag."

There were a few snickers in the room.

Celia Starks asked, "What about Israel? Shouldn't we keep them informed? Iran is likely to retaliate against our closest ally in that region."

"It's not your worry, Celia. I'll discuss with the secretary of state and Jack at CIA," he responded tersely. The president stood and started to leave the room.

Celia Starks stood and watched him leave. She knew she was already on shaky turf with this president but felt compelled to speak her mind. "Mr President, I hope you'll consider waiting before publicly accusing Iran. We don't want to increase tensions in the Middle East needlessly." She quickly looked at Jack Light, who stared stonily ahead, avoiding eye contact.

"Mr President," said Secretary of Defense Ben Cousins. "We should consider increasing our military readiness. This will involve repositioning our carrier fleet and nuclear submarines. The Russians and the Chinese routinely monitor these movements. If they see that you're positioning our military for potential war, they will have to respond likewise. We have to be careful."

"I'm well aware of that, Ben. That's why I have a Cabinet and a DNI. This meeting is over. Ben, join me in the Oval Office."

In the Oval Office, the president signaled for the secretary of defense to sit. "Ben, if I want to use my nukes, what steps do I have to follow?"

"Mr President, Congress is very specific about the process."

"I'm listening."

"First, you meet with your top military advisers in the Situation Room. That would include the secretary of defense, your national

267

security advisor, chairman of the Joint Chiefs, the vice chairman of the Joint Chiefs, and the vice president. If, after that consultation, you still want to go through with the strike, your order is verified. To authenticate the order—"

"Wait, wait," the president interrupted. "What do you mean 'if' I want to go through with the strike? Can military advisors veto my order?"

Cousins said, "The purpose of this consultation is to ensure that you have good advice before pulling the trigger... ah... unless all of the advisors feel you are not of sound mind. Then they can counteract your order." The secretary of defense paused. "Mr President, shall I continue?"

"Yes, Ben."

"So after consulting with your military advisors, if you decide to proceed, a challenge code is read to you. It's usually two phonetic letters like 'Delta-Echo'. You then receive the 'biscuit', a laminated card. It's carried in that briefcase that's always near you. The biscuit has the matching response to the challenge code. The Pentagon broadcasts an encoded message to missile crews, in this case, a submarine captain. Then it's out of your hands, unless a rescinding order is given, which requires a process similar to the launch process."

"I can't just give the order on my own?"

"No. Only after you consult with your military advisors, and they will be evaluating your state of mind very closely."

"Shit, Ben, that dunderhead in North Korea and the ayatollahs in Iran can launch missiles without getting permission from a committee, and I suspect the same is true for Gorky in Moscow. America is at a disadvantage."

"That may be true, Mr President, but we are still the only country in history that has ever used nuclear weapons against another nation."

Chapter Forty-four
Wednesday

After returning from the White House meeting, Director Starks summoned Lynda, Sally, and the head of FBI IT into her office for an eleven thirty meeting.

"Our agents and a forensic team have confirmed that the Irvine condo has been the source of much of the hate cyberwarfare, as well as burner calls to the FSB headquarters in Havana."

She turned to the head of IT. "Have you retrieved any information from the computer recovered from the California condo?"

"Whoever wrote the self-destruct software did a good job. Nothing yet, but we're still trying."

"What about the condo rental payments?" Sally asked.

Starks gave a nod. "Traced to an offshore account in the Cayman Islands. A dead end. The money came from an Albanian bank, via an Estonian bank, and from there, the trail disappears."

Lynda said, "Eastern Europe... that's consistent with money originating in Russia."

"Yes," Starks said. "But it's not proof. Wire transfers zip around the world in seconds. Could've originated anywhere."

"What about the purchase of the airplane?" asked Sally. "Can't we track it by its registration number?"

"That's another dead end. It was bought by a fictitious person with money from an offshore account," Celia responded.

There was silence as everyone in the room was thinking feverishly about where to go next.

Lynda was the first to speak. "I'd like to go to California and work with the FBI team tasked with tracking the other resident of the condo. It may be our best chance to nab someone and get a computer before everything is erased."

Celia Starks considered Lynda's request. She had told the president that the FBI would devote itself to countering the social media cyberwar directed against America. But the FBI had first rate cybersleuths working on this and getting hold of the remaining suspect's computer — intact — could provide the key to deciphering the plot against America.

"Okay. I'll contact Dan Craft, the senior agent-in-charge of the LA field office and let him know you're coming"

At John Wayne Airport's charter air terminal in Orange County, Lynda arrived in the FBI Gulfstream and was met by senior LA agent Dan Craft at one thirty p.m. By 1.50, they were conducting a surveillance action from a vacant condo two doors down from the condo that had been occupied by the terrorists. Two more agents were there with digital cameras, capturing images of the suspect condo and monitoring signals from wireless microphones strategically placed in the perps' condo.

"Do you really think the other suspect will come back?" Lynda asked.

"Long shot," Dan replied. "But we have to cover our bases, just in case. I've been troubled by something, though. Why did the CIA make the first contact? Domestic espionage is clearly the FBI purview, and in a case like this the spade-work would be our responsibility."

"Don't know," Lynda curtly answered, not wanting to divulge that the CIA had an informant who may have revealed the existence of this site. Lynda suspected that the CIA had determined this location based on the cell phone tracking data she provided after the first meeting at Langley. This was a question Lynda hoped Celia Starks would raise with Jack Light.

As far as she was concerned, if the FBI had been the first to interdict the condo instead of CIA operatives masquerading as FBI, the computer would not have been turned on. Instead, it would have been sent straight to FBI headquarters for evaluation. And they would not have allowed the suspect to go unaccompanied to the restroom.

An FBI agent entered the condo, excited. "We've found a neighbor who's behaving suspiciously. Jan is with him. It looks like he knows something. We need someone who speaks Chinese."

Dan called the Orange County FBI office and asked for a Chinese-speaking agent. He told Lynda, "We'll have someone here in a half hour."

Lynda recalled her last annual boot camp. Due to the new geopolitical landscape, it had focused on interrogation techniques of non-English-speaking suspects. She said, "I'm going over there now. I might be able to get something from him. Every minute the suspect is out there, the chances decrease that we will track her down."

"Good idea."

On the walk over, the FBI agent, Pat Smith, briefed Lynda. "The name of the person of interest is Zhao; he's a graduate student at UC Irvine in engineering from mainland China. They have not asked him for ID because at this point, they don't want to spook him. And they have not been able to identify the woman his roommate appears to have gone off with."

Pat further explained. "We've determined the missing suspect is female, based on the clothes left behind. We haven't been able to identify the one that killed herself, but we're circulating her photo and fingerprints to Interpol as well as the intelligence agencies of our allies."

Zhao was sitting on the couch across from FBI agent Jan, who was attempting to engage him in a harmless conversation about the weather and the comforts of the condo.

Lynda put on her best smile and extended her hand to Zhao and said, "I am Lynda Chester."

Zhao was rooted to the couch, unsure what to say now that there were three strangers in his condo. He stood, shook hands with Lynda, and sat back down.

Seeing that he was nervous and maybe scared, Lynda said, "I am an engineer like you. Did you study engineering in China?"

Zhao understood the simple question. "Yes."

Lynda had to loosen him up. "Do you have water?"

"Ahh, yes." He got up and went to the kitchen, returning with a glass for Lynda.

Pat and the other agent took this as an opportunity to do a quick assessment of the condo. Based on items and clothing, they figured there was another person living here.

Lynda asked. "Do you live with someone?"

Zhao nodded yes but said nothing further.

There was a knock on the door; a fortyish Asian American man in a suit but unbuttoned collared white shirt showed his FBI credentials and introductions were made.

Ken Chang sat next to Zhao on the couch. The other two agents headed out to visit the university police department and registrar, hopeful of obtaining more information about Zhao and his room-mate.

Agent Chang started speaking in Chinese. Lynda noticed a change in Zhao's demeanor. He relaxed and was soon fully engaged in the conversation with Chang.

After five minutes, Agent Chang turned to Lynda. "He's afraid he is in trouble and will lose his student visa and be sent back to China."

"Tell him, we are not interested in taking away his visa. We are pleased he is a student in this country. Ask him about his room-mate."

Chang and Zhao conversed for a few minutes before Chang turned to Lynda. "He's reluctant to discuss his room-mate, whose name is Liang Hong, also a graduate student in engineering. I asked him where Liang is now, and he said he doesn't know. But I'm fairly sure he does."

"Ken, I think we need to play a little hardball with him, ratchet it up a notch. This is related to national security and the bomb that went off in Kansas. Tell him if he doesn't cooperate, we'll have to revoke his visa and send him back to China. Don't threaten him with being a spy or going to jail... not yet anyway."

Chang engaged Zhou in another long conversation. The student became animated and was clearly stressed now that his visa was in jeopardy.

"Liang has a girlfriend, and Zhao didn't want to get them in trouble."

"Tell him, all we want to do is talk with Liang and his girlfriend. Also, reassure him if he cooperates with us, we will make sure he keeps his visa."

After more talk, Agent Chang said, "They're staying at the Surf and Sand Hotel in Laguna Beach."

Lynda sprang from the couch. "Stay with him," she told Chang. "And no phone calls."

She sprinted from Zhao's condo back to the surveillance condo. Bursting in, she updated Dan Craft and said, "We need to get to Laguna Beach asap. Do you know the Surf and Sand Hotel?"

"Yes, upscale, and on the beach. It's about fifteen minutes away." He signaled to the female agent, Pat, to come with them.

In the car, Lynda briefed the two agents on the importance of capturing the woman alive as she may be part of the team that had set off the Wichita bomb. "Since her roommate killed herself, we need to assume that the partner might do the same if given the opportunity, so we need to restrain her quickly, and recover her computer before she can activate the self-destruct mechanism."

Lynda placed a call to Director Stark's personal cell, giving her a quick update.

Dan said, "Okay, Jan you restrain the female suspect as soon as we enter the room. Lynda, you locate the computer. I'll detain the male suspect. FBI protocol requires we enter the room with weapons drawn." Dan asked Lynda, "Have you ever done an interdiction and takedown?"

"N... n... no," she stammered. "I spend most of my time behind a computer."

"Okay, you stay in the hall until we've secured the room.

They pulled into the covered alcove of the hotel's entrance and went directly to the front desk, demanding to speak to the manager. They identified themselves and asked for the room number of the suspects.

The manager agreed to open the door with a passkey.

They took the elevator to the sixth floor. The manager indicated the room at the far end on the left. Dan took the key and instructed the manager to go back to her office, but not to speak with anyone about what was happening.

The team approached the room, with Lynda trailing behind. Dan swiped the passkey card across the lock. The light turned green, and he and Jan entered the room with weapons drawn.

Lynda heard: "Freeze, FBI. Do not move."

There were scuffling sounds, then an agent shouted, "Clear!"

Lynda rushed in. An attractive female with red hair was partially clad. Her wrists were handcuffed behind her back, and FBI agent Jan had her restrained. Dan had the male suspect, also handcuffed and sitting in a chair by the window so he could not communicate with the female suspect.

Lynda saw the laptop on the desk with its top closed. She snatched it and put it into the carry case on the floor next to the desk.

After grasping the situation, Larissa said, "I am Russian, and I want asylum."

The two FBI agents looked at Lynda, who they knew was tight with the FBI director. "Wait while I make a call," Lynda said.

She went onto the room balcony with waves from the Pacific Ocean crashing below and dialed Director Starks' private cell. When the director answered after only two rings, Lynda conveyed the Russian's request to defect.

Starks said, "Okay. But I can't guarantee asylum until it goes through a vetting process to see if she really has useful information. Get her on the Gulfstream and back to DC as soon as you can. I'll start the wheels on this end. And bring that damn computer."

"What about her Chinese boyfriend?" asks Lynda. "He wants asylum too, and I think the woman may be more cooperative if she knows he's with her."

"Okay, have the LA agents accompany you. Keep the two suspects apart. No communication allowed between them."

Chapter Forty-five
Wednesday

Two black Cadillac Escalades were waiting in an empty hangar at Reagan International Airport.

Larissa was hustled into the first car with Lynda, where Celia Starks and Jack Light were waiting with a Russian translator. Liang was in the second car with a Chinese interpreter and the two FBI agents.

Through the translator, Celia introduced herself and Jack Light. Larissa said, "My English is good. I do not wish to talk through a translator."

"Okay," Celia said. "You said you want to defect?"

"Yes, that is correct."

"Over the next few days, you will meet different people who will have many questions for you. We will then decide about granting you asylum in the United States."

"I need asylum and protection. My country will try to kill me," Larissa said, wringing her hands, then swiping away a tear. "And my family in Russia; can we get them out."

Jack Light said, "We can protect foreign agents who defect, but we need full cooperation, no information hidden. We can try to get your family in Russia out, but that could be quite difficult."

"We want access to your computer and all its files," Lynda said.

Celia nodded in agreement. "We'll put you up at a hotel tonight with one of our agents. But first you must unlock your computer, so we have access to everything."

"It recognizes my facial pattern, scans my retina, and also recognizes my unique key stroke patterns. Anything different, and it destroys all information and programs."

Celia looked at Jack, and said to Larissa, "We'll keep the computer, and in the morning, you will work at the FBI headquarters with Dr

Chester and our IT people to retrieve all the information from your computer."

"What about Liang?" Larissa asked. "We are asking for asylum together."

Jack Light said, "We will consider his request but no guarantees."

"It is a condition for me to give everything I know about the FSB and its operation for this mission."

Celia asked, "So you admit you are an FSB agent?"

"Yes."

"What do you know about the Kansas bomb?"

"I don't know about that. That was not part of my job."

The FBI director stared hard at Larissa, and said, "But you are a spy and a terrorist. You can be executed."

In a small meeting of select agency heads and the DNI in the Oval Office, the DNI cleared his throat. "Mr President, the heads of the agencies represented here have had their top interrogators and IT specialists working with the Russian defector to secure information from her computer, and from her, personally."

"Give me the bottom line," the president said impatiently.

"Mr President," Celia answered. "Dr Chester, who is on loan from the NSA, has been able to replicate the individual keystroke pattern of the Russian, so we have complete access to her computer."

"Cut to the chase, Celia. What have you found?"

Celia shifted her facial features into a neutral expression. She refused to let this president get to her. "We know that Russia sent three teams into the US. Two were tasked with flooding social media with incendiary information, and we're reasonably certain the third was tasked with detonation of an atomic bomb in Wichita.

Jack Light added, "It was cyberwar against America."

"So the attacks on liberal and conservative media outlets, the NGA, and the rise in anti-Semitic activity like the stabbing of that rabbi in Rockland County were all a result of this cyberwar?" the president asked.

"Yes, Mr President," Jack said. "We have intercepted communications on the dark web from extremist trolls. They're piggybacking on the Russian cyberattacks, amplifying their message and calling to action sympathetic radicals to incite violence."

"What about the bomb?" the president asked.

Celia Starks responded before Jack could monopolize this line of questioning. "We believe the bomb was smuggled under the border in Nogales, Arizona and flown to Wichita. The terrorists escaped into the Mexican desert on the same plane that brought the bomb."

She added, "We have identified Andrei Grushkov as the terrorist leader. The mission was staged and controlled from the FSB headquarters in Havana, Cuba. We surmised this from intercepted cell and satellite calls between Cuba and the US, and it was confirmed by the defector."

"Did the defector confirm the bomb story?" the president asked.

"She claimed ignorance of a bomb. There never was actual mention of a bomb in any of the communications we intercepted," Celia Starks answered.

"It's a very strong circumstantial case, Mr President," the DNI added.

"Did anything on the Russian's computer implicate the Russians in the actual bombing?" the president asked, his voice rising as his frustration grew.

"No, Mr President," Celia Starks responded. "But we retrieved a treasure trove of FSB operational methods."

The president looked angrily at his DNI. "So you *think* the Russians set off the bomb, but we have no direct proof?"

"Mr President, it was a clever deception trying to duplicate an American nuclear bomb, something we feel only the Russians would be capable of. But we have yet to attain definitive proof."

"And what about your informant?" the president said, turning to CIA Associate Director Jack Light.

"As I said, Mr President, she can connect the Russians to the plane, but not directly to the bomb."

Celia Starks stayed silent, enjoying Jack's inability to tell the president what he wanted to hear.

The president said, "Okay, so it's very likely it was the Russians, but no proof of their fingerprints on the bomb?"

No one in the room spoke. All of those present seemed to realize that the president did not want to publicly accuse Russia, and that he was using this lack of concrete proof to let Gorky off the hook.

"We can win a war against any of the second-rate nuclear powers, but I'm not so sure about the Russians. They have as many nukes as we have," the president said.

"Jack," the president continued. "I don't give a good god-damn about keeping your informant's identity secret. Bring her in, offer what you need to, and get her on record implicating Russia in the bombing. If I have proof it was Russia, I can have a back-channel talk with Gorky."

"And then what?" Celia Starks asked.

"Then what?" the president barked. "It gives me something to hold over his head. Something we can use in negotiations on future issues. And then I can point the finger at someone else, like Iran, North Korea, Pakistan, India: any number of suspects."

The president rose and abruptly left the meeting. As Jack Light followed, the president stopped him. "Jack, use your vast spy network. I want to get the Russians who were responsible for the bombing."

"That could be your quid-pro-quo with Gorky for keeping quiet on Russia's involvement in all this," Light said.

"I like it, Jack."

Outside the Oval Office, Celia Starks grabbed Jack Light. "We need to talk... now."

"Okay, let's ride together. I'll drop you at your office."

In the shadow of the White House, Director Starks told her driver to head back to the Hoover building without her. She got into the CIA Escalade with Jack.

"Is this a secure car?" she asked.

Jack scowled. "We're CIA."

"I heard your conversation with the president. We both know the Russian operation is Andrei Grushkov's."

"What are you saying, Celia?" Jack's face darkened.

"I know about your past friendship with Grushkov, and I understand that when you were posted to our embassy in Moscow after the Soviet Union disintegrated, you maintained your relationship with him. It doesn't pass the smell test. 'Top CIA operative drinking buddy with top Russian spy-master'."

"Your agency is tasked with domestic crime. Mine is espionage. Having a tight connection with a top Russian spy is something every intelligence officer would kill for. You never know when it will pay off."

"You heard the president. He wants the top Russian spy on a silver platter."

"Enough with the clichés," Light said. "I haven't decided whether or not it is in the country's best interest to reveal that Andrei Grushkov was head of the Russian operation."

"You mean in the best interest of the CIA, don't you?"

Light ignored her parry. "I'm not sure Gorky would deliver him, anyway. He's going to deny the whole operation. Say it was a group of rogue ex-KGB. We got that from our Russian defector."

"But he might deliver Grushkov in return for the president *not* calling out Russia for the plot, or we could offer Grushkov sanctuary. We could set him up in a safe house in Arizona and pick his brain dry."

Jack shook his head vigorously. "All the background on Grushkov is that he's loyal to Russia. His family has served in the military all the way back to the czars. I doubt he'd turn. Too much of a dark stain on his family name."

"Unless Gorky turns on him first," Celia Starks said. "It's a chess game, Jack. We're banking on anticipating a future move of our enemy."

"That's the spy game. Not like filing subpoenas and arresting perps, which is what the FBI is good at," Light chortled.

Jack's arrogance sent Celia into a slow boil, but she refused to rise to his bait. They were silent for a minute, then Jack said, "I have a plan that may get us Grushkov."

"I'm listening."

"Tomorrow, Celia. Come to Langley. Bring the surveillance tapes from the Long Island airport. You know, the ones your agent Lynda secured. In fact, bring Lynda."

Jack was up to something. But Celia thought it would be beneficial for both agencies to share information and be on the same page, even if his behavior at the last meeting at the White House had raised troubling questions.

In a darkened CIA conference room, Lynda gave the thumb drive with the MacArthur Airport surveillance images to Agent Boyd, whose computer was plugged into a PowerPoint projector. Jack asked Lynda to narrate what was on the screen.

She described two sequences of a Lexus registered to the Russian embassy entering MacArthur Airport and heading toward a private airplane hangar. It remained there about a half hour, left, and returned three days later when the suspect exited the passenger side and went to the open driver's side window.

Jack interrupted Lynda's narration. "Increase the magnification on the image where the perp bends over the open window."

He continued. "The man is Andrei Grushkov, director of clandestine operations of the Russian FSB. The woman he's kissing is Olga Radinova, an IT expert. She's been at the Russian Killingworth Mansion in Glen Cove for a little over a year."

Jack nodded to Tom, who left the room and was back in under five minutes.

Jack said, "I'd like you to meet Olga. She's been an informant for the CIA for the past eight months." He introduced all those present.

Olga Radinova sat at the conference table, visibly trembling. Celia and Lynda watched, surprised, but showing no emotion.

Jack said, "Olga, tell us in your own words what you know about the purpose of the men in the hangar."

She looked around until her eyes rested on Jack. "I am aware that two or three men from the Russian consulate in Manhattan made changes inside a Cessna plane."

"What were the specific changes?" Celia Starks asked.

"I don't know exactly, but it involved building something inside a stripped-down cabin."

"Do you know exactly what their purpose was in modifying the plane?" Lynda asked.

"I'm, ah, not sure, but they were going to fly to Arizona to pick up a package and then fly to Wichita, Kansas."

"How do you know it was Kansas?" asked Lynda.

"There was a sleeper Russian agent in Wichita, Kansas. I activated him in preparation for the arrival of the package."

Celia asked, "What do you think was in the package?"

Olga looked at Jack Light, who nodded. "A bomb," she said.

"How do you know?" asked Lynda.

Olga looked again at Jack before saying, "Andrei Grushkov and I were lovers. I gleaned a few things."

Celia said, "Let me understand. You were sleeping with Andrei Grushkov, and he told you that he was taking a bomb to Kansas."

"Not exactly," Olga replied.

Jack Light interrupted, "How did you work this out?"

"I pretended to be on my cell phone in my car but was really listening to the conversations in the hangar."

"Did Grushkov or any of the Russians use the words 'atomic bomb' or 'nuclear device'?" Celia asked.

Olga said, "Not exactly, but what else could it be? The news has reported radioactivity associated with the bomb that went off in Kansas, where Grushkov was going with a heavy package."

Celia Starks asked, "Olga, how do you feel about Grushkov now?"

"I don't want him be hurt," her voice wavered.

"Are you in love with him?" Jack asked.

"No. It was the job I was doing for you."

Lynda, watching dispassionately as Olga described her feelings toward the man Lynda had an affair with thirty years ago, asked, "So you had a torrid affair with this man over one weekend, and now you betray him?"

Olga looked directly at Lynda and said, "It was not all an act."

"So you do have feelings for him?" Jack Light asked.

"Yes, I met him years ago at a weekend training retreat and have followed his career in the KGB and now the FSB. I always admired him."

"Thanks, Olga," said Jack. "You now are under the protection of the United States government. You will be taken to a safe location. We'll talk again later."

As soon as Olga left the room, Celia said. "I see where you're going with this, Jack. Lure Grushkov to defect so he can be with Olga."

"It's a gamble, but I think it may work. I know Grushkov pretty well. He's been drifting for years emotionally, and Olga might be the hook to land him."

Celia turned to Lynda. "What do you think?"

"Uhm, I just don't know. Our affair was a long time ago. I got the impression that he was Russian through and through."

"What family does he have in Russia?" Celia asked.

"A ninety-three-year-old mother in a state institution, and an older sister he is not close with," Jack said.

Lynda had been wrestling with her feelings, and now, she found herself blurting out, "I don't think he deserves an offer of asylum. His intent was to obliterate Wichita, killing tens of thousands of innocent people, and he succeeded in killing and wounding over a dozen FBI and first responders."

Celia Starks asked, "What do we tell the president?"

"We have to be together on this," Jack said. "We'll tell him that the informant has confirmed that it was a Russian plot, and there was a bomb on the plane."

FBI Director Starks laser-focused on Jack, and said, "Olga did not confirm there was a bomb on the plane."

"Celia," Jack said, "she confirmed it was a Russian operation, and her knowledge of the modifications to the plane and the path of it to Kansas are enough of a smoking gun to convince me and the president."

Lynda had been listening and processing. Olga's information lent the necessary credibility to Russian involvement in the plot. She saw Jack Light as the next head of the CIA, and Celia's tenuous job as the first female African American director of the FBI being strengthened. The president would be satisfied because he would have leverage over Gorky. As the meeting broke up, Lynda retrieved the memory stick of video images of the black Lexus.

Celia, who technically outranked Jack, said, "I'll notify the DNI and request a meeting with POTUS."

In the car back to the FBI, Celia turned to face Lynda directly. "How wedded are you to returning to your job at the NSA?"

Surprised by the blunt question, Lynda asked, "Are you offering me a job?"

"Well, the associate director for Information Technology is retiring January first. We're required to do a search, but I think you'd be a good fit. Our anti-cyberwarfare unit falls under the division as well as all our imaging and pattern recognition activities."

"When do you need an answer?"

"Soon."

"I'd like to do some fieldwork. I don't want to be stuck behind a desk and computer for the rest of my career."

"That can be arranged. You can go through the normal three-week training program for new agents at Quantico. I see no reason why you can't work closely with our field agents on selected projects. You've performed exceptionally in the field on this Russian caper."

Chapter Forty-six
Friday

Andrei Andreievich Grushkov took his seat at the pitted oak table in FSB headquarters in the backroom of Club El Muro Blanco in Old Havana, Cuba. His shoulders drooped, and there were bags under his eyes. As a seasoned ex-KGB agent, he was conditioned to accept casualties, but this time he felt a stake had been driven though his heart. He'd lost more than half his team — all of whom were personal disciples — as close to being his children as possible.

He inhaled slowly, sighed, then looked at Gregory and Yuri, his two surviving team members. In a muted monotone, he said, "You are to be congratulated for the successful execution of your mission. I talked with President Gorky yesterday, and he asked me to inform both of you that you are Heroes of Mother Russia. While he cannot thank you publicly, he looks forward to doing so in private when you return to Moscow."

Grushkov felt an increasing tightness in his chest. The American news media was referring to a dead spy in California, and his contacts in various Russian consulates in the US indicated that Larissa Rubin had defected. He suspected that Irene committed suicide rather than be captured by the Americans, and Larissa probably seized the opportunity to be free. Peter's death was bizarre, and not fully explainable. Grushkov knew that Gorky would consider the mission a failure: two dead agents, a defector left behind, and a bomb that was a dud. Andrei knew first-hand the ruthlessness of Gorky and he feared what may happen to Yuri and Gregory if they returned to Moscow. He also feared for himself, but he was Russian, and would accept whatever punishment Nikita Gorky decided.

He looked at Gregory Borisy and said, "I don't know why the bomb did not function properly."

Gregory said, "Maybe the explosive charges were jolted during transport. We're lucky it didn't explode prematurely."

Yuri said, "I heard that there were problems in the tunnel and getting it on the plane in Arizona."

Grushkov was touched; he realized they were trying to help their mentor understand why the bomb exploded as a dirty bomb rather than a full-blown atomic bomb as intended, but he recalled that profound feeling of doubt when his shaking hand cradled the wires dangling next to the bomb core. He had hesitated. He hadn't been sure about the correct connections. His thinking had been clouded by the thought of all those innocent children.

He looked at Yuri Khodakov, the remaining member of *Snow leopard*. "You and Peter masterfully weaponized the Internet and the dark web to create a hysterical level of discontent in America that snapped when the bomb exploded. You are to be congratulated. I am sad that Peter is not here to celebrate with us, but I think he is in a peaceful place."

"Andrei Andreievich," Yuri said as he wiped a tear from his eye, "I wrestled with how to confront Peter as I saw his relationship with Tom Mahoney evolving in a direction that could only end badly for Peter. But fate took him anyway. I miss Peter and don't know what I will say to his family."

Grushkov got up from the table, went to Yuri, who rose from the pitted oak table. The two men embraced. Grushkov said, "You were in a difficult situation. You may grieve the loss of your friend, and I grieve with you." After several minutes, Grushkov reached under the table and pulled out two unopened bottles of Stoli in a large washbasin afloat in tepid water. "The ice melted an hour ago," he said.

Filling three glasses with double shots, he raised a glass, and his companions did the same. Grushkov said, "We toast the memory of Mischa Asimov, Yuri Khodakov, and Irene Seminova."

"*Nostrovia!*" they all shouted, then swallowed the lukewarm alcohol.

Images of his fallen team members, Olga, his wife Marina, Lynda, his mother, and grandfather swirled before Grushkov.

Ivan, the bartender of the Club El Muro Blanco rushed in and shouted, "You must see this on the television!"

Andrei, Gregory, and Yuri hurried from the back room into the bar and peered at the TV mounted on the wall. The American president announced, "We have identified the foreign perpetrators of the attempted attack on America and will be responding appropriately."

Then the president took a moment to thank several key people who had uncovered the plot. He introduced FBI Director Celia Starks, followed by CIA Associate Director Jack Light, about whom he said, "Working with an agency informant, he was able to pinpoint the originators of the plot, capture one of the terrorists, and kill another." Finally, the president turned to a woman next to him. "I want to introduce the woman who cracked the case wide open, Dr Lynda Chester of the NSA." He abruptly turned and left the room amid shouts from reporters to answer questions.

Grushkov's heart palpitated wildly. He felt dizzy and wobbled to a table in the corner of the bar. Yuri rushed over.

"What is it, Andrei?" he asked.

He drank water, then vodka, waving to Ivan for another. After his third Stoli, Grushkov got up amid protests from his team. "Forgive me," he mumbled. "Need to be by myself for a while."

Alone in the back room, he poured another shot of Stoli from the bottle left on the table. He laid his head into folded arms on the oak table and tried to cope with his feelings. The public announcement of the failure of the Tinderbox Plot was like twisting a knife through his gut; in Grushkov's mind, it dishonored his fallen team members. Hearing the American president gloat over having captured one and killed another of his team was too much to bear. Andrei knew that the American president was a shrewd politician, and the message he was sending was for President Gorky. Grushkov knew it was certain to get under his boss' skin, even if Russia was not specifically identified.

He tried to imagine what game the Americans were playing. He puzzled over why the American president didn't come right out and point the finger at Russia, unless he wanted Gorky to know he knew, and wanted something in return for not blaming Russia. And who was the informant?

"It must be Olga," he said to himself. She enjoyed the good life in America, driving her fancy Lexus and living in her own condo. He also knew the CIA was particularly good at getting people to turn and become double agents. That's what Jack Light had successfully done over the thirty years Grushkov had known him.

Or perhaps the informant was someone else with knowledge of the Tinderbox Plot, like Anatoly in Havana, Alexey or Viktor in Mexico, or a number of others from the New York consulate.

And about Lynda's role? He remembered her superb skill at knitting together bits and pieces of disconnected facts into a coherent picture. She did it with pixels of satellite images; it was how her brain worked. Having her on his tail had been unnerving and had made Grushkov move more quickly than he had liked. He wondered if this had caused him to make mistakes, putting his teams at risk, causing the deaths of Mischa and Irene.

He downed another shot of warm vodka, took an envelope from his jacket pocket and, with unsteady hands, studied his plane ticket to Moscow for tomorrow. He knew that people who displeased Gorky sometimes just disappeared.

Chapter Forty-seven
Saturday

While waiting in the Havana International Airport Premier Club lounge for the boarding call for his flight to Moscow, Grushkov ordered a second iced vodka. He was vaguely aware of two people sitting at the table behind him

"We should talk, Andrei Andreievich Grushkov," said a voice from behind.

Grushkov spun around, knocking over his vodka. It spilled off the table.

Grushkov's eyes widened as he recognized Jack Light and Lynda Chester.

Jack said, "It's been many years, Andrei, but there was always trust between us, even as we were on opposite sides of a Cold War. I have fond memories of our time together while I was stationed in California and Moscow."

Grushkov looked first at Jack, then at Lynda.

"And how is it you are in Havana?" Grushkov asked.

Jack offered a pained smile. "It's no accident, Andrei. We know you're booked on the next flight to Moscow."

Lynda said, "Andrei, we want you to come to America with us. Jack and I were sent to offer you asylum."

Jack lowered his voice. "To Gorky, your operation was a failure and an embarrassment. You know what that means."

"My operation was a success," said Grushkov. "We destabilized America."

"You set off a bomb that could have killed millions of people," said Jack. "It released radiation and killed a dozen government employees."

"So why should I come to America if you will consider me a criminal?"

"We can protect you, give you asylum, and set you up in a nice home somewhere in America where you will be safe from Gorky," Jack added.

Grushkov was thinking of his mother, whom he would never see again. A tear trickled down his cheek.

Lynda seemed to sense his thoughts. "Andrei, your mother died a month ago. We think this was kept from you because your superiors did not want to upset you and compromise your mission."

Andrei took a deep breath and shut his eyes tight, not wanting to shed more tears in front of Jack and Lynda. He rose from his table. "I need to walk."

Jack stood and gently touched Grushkov's shoulder. "It's not safe for you to return to Russia."

"And it's not safe for me in America. You will not ignore that my plot killed many of your FBI team. You will get from me what you want, and then I will be killed or put in prison for the rest of my life."

Grushkov pushed away from Jack, walked into the main terminal, and out to the street and the hot humid air of mid-day Cuba. His mind churned. If what Jack said was true, Gorky would certainly want him and his surviving team members eliminated. In the many years he and Jack had cooperated on issues that were mutually beneficial, both had been straight shooters. He didn't doubt what Gorky was capable of, and he trusted Jack's word that in America he would be protected. But he knew any promises of protection may not be honored by future American administrations, which seemed to change on a regular basis. Further, if he revealed all he knew about the operation of the FSB, he will have betrayed his heritage and his ancestors who died for Mother Russia. Sweat was now soaking his shirt. He looked at his watch. Still twenty minutes until his flight boarded.

He thought of Olga. The chemistry between them had been strong, but it had been more than just physical. They had shared a common background in the FSB, they had laughed and made love. She was the kind of woman he would like to spend the rest of his life with. But should it be in the US or in Russia, he asked himself. If it was in the US, they would both be traitors to their homeland and would have to live with that knowledge for the rest of their lives. If they returned to Russia, they might also be considered traitors there.

He returned to the lounge, to the table where Jack and Lynda were nursing drinks, a half full bottle of Stoli and an empty glass now on the table.

"I will take my chances in Russia. I believe President Gorky will toast me and my teams as Heroes of Mother Russia," he said, filling his glass from the open bottle of Stoli.

He raised his glass. "Might as well finish with a farewell toast."

All three raised their glasses and said, *"Nostrovia."*

In twenty minutes, Andrei Grushkov boarded the large Aeroflot jet and was seated in first class.

The flight attendant offered him a drink while the rest of the passengers were boarding. "Vodka on ice," he slurred, feeling lightheaded.

By the time the drink was on the tray by his seat, he appeared asleep, leaning against a pillow wedged between his head and the window. He was still not awake when a well-dressed man sat next to him in the aisle seat.

Once airborne, Grushkov stirred and there was another vodka on ice waiting for him. The adjacent seat was empty.

He tossed down the drink, and in a few minutes a dark fog engulfed his total being. Like the eye of a hurricane, for a few seconds his mind achieved crystal clarity. Images of his mother, his family sitting around the family dacha fireplace listening to his grandfather tell stories about his war exploits, and of Marina on their wedding night, flashed through an ebbing consciousness. His final image was of the bomb core's colored wires dangling, awaiting proper insertion into the sphere-of-death. He visualized his shaking hand connecting the wires into the wrong slots. At peace, he exhaled a final breath.

After six hours of flight time, the flight attendant shook Grushkov to offer him a meal. He didn't respond. She summoned the senior attendant who then notified the captain.

Andrei Andreievich Grushkov was dead.

The flight attendant said to the captain, "I thought there was a person in the aisle seat, but I checked the manifest, and this seat was never assigned."

When the flight landed in Paris to refuel, the French gendarmerie nationale and the Compagnie Républicaine de la Sécurité (CRS) assumed control. Despite objections from the Russian embassy, they immediately declared the Aeroflot plane a crime scene. After initial processing of the scene, despite further objections from the Russian government, Grushkov's body was taken to the top French forensic lab for processing. Before the plane could be moved to a French hangar for further processing, its passengers were informed that a replacement plane was on its way. They must claim their baggage, check in a second time, and all passengers and crew were interviewed by French police or agents of the French CRS.

At the forensic lab, French and Russian diplomats fought over custody of Grushkov's body which was fingerprinted and photographed. Blood and tissue samples were taken for DNA analysis. After forty-eight hours, the Russian embassy filed a legal complaint with the French government, insisting upon the release of Grushkov's body so he could be returned to his homeland where he was to be honored as a Hero of Mother Russia.

THE END

CPSIA information can be obtained
at www.ICGtesting.com
Printed in the USA
LVHW111444051021
699593LV00011B/72